THE BEST AMERICAN

NONREQUIRED

READING

2014

D0032399

THE BEST AMERICAN

NONREQUIRED READING™

2014

■

EDITED BY

DANIEL HANDLER

INTRODUCTION BY
LEMONY SNICKET

MANAGING EDITOR
DANIEL GUMBINER

A MARINER ORIGINAL
HOUGHTON MIFFLIN HARCOURT
BOSTON • NEW YORK
2014

ISSN: 1539-316x
ISBN: 978-0-544-12966-5

Printed in the United States of America
DOC 10 9 8 7 6 5 4 3 2 1

"Embarazada" by Andrew Foster Altschul. First published in *Ploughshares*, Winter 2013–
2014. Copyright © 2013 by Andrew Foster Altschul. Reprinted by permission of the author.

"Charybdis" by Cole Becher. First published in *The Iowa Review*, Spring 2013. Copyright © 2013 by Cole Becher. Reprinted by permission of the author.

"You Have Harnessed Yourself Ridiculously to This World" and "Currying the Fallow-
Colored Horse" by Lucie Brock-Broido. First published in *Stay, Illusion*. Copyright © 2013 by
Lucie Brock-Broido. Reprinted by permission of Alfred A. Knopf.

"The Robots Are Coming" by Kyle G. Dargan. First published in *The Baffler*, no. 22, 2013.
Copyright © 2013 by Kyle G. Dargan.

"Body-without-Soul" by Kathryn Davis. First published in *Duplex*, 2013. Copyright ©
2013 by Kathryn Davis. Reprinted by permission of Graywolf Press.

"Greencastle," "Nobleboro," and "Sidewalk Poem" by Matthew Dickman. First published in *Wish You Were Here*, 2013. Copyright © 2013 by Matthew Dickman. Reprinted by
permission of the author.

"Seven Days in Syria" by Janine di Giovanni. First published in *Granta*, Winter 2013.
Copyright © 2013 by Janine di Giovanni. Reprinted by permission of the author.

"Mona Eltahawy with Yasmine El Rashidi" by Yasmine El Rashidi. First published in *Bidoun*,
Spring 2013. Copyright © 2013 by Yasmine El Rashidi. Reprinted by permission of the author.

"Episode 15: Street Cleaning Day" by Joseph Fink and Jeffrey Cranor. First released as
part of the podcast *Welcome to Night Vale*. Copyright © 2013 by Joseph Fink and Jeffrey
Cranor. Reprinted by permission of Writers House.

CONTENTS

Editors' Note

Dear Person Who Doesn't Skip Editors' Notes at the Beginnings of Books,

Hello. Welcome to *The Best American Nonrequired Reading 2014*, a collection of journalism, fiction, poetry, comics, stage plays, interviews, and podcast transcripts culled from a mountain of material that was published, posted, or otherwise presented over the previous year. While you were likely wasting your time, a dedicated team of individuals went through this material and gathered together their favorite things.

Who is this team? They are high school students from the San Francisco Bay Area. Some are seniors and some are freshmen. Some go to public school and some to private school. Some talk a lot and some need to be prodded. Some of them believe in aliens and some of them do not. It is irrelevant and perhaps inappropriate to dwell on their physical characteristics, but suffice to say that they are, for the most part, a very good-looking bunch.

They are also good at reading. The team gathered every week, reading two or three pieces during the first, silent hour—an assortment of famed journals and unknown periodicals, popular websites and obscure chapbooks. And then, in the second, more interesting hour, they leapt into discussion with careful thought, heated debate, and diverse and startling opinion. Provocative cheese philosophies were bandied about. Revolutions were subject to raised fists and rolled eyes. There were no fixed criteria and no rules—except for the "no-projectile-launching-of-boba-tea rule," which had to be instated after repeated incidents that will not be elaborated on in these pages.

This thing—the weekly gathering, the ardent reading, the provocative discussion, and the anthology—was founded by Dave Eggers in 2002, and this year Dave passed the torch on to two Daniels, who shared the job of working with the *BANR* team. They did not share it fairly. One was a constant presence and a paragon of organization due to his impressive experience in such matters, while the other was often absent, due to book tours and a grievous injury, and would often crack cheap jokes and offer odd, off-kilter advice. On the other hand, that second person brought delicious snacks that he paid for with his own money.

Longtime readers of these anthologies will note that the new regime has brought a few changes—there is no more "Front Section," in which shorter pieces were once gathered—but that the spirit of *BANR* remains kicky. We hope this collection will introduce you to some new writers and publications and remind you of the immense spectrum and verve of our current writing scene.

Finally, thank you to our peers in Ann Arbor, who have their own committee at 826 Michigan. They met weekly, just like us but with worse weather, and provided much-needed advice.

DANIELS GUMBINER and HANDLER
San Francisco, 2014

INTRODUCTION

RECENTLY IT WAS brought to my attention that a number of young people were cooped up in a windowless basement in the Mission District of San Francisco. Like all decent people, I found this alarming. If memory serves, I said something like "Egad!"

"There's no reason for 'Egad's," explained a literary personage of some sort. "They're sifting through this year's supply of literature."

"Sifting through this year's supply of literature!" I repeated, in a sputtery tone I reserve for repeating astonishing things people have said. "This is an outrage! What sinister slave drivers have abducted teenagers and are requiring them to do their literature-sifting for them?"

"No, no," said the other person, sounding a little sputtery himself. "Nobody is requiring them to do this. They want to do it. They're putting together an anthology and the anthology is called *The Best American Nonrequired Reading*, and it's really quite terrific."

I said something along the lines of "That still sounds suspicious," and it does. For one thing, nobody, young or old, wakes up in the morning and decides to put together an anthology. It's a task requiring a tremendous amount of dull work. In order to find lively pieces of literature one wants to anthologize, one has to read an enormous amount of wretched literature one wants to toss out the window, and in a windowless basement this is even more troublesome than it is ordinarily.

Additionally, literature is slippery and slippery things cause disagreements. Although absolutely everyone agrees on what is best in ice cream flavors (chocolate and peanut butter), seasons (autumn), Eastern European composers (Béla Bartók), inspiring slogans ("To the ramparts!"), or scary movies (*The Lair of the White Worm*), there is a surprisingly vast difference of opinion on what is good to read. So if you have a team of anthologists, you are going to have a team of arguments. "How could you possibly have admiration for that essay and not appreciate these poems?" and, "Anyone who disagrees with me about this comic is a blithering fool!" and, "If you don't like this short story and don't despise this stage play, I'm going to tear my hair out!" are cries commonly heard from an anthologists' den.

Invariably, the most passionate and interesting pieces of writing divide a literary team, and are put aside in favor of less controversial items, and these safer pieces of literature tend to be dull, and then the anthology is dull, and there is only one way to make people read something dull: to require it. Want many people to read what you write? Write something interesting. Want *everyone* to read it? Write something mandatory. From *Dick and Jane* to *How to Redeem Your Airline Miles*, from *To Kill a Mockingbird* to *Do Not Enter*, we read things we would not read under any circumstances simply because we are in circumstances which require us to do so.

Therefore, the idea of a group of young people discussing literature in a room in which nothing can be thrown out the windows, and thus creating an anthology that is "terrific" but optional is laughable, and after I explained this to the literary personage, I laughed out loud scornfully to prove it was so.

"There's no need for a scornful laugh," the person said to me. "You are quite wrong on all counts. These young people were very eager to do this. Wretched literature can be tossed into a recycling bin rather than thrown out a window. Fierce discussion can be tempered by a robust *esprit de corps*, a phrase which here means that an enthusiasm for the project at hand kept disagreements respectful. And the anthology is really wonderful. Look here, I happen to have the manuscript of it right here with me. Peruse it and judge for yourself. Observe how the anthology opens with a deadpan pedagogical pseudo-instructional speculative humor piece, and moves quickly to Bolivian fiction, cult investigation, pet shop philosophizing, activist inquiries, and lyric poetry. Observe the balance of famed and unknown authors, the straightforward and the askew, the dramatic and the subtle, the hilarious and the weepy. Dull, mandatory anthologies, my foot! This collection of literature is so ferociously entertaining and veeringly diversified that we could no more make it mandatory than we could fashion it out of fish! Readers will be drawn to it like yarn to a kitten! Far from being Nonrequired, we could make this anthology Nonrecommended, or even Taboo, or Unthinkable, and still people would come in both literal and figurative droves!"

This person's enthusiasm was contagious, if a bit loud. People were looking. I took the manuscript from him and began to read.

"Very well then," I said, when I finished reading the manuscript a few days later. People were still looking at us. "You are correct. This is a magnificent piece of work. In fact, I would be proud to be associated with it despite having nothing to do with its creation, perhaps by writing an introduction."

"You already have!" crowed this other person in triumph. "I have been surreptitiously recording and transcribing our entire encounter, and will publish it forthwith. I will add nothing but a bland, inspirational final sentence, so that out of the whole anthology, only your introduction will be of the unimaginative, uninspiring sort of writing you were decrying earlier!"

"I knew something suspicious was going on!" I cried in more or less dread, and then said "Egad!" which I think this time was called for.

Have fun reading this anthology, everybody!!

LEMONY SNICKET

Lemony Snicket is the author of the thirteen-book sequence A Series of Unfortunate Events *and the four-book series* All the Wrong Questions, *among (too) many others.*

THE BEST AMERICAN

NONREQUIRED

READING

2014

MATTHEW SCHULTZ

■

On the Study of Physics in Preschool Classrooms: Pedagogy and Lesson Planning

FROM *Ecotone*

Beginning Your Unit

Though it may seem natural to begin your study of the physical universe with the moon, educators working in urban areas should skip ahead to section two, for in cities, especially large ones like New York and Tokyo, the moon is mostly irrelevant. Appearing small and weak behind skyscrapers, it fails to capture the imaginations of urban children and parents alike. They may wonder at the wastefulness of the moon, which sits in the sky contributing nothing when it could very well be used as a site for low-income housing or made into a screen on which the time and the weather are perpetually displayed. Teachers in suburbs and rural areas should begin with a simple observation of the moon. After all, it is thanks to the moon that humankind ever noticed the sky. Something always indicates the presence of nothing.

For this lesson you will keep the children quite late. Take them out to a place where the grass is unmowed and the horizon unobscured. Direct their attention to the subtle curve of the Earth, and let them experience themselves standing on something round, a globe, which lives in constant relation to another globe, which they will see, pale and pocked, above their heads.

Share silence and wonder with them.

Those of us in cities will not bother attempting this. Our skies are deserts. Those of us in cities will wait until day.

The Sun

When day breaks you turn your study to the sun, which works without ceasing to create useful products like light and warmth. Take the children outside for a twenty-four-hour period. Have them don protective goggles and let them stare at the sun. When night falls they will stare at the lack of sun. Have them draw on construction paper their impressions of the sky at various hours. Ask them why the sun appears here and then there. Ask the children where it is when it is not visible. Most likely they will note its slow, steady movement. After sunset they will tell you that it is just over that hill in the distance.

Then take the children to the sun for a twenty-four-hour period. Bring sunscreen with a high SPF to protect their skin and yours. Pack snacks for the long journey there and back. This time the children will observe the movement of the Earth. They will come to understand relativity as a general concept, and one of the children (most likely not more than one, or possibly not even one) will look at you with a new understanding.

Keep in mind that preschool-aged children think that their teachers are simply an aspect of the classroom, existing only for that role, rising and setting just for them. Keep in mind that you believe this too—that the children, at least one of them (Gabriel, age three), were born to hear what you have to say. Look into this child's eyes as the two of you stand on the surface of the sun and you will share an understanding of independence and mutuality and yes, yes, *relativity!* Then gaze off at the setting Earth and forget this shared insight. Fall back into particularity. Return home to Earth, to the classroom, and teach this child as if his ears were made for your words, and he will learn as if the classroom were built for his sake alone.

An Overview of Your Unit

Observation of the moon and sun will lead to observation of the sky, and observation of the sky will lead to observation of the stars. Observation of the stars will lead inward upon itself to that which lies at the center of stars and is witnessed at their death. This we call a black hole, and observation of a black hole will lead to observation of nothing, because a black hole is made of nothing. Learning this, the children will become frightened and depressed. And this will lead to observation of the self, because the children will need an affirmation of that which is not nothing, not emptiness. This will lead to observation of matter and energy. At this point in the year, hatch ducklings in an incubator. Raise butterflies in cocoons. Cook muffins. Finger paint. And then the children, reminded of life and matter, will be ready to turn back to the sky. This time tell them to look past the moon. Tell them to look past the stars. Their eyes will strain into the darkness. They will find the boundary of space-time. This will lead to observation of ultimate truth. And then the year will be over, and the children will leave and grow and forget.

Gabriel, A Case Study

Gabriel (age three) and I sat together and played with Play-Doh.

"Look," he said. "It's a pizza."

"Wow," I replied. "It looks very good."

He reshaped it and said, "Look, it's a car."

"Wow," I replied. "It looks very fast."

He reshaped it again and said, "Look, it's the Earth."

"Wow," I replied. "It looks very round."

He reshaped it again and said, "Look, it's a star."

"Wow," I replied. "It's so bright."

He reshaped it again and said, "Look, it's a quasar."

"Wow," I replied. "It's so luminous and radioactive."

He reshaped it again and said, "Look, it's a pizza again. But this time it has pepperoni."

The Big Bang

Explain the Big Bang to the children at story time. Tell them that once upon a time there was no time. Tell them that this all happened in a place that wasn't a place. Remind each child of his or her mother and how he or she used to live inside her. Ask the children where they were before they were in the belly, and when they answer, you will see that they have understood the story of the Big Bang and may even remember it. Suddenly, you will remember it too, remember the day when infinite density gave birth to matter and distance and collision and emptiness.

Field Trip

A field trip to the moon is recommended for any classroom learning about physics. Remember, ideally—contingent on the urban or non-urban setting of your school—the moon has served as the children's introduction to this course of study, rolling about as it does like a bowling ball in a vast blackness.

Do not invite parents to be chaperones. The moon is a place to be alone.

To prepare for this trip, use Play-Doh to make a baseball-sized model of the Earth as well as another body roughly the size of Mars in proportion to this. Show how the Mars-sized body collided with Earth hundreds of thousands of years ago and sent a portion of our planet hurtling off into space. Show how the moon was cast away and forgotten and how the centuries passed and humankind was born and saw the moon as something foreign and mysterious.

Tell the children that on July 20, 1969, the Earth and the moon were reunited when humankind rocketed into space and landed on the lunar surface. Tell them that the moon thought someone had at last come to take her home. Tell them that humankind did not recognize the moon. Tell them that humankind played golf and then went home without her.

Let the children run and explore. Watch them struggle and writhe. Watch them soar and dance and then become terrified and frustrated and cry and hide in craters. Do not hurry to comfort them. Let them feel abandoned.

As you jet back to Earth serve graham crackers and juice. Read a story aloud. Better yet, sing a soft song and encourage them to sleep as gravity reclaims them.

How to Grow a Star

Having observed the sun and the moon, the children will certainly ask you how it is that energy coalesces into form. Do not attempt to describe it with words, for any such descriptions are nonsense. Rather, demonstrate it inside the classroom.

Clear all matter from a small area. Ask the children to aid you in this by using tweezers to pull particles from the area. This can be a great exercise for the development of fine motor skills. Make sure that a teacher is holding the boundaries of the newly created void at all times so that it doesn't snap shut into a singularity that could possibly consume a child, or the whole school, or the entire Earth and the moon and the planets and all things past and yet to come.

Next have the children add atoms of hydrogen and helium into the void and observe the swirling nebula that results. Record their observations. "It looks like a rainbow," they may say. Or "It's like a sandbox."

The atoms will coalesce into a sphere. Nuclear fusion will begin to take place within the star, rapidly increasing its heat and brightness. The star will begin to glow as electrons shoot off into the void. The children will see heavy elements such as carbon being formed. This will cause planets to form around the star. Pluck the new planets from their orbits and hand each, as it is made, to one of the children.

Have the children paint and name their planets. Place the planets over the cubbies to cool and let the children take them home at the end of the day.

Some personal notes: the first time I attempted this activity I saw that life had emerged on Gabriel's planet. But by the time he showed it to me the inhabitants of this tiny world had come and gone. I looked closely and saw unearthly landscapes and petrified vegetation.

He named his planet "Ortexuan" and when I asked him how to spell it he said "O, t, ɪ, r, r, g, c, 6, y."

A warning to teachers who have never worked with stars before: that day, as the class and I watched our star die, it collapsed in upon itself and formed a black hole. This is exactly what you will want to avoid. All the children were pulled into the black hole and I was nearly pulled in myself. I managed to turn the thing off and pull the children out, but their atoms were all mixed up. It took me the whole rest of the day to reassemble them, and one student (Rachel, age four) never got her freckles back.

Keeping a Tidy Classroom and Thermodynamics

Be sure to keep an organized plan book. Be sure to keep an organized classroom. Organize the toys on the shelves, and the puzzles too. Organize the cabinet where the snacks are kept, placing the crackers to the left and the pretzels to the right. Organize the drying rack where the soppy finger paintings are laid to dry. Organize the children's cubbies where the detritus of their days accrues: the mittens, the lunchboxes, the crinkled crayon drawings.

Never cease in your battle against the second law of thermodynamics, that of entropy, of chaos, of mixing up. Teach the children how things come together, how energy coalesces into matter, into time and place, into life and color and humanity. Do not tell them that life is only a futile last stand against entropy, the inevitable breaking up of things. Only the janitor will learn this lesson. Nod politely to him as you depart from your classroom each day. This man works hard. He sweeps the staples off the floor, vacuums the crumbs from the rug, and wipes the encrusted Play-Doh from the remotest corners of the classroom. And only he fully understands that no matter how hard teachers strive for the opposite, all lessons are only about entropy.

Mapping the Stars

Many children are familiar with connect-the-dots drawings. These can be an excellent introduction to the study of stellar geography.

Give the children blank star maps and have them design and name their own constellations. I recall that in my class, Margaret (age: two point five) and Tommy (age: three) both named their constellations "Mommy," while most of the others called theirs by their own names.

It was Gabriel who connected every star on the map to every other star. He named it the Foof and when I asked him what a foof was he told me that it was a monster that ate itself up and then ate its own mouth.

I desperately wanted to ask for further details, such as how a thing could eat its own mouth, and whether or not the Foof knew he was a foof. No doubt Gabriel would have had some answer for me, but I wasn't ready to let him see how little adults sometimes know.

Concluding Your Unit/The Multiverse

Your classroom's exploration of the physical principles of the universe will never truly conclude.

Move on, but revisit and review by having the children count the atoms in a cracker at snack time, or by asking them to identify the difference in the wavelengths of light reflecting off purple and yellow paints.

The children's capacity to recall the material will surprise you. Gabriel, for example, asked if it were the case that nothing drawn or written down is true. I told him that, yes, nothing drawn or written is true because the truth is too complex to be captured by human efforts. It was then that he showed me a drawing he had made of the singularity in which all matter and energy were contained at the beginning of time.

It was, I was surprised to notice, perfectly accurate, and so I had to recant my prior statement. Being perfectly accurate, this drawing hummed with the desire to know the distance and emptiness and confusion it depicted, and it opened up like a flower into a new universe that runs, to this day, mostly parallel to our own and which can only be witnessed, occasionally, on sheets of construction paper.

"Another foof," Gabriel told me.

Be sure, brave teachers, to recognize such accomplishments. Hang the children's work on the bulletin board. Tell them that their parents will be proud. Perhaps, if the work warrants such a reaction, fall to your knees and let your head become heavy with new insights.

When the children's work is done, tell them that you will be moving on to a new unit. A unit about vegetables and healthy foods, perhaps, or about words that rhyme.

This will be your final opportunity, so fight your own weariness, and beg the children to sit still on the rug just a moment longer.

Speak your closing words about time and space. Remind the children that the two are not separate, that both are relative, that clocks lie, that schedules lie, that time only appears to move in one direction, that the universe is both finite and infinite, and that anything true is impossible to fit inside your head.

Then pack the children up to go home. Sing the good-bye song and send them on their way.

DAN KEANE

■

AP Style

FROM *Zoetrope*

LA PAZ, Bolivia — Police say 24 people were killed in a tragic accident Monday when a bus plunged from a narrow mountain road.

MEMO FROM MEX. CITY:
Not everything sad is *tragic*. Evaluate on case-by-case basis.
More Bolivia context please.

LA PAZ, Bolivia — Police say 47 people were killed Tuesday when a bus plunged from a narrow mountain road.
Bolivia is the poorest country in South America.

MEMO FROM MEX. CITY:
Tragic fine for 47 dead. Just fyi.

LA PAZ, Bolivia — Government officials say a new highway completed Wednesday outside the Bolivian capital will save lives.
The paved route through the mountains replaces a narrow dirt track known as the Death Road, blamed for decades of fatal accidents.
At the ribbon-cutting ceremony local dignitaries smashed clay pots of *chicha*, or corn beer, on the highway's spotless new concrete.
The traditional Bolivian tribute sought favor from the Pachamama, the Earth goddess revered by much of Bolivia's indigenous population.

MEMO FROM MEX. CITY:
Please use *Indian* over *indigenous.*
Indigenous sounds like an endangered tree frog.
Readers know what an *Indian* is.

LA PAZ, Bolivia—A roundtable of foreign correspondents covering this Andean nation declared Thursday that "the most totally Bolivian thing" would be to fuck an Indian.

The table raised their glasses to *cholitas,* local slang for the Indian women who wear the traditional dress of petticoats, shawl, bowler hat, and long braids.

"To petticoats!" a reporter said.

"To what's underneath!" said a guy who sometimes wrote for *Time.*

Reaction was swift from the lone female at the table.

"Jesus," said the freelance radio correspondent. "You colonialist assholes."

LA PAZ, Bolivia—It'll be bowler hats, not bikinis, at a beauty pageant to be held this week for Indian women in the capital of this landlocked country.

Contestants for the title of Miss Cholita La Paz will be judged on the style and authenticity of their hats, colorful skirts, and sequined shawls. The young women will also be asked to dance and to deliver a short speech in the Aymara Indian language.

The grand prize is a college scholarship and an honorary role at city events throughout the year.

MEMO FROM MEX. CITY:
Lukewarm on Indian beauty pageant.
Happens every year? Pls. confirm.
If annual, just send Luis for photos.

LA PAZ, Bolivia—Police say 19 people were killed Friday when a bus plunged from a recently built mountain highway.

Survivors report the bus lost control on a sharp turn and broke through a new guardrail before falling into a deep ravine.

Among the Bolivians who died was a six-year-old girl.

Bolivia is the poorest country in South America.

MEMO FROM MEX. CITY:

In future pls. skip all bus plunges with less than ~20 dead.

Exceptions for holidays, election days, great photos, etc.

File all accidents with foreign fatalities, esp. non-LatAm.

An international agency covers international news.

LA PAZ, Bolivia—Shimmering sequins and fluffy petticoats shared the runway Saturday at the Miss Cholita La Paz pageant, an annual celebration of this city's blend of Indian heritage and urban style.

This year's winner, Patricia Quispe, 23, wowed judges with an electric blue skirt and shawl, gold press-on nails, and a saucer-sized brooch dangling from her black bowler hat.

"I'm proud to be a *cholita*, and proud to be a Bolivian woman," a beaming Quispe told the crowd gathered in a chilly La Paz park.

The new Miss Cholita La Paz works during the day at her aunt's chicken stand in a cliffside neighborhood overlooking downtown. At night she studies business administration at a local university.

Once fitted with her title's golden sash, Quispe stepped down from the stage to be smothered by a joyful mob of round *cholita* neighbors and aunts. One by one they lifted her bowler hat and mashed handfuls of confetti into her hair.

The confetti caught on Quispe's lipstick when she laughed and gathered in great drifts on her sequined shoulders.

High above the park, the Andes turned pink.

MEMO FROM MEX. CITY:

Nice color here but still going to pass.

Strictly local news. But Quispe's a looker, eh?

Tell Luis great photos.

LA PAZ, Bolivia—A reporter shared a taxi home from the club early Sunday morning with a freelance radio correspondent.

The reporter carefully slid a hand across the backseat, but the freelance radio correspondent dozed on against the far window.

Orange streetlights rolled over her face. The reporter imagined the two of them were alone together in the empty maze of a ruined city.

At her building the freelance radio correspondent leaned over and kissed the reporter once on the cheek, as local custom required.

"Fun night," she said. "Dream of your *cholita*."

Not an air kiss, though. Full lips. On her skin he could smell where the club sweat had flash-dried in the mountain air.

LA PAZ, Bolivia — An ambitious campaign to modernize Bolivia's primitive highways takes a big step this week as construction begins on a new route across the country's remote eastern jungles.

Government officials say the Trans-Amazon Highway will promote development and expand trade with wealthy neighbor Brazil.

But Amazonian Indian groups oppose the project, fearing the road will open up their traditional homelands to outside settlement.

MEMO FROM MEX. CITY:
Road-through-virgin-rainforest thing a bit played out these days.
Does Brazil care? Check in with São Paolo.
Maybe a feature when it opens.

LA PAZ, Bolivia — Miss Cholita La Paz has been stripped of her title for wearing fake braids during the pageant, city officials announced Monday.

Witnesses said they noticed the braids coming loose as Patricia Quispe, 23, embraced friends and family after winning the title Saturday evening.

Mothers of the other contestants immediately cornered the judges in the park where the pageant was held.

A harried man from the city's cultural bureau finally agreed to call a new pageant for the following weekend, with strict rules regarding hair.

MEMO FROM MEX. CITY:
Loving Braidgate.
A feature there? Trials of being an Indian in the 21st century?
Interview Quispe re: lifestyle, Internet, globalization, etc.

LA PAZ, Bolivia—A reporter's phone buzzed just as the Miss Cholita La Paz story broke over the office radio.

Do fake Indians still count? :-) a freelance radio correspondent wanted to know.

The reporter sent back a quick, noncommittal *Crazy, right?* and then a professional inquiry: *You filing this?*

No shit I'm filing this, came the reply. *See you in the funny papers.*

LA PAZ, Bolivia—The disgraced Miss Cholita La Paz was approached by a reporter Tuesday at her aunt's chicken stand in a cliffside neighborhood overlooking downtown.

The angry aunt berated the reporter with a greasy chicken knife, but Patricia Quispe, 23, waved her off.

"It's okay. I'll talk."

Freed from its pins, Quispe's short, black hair hung level with her hard-set chin. She said she'd worn long braids since childhood but cut them off last year when she went to Buenos Aires in search of work.

"If you show up with braids, they call you an Indian," she said. "And they pay you a lot less."

Would Quispe call herself an Indian?

"Look," she said. "I'm a woman who works at a chicken stand. I go to night school for business administration. I grew up in the mountains and I wore petticoats—we all did. Then my mother died and we moved to the city."

So no, not anymore?

"Let me finish. I wear jeans to school and maybe I forget a lot of my Aymara. But I spent four months' pay on that outfit you saw Saturday, and it's the most beautiful thing I've ever put on."

The disgraced Miss Cholita La Paz fought back tears.

"Call me whatever you want," she said to the blood-smeared countertop.

MEMO FROM MEX. CITY:
Braidgate draft good. Tell Luis we need a photo.
Amp up "Modern Indian" angle a bit.
Maybe Quispe has a blog? Cell phone?

LA PAZ, Bolivia — More than a dozen people were injured Wednesday in violent protests against the construction of a new highway through Bolivia's remote eastern jungles.

The Trans-Amazon Highway aims to boost trade in South America's poorest country. But Amazonian Indians say the road will carve up their rainforest homeland.

Meanwhile, Aymara Indians in the dry western mountains see the route as opening Bolivia's fertile lowlands to settlement.

MEMO FROM MEX. CITY:
Confused. So we've got Indians vs. Indians here?
Or Indians vs. Civilization? If the latter pls. add to Braidgate final.
Price for car & driver to Trans-Amazon?

LA PAZ, Bolivia — A freelance radio correspondent called Wednesday looking for a ride out to the Trans-Amazon protests.

"Tell me you're going," she said when a reporter picked up. "Tell me you've got a seat for your favorite starving freelancer."

The reporter's budget was too tight for a dozen injured.

"You should go, though," he said. "You could take the bus."

"Jesus, that'd be like an hour for each victim."

"You could meditate on the way."

"You salary boys have no idea."

LA PAZ, Bolivia — The disgraced Miss Cholita La Paz was surprised Thursday to see a reporter return with a photographer just as she and her aunt were closing the chicken stand.

Patricia Quispe, 23, had to rush home and shower before night school, and was hesitant to be photographed in her work clothes.

"Ay, you should have called!" Quispe said, brushing at her stained sweater and worn velvet skirt. "I would have brought a nicer outfit."

Did Quispe have a cell phone?

"Of course I have a cell phone," Quispe said. She scribbled the number and her email address on a scrap of butcher paper. "Promise you'll send me a copy of your story."

The photographer asked Quispe if she'd put on her hat and step into the street to pose, gazing out at the city below.

Did she need to call anyone, maybe?

Quispe laughed. "Now? For the picture?" She pulled a cell phone from a hidden pocket in her skirt and pressed it to her ear. "Like this?"

She should really be talking to someone, the reporter said.

"Then I'll talk to *you*," Quispe said. "Where are you from? Where in the States, I mean."

The reporter always said Texas. Bolivians know what a Texan is.

"A cowboy, then!" Quispe said. "Where's your horse?" She made a pistol of her non-phone hand and fired at the camera. "Bang bang!"

LA PAZ, Bolivia—With a new Miss Cholita La Paz set to be crowned Friday night, reporters on the Patricia Quispe beat wondered if she might need a drink.

A freelance radio correspondent texted a reporter with the suggestion Friday afternoon. The reporter replied that he had already extended an invitation to the 23-year-old Quispe.

Well don't let me get in your way, answered the freelance radio correspondent.

No, you should come! the reporter wrote back. *What if we have nothing to talk about?*

LA PAZ, Bolivia—Judges crowned a new Miss Cholita La Paz Friday after disqualifying last week's winner for wearing fake braids.

The city's cultural bureau adopted much stricter rules regarding hair, which tradition dictates should run in braids all the way to a *cholita*'s waist.

Only half the original contestants returned.

Esmeralda Condori, 19, took the title with a dress of purple sequins and a mouthful of gold teeth.

Judges gamely tugged at her braids for the cameras.

MEMO FROM MEX. CITY:
Nice color but standalone story unnecessary.
Tell New York to just update Braidgate final with new winner.

LA PAZ, Bolivia—The disgraced Miss Cholita La Paz descended the stairs to the basement club Friday in skinny jeans, gold hoop earrings, and a jacket covered in zippers.

A reporter leapt up from his crowded table to introduce Patricia Quispe, 23. A freelance radio correspondent had dragged along two Spanish photographers and a guy who sometimes wrote for *Time*. Quispe gamely circled the table, kissing cheeks.

The freelance radio correspondent nudged the reporter's ribs. "No petticoats," she whispered.

Quispe called for a toast.

"To fake braids and real friends," she said.

As the correspondents drank, she dipped a finger in her glass and flicked a few drops of beer onto the concrete floor. "For the Pachamama," she explained.

The correspondents quickly followed suit.

LA PAZ, Bolivia—The club's floor show was a troupe of stern young men dressed in Indian ponchos and banging on big drums.

A guy who sometimes wrote for *Time* asked the disgraced Miss Cholita La Paz if she'd heard who'd won the pageant to replace her.

"I just came from there, actually," said Patricia Quispe, 23. "My aunt told me I shouldn't go, but I wanted to see. Esmeralda's a really good person. Speaks better Aymara than me, too. I'm happy for her."

"Wait, you were there?" said a freelance radio correspondent. "We didn't see you. You should have come found us."

Quispe shrugged. "I was kind of hiding in the back. It was just easier that way."

The floor show ended and pan flutes roared from the speakers.

A reporter asked Quispe to dance. She stood and smiled. Without the bowler hat, she barely reached the reporter's shoulder.

"Is this a partner dance?" he asked as they stepped onto the floor. "Do we hold hands?"

"Just the one hand, and then you spin me," Quispe said. "Watch."

LA PAZ, Bolivia—A spirited band of foreign correspondents say they lost two members of their party not long after reaching the End of the World.

The End of the World opens when everything else closes. Sweat runs down the blacked-out windows. Peruvians in the bathroom sell twisted baggies of cheap coke.

After a high-volume debate, the correspondents decided the disgraced Miss Cholita La Paz was last seen standing in a back corner. A reporter was leaning close. They were sharing a beer.

Later the police arrived and the bartender went outside to pay the bribe. In the empty street *cholitas* dug for bottles in the trash.

LA PAZ, Bolivia — Every night in the last hour before dawn someone scrubs down the sidewalk below a reporter's apartment.

In bed, through a loose metal window ten floors up, he hears the brush scratch back and forth over the soapy concrete.

The reporter and the disgraced Miss Cholita La Paz, Patricia Quispe, 23, make love without speaking.

Quispe moans *ay* three times, according to the reporter's count. The foreign syllable sends a quiver up his spine.

He wonders whether his gringo *oh* has the same effect.

The scrubbing stops. A bucket empties on the sidewalk. In the dark bedroom a cell phone beeps its low-battery warning.

LA PAZ, Bolivia — Patricia Quispe, 23, said Saturday that a reporter was not her first foreign boy.

The reporter leaned on an elbow in the first breath of gray morning light.

He was a backpacker, Quispe said. A couple years ago, before she went to Buenos Aires. From Australia, or maybe New Zealand.

"You see them downtown all the time, and if you're young and dressed *cholita* they just stare at you," she said. "I'm not stupid. I know what they're thinking."

The reporter gazed at her clothes on the floor. Jeans. Wadded-up socks. Knock-off Pumas, the logo a bird instead of a cat.

"He wanted me to take my braids down," Quispe said. "I said, 'No way—you know how much work these are?'"

LA PAZ, Bolivia — Studies have confirmed there is no less cowboy a gesture than fumbling for a pair of glasses on the nightstand.

A reporter offered breakfast. Patricia Quispe, 23, had chickens to sell.

Quispe pulled on jeans, shoved her socks into the pockets, and slipped her bare feet into fake Pumas.

She kissed the reporter at the door, walked to the elevator, and punched the button.

"*Chau chau,* Texas."

MEMO FROM MEX. CITY:
Braidgate getting great play online all morning.
New York loved it, wants to know what else we got.
What else we got?

LA PAZ, Bolivia—A reporter sat in his pajamas Saturday afternoon eating aspirin and imported U.S. cereal.

His cell phone buzzed, and he stared at it a long time before picking up.

"So, you a proper Bolivian now, or what?" the freelance radio correspondent asked.

"Um," the reporter said.

"Turn on your TV and call me back."

LA PAZ, Bolivia—One protester is dead and dozens more injured as violent clashes continued Saturday between police and Amazonian Indians blocking construction of a new highway through Bolivia's remote eastern jungles.

Television news footage showed opponents of the Trans-Amazon Highway setting fire to a bulldozer before being beaten back by police.

Police say the unidentified protester died from a heart attack suffered during the riot. Protesters claim the man was killed by a gunshot.

Aymara Indians in the dry western mountains, eager to settle the fertile lands along the proposed route, plan to march in the capital tomorrow to demand the controversial project continue.

MEMO FROM MEX. CITY:
Stay in La Paz for marching Indians.

Tell Luis to buy highway pix from a local shooter.
Keep car & driver on standby. Deaths continue, you hit the road.

LA PAZ, Bolivia—A freelance radio correspondent called Saturday night looking for a car and a driver.

"C'mon, one dead," she told a reporter. "You gotta go."

"Salary boy's stuck on the desk."

"Well, fuck it, then. I got savings. My producer wants this bad."

The reporter read off his list of drivers, all except Ramon. Ramon was the best, and Ramon was on standby.

"Thanks, I owe ya," said the freelance radio correspondent.

"Let me call you for some color."

"Buy you a drink when I get back," she said. "You want color, you get your ass down there yourself."

LA PAZ, Bolivia—An American journalist was killed Sunday when her car plunged from a recently built mountain highway.

Kate Ballantine, 28, was rushing to cover violent clashes between police and Amazonian Indians over the construction of a new route through Bolivia's remote eastern jungles.

The Bolivian driver was also killed.

MEMO FROM MEX. CITY:
Awful. Did you know her? Can you expand a bit?
Something short. Remember: desk closes early Sundays.

LA PAZ, Bolivia—An American journalist was killed early Sunday when her car plunged from a lonely mountain highway.

Kate Ballantine, 28, of San Francisco, was traveling overnight to reach the site of violent Indian protests. The car's driver was also killed.

Ballantine had been working as a freelance radio correspondent in Bolivia for six months. Her producer in New York called her death "a tragic loss for our listeners and for Bolivia, a place whose story she told with remarkable insight and compassion."

Ballantine had brown eyes and a quick smile. She swore like a proper journo. A reporter was working up the courage to kiss her before the rains came.

Fog hangs low in the Andes at night. The few lights are scattered and dim. Police do not know how long she lay down there in the dark.

The wheels stop spinning. The insect songs resume. The very farthest point from home.

MORE KATE HERE I can't.

I think the driver's name was Javier.

MEMO FROM MEX. CITY:

Thanks. We'll cut from here.

Take a few days, man. Whatever you need.

Last thing: SF desk still closed. Any family contact info for comment?

LA PAZ, Bolivia—A reporter shared a taxi home from the wake with a guy who sometimes wrote for *Time*.

"My parents want me to come home," the guy said. "Like this is the only story they've read the whole time."

The taxi crept along under orange streetlights. It was dark but still early. The radio recited its evening news.

The guy checked his phone. "I mean, Kate would want us to stay, right?"

LA PAZ, Bolivia—Police say a man narrowly escaped death when his neighbors tried to bury him alive in the concrete pylon of a new bridge.

Residents of the small city of Caracollo, 110 miles south of the capital, La Paz, believed the bridge would collapse without an offering to Pachamama, the Andean Earth goddess.

Witnesses told a Bolivian television station that the man, described as a homeless drunk, was passed out in the street when town elders selected him for the sacrifice.

But as they lowered him into the concrete mold, the man woke and scrambled out, assaulting several people before police arrived.

Bolivia is the poorest country in South America.

NATHANIEL RICH

■

The Man Who Saves You from Yourself

FROM *Harper's Magazine*

NOBODY EVER JOINS A CULT. One joins a nonprofit group that pro-
motes green technology, animal rights, or transcendental meditation.
One joins a yoga class or an entrepreneurial workshop. One begins
practicing an Eastern religion that preaches peace and forbearance.
The first rule of recruitment, writes Margaret Singer, the doyenne of
cult scholarship, is that a recruit must never suspect he or she is being recruited. The second rule is that the cult must monopolize the
recruit's time. Therefore, in order to have any chance of rescuing a
new acolyte, it is critical to act quickly. The problem is that family
and friends, much like the new cult member, are often slow to admit
the severity of the situation. "Clients usually don't come to me until
their daughter is already to-the-tits brainwashed," says David Sullivan, a private investigator in San Francisco who specializes in cults.
"By that point the success rate is very low."

Sullivan became fascinated with cults in the late sixties, while attending Fairview High School in Boulder, Colorado. It was a golden
age for religious fringe groups, and Boulder was one of the nation's
most fertile recruiting centers, as it is today. (There are now, according to conservative estimates, 2 million adults involved in cults in
America.) "You couldn't walk five steps without being approached
by someone asking whether you'd like to go to a Buddhist meeting,"
says John Stark, a high school friend of Sullivan's. Representatives

from Jews for Jesus and the Moonies set up information booths in the student union at the University of Colorado, a few miles down the road from Fairview High. Sullivan engaged the hawkers, accepted the pamphlets, attended every meditation circle, prayer circle, shamanic circle. When the Maharishi Mahesh Yogi led a mass meditation session at the university, Sullivan was there, watching from the back of the lecture hall.

Sullivan was not religious. Though raised Catholic, by high school he considered himself a "hardcore atheist." Before the family moved to Boulder, his father had managed a used-car dealership in Salina, Kansas. His mother worked in a pawnshop. On Thursday nights, during the late shift, Sullivan sat with her at the counter, where he met criminals, alcoholics, and grifters trying to stay one step ahead of bill collectors. He saw how people could be manipulated if you exploited their weaknesses. He learned about desperation and the lies people told to arouse sympathy. From his grandfather, a funeral-home director who, Sullivan suspects, forged death certificates for the local Catholic church, he learned how to keep a secret. The suicide of a gay priest was called a heart attack. The botched abortion of a pregnant nun was pneumonia.

During spring break in 1968, inspired by *On the Road*, Sullivan and Stark set off on a tour of the Southwest in Sullivan's baby-blue Pontiac convertible. They visited Drop City in southern Colorado, eating brown rice and tofu under geodesic domes, and the New Buffalo Commune outside of Taos, New Mexico, washing dishes after the communal meal and hitting on the women. Stark remembers how excited Sullivan would become when he entered these communities. "He had a wanderlust, a powerful urge to immerse himself in these different cultures." When they spent the following summer in Mexico City, Stark noticed that Sullivan had begun to speak with a Mexican accent.

"There was a soul-searching element of it," says Sullivan. "But I was also curious to know what the gurus were getting out of it. And I wanted to figure out how they picked up all those girls."

The spiritual groups, he soon realized, shared a simple tactic: they demanded that their followers suspend critical thought. "They'd say, 'You have to break out of your Western mentality. You're too judgmental. You have to abandon your whole psychological-intellectual framework. Your obsessive materialism is blocking you from seeing the truth.'

"I became disturbed by how dramatically they transformed people, and in such a short period of time. They could take some regular American kid and all of a sudden he's wearing saffron robes, walking around barefoot, all painted up, with a tiny ponytail and shaved head, dancing for hours, selling flowers and incense, living on the floor and eating disgusting food, repeating *Hare Krishna, Hare Krishna, Krishna Krishna, Hare Hare, Hare Rama.* They persuaded a lot of intelligent young people to drop out of college, fuck up their whole career track, break up with their boyfriend or girlfriend, and go off to some retreat. Next thing you know, they've lost contact with their family, they're scrubbing latrines with toothbrushes and liquidating their personal savings."

In 1974, Sullivan briefly dated a woman whose grandparents had joined something called the Peoples Temple in San Francisco, led by the Reverend Jim Jones. Sullivan's girlfriend called him one day in tears. Her grandparents had announced that they were following Jones to a settlement he was founding in Guyana. They had already packed their suitcases, but Sullivan helped persuade them not to go.

He received another call around the same time from a friend whose sister was being initiated into a group called the Divine Light Mission. The DLM's leader was a pudgy thirteen-year-old boy from Haridwar, India, named Prem Rawat. He was said to be the reincarnation of his father, the Perfect Master Guru Maharaji, the founder of the DLM, who died when Rawat was eight. The DLM had millions of followers in India, but its adolescent guru wanted to bring his message to America. He arrived in 1971, preceded by a press release: "He is coming in the clouds with great power and glory, and his silver steed will drift down at 4 p.m. at Los Angeles international airport, TWA Flight 761." A crowd of reporters and screaming young acolytes greeted him at the airport. The DLM incorporated as a tax-exempt church in Colorado and established an ashram in Wallstreet—an abandoned town ten miles west of Boulder that had been conceived, in 1897, as a socialist utopia.

When Sullivan arrived in Wallstreet, suppliants were lined up alongside a creek outside the ashram, waiting to be granted admittance to the Perfect Master's chambers. Once inside, they bowed before the guru's feet, made an offering of a *khata*, a ceremonial scarf purchased at the gate for a buck fifty, and received a blessing. Then they sat and listened for hours to the boy's droning pronouncements:

"The lotus flower grows in filthy water, yet it is pure."

"You do not want to just polish the car, the outside. You want to work on the inside."

"When we die, we will become one with God. It will be like a drop of water that falls in the ocean. Can you take that same drop out again?"

Sullivan stood in the back and watched as the boy gawked at the breasts of the American girls who bowed before him. (Three years later, at age sixteen, Rawat would marry a twenty-four-year-old Pacific Southwest Airlines stewardess named Marolyn Johnson.) But the boy did not interest Sullivan nearly as much as did the boy's mother.

Mata Ji, "Holy Mother," was a large, buxom woman in a sari who wore wraparound green-tinted sunglasses. She stood behind her son, scrutinizing every visitor. Occasionally, displeased by something her son said, she leaned close and whispered into his ear. The boy would stiffen, his eyes widening, and nod abjectly. When he repeated her lines she rewarded him with round pieces of taffy, hand-feeding him as one might a trained monkey. Holy Mother caught Sullivan staring. When Sullivan began to ask skeptical questions to some of the followers, a lackey asked him to leave.

Back in Boulder, Sullivan found his friend's sister. She was a smart, pretty girl from the East Coast with artistic aspirations and a trust fund—an ideal recruit.

Sullivan met her in Boulder's Beach Park. The conversation did not get off to a good start.

"How can you possibly sit in judgment of an ancient Eastern religion?" she said. "In India they have a deep and powerful understanding of life. We in the West, we're spiritually impoverished. We're a new society without traditions. Their civilization has been around for aeons!"

"They've been conning people for centuries," said Sullivan. "That's the only thing that's ancient about this."

"The Perfect Master says humility is a good thing, poverty is a good thing, manual labor is a good thing. What's wrong with that?"

"If that's the case, then why doesn't he ever lift a finger? Why does he fly first class or in chartered jets?"

They went back and forth like this for an hour. Finally Sullivan took a different approach.

"Forget about their philosophy," he said. "Let's focus instead on who is really in power."

He explained what he'd seen at the ashram, the way the mother dominated the son. Sullivan knew that the girl had come to Boulder to escape her alcoholic mother.

"If you join the DLM, you're not going to be working for that little boy," said Sullivan. "You're going to be working for Big Momma."

That cut it. She stopped visiting the ashram, finished college, and got a master's degree in fine arts. The Divine Light Mission, she realized, was not her calling. But Sullivan had found his.

She introduced herself as Stella Zrnic, a twenty-four-year-old Croatian immigrant who had recently moved to San Francisco. She knew nobody in America and hoped that Dr. Kurt Robinson might help her. She had found Dr. Robinson's email address on a website that offered dream interpretation. In the About Me section of the site, Dr. Robinson had written: "I am a true subconscious communicator."

"I'm writing to you because of the dreams and nightmares that I cannot get rid of," Stella began her letter.

Dr. Robinson responded immediately. "Give me a call," he wrote, providing a private phone number. "I can help you."

Soon they were talking on the phone every day. Dr. Robinson's voice was cheerful, friendly. He didn't sound like any therapist Stella had ever met.

"It was brave of you to move to a strange country without knowing anybody. You are very nice, and very smart. But I worry about you."

"You do?"

"Of course I do," said Dr. Robinson. "You're too young to be so unhappy, to be contemplating suicide."

He asked about her dreams.

"I have nightmares where someone is chasing me," she said.

Dr. Robinson didn't seem particularly interested in that. She tried again. "I had a dream about my mother having sex with my boss."

"Describe it for me." After she did, he said, "Describe it again — in more detail. I want to see how your mind works."

He told her to read his book, which was available on his website. It was confusing, and terribly written, but she persisted because he kept asking her about it. He was thrilled when she told him that she'd enjoyed it.

"Have you been in any serious romantic relationships?"

"I was seeing someone in Croatia. But we've been growing apart since I moved to America."

"How old were you the first time you had sex?"

"Sixteen."

"Was it a positive experience for you?"

He mentioned that he led a psychology workshop at his home in Orange County, California. He hinted that his students lived with him.

"They want to learn how to be happy," he said. "I'm here to help them."

"Can I visit your workshop?"

"I can cure people from a distance. My soul can travel outside of my body."

She pressed, but Dr. Robinson demurred. There were no openings available, and a long wait list. Besides, she wasn't mature enough. If they continued to speak regularly, however, she might yet prove herself.

"It's just that I miss my family," she said. "And my old friends."

"But you don't need them anymore. We'll be your family. We'll be your friends. Do you trust me?"

"Yes. I think so."

"I need to be certain," he said.

"How will you be certain?"

"Do you have a camera?"

The psychological methods used by a cult leader are the same as those used by con men, advertisers, and politicians. As Margaret Singer writes in *Cults in Our Midst*:

> Cult leaders and con artists are opportunists who read the times and the ever-changing culture and adapt their pitch to what will appeal at a given moment. These manipulators survive because they adapt and because they are chameleon-like. So, at some times we get cults based on health fads, business-training programs, get-rich-quick schemes, and relationship improvement seminars; at others we get fundamentalist religious

cults, Eastern meditation groups, identity or hate groups, longevity groups, and so forth.

Singer, who died in 2003, was a mentor to Sullivan. "She was the most knowledgeable and intuitive person I ever met," says Sullivan. "She taught me how to recognize the influence of a cult leader, even in people who disguised their connection to a group. She taught me how to keep my composure. And, most invaluably, she taught me how to resist being programmed."

Like Singer, Sullivan doesn't think that any cult leaders are true believers. "Some of them come to believe their own bullshit—they almost have to in order to be convincing. But on a deeper level they know they're full of shit. I say that because the guru's teachings will always correspond with his desires. For example, if there is a pretty young convert, the Holy Spirits will always decide that she has been specially ordained to be the leader's consort, whereas the homely, hardworking woman will always be reserved for one of his schmucks. It's the same thing with money—the richest devotee is always considered the most devout.

"Some leaders do make mistakes. They surround themselves with a small circle of sycophants and start to believe too much in their own powers. These are the ones, like David Koresh or Jim Jones, who are most likely to take everyone down with them in a grand extension of their narcissism. And even so, they resort to mass suicide only when they come under threat and have no other way out. Marshall Applewhite of Heaven's Gate, for instance, had a terminal illness. But the most powerful cults, like Scientology or est, don't for a minute believe their own bullshit, at least not at the higher levels. The people in control know it's a game of money and power."

Sullivan first worked with Singer in the early nineties. One case involved a woman posing as a psychologist, who had persuaded several of her male clients to undergo sex-reassignment surgery. (The men later alleged that they had been brainwashed.) Singer also collaborated with Sullivan on an investigation of a therapist based in Carmel, California. Sullivan's involvement began when he received a call from a lawyer named John Winer.

"I've never had a dilemma like this," said Winer. "I have a potential client, a woman living in Carmel, who alleges outrageous things against her therapist. It sounds crazy, but I'm convinced she's telling the truth. If she is, it's a huge case. But then I deposed the therapist, and either *he's* telling the truth or everything is a lie."

The woman claimed that her therapist, Dr. James D. Nivette, had seduced her and turned her into his personal sex slave. Nivette flatly denied this, and he seemed trustworthy. He was beloved in his community: a consultant for the Monterey Police Department, a volunteer at the local VA hospital, and a professor at Monterey Peninsula College. His patient had a personality disorder, he said, and had fallen in love with him. When he rebuffed her, she concocted an elaborate sexual fantasy.

The woman's story did seem outlandish. She claimed that Nivette worked for a clandestine government agency more secretive than the CIA, and that one day he had taken her to a remote trailer park near Napa Valley (she couldn't remember the exact location) where everyone addressed him by a code name. He drove a black Porsche with a license plate that read ZAUBER, German for "magic." And he really *did* have magical powers, she claimed—in fact, he was a practicing wizard! He had also served as a fighter pilot during the Vietnam War and was shot down while flying over China. At the POW camp he seduced a female guard, who helped him escape.

She said that after she tried to end the relationship, Nivette climbed through her window in the middle of the night and crawled into her bed. She awoke with a pistol pressed against her temple. "If you open your mouth," he said, "I'll kill you and I'll kill your daughter." He raped her, then slipped back out the window.

Winer hired Sullivan to find out whether there was any evidence to support the woman's story. The reason he chose Sullivan, he says today, "is his knowledge of psychology. . . . He's very creative in the way he approaches a case. He is able to talk to clients in a way that makes them feel he understands them. People say things to him that they wouldn't ordinarily say."

Sullivan drove to Carmel and interviewed Nivette's accuser. He examined Nivette's public records at the local courthouse. He spoke to Nivette's sister and his elderly mother's caregiver. He interviewed security guards at Monterey Peninsula College. After two days, he called Winer.

"Don't tell me," Winer said. "She's out of her mind."

"No, man. Even worse. She's telling the truth."

Nivette, Sullivan had found, had a history of sleeping with his young female patients. If a woman refused his advances, he diagnosed her as delusional and had her committed. Nivette was so powerful in the community that nobody reported him. He collected guns and swords and intimidated his mentally fragile patients with talk of mystical powers and secret government connections. He did have FBI clearance, but it was only to work at the VA, where he counseled Vietnam vets with post-traumatic stress disorder. The FBI hired him because he claimed to be a Vietnam veteran, but Sullivan discovered that this was a lie—during the war Nivette had been a student at UCLA. Sullivan also found, in Texas, another victim of Nivette's. She confirmed the story of the Napa trailer park and gave him directions to it.

Winer accepted the case. Margaret Singer was hired to serve as an expert witness, but Nivette agreed to a pretrial settlement. Penniless, he left Carmel and disappeared.

A few years later, in 1997, an eighteen-month-old boy was found abandoned on a street in an industrial section of San Bruno, near the San Francisco airport. On the same day, the body of a young woman named Gina Barnett was discovered in an apartment in Folsom. Barnett's boyfriend identified the San Bruno infant as her child. The father, he said, was James Nivette. Police learned that he had shot Barnett and ditched his son on the way to the airport, then fled to France.

Nivette was extradited four years later. He is currently serving eighteen years to life at the California Men's Colony in San Luis Obispo.

"Croatia has produced a lot of great tennis players," said Dr. Robinson. "Goran Ivanišević. Novak Djokovic."

"Djokovic is Serbian."

"Do you play tennis? I'm actually an excellent tennis player myself."

Stella spoke with Dr. Robinson for hours at a time. He bristled when she called him Doctor. He preferred Teacher. He explained that the world programs you in ways that limit your freedom, and that it was his job to deprogram her. If she didn't pick up the phone immediately when he called, he became furious.

"What were you doing that you couldn't pick up the phone? Be honest. Were you out with a boy?"

"My phone was at the bottom of my purse. I didn't hear it ringing."

"I'm taking time away from my practice to talk with you. Do you know how many people are on my waiting list? How many psychiatrists come to me for advice because their methods are ineffective? I'm going to have to think about whether I want to speak with you again."

She apologized and promised to carry the phone in her hand at all times.

Dr. Robinson sighed. "I know it's hard for you. My main goal is to help you grow. And you are beginning to grow. But in order to reach the next dimension, you need to allow yourself to be more free."

"I'm trying."

"Have you taken the pictures of yourself like I asked you to?"

"Yes." She had taken photographs of her face.

"Send them to me. I want to see how free you are."

Dr. Robinson liked the photographs she sent.

"You're beautiful," he said. "But I can see that you're not completely free. Can you do something for me?"

"Yes."

"Stand in front of the mirror fully naked. Take a picture of your body."

"I don't know if I can do that."

"Don't you feel comfortable naked? You're a unique, beautiful human being. You have to trust me. When you show me the most intimate parts of yourself I can connect with your real nature, and then I can lead you to your true self."

"I'll try."

"There's a girl here with us who reminds me of you. Her name is Kati. She recently immigrated, too—from Turkey. You would like her. Maybe one day you can come visit us. But first you must prove to me that you're ready."

Although most cults use the same basic psychological techniques, they each have their own codes, symbols, and lexicon. Often the only way to reach an indoctrinated member is to communicate in the cult's language. In order to master this vocabulary, Sullivan must join the cult himself.

"David is a chameleon," says Patrick O'Reilly, a psychologist specializing in undue influence. "I've seen him work closely with gunrunners, psychopathic murderers, cult leaders. He's excellent at assimilating to any subculture, and he is relentless about getting information. He has an uncanny ability to become whatever it is the person is looking for."

During the winter of 2001, Sullivan infiltrated an organization based in Salt Lake City called Impact Trainings. The group, which is still active today, placed advertisements for its "Harmony" seminars, which promised to "empower the human spirit toward a free, unconditional loving and joyful life." The seminars were held in large, windowless warehouses and lasted as long as four days. They were led by "facilitators" who established psychological control over the trainees through public humiliation.

Two days into the seminar, Sullivan found himself hiding behind the warehouse, lying prostrate beneath some bushes, whispering into a dying cell phone.

"I think they're going to kill me," he said. "My cover's blown."

Sullivan hadn't slept since the seminar started. He had been forced to subsist on a near-starvation diet: sugar pops and water. (Protein deprivation is a common tactic; without protein you can't think.) All he wanted was to return to the warehouse, announce who he was, try to persuade as many people as possible to leave, then run outside to his rental car and race to the airport. But Kim Kruglick, an attorney who had hired Sullivan on the recommendation of Margaret Singer, wouldn't hear of it.

"What the hell are we paying you for?" Kruglick said. "Get back in there!"

"You don't understand," Sullivan whispered. "I'm at the end of my rope. I can't take it anymore."

"But you can't leave now. You haven't even been *reborn* yet!"

The phone died.

Kruglick was serving as a defense attorney in a bizarre murder case in Marin County. On August 7, 2000, nine nylon duffel bags containing dismembered body parts floated to the surface of the Mokelumne River near Sacramento. Early that morning, Marin County police arrested Glenn Taylor Helzer, thirty, a charismatic, handsome former

Morgan Stanley stockbroker; his brother, Justin, twenty-eight; and Dawn Godman, twenty-six, a depressive, overweight woman who lived with the Helzers at their home in Concord, California.

Godman had met the Helzer brothers a year earlier, at a murder-mystery dinner hosted by the Latter-day Saints Temple in Walnut Creek. The Helzers stood out from the rest of the congregation. They dressed in black and spoke in koans. They had been raised in a strict Mormon family, but Taylor was beginning to stray. He had attended seminars conducted by Impact Trainings and encouraged Godman to go through the Harmony training. After she completed the first two levels, Taylor announced that he would take over as her personal trainer.

Inspired by Harmony, Taylor planned to start his own self-help group, Transform America, part of a grand scheme to bring about Christ's millennial reign. He decided that God had put him on earth to take over the Mormon church and become its true prophet. His younger brother and Godman were his first two disciples.

God told Taylor that the best way to overthrow the Mormon church was to adopt Brazilian orphans and train them to be assassins. Once they became teenagers, the child mercenaries would execute the fifteen highest-ranking officers of the Mormon church, preparing the way for Taylor's ascension. But Taylor needed money to finance this operation.

One idea was to import underage girls, again from Brazil, and use them to blackmail Taylor's married clients at Morgan Stanley. Another was to have his girlfriend, Keri Mendoza, pose for *Playboy*. This plan worked — the magazine accepted Mendoza's photos — but after she was named Playmate of the Month for September 2000 she broke up with Taylor and kept the money for herself. (At the Helzers' murder trial, Mendoza testified that the plan to import underage Brazilian girls "didn't feel right to me in my heart.")

On July 30, 2000, the Helzers and Godman kidnapped Ivan and Annette Stineman, two of Taylor's elderly banking clients. Taylor ordered Ivan to write Godman a check for $100,000. Taylor then beat Ivan to death, and Justin cut Annette's throat. Later that day the Helzers killed Taylor's girlfriend, Selina Bishop, who they worried might be able to connect them to the Stineman murders; Bishop's mother and a friend were staying at her apartment, so they were killed, too. The Helzers butchered the five corpses, mixing up the bodies in different duffel bags, rented Jet Skis, and dumped the bags in the river. God had neglected to educate Taylor in the chemistry of decomposition, however, and several days later, when the remains began to leach gases, the bags floated to the surface.

Godman could avoid the death penalty by testifying against the Helzers. But she still believed that Taylor was a prophet and that she would soon transcend the prison walls and reunite with him in heaven. She refused to speak with her lawyers; in fact she refused to speak with anyone who hadn't been reborn through Harmony. That's when her lawyers called David Sullivan.

The Harmony trainings were led by a man called the Trainer. He had a sonorous voice, a helmet of hair, and impeccable self-confidence. His enforcers were called Angels. On the first day, the Trainer conducted an exercise in which each trainee—there were about eighty in the class—confessed his or her greatest failures. Then the trainees were given new names. A victim of incest became Daddy's Joytoy; a woman with a history of cutting herself was Slice and Dice; an unmarried pregnant woman was White Trash Slut. It was forbidden to call anyone by anything other than his or her nickname. Because Sullivan "thought too much," the Trainer christened him Anal-Cranial Inversion.

Trainees were taught that they were responsible for their misfortunes. Daddy's Joytoy, for instance, was told that she had seduced her father. An obese woman was forced to wear a cow costume. At one point the Trainer singled out a pretty blonde who kept one of her hands in her pocket at all times.

"Be honest with us," said the Trainer. "You despise your husband. You despise your children."

"That's not true," the woman said. "I love my family."

"Take your hand out of your pocket."

She shook her head pleadingly.

"Hold up your hand!"

Sobbing, she obeyed. Her fingers were fused together in the shape of a triangle.

"See how ugly your hand is?" said the Trainer. "That's the ugliness you carry around inside of you!"

The night before Sullivan called Kim Kruglick from the bushes, the trainees were divided into groups of seven. Each group member was made to stand silently while the others took turns screaming in his or her face. They stood as close as drill sergeants, so you could feel their breath and spittle.

"You are scum!"

"You're a rip-off! You're incapable of love! You've wasted your life!"

"Prostitute!"

"Fat ass!"

"Pervert!"

To avoid suspicion, Sullivan yelled as vociferously as the others, but he was beginning to wonder how much longer he could hold up. One young woman in his group was so anguished that, in the middle of her session, she started vomiting quietly down the front of her dress.

Sullivan became especially concerned about the attentions of one fellow trainee, an attractive, poised woman with dark, intelligent eyes. He didn't remember her name, but privately he thought of her as the Observant One. He caught her staring at him and wondered whether she had been planted by the Angels.

After the screaming exercise, the Trainer gave a new command: "Walk around the room and find the person you most despise."

The Observant One grabbed Sullivan immediately.

"*You*," she said. "Anal-Cranial Inversion."

The trainees were told to sit with their partners and spend fifteen minutes talking about how much they hated each other. As soon as they were alone, the Observant One leaned forward.

"I chose you because I don't think you're like the others," she whispered. "I think you're a spy. Or maybe the police."

Sullivan began to wonder whether he could outsprint the nearest Angel to the parking lot.

"I don't know what you're talking about," he said. "You got me all wrong—"

"You have to get me out of here."

"What?"

"Please. You're the only hope I have left."

An Angel passed near them.

"You're despicable!" said Sullivan loudly. "You're a liar! You're beneath contempt!"

The Angel walked away.

"I was forced to come here," the woman continued. "I had cancer. My fiancé left me. My boss took over my life. He told me that I had to attend the training. But I can't take it anymore."

Sullivan empathized with her. Two years earlier he had been diagnosed with liver cancer, and his girlfriend had abandoned him in the middle of treatment. He wanted to help the Observant One, but he couldn't jeopardize the Godman case. He told himself not to break character. Then he broke character.

"Listen," he said. "You're going to put us both in serious danger if you don't do exactly as I tell you."

He pointed out the surveillance cameras. There was a control room where the Angels watched video monitors. He would wander into the control room and make a scene. As soon as the Angels glanced away from the monitors, she would have to escape. To buy time after she left, Sullivan would claim that she was in the bathroom being sick. When they finally realized she was missing, she'd be in Wyoming.

Two hours later, when the Angels discovered that the Observant One had escaped, they turned their attention to Sullivan. He was ordered to stand in the Humiliation Box. The Angels took turns shouting into his face. He was not allowed to sit, go to the bathroom, eat, or drink. When Sullivan got back to his room that night it looked like it had been searched.

The next morning, hoping to discourage further suspicion, Sullivan embraced his activities with renewed vigor. During a session in which the trainees were asked to deliver self-debasing monologues, Sullivan became so overwrought that he punched his chair until his knuckles bled. An Angel brought him a bag of ice. But he knew he'd have to do more.

The Trainer began his redemption speech. This is the second part of the brainwashing process; after being broken down psychologically, the initiate is overwhelmed with acceptance and love.

"No matter how low you've sunk," said the Trainer in his booming, paternal voice, "I can offer you a way out. If you are willing to take my hand, we can move forward. We can find our way to a new life—"

Sullivan jumped to his feet.

"Yes!" he cried. "I feel it!"

The Trainer and the Angels looked at him in astonishment.

"Oh sir," said Sullivan, "oh *sir*, can I please express what's inside me right now?"

"Sure, Anal-Cranial Inversion," said the Trainer. "What is it?"

"May I?"

The Trainer shrugged and handed Sullivan the microphone. Before the Trainer had time to reconsider, Sullivan leaped onto the stage and belted out, in a trembling baritone, the first lines of "The Impossible Dream (The Quest)," from *Man of La Mancha*. He built it gradually, the emotion in his voice rising. The crowd watched in awe. Some of the trainees began to sob. The head Angel embraced Sullivan. By the end, many in the audience had joined in and they all sang together, louder and louder, teary and off-key: "To dream . . . the impossible dream!"

Anal-Cranial Inversion had been redeemed. He graduated the training and was pronounced reborn. The Trainer even invited him to the training for Angels. He had been deemed worthy to brainwash the next group of initiates.

Sullivan returned for the second training a month later, and then attended one of Godman's pretrial hearings. He got her attention while sitting in the audience, flashing hand signals he had learned at Harmony: an open palm with four fingers spread wide, indicating that he was a trusted, heart connection. Godman beamed. When he visited her jail cell, she welcomed him with a wide, blissful smile. She believed he had walked through the prison walls, that he was Archangel Michael, come to save her.

He met with her regularly for six weeks. Slowly she began to realize what had happened to her.

"Taylor wasn't a prophet, was he?" she finally said.

"No," said Sullivan. "He's not a prophet."

She broke down.

"You mean we killed all those people for *nothing*?"

Godman testified against the Helzers. Today Taylor is on death row at San Quentin; Justin committed suicide in prison earlier this year. Godman is at the Valley State Prison for Women in Chowchilla. She will be eligible for parole in 2043.

"You were supposed to call twenty minutes ago."

"I'm sorry," said Stella. "I had bad dreams. I overslept."

"You're like a little puppy. If I let you in my house, you would put your dirty paws all over the furniture, soil the carpet, drink from the toilet."

"Last night—"

"Listen to me!" said Dr. Robinson. "You never listen to me. It's all your father's fault—he never showed you enough affection. He was too tough on you. That caused great damage."

"Yes, Teacher. I know."

"You are just like Kati. The intimacy problems, the troubled background. Unlike you, however, she is diligent, committed, and responsible. Is there a street you walk down every day on the way to your babysitting job?"

Stella couldn't tell whether Dr. Robinson was being rhetorical. Dr. Robinson was often being rhetorical.

"I asked you a question."

"Yes," she said. "There is such a street."

"Have you ever felt that this street is beautiful one day but ugly the next?"

"I guess."

"Of course you have! That's proof, you see, that reality is all in our heads. It's not the street's fault. The street is always the same. It's us—we're the ones who change. You understand?"

She murmured her assent.

"Have you begun to perceive the benefits of our conversations?"

"I feel better, but I don't know why. Last night I had a dream that I was a turtle, and my shell was peeling off."

"That's very good. The shell, you see, is the hardness in you. And you must peel it away in order to access the real Stella. You are making progress."

"Yes, Teacher."

"One thing concerns me, however. In the pictures you sent, you're wearing a dress. You're wearing tights. Everything is covered."

"I don't feel comfortable taking naked photographs of myself."

He told her again about Kati, who had been raised by religious parents and found it difficult to "open herself up sexually." But he had treated her, and now she was taking many photographs of herself. First she relaxed in front of the camera. Then she was able to relax in bed.

"Poor Stella. You still have so far to go. This is part of your deprogramming. This shyness about your body is not you. It is what the world is telling you to do."

"Yes, Teacher."

"I'm trying to help you to be free," said Dr. Robinson. "But you have to work at it, too."

Stella sent him naked photographs of herself. They were demure, low exposure, her legs crossed, her hands over her breasts, though in one photograph she revealed a nipple.

"This is just you being closed," he said. "You're not trusting me enough. You are disappointing me so painfully. You will have to prove yourself to me in another way."

When an acolyte absolutely cannot be deprogrammed, when she is too far gone to be reasoned with, there is only one strategy left: destroy the entire cult. Several years ago Sullivan received a call from a man in Marin County who owns a chain of retail stores. The man's niece, Judy, had become a devotee of someone who called himself Swami Sebastian. The Swami was a tall, good-looking black man who wore turbans and flowing white robes, spoke in a Nigerian accent, and claimed to be the reincarnation of Christ. He named his group the Mother Divine Love Foundation and placed flyers around Marin County:

Are you feeling a deep urge to make changes in your life? Are you feeling a burning desire to connect with the wholeness of yourself? Then reach out and Touch Yourself with a 30-minute session of phone dreaming. Learn to access and develop your own line of inner communication and experience the internal freedom and sense of renewed energy as you release the blocks to living life to its fullest.

Other flyers were more explicit:

Experience Sexual Healing
The Tantricka, Enlightened Mystic
The Traveling Wanderer from

> Eternity to Eternity has come to
> America and is sharing the joy &
> ecstasy of:
>> Tantric
>> Explosion
>
> 8 p.m. to 10 p.m. FRIDAYS
> Share the fruits. Taste the nectar of
>   this Divine Being.
> Explore the ancient secrets of Africa,
>   Asia and the Caribbean
> Flexible Financial Arrangements
>   Available

The Swami's disciples, mostly young women, lived with him in a house in Bayshore, just south of San Francisco. They called him Abba. He explained that he was the personification of all good and all evil. In Nigeria he had been an African warrior, and when he was a young child Haile Selassie had touched his head and pronounced him a divine spiritual being. Judy had conceived a son with Abba.

The Swami owned a juice bar on Capuchino Avenue in Burlingame called Sebastian's Take Outrageous. He used it to recruit new members. Judy, who was in her late thirties, was his oldest and plainest disciple. But she was also the richest. Abba rechristened her Blessing and told her that her role in life was to bestow blessings. This meant that she was to fund his refuge for women and babies in Jamaica and to support him with a monthly income. So far she had given him more than $35,000. Judy's family had succeeded in getting her to leave the Swami once before, but after three weeks she returned, and the family began to receive threatening calls and letters. Cars with tinted windows would drive slowly past their home.

"I promised my wife I'd help Judy," said Sullivan's client, "but we have two young children, and I don't want to put them at risk. I'll pay you to get her out, but I don't want this maniac to know I'm involved."

Sullivan staked out the Swami's house. In addition to Blessing, the Swami spent a lot of time with a stunning young woman named Heather. Heather had long, dark hair, pale skin, and dark eyes—an ideal temple love goddess. The Swami had renamed her Hathaya.

When the Swami arrived home one day, Sullivan took photographs with a telephoto lens, then sped away. He made sure the Swami saw him.

"Come back here!" screamed the Swami, running after Sullivan's car, middle fingers raised. "Who are you, motherfucker?"

A funny thing happened when the Swami cursed: his accent disappeared. He didn't sound like a Nigerian anymore. He sounded like an American.

Sullivan had his operatives tail the Swami. They reported that he left home each morning with three or four of his acolytes and drove to different houses in a white Cadillac. Every stop was the same: he'd knock, a woman would greet him warmly, and he'd enter the house, sometimes with the girls, sometimes without. He'd stay about an hour, then leave, often carrying a bulging envelope.

Sullivan visited Sebastian's Take Outrageous while the Swami was on his rounds. There were bags of oranges piled up in the bathroom, bundles of wheatgrass stacked on the floor, and the serving area was grimy with rotting fruit. Sullivan noted that the business license was expired, so he called the local health board. An officer showed up the next day and ordered the juice bar to close until a new license had been procured.

Sullivan researched the LLC listed on the business license and discovered it was controlled by a man named Delroy Miller. He ran a background check on that name and found that Miller had a criminal record in a small town outside Fort Worth, Texas. Sullivan looked up the number for the police department there.

"Delroy!" said the sheriff when Sullivan called. "What's ol' Delroy up to these days?"

"He's in California now."

"Better you than us."

"Tell me, what kind of trouble did he get into back in Texas?"

"Delroy was just a flimflam man. Sometimes he cut fraudulent checks. Sometimes he was a preacher accepting donations. Sometimes he had an aluminum-siding and roofing business. He'd get the deposit and skip the work. Or he'd case the house and send his buddies to burglarize it a week later. He did some time, and when he got out I told him he better move on. So he did. Has he been arrested?"

"No. He's found a new calling."

"What would that be?"

"Well, sir, Delroy isn't Delroy anymore. He calls himself Swami Sebastian, and he has a sex cult in a small town south of San Francisco."

"No shit. A *swami*." Sullivan heard the sheriff talking to another officer. "You remember Delroy the Jamaican? Yeah, well now he's a goddamned sex swami in California!"

"Do you have any background on the guy?" asked Sullivan. "Do you know where he came from?"

"He had some trouble in Georgia, if I remember correctly. Savannah."

Sullivan called the Georgia Bureau of Investigation and found an agent who remembered Delroy Miller.

"He used to dress like a pimp," said the detective. "He was a member of the Rude Boys, a Jamaican drug gang, and he hooked up with the local mafia down here. They run drugs from Jamaica through Florida and up to Georgia. Your man must have had some problems with these fellows, because he left in a hurry. We heard he ripped off Little Nick, the guy who runs the local outfit."

Little Nick owned a sports-memorabilia store in Savannah. Sullivan called the store.

"I'm looking for Nick."

"Who's this?"

"He doesn't know me. But I have some information he might appreciate."

There was silence. Then another man picked up the phone.

"Yeah?" Nick was not a native Georgian. He had a New Jersey accent.

"Do you remember Delroy Miller?"

"What's it to you?"

"He's set himself up here in California as a swami. He's got a bunch of young girls worshipping him. Some of the girls' parents aren't too happy about it, and they'd like to see him gone. I understand you might have some unfinished business with him."

"What's in it for you?"

"Nothing. I'd just be happy to reunite you two."

Nick laughed and took down the Swami's address. Sullivan called the house in Bayshore.

"What is this about?" said the Swami in his thick accent.

"We haven't met, but you know who I am. I've been taking your photograph. I called the health board on your juice stand."

The Swami started cursing.

"Calm down," said Sullivan. "I'm about to do you a big favor."

"I don't need favors."

"You remember Little Nick from Savannah?"

The Swami ditched the accent.

"You know Nick? What's this about?"

"Nick has your address."

"How did he get it?"

"I gave it to him. He's catching a flight this afternoon. That puts him at your doorstep in about eight and a half hours."

The Swami hung up.

One of Sullivan's operatives was at the Swami's house. He watched as the garage door opened and the Swami's women ran about frantically, loading boxes into a van. The Swami yelled at them to move faster. Judy was trailing him in a near-hysterical state.

"Where are you going, Abba?" she wailed.

"Shut up, woman! Get out of my way!"

That night Sullivan called his client.

"The Swami is on an airplane and he's not coming back."

"Yeah, I just heard from Judy," said his client. "She's a wreck."

Abba had told Judy that she and the other disciples were unworthy of him. He had wasted too much time on them already and refused to tolerate their ignorance any longer. Only Hathaya, beautiful Hathaya, had sufficiently proved her devotion. Only she would accompany him to the promised land. Yes, Hathaya was the most holy.

"I'm running, panicked, through a dark jungle. There are hundreds of eyes in the bushes watching me. A creature is pursuing me, something strong and extremely fast, and when I glance back I see it's a lion. But then I notice that I have claws and fur, and I realize that I'm not me at all — I'm a puma. I don't feel afraid anymore, because I'm big and powerful, and I want the lion to attack. And he does! The lion leaps on my back.

We're writhing around, biting each other, I feel very warm, and the next thing I know we're having fierce, passionate sex, our bodies are merging into a single body—"

"Yes," said Dr. Robinson, his voice high with excitement. "You're beginning to apprehend the undiluted truth! Finally you are allowing me to heal you."

"Can you explain the dream?"

"Of course. You're the puma. And I'm the lion."

"I see."

"You're entering a new dimension. Your fears are vanishing. You are ready."

He explained that the others were excited to meet her. Especially Kati. But Stella would have to be eased in slowly. Dr. Robinson would meet her first, alone, so that he could prepare her. He had already picked out a motel.

Stella Zrnic, thanking him profusely, hung up. And Stela Jelincic, a thirty-four-year-old writer who moonlights as an operative for David Sullivan, dialed her boss.

"It worked," she said. "He's hooked."

Sullivan took down the motel's address. Then he called Kati's mother to say that he had finally captured the monster who had brainwashed her daughter.

KAREN MANER

■

Hugo

FROM *The Colorado Review*

AFTER WORKING AT a family-owned pet store in Ohio for a number of years, I took to entertaining myself by predicting, within moments of their walking in the door, what customers would buy. At first it was a matter of demographics and statistical probability. For example, slightly underweight males aged eighteen to twenty-four demonstrated a marginally higher interest in iguanas than the average customer, whereas slightly overweight males in the same age bracket expressed more interest in bearded dragons. White females aged thirty to forty-five with small children in tow gravitated toward hamsters or other small, easily squashable, unexpectedly hazardous pets, while white females aged fifty-five to seventy with small grandsons in tow often left with a bloodthirsty reptile, unassuming in appearance, that would be returned, for a full refund, later the same afternoon.

After a while, my successes convinced me that I could not only predict what people would buy, but also intuit why they would buy it, and I divided the customers purchasing pets for themselves into two categories: mirrorers and acquirers. A mirrorer is a prospective pet owner who, knowingly or not, worships a particular aspect of his or her own personality or appearance and wishes to see the same characteristic in his or her animal companion—the combative ferret owner, for example, or the nihilistic scorpion enthusiast. Acquirers, on the other hand, select pets based on a perceived lack and what they want others to assume about them. A young wallflower might, for example, purchase a corn snake as a way of suggesting that her isolation is by choice, a symptom of her elusive and dangerous nature.

During the time I was doing all of this sizing up of others, my own pet was a blue betta fish named Hugo who suffered from debilitating scoliosis. Viewed from above, he resembled a teal sperm, but he rarely could be viewed from this angle thanks to the unusual buoyancy provided by the gas and food matter perpetually blocked by the S curve of his body. He drifted on his side, at the surface of the water, one glassy eye forever fixed on heaven. It didn't occur to me then to consider what owning Hugo might say about me. Rather than placing myself in either the category of mirrorer or acquirer, I believed myself to be of a rarer and better class, that of the true animal lovers, and I assumed that others would share this perception of me.

When I found him, he had been sequestered in a cubbyhole under the cash register, deemed too hideous for public view. In all fairness, it was true that his appearance didn't inspire confidence in our store, or in his species. Healthy bettas were a sad enough sight. Customers often lamented the drinking cups they were shipped and stored in, to which my coworkers and I would reply, "In the wild, they live in the shallow rice paddies of Thailand," as though there existed no greater horror. Hugo was the greater horror.

For several weeks I checked his cup daily, shook it to make sure he wasn't dead, dropped in a dried bloodworm or two, and watched him spin in wild circles around and around the food. When I decided to take him home, my manager charged me full price and said, "Are you sure you want that thing?" It felt good to spend forty dollars on a two-gallon aquarium, colorful pebbles, a miniature Atlantean castle, and a plastic clump of seaweed, knowing that Hugo would have a better life with me; it felt even better to do so knowing that it would leave others perplexed and maybe a bit awed.

I'd like to think that I wasn't aware of the latter effect until after I'd already decided to buy Hugo, that I'd thought initially only of his benefit and not my own, but I can't remember now. I might have bought him because I felt an affinity for him, seeing in him a feebleness I find harder to face in myself. Or I might have needed him to remind myself and others of my capacity for good, in which case I wasn't being good at all.

* * *

I've kept pets all my life, but over the course of my employment at the pet store, I began to question whether it was ethical to do so. It started as an occasional queasy stirring or inchoate guilt. In the way that biting into a bit of gristle transforms "food" into something harder to swallow, a small disaster at the store would remind me that many of the "goods" I was peddling were capable of looking at, and possibly thinking about, me, and for an instant, everything would seem surreal and obviously wrong. In one such moment, a coworker dropped the wrong end of an electric pump into one of the saltwater tanks while cleaning and—thanks to a shared water source and filtration system—electrified nine aquariums at once, leaving their colorful inhabitants bobbing on the surface like Froot Loops. Another time, a customer mishandled an iguana, broke off its tail, and tossed both back into the cage in shock. The tail bounced and spun on the bark substrate, leaving spots of blood on the glass door with every flip, and the young man asked for a discount on either the damaged iguana or its cage mate, and a job application. There was the unmarked bag in the staff freezer containing a dead cat; the item "Pull Dead" on the nightly checklist; the flattened hamster in the stockroom that had somehow been placed in an empty aquarium that was subsequently placed at the bottom of a considerable stack of empty aquariums; the pond owner who told me, with delight, that she had dreams of decapitating blue herons with the rusty shovel she kept by her kitchen door; the man who squeezed the mouse down the length of his snake, like toothpaste in a tube, when it wouldn't eat; and of course, the rabbit that had been kept in a cage roughly one inch longer than itself, whose owner wished to return it for a refund or in-store credit when it contracted two eye infections, a respiratory infection, and a severe case of diarrhea. And there was the moment in which I heard the following story from a coworker and decided it was as likely to be true as untrue: One day the assistant manager got a call from a gentleman who said his son had just brought home a guinea pig from the flea market. The man wanted to know if the guinea pig could be kept in the cardboard box it had come in or if he needed to buy something larger. The assistant manager recommended he keep the guinea pig in either a cage or an aquarium with some wood chips. About an hour later, the man called back and said, "He swam around for a while, but he's dead now."

By the end of my two and a half years at the pet store, I had developed a pessimistic outlook on human-animal relations, and I went so far as to announce to friends and family that I was quitting the job for moral reasons: I could no longer support an industry that enabled carelessness, abuse, and neglect for the sake of profit. There needed to be stricter requirements regarding who could own animals—mandatory personality tests, comprehension quizzes, documentation, or hard evidence showing that the prospective owner possessed all of the necessary equipment to care for an animal—to prevent neglect out of ignorance or apathy. But taking a moral stand implies having a sense of right and wrong, and I can't say, looking back, that I had such an understanding. I had compiled a list of wrong ways to treat animals from very obvious examples, and my logic assumed that by preventing these things from happening, a person or industry would be promoting the right ways to treat animals. But really this approach only results in a code of conduct that is *not wrong*, not necessarily one that is *right*, or alternatively, *not cruel* but not necessarily *kind*.

Many, if not most, Americans have a proprietary relationship with nature, but in the case of animals, we view some as property and others as companions, and the lines of division are largely arbitrary and inconsistent. Many cat owners claim to be owned by their pets, not the other way around. Dog owners often describe their animal companions as "members of the family," and pamper them with their own Christmas stockings, wardrobes, place settings, and afternoon outings to canine pastry shops. Not all cat and dog owners act this way, of course, and the ones who do could be considered eccentric, but such behavior still lies well within the accepted boundaries of sanity, while organizing a schedule around the whims of a leopard gecko or taking a guinea pig out for gourmet yogurt drops at a '50s-themed, rodents-only milkshake parlor does not. In other words, what goes for one animal does not go for another, which presents an ethical quandary for me.

Take, for example, the case of the humble feeder rodent. With soft fur, velvety ears, pink noses, and delicate whiskers, they meet most of our standards of cuteness; even so, mice and rats get a raw deal, more often being food for other pets than pets themselves. On one of my first days at the store, a customer approached the counter and asked for a frozen pinkie. It must have been obvious that I had no idea what he was talking about, because before I could ask, he directed me to the bottom shelf of the store's freezer, where I found an assortment of paper and plastic bags containing rats and mice. After meeting quiet deaths en masse in a CO_2 chamber, they'd been frozen in various stages of development—some the size of a sneaker, others not quite as big as a thumb—but all shared the common feature of being as solid as a forgotten TV dinner. The pinkies, it turned out, were hairless newborns, stored by the dozen in plastic sandwich bags to be sold as food for small reptiles. Some of their undeveloped feet and tails had broken off during shipping and settled to the bottom of the bags, while others had been collected in a sack marked for discount sale and labeled "Parts."

Rodents destined for live feeding spend time in the mad scramble of pet-store feeder cages. I can't speak for all stores, but when new rodent shipments came in, our cages were usually packed to the brim—say, thirty mice in a plastic container the size of a large shoebox. Sometimes one would manage to climb onto another's back, reach the bars of the lid, and hang over the frenzy, as if from a stage, preparing to fall into the crowd at the best concert of its life. And very occasionally one would be singled out by the others and partially eaten, left to run around with a black, fleshy hole in its back or head until either someone noticed and lifted it out by the tail, or the wound was widened.

When I think about it, the lives of feeder mice bear a striking resemblance to those of the abject humans who populate our post-apocalyptic, alien-takeover, dystopian fictions; and yet, I had time to consider their existence four days a week for thirty months without considerable distress, and even now I find myself having to create thought experiments to inspire my own concern on their behalf. How long would I have held a job at a facility keeping dozens of kittens in a glass tank, scrambling over each other and eating one another out of stress and desperation, for the sake of selling them as food to Nile monitors or alligators at a local tourist attraction? Not long, I imagine.

Mice just aren't pitiable enough without mental gymnastics. Being generally fond of four-legged mammals, especially those with whiskers, and having had no negative experiences with mice, I have to assume that my lack of concern for their situation comes from being accustomed to the idea of it. Having long been associated with filth and plague, mice have come to be known almost universally as pests, not pets, and this low level of perceived lovableness has resulted in a now decades-old exclusion of Rodentia from the scope of human concern, including mine. There are few things mice can do to draw considerable sympathy from a person like me, short of being animated or getting eaten right in front of me by an even less pitiable creature.

I've heard arguments defending these apparently automatic inclinations to empathize or not empathize. There's the biblical defense that animals were put on earth for our use, but I've always assumed there was an understanding of "within reason" or "without cruelty" inherent in that proclamation, though I'm not the appropriate person to defend such an assumption. And then there are more scientific defenses, such as the argument that most animals don't have the capacity to understand what's happening to them and therefore don't care. But this argument calls to mind my friend's grandmother, who spent several years forgetting who her husband and sons were, then several more years wandering the halls of a special facility and defecating in potted plants because she had no idea who she was, where she was, or when she was. In spite of everything she didn't know, she seemed certain that she was terrified, even if she couldn't grasp how often she was terrified, which was most of the time. Again, I come back to the question of kindness and cruelty, and I think that the line between them has less to do with what the person or thing being acted upon knows and more to do with what the person doing the acting knows. So knowing that I am inclined to care more about some creatures than others; knowing that I sometimes have to think my way into compassion and that it can take me a good long while to do this or even to consider whether I should try to do it; knowing that instinct and emotion are at once influential and inconsistent; knowing, in other words, that I exhibit an emotional tolerance for treatment that my rational mind tells me should be intolerable, should I really trust myself to be kind?

* * *

After bringing him home, I decided that the best place for Hugo would be on the nightstand, as it was an appropriate distance from the windows, not too high or too low for him to watch my daily go-ings-on, and not in my way. Once he was established there, I set about the task of curing his constipation. Several fish-health websites suggested that variety was the key to clearing a blockage, so at three o'clock every afternoon, I sat, staring down into his tank, pushing around a shriveled bloodworm or a shelled pea or a chunk of dehy-drated shrimp on the surface of the water with a bobby pin, trying to place it either in his mouth or somewhere along the trajectory that his twisted body would take. At first the process took up to half an hour, with Hugo hurling himself at the food but invariably whirling past it at least five times, but after a few weeks I could almost envi-sion a semicircle drawn in the water, extending from his mouth, and we could pull it off in one shot.

For the first month, Hugo spent most of his time propped against the upper leaves of his artificial plant. It was hard to look at him other-wise. Watching him float, I imagined myself drifting over deep water, helpless and forced to stare down into the depths, wondering about predators below. This was backward, of course. For Hugo, the im-mense shadows came from above, from the white void of the ceiling he was constantly drawn to. At times he seemed seized by sudden ter-ror and determination, and he would dive straight down with a splash. Then, halfway to the bottom, his forward momentum would stop and his body would quiver against an invisible barrier for a moment be-fore falling limp and rising again, without resistance, to the surface.

In the second or third month, Hugo achieved a complete descent. The first few times were graceless nosedives into the gravel followed by the same limp rise as before, but after repeated attempts, he man-aged an effortful though precise parabola down to the bottom, past his castle, and back up to the top. He began to do this several times a day, then once an hour, and although he still couldn't resist buoyancy for more than a second, he at least played an active role in his ascent, which—at the risk of anthropomorphizing too much—must have felt very satisfying.

His body was still curved, but the swelling around his middle had decreased and his color had brightened. This is not to say he ever possessed a lively appearance. Every time a person met Hugo for the first time, the most she or he had to say was "hmm," and every visit after that—regardless of how many times she or he had already seen Hugo—began with the visitor approaching the aquarium, growing tense, and turning to me with a nauseating look of exaggerated pity, believing him to be dead. The scene made me cringe every time it played out, and I tried to remember to always be the first one in the room, to say "hello" to Hugo and show there was no need for alarm.

I spent six months enjoying Hugo's progress, our routine together, and the pride and satisfaction that come with being both relied upon and reliable. Then one day I came home and found Hugo gray and cloudy eyed, floating at the surface as always, but with his tail fin hanging straight down. I know there are people who would laugh at me for it, but I cried. To my surprise, the crying had less to do with a feeling of loss and more to do with the sudden thought that Hugo might have lived a terrible life. I had been aware all along, of course, that he was crippled and couldn't shit, but for me there had been moments of excitement, breakthroughs, and meaning—but maybe for him, it occurred to me then, it was all just an endless series of moments inhabiting a broken body, each one instantly supplanting the last. It sounds melodramatic, I'm sure, but for the first time, I looked at Hugo and had nothing to show for all the good deeds I'd been doing, and in the absence of such reassurance I became aware of all I hadn't been doing.

I hadn't, for example, replaced his water on as strict a schedule as I could have. I hadn't bought him a heater when the power had gone out for a week in the middle of winter—a stress that could have killed even a healthy fish. I hadn't purchased an aquarium stand, although I'd intended to, so he'd spent six months inches away from the phone and an alarm clock I've always referred to as the "Sonic Boom," an alarm clock designed to accommodate deaf and blind persons, which comes equipped with flashing lights and a vibrating disk to insert under the mattress, and whose snooze function was used at least seven times every morning.

I wondered how many heartbeats he'd wasted attempting to escape the howling of the devices that surrounded him, whether maybe he'd grown accustomed to it and had ceased to think about it, as I had, but then I remembered the likelihood of his short memory. I considered that Hugo's life with me was at least much better than the one he had been living under the cash register in a plastic cup. That seemed obvious. It also seemed obvious that "better" wasn't good enough; that not being unkind to Hugo was not the same as being kind; that cruelty isn't always something one sets out to do, but kindness is.

I buried Hugo under a bush by the front stoop with his Atlantean castle marking the spot, and I regretted that if I'd invested in a tiny headstone, the epigraph might have read, "He swam around for a while, but he's dead now."

A little over a year ago, a news story broke about a husband and wife, Terry and Marian Thompson, recently separated, who owned a private zoo in Zanesville, Ohio, about two hours east of my hometown. Terry had been cited on multiple occasions for animal abuse and neglect, but the couple had maintained throughout the years that their zoo was a sanctuary for exotic animals that would otherwise be homeless or put down. One Columbus Zoo official testified that the couple kept primates in small birdcages and a bear in a cage with little room for movement, covered in its own feces, and neighbors complained of numerous animal escapes, fear for their children's safety, and sleepless nights listening to lions bellow.

All of this came to light on October 18, 2011, when sixty-two-year-old Terry Thompson took a last walk around his property, opened the pens and gates that held nearly sixty exotic animals, and shot himself to death. When the police arrived, they found dozens of large cats, bears, wolves, and primates wandering the facility. Others had already escaped into the countryside, and some were heading for the highway. Signs were placed on roadsides warning citizens of roaming wild animals, schools were closed, and everyone was advised to stay indoors. With little daylight left and the team equipped with tranquilizers still an hour away, the sheriff issued a shoot-to-kill order on any animal seen leaving the property. Of the fifty-six animals that escaped, six were captured: three leopards, two monkeys, and one bear. Of the other fifty, one monkey was presumably eaten by one of the large cats, and the remaining forty-nine—including seventeen lions and eighteen endangered Bengal tigers—were shot to death.

The story gained instant national attention, and the question asked again and again was "How did this happen?" The embarrassing answer was "No one ever said it couldn't." Prior to the incident in Zanesville, Ohio's laws regulated the import of non-native species, but nothing was required to *own* a non-native animal as long as it wasn't part of a public exhibit. If the Thompsons' private zoo had contained a collection of native species, such as spotted salamanders, American toads, or red-eared sliders, it would have been regulated. But tigers? No problem.

It was chilling to consider what might have happened in the Zanesville case, and the possibilities were significant enough to motivate Ohio's legislature to create a law mandating the registration of exotic animals and banning the ownership of big cats, crocodiles, hyenas, and snakes over ten feet long, among others. Exceptions would be made for individuals who owned these animals prior to the law being put into effect. Such owners would not be required to give up their animals as long as they obtained permits for them. The new law was announced in the summer of 2012, eight months after the disaster, and upon hearing about it, I was relieved—except I couldn't help feeling that the point had been missed. The commonality among all the animals listed in the new legislation is that they pose a threat to humans, but for me, Zanesville demonstrated the threat humans pose to animals.

The day after the shootings, Marian Thompson arrived at the property to find the surviving animals being prepped for transport to the Columbus Zoo, and she pleaded with the zookeepers: "You're taking my children." I don't doubt that what she felt in that moment was despair. I don't doubt that what she had felt for her animals over the years could only be described, by her, as love. And I can accept that she believed, or had come to believe, that she and Terry were in fact rescuing those animals. It might even be true that whatever circumstances they took them from were far worse than the ones they ended up in. But that shouldn't be good enough.

In April state officials announced that five of the animals rescued from Zanesville—one leopard had been euthanized at the zoo—would be returned to the care of Marian Thompson. The state had no choice. Even the new law, which hadn't been passed yet, wouldn't prevent it. At least one official was optimistic, and said, "I truly believe after all these goings on that she will be making a good effort." It seems an odd phrase to put faith in: *A good effort*. Words scrawled on the top of a composition paper that needs restructuring, rethinking, and rewriting. Words said to the child whose soccer team just lost the match. Words that mean a noble and admirable coming-up-short.

It reminds me of how, when I was a child, I used to tell my mother that someday I would own a farm where cats with missing eyes and amputated legs, cats that no one wanted to take home from the shelters, could frolic and be free. It wasn't an entirely thought-out plan, and not one I've ever attempted to make a reality—now I see a lot more opportunities for birds of prey and coyotes than I do for freedom and frolicking—but I still believe that it was a well-intended dream from a charitable heart. At the time, others did too, and I received my due praise. In third grade, I wrote a series of journal entries describing an injured kitten I was nursing back to health and sheltering in the hollow of a tree in my backyard. There was no kitten, there was no hollow, but it was a nice story that earned me many encouraging stickers and compliments from my teacher. Much later on, when telling people about my decrepit Hugo and his shelled peas, I earned looks of amazement and responses such as "You must be more patient than I am." Meanwhile, I made sweeping statements about the general pet-owning population and quit a job as a way of taking a moral stand while actually doing nothing—I was told it was good to stand for what one believes in, and I felt much better about myself once I had done that big showy nothing. It occurs to me that I have been making *a good effort* all my life with hardly any good and hardly any effort at all.

Sometimes the idea of a thing overwhelms the reality of it. We want to believe we're good, we want others to believe it, and they want to believe it too. The problem arises when we forget to look closely and mistake seeming kind for being kind, when stated intentions become cause for congratulations or at least forgiveness, even if they are self-serving or nothing more than flights of fancy, or end up buried by the front stoop or shot on the neighbor's lawn.

There is an unpleasant part of me that still finds all of the thought I'm putting into the issue of animals and people silly, because after all, there is a natural hierarchy in the world and humans are at the top of it. To that part of myself I say that, if anything, it is precisely our ability to be moral, to think things through, and to make the right decision that makes us superior. So I arrive at the very basic question of whether kindness and ownership are even compatible.

Already, I'm stuck. Kindness, as I understand it, is setting aside the self, recognizing suffering and alleviating it, being generous and compassionate, considering what would be the best state of being for another, and taking steps to make that a reality. But there are difficulties in determining an ideal existence for an animal—what would make it "happy," for lack of a better word. Without knowing what's going on in the minds of animals, or even assuming that they're just small minded, the most practical course of action seems to be trying to make their existence as natural and normal seeming as possible. In other words, leaving them be. And with this being the most obvious path to happiness for an animal, it is hard to imagine that we wouldn't want to offer it to our loved ones, our pets. And yet, as the feeder-mice vendor Rodentpro.com points out, "If we wanted our animals to enjoy a natural state, we never would have acquired them."

YASMINE EL RASHIDI

■

An Interview with Mona Eltahawy

FROM *Bidoun*

MONA ELTAHAWY HAS A KNACK for inspiring hatred. Egyptian activists and bloggers have called her an alien, man-hating, woman-hating, out-of-control psychotic. Non-Egyptian bloggers have called her a Muslim Nazi bitch. Pam Geller, the fulminator behind the Ground Zero Mosque scare, called her a "fascist savage." A cover story on "misogyny in the Middle East" for *Foreign Policy*—titled "Why Do They Hate Us?" and illustrated by images of nude women painted black, only their eyes showing, like human hijab—generated tens of thousands of angry words in response. Sondos Asem, the young female spokesperson for the Muslim Brotherhood, decried her "one-dimensional reductionism and stereotyping." There were parodies, character assassinations, death threats. Most people would wilt in the face of all this vitriol, ridicule, and angst.

Most people are not Mona Eltahawy.

Eltahawy, a journalist-turned-pundit–activist, seems to rather enjoy it. Since the revolution broke out in Egypt on January 25, 2011, this media-savvy New York–based Egyptian has fashioned herself its global spokesperson. And in the intervening two years, she has found a new career as a provocateur. Besides her numerous articles, she has taken her activism into the proverbial street. In November 2011, she took part in the protests on Mohamed Mahmoud Street in Cairo; an ordeal with police and military intelligence followed, including a sexual assault and broken limbs. In September 2012, she defaced a

Geller-sponsored advertisement in the Times Square subway station (IN ANY WAR BETWEEN CIVILIZED MAN AND THE SAVAGE, SUP-PORT THE CIVILIZED MAN. SUPPORT ISRAEL. DEFEAT JIHAD) with hot pink spray paint, before being dragged off by transit police.

As with most everything else she does, these provocations are documented exhaustively on Twitter.

I should say that I went to meet Eltahawy in Harlem last November still outraged by her *Foreign Policy* article, and by half a dozen other things she had written. I arrived at a café near her home prepared for a fight. Mona—everyone calls her Mona, whether they like her or not—unhinges many of us with her seemingly boundless self-regard, her bluntness, her eagerness to court controversy, and her—well, her one-dimensional reductionism. But in person, I found myself disarmed by her honesty and her thoughtfulness. She has a quite nuanced understanding of the criticisms leveled against her, even as she strenuously rejects them. By the end I found myself admiring the very shamelessness and outrage that make so many of us uncomfortable.

At one point in our exchange, Eltahawy described her night in jail after the subway graffiti incident. After a period of discomfort and mutual distrust, she bonded with a cellmate, comparing life stories and tattoos. And they joked about the unlikely pair they made: the drug dealer and the protest-itute.

YASMINE EL RASHIDI: You had a day in court yesterday.

MONA ELTAHAWY: Yes, you caught me at a great time. They offered me a plea deal that would guarantee me no time in jail, but I turned it down—two days in community service and two fines, including my favorite, which is almost eight hundred dollars for the Gucci sunglasses of the woman who came between me and the ad.

EL RASHIDI: What is the exact charge?

ELTAHAWY: Charges: criminal mischief, possession of a graffiti instrument, and making graffiti.

EL RASHIDI: You woke up that morning, September 26, and thought, I'm going to spray-paint that ad?

ELTAHAWY: Oh yeah. I had business meetings that day and it was very frustrating to me that I couldn't go immediately over to the ads that morning. But at least I had a lot of chances to tell people, "Look, I'm going to go spray-paint this ad and I might get arrested today, so don't worry if you don't hear from me for a long time." I was texting and direct messaging friends on Twitter all day.

EL RASHIDI: So you knew that you could get arrested.

ELTAHAWY: Yeah, and I'm still going to plead not guilty because I don't believe I did anything wrong.

EL RASHIDI: You wanted the attention . . .

ELTAHAWY: Absolutely. I wanted to get arrested. The way I looked at it was, those ads cost six thousand dollars. I don't have six thousand dollars. What I do have—my capital is not financial, it's my media profile. People know who I am. So I was not in a position to create an alternative ad—people said that's what I should have done. And in any case those alternative ads people were making, as on point as they were, weren't challenging enough. They were too polite. I was so frustrated, especially by what was happening on Twitter.

EL RASHIDI: On Twitter?

ELTAHAWY: My initial frustration was with Twitter. People were just venting about these ads. And believe me, I love Twitter. Love it. I *live* on Twitter. But there are times when you hit the wall and you need to get out. Like the revolution in Egypt. Against these ads, you need people on the ground, making it socially unacceptable to be racist and bigoted. We need a revolution, not alternative ads. I'm too angry for alternative ads.

EL RASHIDI: What are you angry about? Or is it a general state of being?

ELTAHAWY: You know, Yasmine, over the past few weeks I've truly been unraveling. It was the anniversary of the attack. I went back to Egypt for it, joined the Mohamed Mahmoud Street marches and memorials on November 19. So I've been feeling very torn up. The past few weeks have been the worst in my life, worse even than when I was attacked. I've been so low on energy and inspiration. At my rock bottom. But what happened yesterday in court completely reenergized me! It brought me back to life, because it reminded me of why I did what I did. It reminded me of the many fights I've had—and it reminded me just how much I love to fight. I love to fight! [Laughs]

EL RASHIDI: Following you on Twitter, one might think you *live* to fight?

ELTAHAWY: I think that those of us who are privileged enough to travel between cultures, to travel globally—one of the ways we can be most effective is find the place where we are a minority and poke away at those places. So in Egypt, for example, it's a minority position to say that you are secular and want to keep religion out of politics. It's a minority position to be a radical feminist. To say that they hate us, and that is why we don't have any rights. I've found that for me that's the most effective thing, to poke at the painful places.

EL RASHIDI: But you live in America.

ELTAHAWY: Yes, and here I'm in the minority as a Muslim. So I'm a secular, radical feminist *Muslim*, and people have to accept that. And the spray-painting is a part of it. I mean, all the protests that have happened over the past few years—the Danish cartoons and all that—including the ones against the ads over the summer, are most visibly led and promoted by a very right wing among Muslims. And they are most visibly promoted by a very right wing among non-Muslims, as well. What I try to do with my work is to place myself between the two right wings. And what I hope to do with this protest in the subway is to take that sense of ownership away from them—to say that I am offended. Even a Muslim who looks like me, with my pink hair and tattoo, who defended the Danish newspapers' right to publish those cartoons, is offended.

EL RASHIDI: Your critics say that you conveniently switch between your many identities to suit the news of the moment. American? Egyptian? Muslim?

ELTAHAWY: We all have multiple and layered identities. The American in me, for example, believes that what I did is part of the long line of civil disobedience in this country. The only way this country has changed is through civil disobedience. From the civil rights movement to the protests against the war in Vietnam — they all involved breaking the law out of principle. And that's what I did. I wanted to get arrested. I did it out of principle. And I would do it again.

EL RASHIDI: I knew you in 1997. You worked at Reuters, had dark hair, no tattoos, you dressed somewhat differently. And you seemed sort of . . . *timid?* What happened? [Laughter]

ELTAHAWY: I think I'm just much more visible in my fight now. I think what has happened in my adult life is that the fight that has always been internal has externalized itself, more and more. I mean, I wore hijab for nine years.

EL RASHIDI: Yes! I thought I had a memory of that.

ELTAHAWY: Oh yes, from sixteen to twenty-five I wore it by choice. And that speaks to the kind of pressure that women are under.

EL RASHIDI: You were pressured to cover your hair.

ELTAHAWY: We moved to Saudi Arabia from the UK when I was fifteen. (We had left Egypt for the UK when I was seven.) It was a huge, huge, shock to my system to go to Saudi. The way the men looked at me was just horrendous. We went on hajj soon after we arrived, and I was groped beside the Kaaba, as I was kissing the black stone — the heavenly white stone that was tainted black by the sins of humanity. I was fifteen, it was the first time in my life I was dressed like this—like a nun—going to perform one of the five pillars of Islam in the holiest place on earth for Muslims. And I was groped! This guy has his hand up my ass as we are doing tawaf. I had never been touched in any sexual way before—I didn't know what to say. I burst into tears. It took me years to tell my parents what had happened. Maybe ten years. I was so ashamed, even though I had nothing to be ashamed of.

So I got very difficult and troubling messages about my body. Which is why I have a lot of trouble with niqab, because that's how it started with me. I felt so violated I just wanted to hide. And it's very wrong, that the way we feel we can protect ourselves is to hide. It goes right back to what's happening to women in Egypt today—women are blamed for sexual violence. They are told, "If you cover up, you will be okay."

EL RASHIDI: But you uncovered, eventually.

ELTAHAWY: When I put on the veil I literally thought that I was striking a deal with God—"They tell me that I should cover my hair to be a good Muslim. Well, I'll do that, but please help me not go mad." And I was going mad.

For many women hijab is an integral part of their identity and they're very comfortable. I respect that. But to me it was very uncomfortable. The internal me and the external me were so far apart. It took me eight years to take it off. And the fight you see today is one I've had inside me all along, it just needed all this time to become so visible.

EL RASHIDI: You wrote an article in *Foreign Policy* last spring that made people very, very angry: "Why Do They Hate Us?"

ELTAHAWY: There was no sinister plot, like people think. It's really simple. They wrote and asked if I would like to write a piece on women's rights, and I said yes. And I think it's really disingenuous of the people who are asking why I wrote it for *Foreign Policy*, and why in English—it got to them, didn't it? It found its intended audience. Secondly, no Arabic-language publication would ever have published that, and none would have invited me to write it. I used to write in Arabic. I had a weekly column in *Asharq Alawsat*, until they banned me.

EL RASHIDI: What happened?

ELTAHAWY: They never give you a reason, they just drop you. But it might have had something to do with the anti-Mubarak Kifaya protests in 2005. I had been called into state security for an op-ed I wrote in the *International Herald Tribune* entitled "How Egypt Hijacked Democracy." Anyway, the point is, I have experience with Arabic language media and I know they would never touch this subject, especially since I wanted to talk about religion and culture and how it creates this toxic mix, this mess we live in. And in the age of social media, I found that the people I wanted to reach were exactly the ones I reached, because the piece was available online.

EL RASHIDI: I woke up one morning and logged onto Facebook or Twitter or both, and that piece was everywhere.

ELTAHAWY: I know! It's like I set the world on fire!

EL RASHIDI: So you were happy with the reaction?

ELTAHAWY: It was an interesting and gratifying and gruelling experience. The attacks were very personal. As a writer, I know that on any given day, twenty-five percent of the people will disagree with what I say. But it's the way that they disagree that makes it really interesting. It would be an interesting experiment to change the byline on that piece and see how they would react.

EL RASHIDI: But let's face it, the images were offensive—chosen, it seemed, by that very right-wing contingency you spoke of earlier?

ELTAHAWY: I know many people reacted in a very gut way to them, but I had nothing to do with the images. I didn't choose them. They didn't run them by me.

EL RASHIDI: Were you surprised when you saw them?

ELTAHAWY: You know, overall, I'm very proud of the piece. I'm very pleased with that piece. And in fact I'm going to write a book based on it over the next few months. So for those people who say I generalize and skim the surface, well, it was only three thousand words, and now I'm going to turn it into sixty thousand.

EL RASHIDI: People are going to love that.

ELTAHAWY: I want my book to be called *Headscarves and Hymens*, because for a very long time I've been working on a theory that we women from our part of the world are identified by what's on our head and what's between our legs—the presence or absence thereof. What do you think? [Laughs]

I obviously want to provoke. I've been writing for more than twenty years, I know what I'm doing. With that article, I wanted to provoke and I was very gratified by the response. I'm glad that it hit people in the gut, because it's outrageous what's happening. I am astounded that people are more outraged by what I wrote and how I wrote it and where I wrote it and how it was headlined than they are about what actually happened to the women I wrote about.

EL RASHIDI: We have a knee-jerk hypersensitivity to the West.

ELTAHAWY: The irony is that we have this hypersensitivity while at the same time we are always saying, "You don't matter, you are not the center of our universe." *That sensitivity makes them the center of our universe.* That's another reason why I wrote it for *FP*.

EL RASHIDI: The love-hate-need problem.

ELTAHAWY: I made a point in that piece that I think is important. For that audience, which includes foreign policy pundits and diplomats—you are going to be sitting down with our government, which is largely dominated by Islamists, and they will tell you to mind your own business. That the way we treat our women is religious and cultural. That you can't interfere. And this is where the international community has to stick to its conscience, because there are international standards by which you have to treat human beings, including women. And if you don't treat them by those standards, then you have to be willing to say, We aren't going to do business with you. We're going to boycott you. *This has to happen.* We as women are always being sold out. We're sold out before anybody.

El Rashidi: Like Saudi Arabia and America?

Eltahawy: Exactly! How can you have a strategic ally that treats fifty percent of its population like children? It's gender apartheid. The world boycotted South Africa. If the world can boycott South Africa, it can divest from Saudi.

El Rashidi: But the US props up Saudi because of oil. And it's now propping up the Muslim Brotherhood in Egypt in the name of long-term stability . . .

Eltahawy: Absolutely. The US props up any government that will guarantee stability. They supported Mubarak before the Brotherhood. Anyone who guarantees that oil will flow freely and the Camp David agreements will remain untouched. I don't see a sinister plot in which Obama sat down and said he would help the Brotherhood rise to power, I really don't. What I see, and what I hate this administration for, is him asking, "Who's going to keep everything running so that our interests aren't jeopardized?"

And that's where, as an American, I say, "This is a fucked-up foreign policy."

El Rashidi: But you voted for Obama?

Eltahawy: I voted for Obama because I was standing up to the Christian Brotherhood of America. And if these old, ultraconservative fundamentalist lunatics could be defeated by a coalition of women, youth, and minorities here in this country, then why the hell can't we do that in Egypt? That's our responsibility. We didn't need America to get rid of Mubarak. And please quote me on this—as an Egyptian American, I say, "Fuck the Americans. Who are the Americans? We are in charge. We control our destiny, not the Americans."

EL RASHIDI: You've often been criticized for what people see as serving Western policy makers the kinds of narratives about Egypt and the Middle East that fuel stereotypes. Are those the people you want to reach?

ELTAHAWY: I reach people who speak English, yes, and I have a large following in America, it's true. But I'm also reaching people who speak Arabic. A lot of people on Twitter—the very same people who were angry at me over that *Foreign Policy* article—they were venting on Twitter and Facebook in English. They speak Arabic, too.

I wrote that essay understanding very well that I'm privileged. And I wrote that essay trying to look beyond my privilege. I wrote that essay to address people who are also privileged, and to ask them to look beyond that privilege.

I was interviewed by BBC *Hard Talk* a few weeks ago, and one of the questions that Stephen Sackur asked me was, "After what happened to you, where they beat you and broke your bones and sexually assaulted you—don't you think that this essay was written out of personal anger?" Of course it was written out of anger, just not the anger he was talking about. My anger was a product of the realization that if I wasn't who I was, if I didn't have the privileges I have, I might very well be dead. If I didn't have a high media profile, when I sent out that tweet saying I had been arrested, Al Jazeera and the State Department wouldn't have picked up my story. Certainly not as quickly as they did. This hashtag #freemona wouldn't have started trending globally in fifteen minutes. I probably would have died or been gang-raped or something horrendous.

I was so disheartened and angry by those people who verbally attacked me. We have to look beyond our privileges and see how horrendous it is to be a woman in so many parts of the Arab world. Clearly the women I'm writing about are not going to read my *Foreign Policy* article, and even if they did, so what? They're not the audience. That audience, my audience, is those who know how bad it is, and yet their privilege prevents them from being outraged enough. And it's that outrage that will make our revolution really succeed. The revolution to get Mubarak out of our heads! Mubarak is still in our heads. He's called Morsi now!

EL RASHIDI: I know. It feels, at times, like it's a farce . . .

ELTAHAWY: It is, it is! And it couldn't have happened any other way because we had nothing else available. The revolution is not over, but it will not succeed until we get women involved, too. That's the social and cultural revolution.

EL RASHIDI: Many say that the Muslim Brotherhood will serve as a catalyst for the real revolution.

ELTAHAWY: The Muslim Brotherhood is going to help really pinpoint this. You hear how Morsi talks. You hear how the Salafis talk. You see how women are addressed in the constitution. Mubarak is still up here. [Points] He's in prison now but still terrorizing our minds. Unless we get him out of our heads the revolution is fucked.

EL RASHIDI: Just the Egyptian revolution, or are the Tunisians and Libyans and Syrians angry enough?

ELTAHAWY: In Tunisia, Bouazizi was angry enough to set himself on fire. And that's the analogy I set up in my essay. And in so doing, he ignited these revolutions. The revolution he started has to be completed by women, because that's what will create the kind of shift I talked about in the US, where half the population stood up to the old ultraconservative men.

EL RASHIDI: You just came back from a visit to Cairo. From what you saw, what do you think it will take?

ELTAHAWY: For the longest time, the Brotherhood has been surrounded by this protected halo of religion, which they utterly abuse.

You know how sentimental people are about religion—you can't touch it. Well, once they created a political party and moved away from just a wishy-washy ideology, then it became fair game. Once they entered politics and the dirt of politics, became tainted by politics, they came to deserve all the things we chanted last week—that the people want the fall of the regime.

El Rashidi: What do we do?

Eltahawy: The first step is to break the halo of the sanctity that they surround themselves with. This religious thing. Egyptians have to recognize that they are religious and have faith and that they don't need the Muslim Brotherhood and the Salafis to give them this patina of faith and purity. We don't need them to represent us religiously. The revolution will truly continue when we recognize that they are not our consciences but our elected representatives.

El Rashidi: And women?

Eltahawy: Well, when it comes to women, I don't know if the shift is happening enough. I see more and more coalitions being formed and people on the ground wanting to protect women, but I also see this bizarre, bizarre rage—and these weird combinations of power and sex—in which young men who are courageous enough to face up to our brutal police force, even as they are making their escape from the shooting and the tear gas, manage to find the wherewithal to think, "I'm going to grab her ass." How?! It leaves me speechless. *That's* the shift we need to work on. We need to address this horrible cocktail, this toxic mix of power and sex. These men are high on courage and power. They are the barrier we have to address. They are the mini-Mubaraks.

El Rashidi: So what happened to those mini-Mubaraks during the eighteen days of uprising in 2011? Why were they so respectful of women in the square? Because Tahrir seemed a somewhat utopic place, didn't it?

Eltahawy: I wasn't there for the eighteen days the way you were, and I heard from people what you say—but I also heard from people that there was a reluctance to talk about any sexual assault that was happening because people didn't want to taint the revolution. I understand that kind of power, because it took me a very long time to be able to look at the revolution objectively because it was something I, like so many of us, had wanted for such a long time. Egypt is a very misogynistic country and that was not going to go away after eighteen days. That's the social revolution that I'm talking about, and the one that interests me much more. I'm not interested in the politics. I'm interested in the personal as political.

EL RASHIDI: In a conversation with Gloria Steinem at the Hammer Museum in late 2010, an Israeli woman in the audience said that it is very easy for you to be sitting in your New York apartment speaking about the situation in the Arab world, but why aren't you there, on the ground, fighting the fight? You got very, very angry. But many of us have wondered that—why *aren't* you living in Egypt?

ELTAHAWY: It's a legitimate question, and I've been asked it many times, it's true. But the answer is varied. First of all, I've reached a stage where I can get the message out about Egypt without having to be there. And there are enough people on the ground to keep all this going without me personally having to be there. It didn't need Mona there to tip the scale. I felt at that time, during the eighteen days, I could contribute more by being here and literally shaking the media. People said I was literally jumping out of the TV. You know I would go on CNN and the BBC and I would challenge them—they had headlines like CHAOS IN EGYPT and I'd said to them, "This is an uprising, this is a revolution, stop saying *chaos in Egypt!* This is the most important time in my people's lives!" And then the *New York Times* and Michael Moore said five minutes later they changed it to UPRISING IN EGYPT. If I can do that, then I feel I'm contributing much more here then there.

But I have come to realize over the past two years that the social revolution is much more important to me than the political one, and that to do what I really want to do I have to be on the ground. So I'm actually moving back, next month.

EL RASHIDI: Do you feel that you will get a warm reception in Egypt?

ELTAHAWY: I don't speak for anyone—I only speak for myself. But in doing so, and in becoming so visible with my speaking, I know I represent something that needs to be there in Egypt right now. So many young men and women come up to me, and we have these conversations that are very important. For that I need to be back. And I need to write this book.

But in going back I can't lose my connection to *here*, either. To keep Egypt on the international stage, I need to keep my connections here. This poster that I spray-painted in New York—hardly anyone recognizes me here. But in Egypt, it was insane, insane. I was waiting for a cab in the street and a woman got out of her car and said,

"Are you Mona? I need to shake your hand, I've watched that video ten times, let me give you a lift." She *stopped her car*, on the corniche!

EL RASHIDI: Could you actually tell us the story of the attack, just for the record?

ELTAHAWY: I was at a conference in Morocco, and on the night train from Tangier to Marrakesh. It sounds very romantic, but I spent all those eight hours on the top bunk of the sleeper compartment on this train just crying, following the news from Mohamed Mahmoud Street in Cairo, where there were clashes. One woman tweeted about how this older man came up to her and said, "What are you doing here?" and she told him she was fighting like everyone else. And he said to her, "No, your place is back there in Tahrir. You're educated—Egypt and its future need you. I'm poor and uneducated and I'm probably going to die here. After we finish what we're doing here, Egypt needs you to rebuild it and lead it to the freedom that we're fighting for here."

EL RASHIDI: Goose bumps.

ELTAHAWY: It gives me tears just thinking about it. And then there was this awful picture of a father in a morgue who had just identified his son. It just tore me up.

And then finally there were all these stories coming in of boys as young as twelve years old, probably street kids, some Ultras—who have my ultimate respect since they've been fighting the police since 2007—going into Mohamed Mahmoud knowing they might die. They were writing their mothers' phone numbers on their arms—so that if they ended up in the morgue, people would know who to call.

EL RASHIDI: So you went back to Cairo.

ELTAHAWY: I'd arranged to meet an activist friend outside the Mugamma. Just before I left the hotel my brother called and begged me not to go to Tahrir. He said a relative of ours had just been killed. He was one of the two people who had been killed in Alexandria a few days earlier. He was in his thirties, the father of two young girls—shot dead. I promised my brother I would stay out of trouble. Instead I went straight to Mohamed Mahmoud to meet my fate.

Well, not straight—we had to take a side street because they were blocking the Mohamed Mahmoud crossroads. We went through Bab El-Louk. There was a battle happening right at the main gate of the American University—sirens, tear gas, all this stuff. I was tweeting all this time, and at one point my friend Maged turned to me and said, "Mona, your life is worth more than a tweet, put that thing away." So I put my phone away, and we made our way to the front line.

And we're there, driven by adrenaline, pushing forward, past the ambulances, ducking from the tear gas, pushing, pushing, pushing. We went literally up to the metal barrier. And so I stood up on this rock that was there and I took pictures of these bastard security guys on the other side. Then this man takes my hand and says, "Stand up and take pictures, I'll hold you." I thought it was a bit odd that an Egyptian man was offering to hold my hand like that, but I kept going. And then they saw us and started shooting, so I ducked, and they stopped. These guys next to us were like, "Run!" So we ducked into a tiny fast food place.

We now know that they were *mundaseen*—plainclothes thugs. We didn't know this at the time. We thought they were with us. So we ducked, ran into the shop, and all this time the guy was still holding my hand. And then he started trying to take my smartphone. And I'm like, "Leave my phone, *ya hayawan, ya hayawan*" (you animal). And here we are, cramped in this small place, and one of them gropes my breast! So I start hitting him. We're being fired at and he has the headspace to grope me!? And Maged is like, "Mona, we have to go, this is not the time." But I'm like, "No, no, I'm not done." I was punching him so hard that one of his co-thugs actually tried to protect him from me because I was so enraged.

And then suddenly, there were riot police around us and everyone disappeared. I thought Maged had gotten away, but they'd actually taken him to a place where he could see me being beaten, and they were beating him there.

So I'm in the shop, and I'm thinking, it's just me and these guys, I'm a woman, what are they going to do. Ha! Beat the living daylight out of me is what they did. They were whacking me on the head and I was trying to protect my head with my arms, which is why this bone broke, and this bone broke. [Gestures] They beat me so hard that the bone broke inward, like this.

So after this beating, during which I dropped my smartphone, they took me into this room on their side of the barrier, where they sexually assaulted me. Hands here, hands here, hands between my legs, hands in my trousers. I'm literally plucking hands out of my trousers and saying *No* and they're beating me, pulling my hair, calling me a *sharmouta* (slut). And in the middle of all this beating, I fall to the ground. At first I wasn't sure if I remembered correctly that I'd fallen to the ground, but then my bum hurt so much that I knew I had. And I remember this voice inside me said, "If you don't get up now you are going to die." Something made me get up.

Then they started dragging me to this street that connects to the interior ministry and they took me to this small alleyway that led to the back of the ministry, where their supervising officer, who was in plainclothes and a leather jacket, said to me, "You're going to be fine now, you're going to be okay," as their hands were still all over my body.

And into this new scenario arrives this older man in military fatigues who says, "Get her out of here." They took me into an office inside, and the sexual assault ended. But it was just me and the men sitting there. I kept telling them my arms were broken and I needed a doctor. I could tell from the swelling. And they kept saying, "Put your fingers together, you're fine, see." And I'm like, "But it's my arms that are broken, you morons."

And then I made a point of telling every single man who came to question me that I had been sexually assaulted. Their reactions were amazing. They'd look away, they'd stammer, they'd ignore me. They'd say things like, "For sure it was crowded." And this judge who was there to negotiate terms of a truce with them, said, "Well, what did you expect, you have no ID." And I'm like, "Because I have no ID I deserve to be violated?" And he's like, "How were they to know who you were?" Which is bullshit, because they knew who I was.

El Rashidi: Were you scared?

Eltahawy: No, I was fed up. But I was seriously concerned that they would charge me with being a spy, because I'm a dual citizen. And I'd lived in Israel, which is extremely unpopular with many Egyptians, and it could have easily created a case by which public sympathy could be on their side.

At one point, some activists came in to try to negotiate a truce, and one of them had a smartphone and I got him to put me on Twitter. I tweeted "beaten and interrogated at interior ministry" and his battery died literally ten seconds later.

Then this general appears—he might have been a famous one, I don't know—and he turns to me and asks, "Why are you here, my girl?" I was like, "I don't know, maybe you can tell me." I told him, "Look, can you either charge me with something, so that I can know where I stand, or let me go home since I've been here for six hours." He told me I was going, and then these two military guys appear, and when I ask them where we're going, they say military intelligence. I refuse to go. I'm a civilian, why should I? Then one of them tells me to stop this Bollywood drama, that I'm going whether I like it or not.

So we get into a rickety jeep, every bump I'm feeling in my broken bones, until we get to the military intelligence headquarters by Tiba Mall. It's freezing and they keep me waiting outside for two hours until the supervising officer finally sends orders to bring me in, where they blindfold me and keep asking me questions like, "You're Jewish, right?" And I'm like, "My name is Mona *Ahmed* Eltahawy, where did you get the Jewish from?" And he's says, "The file that has come with you from the Interior Ministry is filled with information . . ."

I mention this because six hours later, they have the nerve to tell me, "Look, Mona, we have no idea why you're here." They were playing good cop, bad cop.

Finally some kind of officer walks in, the first thing I ask him is, "Why am I here?" and he says that it's just a procedure to verify my identity. So we do this whole song and dance about identity again. And he keeps coming and going and disappearing for an hour, and he'd come back and be like, "Look away, look away," which was ridiculous since I was wearing a blindfold.

And in the middle of all this, as I'm telling him I was sexually assaulted, all he wants to talk about is the dirt on my hands. "It looks to me like you were throwing Molotov cocktails," he said. "Look at your hands!" I told him that the dirt was from when his men were sexually assaulting me. And he says, "How do we know you're not a spy?" Eventually I said, "No more questions. Either let me go or charge me and bring me someone from the American Embassy or a lawyer." And he pounces: "The American Embassy? Are you ashamed of being an Egyptian? Are you renouncing your nationality?"

I said, "Look, after hours of people of my nationality beating me, sexually assaulting me, ignoring me, refusing me medical attention—after all these things, I want someone here that I can trust. And if that someone is from the American Embassy, I don't care. I want someone in this room with me that I can trust."

And then literally in the eleventh hour he comes back in and says, "Okay, you can take off the blindfold now." That's when he tells me, "Look, Mona, we don't know why you are here." So who the hell does!?

Then they did this song and dance: "We're very sorry what happened to you, we're going to investigate—can you write down what happened?"

Write it down? For the millionth time, my arms are broken!

So, he records my statement with his iPhone, takes pictures, apologizes again, insists that they have no idea why I was sent there—after they had already told me that my "file" is full of incriminating evidence!

The most climactic moment, I think, was when this guy tried to play the elitism card. "The guys who did this to you," he said, "you know who they are—they are the dregs of society. We drag them up, we scrub them clean, and we open a door in their minds." He clearly thought I would get mad and say, "Yeah, those barbarians!" But instead I said to him, "Who made them live like this? And then you're surprised we had a revolution? And then you ask me why we're fighting at Mohamed Mahmoud?" I was basically defending the men who had sexually assaulted me against this bastard who thought he could play the class card.

Anyway, so then he gives me fifty pounds and tells me to take a cab and go home. Just hands me an envelope with money and his name and number, "in case I need anything."

EL RASHIDI: Surreal.

ELTAHAWY: Completely. So I walk out, find a cab—which is playing patriotic music—get to the hotel, pay the cab the whole fifty pounds, since I wanted none of their filthy money. And then a Tweep, Sarah Naguib, takes me to the hospital, and at the hospital—and this is very telling—I'm at the emergency room and I'm telling them I was sexually assaulted and this female nurse says to me, "How can you let them do that to you? Why didn't you fight them off?"

So this *entire* night is the microcosm of everything I've been talking about. From the nurse who didn't think I fought them off hard enough, to these good cop/bad cop guys, to them telling me that my sexual assault was by the animals of Egyptian society—which they have created, you know. That whole night, it changed my life.

EL RASHIDI: In what way?

ELTAHAWY: In the way that it brought me to where I am now, being a writer with casts on both hands, only being able to use a touchpad with one finger. It took the fight that I used to use my words for to my body. My body became the source of my activism. Whether it's me appearing on TV and talking about what happened, or my hair, or my tattoos.

EL RASHIDI: So the hot pink hair is post-assault?

ELTAHAWY: Oh yes. When my arms were broken I vowed that when I physically healed—because emotionally I haven't—I would celebrate my survival by dyeing my hair red. For me red is a very defiant color. And in the same way that I now go back to Egypt every month to tell the authorities they can't keep me away, the hair also says, "I am here."

Don't you love it? People tweet me at airports to say they saw me—you can't miss the red!

EL RASHIDI: And the tattoos?

ELTAHAWY: The tattoos just came to my head. Look [holds out forearm], this is Sekhmet. I was on a speaking tour in Italy, at this museum in Turin where there are many of our national treasures that we supposedly sold to some rich Italian man two centuries ago. And we're in this room, and the director of the museum says, "And this is the ancient Egyptian goddess Sekhmet—we have nineteen of her statues in this room, and she is the goddess of retribution and sex." And I thought, "Oh! *I want that!* Retribution and sex!" I was like, "Sekhmet is my woman." So I decided on Sekhmet here, to celebrate my ancient Egyptian heritage. And on the other arm, I'm going to get Arabic calligraphy of *Mohamed Mahmoud* and *Horreya*, to celebrate the street, and the Arabic script.

EL RASHIDI: So the tattoo is also post-accident?

ELTAHAWY: In August! I went red, and then went straight to the tattoo artist. This is Sekhmet à la Molly Crabapple, an artist friend who designed it. Sekhmet has the head of a lioness and the serpent on top and all that, and she looks like a hieroglyph, obviously. And her dress is usually red, and the color red is generally associated with her because she's associated with blood and war. According to legend, when humans turned against her father, the sun god Ra, she went on a rampage. And to stop her, the priestesses created this concoction that was a mix of wine and possibly opium and other things, and they poured it on the ground ahead of wherever she was about to go. And when she arrived they said, "Look, Sekhmet, you've killed everyone already, the blood is here on the ground." So this concoction calms her down, calms her bloodlust, and then they have an orgy to celebrate.

EL RASHIDI: So you have bloodlust?

ELTAHAWY: [Laughs] Well, the reason for the tattoo is because of the boys who wrote their mothers' numbers on their arms at Mohamed Mahmoud. Sekhmet is my mother in that kind of symbolical way.

I didn't choose this scar [points to her hand], I'm very proud of this scar, but they left this mark on me. I wanted to put markings on my body that I did choose, that celebrate my survival.

Last summer I lost this suitcase that totally tore me up. I had a breakdown over losing it. It had a lot of Azza Fahmy jewelry that I'd been collecting for a very long time and that was very dear to me and that I'd wanted to give to my sisters and nieces when I died. And a lot of clothes . . . things that were really dear to me. It got lost in transit somewhere.

I had a breakdown over this in Cairo and I realized that it was a displaced kind of trauma. I don't know what I lost when they attacked me last year — but any kind of attack like that, you lose something. You just don't know what it is. So I was like, "You know what, no one can ever take my tattoo away from me — this can never get lost." It was a way of figuring out what I can and can't lose, changing myself in a very obvious physical way, and emotionally, too — though I don't know where I'm going to end up. I'm trying to have this out in a very public way, through Twitter. I tell people all of this, and I want to write an essay about it. A lot of my detractors will say it's for narcissism and self-promotion. They're entitled to their opinions. But I'm doing it for a reason — I think that we don't talk about trauma enough, we don't talk about vulnerability enough. When I am in Egypt, everyone I know is traumatized. They're not able to put it into words. So I'm trying to go through my trauma — very publicly — as a way for those who can't have that very public discussion to watch it happen. Perhaps to recognize the relationship between strength and vulnerability. I'm hoping that it will help someone.

EL RASHIDI: Hearing you, I wonder if the anger toward your piece — which as you know I was angry about, too! — was actually discomfort at issues that many women in the region face but are unable to speak about? That you are able to be so vocal about things that women are made to feel ashamed of.

ELTAHAWY: We've been told to be silent about it. Twelve other women were sexually assaulted. You know the organization Nazra? They contacted me and they said, "Will you join this lawsuit with us?" and I said, "Of course." And they said to me, twelve other women have gone through what you've gone through, but none of them want to pursue it. They can't, for whatever reason.

EL RASHIDI: But you can?

ELTAHAWY: I'm older, I'm forty-five. I'm not a virgin. I was married, I talk about sex openly. I'm a public figure. They can try to shame me, but it's almost like I'm beyond shame. So for all of these reasons I'm obliged to talk about this stuff in a way that a twenty-six-year-old Egyptian virgin can't. And I'm not speaking for her! I'm speaking about my experience, but in so doing I hope I can help others say, "This is what happened to me."

Blue bra girl — and I hate that term and I never use it — she's been silenced by her family. They won't let her speak. It's outrageous, Yasmine! They might as well just put tape over our mouths! And then they get *angry* that I wrote an essay in *Foreign Policy*?

EL RASHIDI: What about —

ELTAHAWY: Wait, let me tell you where the men's rage comes in, because a lot of men wrote to me after what happened, and their reaction was this:

Dear Sister Mona,
    I'm so sorry about what happened to you. I want to bow down before you and kiss your feet because I was not able to protect you. But I vow to you, that I will not rest until I avenge your honor.

So I think, This is very interesting. I write back and I say:

Dear Brother So-and-So,
    I am so grateful for your support.
    Thank you. I am very moved.
    But.
    My honor is intact. Nothing has happened to my honor.
    And let's vow together to restore Egypt's honor. Men and women together, because that's how our revolution will succeed.

                                                                    Sister Mona

The regime does these things to us because they know it emasculates our men. Our bodies are the battlefield, the nexus of power and sexuality. So the regime does this and our men—even men very close to me, including men I'm emotionally involved with—feel emasculated, and they want to go back and take revenge. Or, because I was on the front lines and they weren't, they feel emasculated in *that* way. I'm like, I'm not responsible for your masculinity issues. I've got enough to deal with!

But that nexus of power and sexuality is the revolution that I want to fight. Which is why I'm going back to Egypt. We weren't ready for that in the eighteen days. Now that more and more people see what I wrote about in my essay because they go to the protests and they get groped by the very men who were keeping the physical revolution alive against the police, we can start talking about this revolution. Why are these young men who are so courageous groping me as they are running away from bullets?

And this is where I enter now and say: because the revolution is happening over our bodies. And unless that nexus of power and sexuality is reckoned with, there is no future. That's what I want to do in Egypt—I want to work against sexual violence. There are so many people on the ground working on this, but they're just not working horizontally. If we put all the different initiatives under one umbrella, we can have a national campaign. I'm going to be working with the group Baheyya and their community of artists, writers, musicians, going into the rural areas we normally never see, reaching out to people. Working holistically, with doctors, creating female police units in precincts, getting rape kits and crisis lines and free therapy in place. Working with the Ultras to get awareness down to the streets. Working with football stars like Abu Treika to make a billboard that says, REAL MEN DON'T GROPE.

It's going to take years, but I'm totally fired up about it. So this will be the activist part of what I do in Egypt, where—again—my body becomes a tool. I never called myself an activist before now, but after Mohamed Mahmoud, I've become an activist, as a kind of therapy.

EL RASHIDI: When we first corresponded you replied to my email by apologizing for the tardy reply because you had been busy responding to hate mail.

ELTAHAWY: Every single day! I read it all, I respond to lots. But sometimes when I begin to read it and it's like, "You cunt, you bitch," I realize there's no point.

EL RASHIDI: It doesn't upset you?

ELTAHAWY: When it comes from the right wing, I expect it. When it comes from what should be allies on the left, that hurts more.

EL RASHIDI: I notice that some of the people on Twitter who I know used to hate you, despise you even, are now flirting with you on Twitter.

ELTAHAWY: I know! It took a few months, but I think people have come around, especially as more and more women face the kind of assault I did. And I'm glad people are coming around—we need to move beyond that knee-jerk position.

EL RASHIDI: I don't see the Muslim Brotherhood being too thrilled about your return.

ELTAHAWY: It's true, but I plan to make a very public appeal to Morsi, to say, "Look, you claim to be the president of all Egyptians, you could have really helped things when you were in Tahrir opening your jacket saying, 'Look look, no bulletproof vest.'" He could have said something about the price Egyptian women have paid.

EL RASHIDI: How did you feel about Morsi's win and that speech in Tahrir?

ELTAHAWY: I was much more depressed than I expected. I think we have five or ten years of really hard work on the ground to get to the point where we can get rid of what the military dictatorship of the past sixty years created and begin to build the country we hope for. If we don't look ahead, the revolution will die. And we have to be optimistic. Our optimism is our biggest weapon. If there's no optimism, forget it—pack the whole thing in. I think Morsi is an ineffectual, utterly unprepared nobody. He was just a fill-in, like a spare tire. The problem with him is he's a soft cuddly grandpa, uncle-looking guy, which made a lot of people say, "He's kind, give him a chance." That's crap.

EL RASHIDI: What's your take on the Brotherhood?

ELTAHAWY: They're too ingrained in collective thinking. It's not rocket science—the Muslim Brotherhood is a microcosm of the regime. The Supreme Guide is Mubarak. A top-down structure, just as the country had when Egyptians said *no*. So they need an internal revolution.

But they're organized! They're out there doing things, and all we can think of is Tahrir. The extent of our political imagination is, "Let's go to Tahrir!" I love Tahrir and wish I were there right now, but for God's sake, people.

EL RASHIDI: What about Brotherhood defectors, like Abdel Moneim Aboul Fotouh?

ELTAHAWY: [Shudders] Who are you? You told every political faction that you were what they wanted. To the left you were a leftist. To the

Islamists, an Islamist. You represent nothing man, *nothing*. Not a fan. Don't buy the soft, cuddly, Islamist guy.

EL RASHIDI: So are you categorically anti-Islamist?

ELTAHAWY: No. I have a platform, and it's more than being anti-Islamist. My platform is to create a ceiling of freedom that is high enough in Egypt that it encompasses everyone's freedoms. What last year has done for me is that it has moved me beyond reacting to their agenda. With my essay, with my arrest, with the kind of stuff I want to do now, I'm creating an agenda that other people have to react to. Now, whenever anyone writes something about women's rights in the Middle East, they always mention my *Foreign Policy* piece. It has put a flag on the ground that you have to respond to. And that, for me, is taking away from them. In the past it was *their* flag people had to respond to. Now it's mine.

MATTHEW DICKMAN

■

Three Poems

FROM *Wish You Were Here,* a chapbook

Greencastle

I like the dark inside
the hotel room
because it reminds me
of the dark inside
of an apple
before you cut it in half.
How the core
is like a ribcage some bird
left behind
after it was eaten
and the wind and the rain
had its way with it
and basically that's what
this room is
and what I am too, wondering
how to get outside
when I'm the kind of person
who looks at his shoes or hands
only sees a kind of dark shape
or something like the unnamed
color of molecules.

I'm in Greencastle trying
to express myself
by not being, not moving.
I'm closing my eyes like two
refrigerator doors and thinking
of garbage cans and ponds,
I'm thinking about your feet
and sawdust and rockets.
I'm thinking about all the things
I haven't done
like burying an animal
by myself or how I've never been
on a rollercoaster but feel
anxious about them.
I want to say Greencastle
over and over until it means
something, until there's a hero
walking the perimeter
of the castle wall, dragging
his sword because his horse
is lost in a dark green forest
and his men are gone, trying to
find a way in, a way over the moat,
a way through the thick stone,
even though inside
the tables and chairs have all
been set on fire,
even though the food was eaten
years ago, even though
the king is dead
and everyone in the castle left
when he left. They just
threw their hands in the air
and said fuck it! It's funny
to be in a hotel room and only
think of leaving. Good-bye

to everything green. Good-bye
to the castle and the castle
walls. It's funny being here but not
knowing why, or sitting
on the floor like a pillow
that's fallen off the bed,
and smiling a weird wet smile,
and watching television, watching
the pixels move around
the screen, instead of being dead.

Nobleboro

All my friends are swimming
in the lake
in my hands, all of them have taken
off their clothes,
finally and at last. I want
to say this has something important
to do with the idea
of urban ecology, something to do
with the kind of lamps
psychotherapists choose and if the lamps
are bought at Target
or if they are bought at Crate & Barrel,
but maybe it doesn't matter.
Maybe I should just come out
and tell you that I have no idea
who I am. I thought by now I wouldn't feel
like I've just taken a muscle relaxer
designed in a very clean lab
in Arizona, intended to relax the muscle
of the self, that inside, oh—
is it all right if we talk about this?
that inside I feel like a very big suitcase
with a white handkerchief

floating in the middle of it, that
and like all the air in a balloon
some child is letting out in one long scream
between her fingers. In Nobleboro
the loons are crying or calling, I'm not sure
if they miss their parents
or if they are trying to convince
other loons to fuck them. I'm not sure
if they are anything like me or if they are
anything like you. Either way
I have found it impossible
to sleep without them,
without wondering how they are
and if they love me. Did you know
that I am swimming through the lakes
inside all my friends' hands? It feels good.
It feels like I never want to leave
even though soon I will have to. Soon
I will walk into a store
and the man behind the counter,
behind the lighters and incense, the gum
and maps, will be the death
that was promised the night my father
entered my mother
like a man entering a lake, free and cold
and with wonder. The man
behind the counter will be so happy
to see me and he will be sweating a little
and will smell like a pine
air freshener, and I will think about Erin
and Anna, Nick and Tony,
and he will say,
yes, them as well, and did you bring anything
to swim in or are you just going to go naked?

Sidewalk Poem

My mother worked like a dog
for so long it's nice to see her
be the owner—
There are only, really, one million
two hundred and ten ways
to die. The five main ones being
your father drinking, your father
breathing, your father touching
anything at all, your father
listening to Opera, your father
looking at you and saying
I see you. Like Pope Francis
looking at a girl's knees
when he was twelve and what
made him love Jesus
crawled out of his lunch pail
right as she crossed her legs
in the sign of the cross. Actually
there are only ten ways to die
but I'm too afraid to say. I'm brave
enough to walk home, though.
Brave enough for the dark
if there's a cross in it, a telephone
pole or a weirdly shaped tree,
if there's a dog being walked,
if there's a dog at all. I want to
take this opportunity to say
that the Gettysburg Address
is the Money-Shot of any speech
I have ever read aloud to my mom
and dad, which is to say
if you are ever, even a little bit,
afraid just know that other people
are too. It's not just you

standing in the spice isle
at the grocery store
asking where they keep the anus
extract or if you can use vanilla
instead. In years to come,
when you sign all your letters
with your mind only, know that
someone is alone in their bed
with a body sort of like the body
you have and that she believes
that she is dying. That she is
thinking about her porous mother
and Scotch-taped father. You go
anywhere in the world, even inside
your own self, and your mom
and dad will be right there
like two warm eggs
with a little chocolate and blood
inside them. I'm sorry, I was just
walking home and thinking
about my mom, and thinking about
my dad and saw one of those
blue bags people use to pick up
after their dog, because they love
that stupid dog so much, even
though it's not a baby and even
though they can't have sex with it,
not really, not the way you and I
have sex, with a ball and a stick,
calling each other in from the dark,
whispering good boy
and whispering good girl.

AMOZ OZ

■

Two Women

FROM *Between Friends*

EARLY IN THE MORNING, before sunrise, the cooing of pigeons
in the bushes begins to drift through her open window. The throaty
sound, steady and unbroken, soothes her. A light breeze blows across
the tops of the pine trees and a cock crows on the slope of the hill. A
dog barks in the distance and another one answers it. Those sounds
wake Osnat before the alarm clock rings, and she gets out of bed,
turns off the alarm, showers, and puts on her work clothes. At five
thirty, she leaves for her job in the kibbutz laundry. On the way, she
passes Boaz and Ariella's apartment, which looks locked and dark.
They must still be sleeping, she thinks, and that thought stirs neither jealousy nor pain in her, only a vague disbelief: as if everything
that happened had not happened to her but to strangers, and not two
months ago but many years before. In the laundry, she switches on
the electric light because the daylight is still too faint. Then she bends
over the waiting piles of laundry and begins to separate white from
colored and cotton from synthetic. Sour body odors rise from the
dirty clothes, mingling with the smell of soap powder. Osnat works
here alone, she keeps her radio on all day to ease the solitude, though
the humming of the washing machines muffles both the words and
the music. At seven thirty she completes the first round, empties the
machines and reloads them, then goes to the dining hall for breakfast. She always walks slowly, as if she's not sure where she wants to
go or doesn't care. Here, on our kibbutz, Osnat is considered a very
quiet woman.

At the beginning of the summer, Boaz tells Osnat he's been in a relationship with Ariella Barash for eight months and has decided that the three of them cannot go on living a lie. So, he's made up his mind to leave Osnat and move his things to Ariella's apartment. "You're not a little girl anymore," he says. "You know, Osnat, that things like this happen every day now all over the world, and on our kibbutz, too. Luckily, we don't have children. It could have been a lot harder for us." He'll take his bicycle with him, but leave the radio for her. He wants the separation to be as amicable as their life together has been for all these years. He completely understands if she's angry with him. Even though she doesn't really have anything to be angry about: "The relationship with Ariella wasn't meant to hurt you. Things like this just happen, that's all." In any case, he's sorry. He'll move his things out right away and leave her not only the radio, but everything else, including the albums, the embroidered pillows, and the coffee set they received as a wedding gift.

Osnat says, "Yes."

"What do you mean, yes?"

"Go," she says, "just go."

Ariella Barash was a tall, slim divorcée with a slender neck, cascading hair, and laughing eyes, one of which had a slight squint. She worked in the chicken coop and was also head of the kibbutz Culture Committee, responsible for organizing holidays, ceremonies, and weddings. In addition, she was in charge of inviting lecturers for Friday nights and ordering movies for Wednesday night showings in the dining hall. She had an old cat and a young dog, almost a puppy, which lived together peaceably in her apartment. The dog was frightened of the cat and would politely give it a wide berth. The old cat would ignore the dog and walk past as if it were invisible. The two of them spent most of the day dozing in Ariella's apartment, the cat on the sofa and the dog on the rug, indifferent to one another.

Ariella had been married for a year to a career army officer, Ephraim, who left her for a young woman soldier. Her relationship with Boaz began when he came to her apartment one day wearing a sweaty work singlet stained with machine oil. She'd asked him to drop by to fix a dripping tap. He had on a leather belt with a metal buckle. As he bent over the tap, she stroked his sunburned back gently several times until he turned around without putting down his screwdriver and wrench. Since then he'd been sneaking into her apartment for half an hour here or an hour there, but there were those on Kibbutz Yekhat who noticed the sneaking around and did not keep that discovery to themselves. People on our kibbutz said, "What a strange pair; he hardly says a word and she never shuts up." Roni Shindlin, the comedian, said, "The honey is eating the bear." No one told Osnat about it, but her friends showered her with affection and found ways to remind her that she wasn't alone, if she needed anything, the slightest thing, and so on and so forth.

Then Boaz loaded his clothes into his bicycle basket and moved to Ariella's apartment. He'd come back in the afternoon from his job in the garage, take off his work clothes, and go into the bathroom for his shower. From the doorway, he'd always say to her, "So, anything happen today?" And Ariella would reply in surprise: "What should've happened? Nothing happened. Take your shower and we'll have coffee."

In her mailbox, which was on the far left side of the mailbox cabinet near the entrance to the dining hall, Ariella found a folded note in Osnat's round, unhurried handwriting:

> Boaz always forgets to take his blood pressure pills. He needs to take them in the morning and at night before bed, and in the morning he has to take half a cholesterol pill. He shouldn't put black pepper or a lot of salt on his salads, and he should eat low-fat cheese and no steak. He's allowed fish and chicken, but not strongly spiced. And he shouldn't gorge himself on sweets. Osnat.
> P.S. He should drink less black coffee.

Ariella Barash wrote a reply to Osnat in her sharply angled, nervous handwriting and put it in her mailbox:

> Thank you. It was very decent of you to write to me. Boaz also has heartburn, but he says it's nothing. I'll try to do everything you ask, but he's not easy and he couldn't care less about his health. He couldn't care less about lots of things. You know. Ariella B.

Osnat wrote:

If you don't let him eat fried, sour, or spicy foods, he won't have heart-burn. Osnat.

Ariella Barash replied several days later:

I often ask myself, what did we do? He suppresses his feelings and mine keep changing. He tolerates my dog but can't stand the cat. When he comes home from the garage in the afternoon, he asks me, So what happened today? Then he takes a shower, drinks some black coffee, and sits down in my armchair to read the papers. When I tried giving him tea instead of coffee, he got angry and grumbled that I should stop trying to be his mother. Then he dozes in the chair, the papers fall on the floor, and he wakes up at seven to listen to the news on the radio. He pets the dog while he listens, mumbling some indistinct words of endearment. But if the cat should jump onto his lap asking for affection, he heaves him off with such disgust that I cringe. When I asked him to fix a stuck drawer, he not only fixed the drawer, but he also took apart and reassembled two wardrobe doors that squeaked, and asked with a laugh if he should fix the floor or the roof too. I ask myself what it was about him that attracted me and sometimes still does, but I have no clear answer. Even after his shower, his nails are black with machine oil and his hands rough and scratched. And after he shaves, there's still stubble on his chin. Maybe it's that constant dozing of his — even when he's awake he seems to be dozing — that tempts me to try and wake him. But I manage to wake him up for only a short while, you know how, and that doesn't always happen either. Not a day goes by when I don't think about you, Osnat, and despise myself and wonder if there can be any forgiveness for what I did to you. Sometimes I tell myself that maybe Osnat didn't really care so much, maybe she didn't love him? It's hard to know. You might think that I actually chose to do that to you. But we don't really have a choice. This whole business of attraction between a man and a woman seems suddenly strange and even a bit ridiculous. Do you think so too? If you had children, you and I would have suffered a lot more. And what about him? What does he actually feel? How can anybody tell? You know so well what he should and shouldn't eat. But do you know what he feels?

Or whether he feels at all? I once asked him if he has any regrets and he said, "Look, you can see for yourself that I'm here with you and not with her." I want you to know, Osnat, that almost every night after he falls asleep, I lie awake in bed and look at the moonlight coming into our dark bedroom through the crack in the curtains and ask myself what would've happened if I'd been you. I'm drawn to your stillness. If only I could absorb some of that stillness. Sometimes I get up and dress and walk to the door, thinking that I'll go to you in the middle of the night and explain it all, but what can I explain? I stand on the porch for ten minutes, look up at the clear night sky, locate the Plough, then get undressed again and go back to lying awake in bed. He's snoring peacefully and I feel a sudden longing to be somewhere else entirely. Maybe even in your room with you. But please understand, this only happens to me at night when I'm lying awake and can't fall asleep and don't understand what happened or why, and I just feel such an intense closeness to you. I'd like to work in the laundry with you, for example. Just the two of us. I always carry both your short notes in my pocket and take them out to read over and over again. I want you to know how much I value every word you wrote and also, even more, how impressed I am by what you didn't write. People on the kibbutz talk about us. They're surprised at Boaz; they say that I just walked past, leaned down, and plucked him away from you and that he, Boaz, couldn't care less about which apartment he goes to after work or which bed he sleeps in. Roni Shindlin winked at me near the office one day, grinned, and said, So, Mona Lisa, still waters run deep, eh? I didn't answer him and walked away in shame. Later, at home, I cried. Sometimes at night I cry, after he falls asleep, not because of him or not only because of him, but because of me and because of you. As if something bad and ugly happened to both of us that can't be fixed. Sometimes I ask him: What, Boaz? And he says: Nothing. I'm attracted to that blankness — as if he has nothing, as if he came straight from a desert of solitude. And then—but why am I telling you this? After all, it hurts you to hear it and I don't want to add to your pain. Just the opposite; I want to share your loneliness the way I wanted to touch his for a moment. It's almost one in the morning now, he's asleep, curled up in fetal position, the dog at his feet, and the cat is lying here on the table, his yellow eyes following the movement of my hand as I keep writing and writing by the light of a gooseneck lamp. I know it's pointless, that I have to stop writ-

ing, that you won't even read this note, which has stretched to four pages. You'll probably tear it up and throw it away. Maybe you'll think I've lost my mind, and I really have. Let's meet and talk? Not about Boaz's diet or the medicine he needs to take. (I really do try not to let him forget. I try, but don't always succeed. You know that stubbornness of his, which seems like disdain but is more like indifference.) We could talk about totally different things. Like the seasons of the year, for example, or even the star-filled sky of these summer nights: I'm interested in stars and nebulas. Maybe you are too? I'm waiting for you to write a note telling me what you think, Osnat. Two words will do. I'm waiting.
Ariella B.

To this letter, which was waiting in her mailbox, Osnat chose not to reply. She read it twice, folded it up, and put it in a drawer. Now she's standing utterly still, looking out of her window. Three kittens are by the fence: one is busy biting its paw; another is crouching or maybe dozing, but with ears pricked suspiciously, as if catching a thin sound; and the third is chasing its tail, constantly falling over and rolling softly onto its back because it's so young. A gentle breeze is blowing, just enough to cool a cup of tea. Osnat moves away from the window and sits down on the sofa, back straight, hands on her knees, eyes closed. It'll be evening soon and she'll listen to light music on the radio and read a book. Then she'll undress, fold her after-work clothes neatly, lay out tomorrow's work clothes, shower, get into bed, and go to sleep. Her nights are dreamless now, and she wakes before the alarm clock rings. The pigeons wake her.

JANINE DI GIOVANNI

■

Seven Days in Syria

FROM *Granta*

1. Hossam

When my son was born, I was unable to cut his nails. It was a visceral rather than rational reaction. I would pick up the tiny baby scissors, look at his translucent fingers, clean and pink as seashells, and feel as though I would retch.

One night, in the hours between darkness and light, the time when the subconscious allows the source of such neuroses to become clear, I understood my inability to perform such a straightforward task. I had a vision of the Iraqi man I once knew who had no fingernails.

In the dying days of the Saddam regime, I had an office inside the Ministry of Information. It was a sinister, paranoid place. Journalists begged, bribed, and pleaded to stay inside the country to report. We were followed, videotaped; our phones were tapped. We all knew that our hotel rooms were equipped with hidden cameras. I dressed and undressed in the darkened bathroom.

Every Monday morning, the man with no fingernails arrived in my office and stretched out his hands, utterly unselfconscious that in place of nails were raw beds of flesh. He had come for his weekly baksheesh. His job was to get the money to seal my satellite phone so I could not use it unless the ministry listened in. Most of us had to pay our way to get anything done, and aside from the fee the ministry charged, we gave a baksheesh to get it done faster.

Every time the man arrived and I looked at his hands spread out, I immediately felt a wave of panic, which turned to nausea, and yet I could not take my eyes off the place where his fingernails had been ripped off. Questions that I could not ask him raced through my mind. What had he done to deserve such agony? Was he an informer? Had he tried to escape Iraq and been caught? Was he part of the secret network attempting to overthrow the dictator? I never asked. Nor would he have answered. We were living in a republic of fear. He became one of those shadowy figures one holds in one's mind forever, hovering on the fringes.

The man, whose name I never knew, seemed to bear no resentment that he had been disfigured in such a public way. Because hands are one of the first things we usually notice about someone, every time he stretched out his, one knew immediately he had done something.

Or perhaps he had done nothing at all. Perhaps it was a horrible mistake. Such things happen all the time under dictatorships. People get locked up for years, forgotten, then the key turns and a jailer says, "You can go now." They never know why.

The day Saddam's regime fell, in the feverish chaos, I went to search for the man with no fingernails to open the seal so I could use my sat phone. But he, like most of the regime staff, had fled.

I went back to Iraq many times after that, but I never saw the man with no fingernails again—except in my dreams.

In northern Lebanon, in a town now inhabited by the Free Syrian Army (FSA) and many fighters who are recovering from severe injuries, I do what I do in most war zones: I go to the nearest hospital. In the hallway of a small rehabilitation clinic, I pass a man who recently had twenty-nine bullets removed from his body. Then I meet a paralysed man strapped to a board who is playing with a child—an orphaned child. The man had been badly beaten and left with a fractured spinal cord.

"Every time they hit me," he said, "they screamed, 'You want freedom? OK, take this! Here is your great freedom!'"

Then I meet a man I am going to call Hossam, a student of human rights law, who sits on a bed trying to re-enter the human race.

He is twenty-four years old and dressed in baggy dark trousers, a T-shirt, and has a full beard and a shy but gentle demeanour. He keeps trying to buy me packs of Winston cigarettes, but I keep refusing, and he keeps insisting, gently, that he must give me a gift. On his hands and arms I see cigarette burns that I suspect are not self-inflicted.

On another bed, pushed against a wall, a fourteen-year-old boy sits and listens. When I suggest he leave the room for the interview, which I know is going to be painful, the boy explains that his father was killed in front of him, so he can take whatever else is about to come.

Hossam is Sunni and religious, but he still shakes my hand and gets off his bed, limping, to get me a chair. He tells me that he comes from an educated family—his father a civil servant, his brothers all university-educated.

Then he begins to tell his story without words. Slowly he removes his T-shirt. A thick, angry scar that begins under his mid-breastbone swims down to the proximity of his groin. He sighs, lights a cigarette, and starts to talk in a low voice.

Hossam comes from Baba Amr, the district of Homs, Syria's third-largest city, which became an icon for the suffering of civilians when it got pummelled and overrun by Syrian government troops and paramilitary units beginning in December 2011. He admits that he was one of the organizers of the first peaceful demonstrations against the government, but denies that he is a member of the FSA.

"It was about freedom and rights at first," he says. "Then came bullets."

On 8 March 2012 at about 7:30 p.m., there were shouts outside the door of his family home. He heard men speaking a foreign language that he believes may have been Farsi. At first he refused to open the door. "I said, 'We are civilians! We have rights!'"

But the soldiers—who he said were not wearing uniforms, meaning they could have been paramilitary—fired intimidating shots, and his brother opened the door. The men shot the young man through the chest at close range, and the force of the bullet pushed him against a far wall where he fell, dying.

They swarmed into the house like bees. Hossam thinks there were about thirty of them. They shot Hossam in the shoulder and in the hand as he tried to cover his face for protection from the blow he thought was coming. He holds up his deformed fingers, and touches the angry red circle on his shoulder blade. The impact of the bullet made Hossam reel backwards, and he ended up lying next to his dying brother, looking him straight in the eye.

"I was watching the life go out of him," he says quietly.

The men then picked him and his brother up by their feet and hands and hauled them, along with several dozen men from the neighbourhood, to a truck and threw them in, one on top of the other. They said they were going to use them as human shields. Some of the men in the truck were already dead, many were badly beaten and lay groaning in agony. Others had been shot.

"One guard pulled a man up by his ear and said, 'Say Bashar al-Assad is your God.' The man replied, 'I have no God but God,' and the guard shot him and tossed him onto the pile of bodies."

Hossam was bleeding but his brother was closer to death. They took all of them off the truck when they reached the military hospital, and the minute they closed the doors, they began to beat Hossam brutally with sticks of plastic and wood.

Hossam's brother and the other men were flung into an underground room that served as a morgue. This was the same room where, from then on, Hossam was thrown every night to sleep after he was tortured, on top of the dead bodies. He described how he would lie awake listening to people breathing their last breath.

On the first day, Hossam's torturers, who were Syrian and told him they were doctors, brought him to something like an operating room. There were about four of them. They strapped him down.

"Are you a fighter?"

"No, I'm a student."

"Are you a fighter?"

They held his penis and took a blade and said, "Okay, cut it off."

They pressed the blade into his flesh, enough to draw blood, then began leaning painfully on his bladder, forcing him to urinate.

"Why do you want to kill me?" Hossam asked.

"Because your people are killing us," he was told.

Then they electrocuted him. This went on for three days. Beatings, burnings, cuttings. The worst, he says, was "the cutting."

"They came for me. I lay down on a table and closed my eyes. I saw them cut my gut with a scalpel." He tells me that he must have been in shock because the pain did not seem to reach his brain. "Then they lifted something out of my body—I felt pulling. It was my intestine. They stretched it. They held it in their hands and laid it on the outside of my body. They made jokes about how much the rebels ate, how much food was inside my intestines. Then they sewed me back up, but in a rough way so that there was skin and blood everywhere."

He tells me his stomach was "open" for two days before they properly stitched the wound closed.

The next day the torturers—who clearly must have had medical knowledge—punctured Hossam's lung. They cut an incision that runs from under his nipple to the middle of his back. They inserted what he described as a small plastic suction tube.

"I felt the air go out of my lung," he says quietly. "My right lung had collapsed. I could not breathe."

Hossam is alive only because on the third day of his torture he was left hanging upside down for nearly five hours. He tells me how he was "used as a punchbag by nearly everyone that went by as a way of having fun," until, later that day, when it was quiet, a doctor suddenly knelt before him.

He whispered, "My job is to make sure that you are still alive and can sustain more torture. But I can't watch this any more." The doctor shook his head.

"Your heart has technically stopped twice, once for ten seconds and once for fifteen." He leaned forward and opened a notebook.

"I am going to close your file and write that on the second attempt to revive you, I failed. Do you understand what I am saying? You are dead."

As the doctor walked away, he said, "If Allah intends you to live, you will find a way to get out of here."

It took several minutes for Hossam to understand what the doctor meant. He was giving him a chance to escape, to live. The doctor ordered that Hossam be taken down from his ropes, and he was tossed back into the morgue. As he lay there, he thought of his dead brother, somewhere under the pile of bodies.

Hossam's story is so grisly that, in spite of his obvious wounds, part of me, a small part of me, wonders if it can be true. How can someone actually survive such treatment? This is what torture also does. In its worst form, it makes us doubt the victims.

After an hour among the dead, in pain so brutal that he could think of nothing but the blood coursing through his ears, a nurse came into the room. She whispered that she had been paid by the FSA to bring out any men who were still alive. She told Hossam to follow her instructions carefully: she would give him a Syrian government uniform, and a number, which he must memorize. She made him say it twice. He mumbled that he could stand no more, and she gave him an injection of painkiller. Then, she gently lifted him up and helped him put on the uniform.

With his arm around the nurse for support, they walked out of the courtyard of the military hospital. It took twenty minutes to walk a few feet; but he tells me that it felt like days. A guard asked him for his serial number. He gave the number the nurse had rehearsed with him while she looked on nervously.

At the gate, a car was waiting. It was someone sent by the FSA. They opened the door and the nurse helped him in and turned away without looking back.

He was free.

2. Daraya

Daraya, a suburb seven kilometres south-west of Damascus, was once known for its handmade wooden furniture. It is also allegedly the place where Saul had a vision of God, became a believer and apostle, and headed for Damascus.

In August 2012, more than 300 people, including women and children, were killed—the town was "cleansed." It marked a turning point in the war. I was driven by a Sunni resident, Maryam (not her real name), and we passed easily through the government military checkpoints manned by young boys with stubble and Kalashnikovs who looked as though they would be more comfortable in discos than in this war zone.

Maryam's family came from Daraya, but they had been at their holiday home near the coast when the massacre took place between 23 and 25 August. As we drove, she took in the destruction with a certain sangfroid, but it was clear that she was shocked. She had not yet decided if she supported the government or the rebels. But as an open-minded, educated woman, she wanted to see for herself what was happening in her country.

The government line was that the massacre was a prisoner exchange gone wrong; the FSA said it was an attack and cleansing operation.

"Syrians could not do this to other Syrians," she said, her voice shaking. It appeared as though the government tanks had rolled right through the centre of town, destroying everything in sight, crushing the street lights, the houses, even the graveyard walls.

There were shattered windows and glass everywhere and I saw a lone cyclist with a cardboard box of tinned groceries strapped to a rack over his back wheel. But there were no other civilians on the streets. The buildings appeared crushed like accordions; it looked as though people had either hidden or run away as fast as they could.

The Syrian opposition was giving figures as high as 2,500 massacred, but the local people I managed to find told me the number was closer to 1,000 people killed, mainly men and boys.

One month on, there are still no clear figures, but the number 330 is usually quoted. But everywhere I went that day in Daraya, I encountered the distinctive smell of the dead decaying.

I met one of the witnesses, a man who had just been released after six months in prison. His crime? There were often demonstrations in the streets. But this man said he wasn't even at a demonstration when he was arrested.

"They picked up the wrong guy and forgot about me." He had been led outside in the prison yard, naked but for his underwear in the freezing winter cold, doused with icy water, then left hanging from ropes for hours and beaten. But somehow, he survived.

After a while, Maryam and I went to look for the gravedigger to see if he could give us a count of the dead. There was a crowd of people gathered who were reading a sign put up by desperate families—a list of the missing. They told us that they came every day to see if they could find their loved ones. One man told me he had been looking for his elderly father for three days before finally finding his body decaying in the heat on a farm outside Daraya, along with the bodies of several young men.

"But why kill an old man? Why?" Then he said what I kept hearing, over and over on this trip: "Syrians cannot do this to other Syrians."

3. The Balloon Has Not Yet Burst

My first trip to Syria was in the stifling heat of summer. I arrived in a local taxi from Beirut. The first thing I saw once I crossed the border was the enormous colour portrait of the leader, common to all autocratic regimes. This was of the youthful, triangular face of Bashar al-Assad.

The second thing that attracted my attention was a Dunkin' Donuts, which seemed odd, even in a sophisticated country like Syria. I was aware I was entering what has been called the second most dangerous regime next to North Korea, so I was shocked to see such an American symbol. It's the kind of thing one would expect to find on a US airbase in Kandahar, for example, with well-fed American soldiers, rather than skinny, suspicious-looking Syrians, lined up to buy pink-sprinkled donuts.

As it turned out, the Dunkin' Donuts was a fake. It only sold toasted cheese sandwiches. I bought one, watched all the while by three men with moustaches, smoking cigarettes—clearly Mukhabarat, the infamous Secret Police.

In Damascus, people whisper when out in public. When a waiter arrives at a table, people stop talking. The Mukhabarat are often so obvious that they could have come straight from central casting. They could easily have been the same men who followed me in Iraq a decade before—the same cheap leather jackets, the same badly trimmed, downward-turned moustaches.

I had come to Syria because I wanted to see the country before it tumbled down the rabbit hole of war. That first trip in June 2012, Syria was on the brink. I checked into a hotel where the United Nations military observers who were there to monitor Kofi Annan's six-point plan in an attempt to bring peace—glum-faced men who were no longer allowed to operate because they had been shot at too often—sat drinking coffee after coffee and making jokes about the Russian hooker bar downstairs.

One Thursday—the start of the Muslim weekend—I came in after an exhausting day of talking to people who were uncertain whether or not their country would exist in a year or two. They were Christians, but liberal. They did not support the government's crushing of peaceful protests at the beginning of the uprising; on the other hand, they were terrified of what was coming next.

"Jihadists?" they asked. "Salifists?" This is what everyone was worried about, what everyone claimed to distrust: "Who's next?" Syria, like Bosnia, is multi-ethnic: home to generations of Greek Orthodox, Christians, Sunni Kurds, Shias, Alawites, and even a residual population of Jews—"a melting pot," as the foreign minister's spokesperson, Jihad Makdissi, a Christian with an Islamic name, has called it. But for how much longer was that melting pot going to hold?

To get the weekend going, the hotel sponsored a pool party that looked to me, with the smoke rising in the background from shelling in the southern suburbs, like a re-enactment of Sodom and Gomorrah.

A half-dressed Russian woman danced onstage by the pool, gyrating her skinny hips. Voluptuous wealthy Syrian ladies—all teased hair, glossy lips, and silicone-enhanced bosoms—strutted in bikinis and high heels. Men also wore the briefest of swimming trunks and drank what the Levants call "Mexican beer"—Lebanese beer served with a slice of lime in a salt-rimmed glass.

The party was obscene in a city that was verging on civil war. I stood on my balcony and watched this denial of the drum roll of impending carnage. These people's lives were falling apart. But the balloon had not yet burst.

4. The Believers

For two weeks running, I witnessed the fevered hedonism of the Thursday-afternoon pool parties at the Dama Rose Hotel. The first week was like every other. The hairdressers were full of ladies of leisure getting hair extensions, mani/pedis, and false eyelashes. The roads were clogged with luxury cars heading outside the city to amusement parks — the ones that were still open — en route to country villas for parties, weekend picnics, or dinners. Restaurants such as Naranj, which takes up nearly half a block in the Old City and serves traditional Arabic food to the elite, were packed.

But what was unusual about the Dama Rose pool parties was that they were taking place in a hotel that was, ironically, also home to those 300 frustrated United Nations soldiers from fifty different countries who had been brought in to monitor the situation.

From 14 June onwards, when their operations were suspended because it became too dangerous for them to work — their convoys had been attacked, shot at, and harassed — the men sat around in the hotel lobby, looking bored, just like the Mukhabarat.

The blasting house music wafted up to the third floor where Major General Robert Mood, who was then head of the UN Supervision Mission in Syria, tried to negotiate ceasefires, and where his civilian staff shut the windows, put their heads in their hands, and wondered what the hell was going to happen to their mission. It would be suspended a few weeks later and Syria would be added to the long list of United Nations failures.

That first week, people danced around to a pumped-up version of Adele's "Someone Like You," but by the second week, there was an air of sombre reflection to the party. People drank, the house music blared, the UN staff complained about the noise, but the Russian dancer was gone. And this week, people left early, rushing to their 4x4s with distinctly worried looks on their faces.

In the distance, beyond the pool, towards the al-Marjeh neighbourhood, just across from the Justice Courts, there was a larger curl of smoke: two car bombs had exploded earlier that day in the centre of Damascus.

I had left town that morning to visit a remote convent where pro-government — meaning those who support the regime of President Bashar al-Assad — nuns made apricot jam and spent their days praying to the relics of Takla, an ancient Christian saint.

Takla had been an early convert of Saint Paul, who was running from the Romans when she found herself facing an enormous mountain. Miraculously, the mountain opened to let her pass and make her escape. Syrians and others from all over the Middle East came to be healed at the place of that miracle.

Like many people who support Assad, the Greek Orthodox nuns feared a fundamentalist Islamic regime in their country. I sat with one sister who wore an old-fashioned wimple and served me sugared coffee and biscuits. She spoke Aramaic, the ancient language of Christ, and vehemently defended the regime.

The nuns would not believe that Syrians could massacre each other, she said. When I pointed out that earlier in the summer the United Nations had released a report pointing a finger at the Assad regime for the massacre of civilians at al-Houla, she ignored me, asking a younger nun to bring in a plate of sugared apricots.

This was the same week that the offices of a pro-government television station had been bombed and a firefight had broken out between opposition and pro-government forces. And yet, in Maaloula where the convent was situated, in this village that lay on the road between Damascus and Homs, I felt an unexpected sense of peace.

I remember thinking this would be a good place to hide if full-scale war broke out, and I slipped away from the nuns to explore the convent. Downstairs, the nuns slept in monastic cells, which looked out over the mountains where Saint Takla had fled. In the courtyard, I saw Syrian couples who had come here to pray for fertility or for the healing of various ailments: you went into a candlelit cave and held a wooden foot, or stomach, or arm, or whatever part of the body ailed you, and prayed to Saint Takla.

The sun bore down on the car on the road back, and in contrast to the cool convent with its sense of hushed protection, the Damascus bomb site stank of burned rubber. Skeletons of charred cars remained. It was a miracle that no one had been hurt by these explosions caused by "sticky bombs"—handmade bombs taped to the bottom of a car at the height of rush hour, just across from the Justice Courts.

"Real amateur hour," one UN official said to me later. "The bombers didn't know what they were doing—it's just a scare tactic to make the people hate the opposition."

And it worked. People blamed the opposition and "foreign interventionists" for the explosions. Crowds of people gathered, angry that their city was quickly falling victim to the devastation that was spreading across the country.

"Our only friend is Russia!" one well-dressed man shouted, his face contorted with rage. "These are foreigners that are exploding our country! Syria is for Syrians!"

It is a common belief that the bombs and the chaos spreading throughout the country are being caused by a "third element." Especially in Damascus, which has long been an Assad stronghold, people refuse to believe that the opposition will rule their country without turning it into a fundamentalist Muslim state.

Damascus has many faces. There are the opposition activists who are working night and day to bring down Assad, the ones who meet me in secret. Sometimes, when I return to my home in Paris, I hear news through the grapevine that they have disappeared. These are the ones who risk going to jail for up to forty-five days without charge. Even peaceful protesters have been thrown in jail simply for demonstrating. Their families are not told of their whereabouts.

Twice I visited the Damascus Opera House — the second grandest in the Middle East, in this city named by UNESCO in 2008 as the Arab Capital of Culture.

"I do not want to give the impression that we are like the *Titanic* — the orchestra plays on while the ship sinks," explained one classical musician. We were sitting in her office and she motioned overhead, meaning the room was probably bugged.

On another visit, I went to see the Children's Orchestra practising, led by a visiting British conductor. When I mentioned that he was brave to be there, he said, with a worried look, "Should I get out soon? How long do you give it before all-out war?"

I reassured him, but in fact, I thought, the country was already in a full-scale, if guerrilla, war.

Some of the musicians were very young — around eight — with tiny hands holding their instruments, but others looked like teenage kids anywhere — Brazilian surfing bracelets, baggy jeans, long flowing hair. They practised the incredibly touching song of innocence, "Evening Prayer," from Humperdinck's *Hansel and Gretel*.

I sat for a good while watching the fresh young faces of the children intently reading the musical scores and holding their instruments with care, and wondered what this room would look like if I returned at exactly this time next year. How many of these boys would be sent to mandatory military service? How many would flee the country? I tried not to think about whether any would no longer be living.

Maria Saadeh (Arabic for "happiness") lives in Star Square in the old French mandate section of Damascus, in a 1920s building that she helped renovate. A restoration architect by training (educated in Syria and France), she was recently elected, without any experience, as the only Christian independent female parliamentarian.

The Christians are frightened. On Sundays during my stay, I go to their churches—Eastern Christian or Orthodox—and watch them kneel and pray, smell the intense wax of the candles, and see the fear on their faces. Will we be wiped out?

The Christian minority fears that if a new government—and perhaps a Muslim fundamentalist one—takes over, they will be cleared off the face of Syria, off the face of the Middle East, the way the Armenians were driven out of Turkey and massacred in 1914.

"Christians to Beirut, Alawites to the coffin," is one of the chants of the more radical opposition members.

Maria seems confident for the moment. She sits on her roof terrace in a chic apartment building, her two adorable children, Perla and Roland, peeking their heads through the windows and a Filipina maid serving tea. It could be an ordinary day in peacetime—except that, earlier that day, in another Damascus neighbourhood, there was a car bomb and no one yet knows the number of people killed.

Earlier in the week, I had gone to a private Saturday-night piano and violin concert where the director-general of the Opera House, an elegant woman of mixed European and Syrian background, performed Bach, Gluck, and Beethoven.

The concert was held at the Art House, an elegant boutique hotel built on the site of an old mill that has water streaming over glass panels on parts of the floor. The audience was sophisticated. There were women in spiky heels and strapless black evening gowns mingling with artistic-looking bohemian men in sandals and casual chinos, and their children.

Everyone rose at the beginning of the concert to pay homage to the "war dead" with a minute of silence. The violinist wore a strapless red silk dress and high heels, and received a standing ovation. Afterwards, the audience filed out to an open-air restaurant where champagne was served. I overheard several people talking in hushed voices about what had happened around the city that day: explosions, fighting near the suburbs.

"A symphony," one man said, toasting hopefully with his glass of champagne, "that we will live through for the next few years."

5. Firis

One steaming Saturday morning, I drove to the neighbourhood of Berzah, which is a toehold of the opposition inside Damascus. There are frequent protests here, and the government soldiers crack down with arrests, shootings, injuries, and deaths. Berzah is known as one of the "hot spots": areas around Damascus where it is evident that the war is now creeping closer. Douma, where dozens of people were killed in one day in July, is another hot spot. These days the hot spots are engulfing Damascus.

Berzah is also the site of the government-run Tishreen military hospital. One morning, I go to a funeral for fifty soldiers, all killed fighting for Assad. I watch silently as men load the mangled bodies—disfigured and broken by car bombs, IEDs, bullets, and shrapnel—into simple wooden coffins, which are then secured with nails before being draped with Syrian flags. The men then march with the coffins, in full military style, to the sound of a marching band, into a courtyard, where families and members of their regiment wait, many of them weeping. It is an acute reminder of how hard Assad's forces are getting hit by the opposition, who are resorting more and more to guerrilla tactics. A senior official at the hospital, who refuses to give his name, says that 105 soldiers are dying every week.

Upstairs, on the seventh floor of the hospital, a thirty-year-old major lies under a sheet, his right leg and arm missing. At the end of May, Firis Jabr was in a battle in Homs where he says he was ambushed and gravely injured by "foreign fighters: Libyans, Lebanese, Yemeni."

Despite the fact that he is now missing nearly half his body, and his anxious fiancée is standing attentively near his bed, Firis, who is Alawite—an offshoot of the Shia religion to which the Assad clan and many of his followers belong—has a huge smile on his face. He introduces me to his mother, whom he calls "Mama" when I ask her name, and she makes us coffee from a small hotplate in the corner of the room. She serves Arabic pastries with pistachios. She tells me that she is a widow and Firis is her eldest son.

Like nearly all the government supporters I meet, Firis says that he believes in Assad and will continue to fight, as soon as he is fitted with his prosthetics.

"I have two loves," he tells me, trying to lift himself up with his useless side, "my fiancée and Syria."

Later I meet a Syrian friend for tea. She shakes her head sadly when I tell her about Firis.

"It has started," she whispers sadly. "The beginning of the end of what was Syria."

6. Among the Alawites

On my second trip to Syria, a little more than a month later, I felt I was in a different country. The evolving war had become a real war. The faux light-heartedness that had existed—like a balloon—had been popped. Four men in Assad's closest circle had been assassinated, probably with the help of FSA members who had infiltrated the government. People were expecting the fall of Damascus, or worse. There was heavy fighting in other parts of Syria—in Idlib, Aleppo, and in the suburbs of Damascus.

I was told by a local reporter that 2,000 people had fled the capital alone. Refugees were flooding the Turkish, Jordanian, and Lebanese borders. There were fears for the winter.

The Dama Rose Hotel pool parties had halted. The UN had been pulled out except for a skeleton staff; one night I watched a strange karaoke evening—an attempt to be jolly in a miserable place—in the bar. I sat smoking a narghile—a water pipe—and listened to shelling coming from inside Damascus.

I went back to Homs to see some of my Syrian friend Maryam's relatives, and had lunch with her family. Everyone ate quietly while we heard the shelling emanating from a nearby government base. Then, while the older ladies rested on sofas for their after-meal repose, I spoke quietly to the men, asking if they were frightened.

Many people had left, they told me, or were leaving, and they pointed in the direction of the sound of the shelling: "This is the background music of our lives."

The next day, we drove towards Latakia, in the Alawite heartland, to see the mausoleum of Hafez al-Assad, the father of Bashar, who had been president from 1971 until his death in 2000. I drove down with Maryam and her husband, passing through checkpoint after checkpoint, and as we got closer to Qardaha, where Assad is buried, there were stone lions everywhere—*assad* means "lion" in Arabic and it's the name Bashar's grandfather had adopted.

Maryam, who wears a hijab, said, "We are in the land of Alawites now." She paused. "I feel uncomfortable."

But at the Assad family mausoleum, the guards—young men in sombre blue suits—were friendly; shocked, even, to see a foreigner. They gave me tea and escorted me inside to the green-covered graves where Hafez and two of his sons are buried. They said Hafez had been the first Alawite to go to high school. The air was heavy with the scent of roses and incense. I looked at an empty corner and wondered if the current president, Bashar, was going to find his place there, sooner rather than later.

"We may never see this again," Maryam's husband said as we left, passing another lion. "If the regime crumbles, the opposition will tear this place down to the ground."

When we left, we climbed higher into the green Jibal al-Alawiyin mountains and stopped to eat at a roadside restaurant. A river rushed below us. The waiter was blue-eyed—many Arabs in the Levant are, but in particular Alawites—and said he had moved to Latakia when he was a child. As an Alawite he constantly felt marginalized: even as part of the minority that controlled the country. Seventy-four percent of the country are Sunni Muslims, yet the Alawites control most of the government jobs and postings.

"The Europeans don't understand us," the waiter said as he brought platters of barbecued chicken and bottles of beer. "As Syrians, we are all losing so much."

At another table, two Alawite businessmen offered us *rakija*, a form of brandy made with anise, and came to join our table. We spoke openly of politics, but when I mentioned the regime's reputation for torture and detention, there was visible stiffening.

"That does not happen," one of the businessmen said. "It's propaganda."

Then the men excused themselves politely and left; Maryam was embarrassed.

"You should not have asked that," she remonstrated quietly.

"But it's true," I said.

She turned her face away, and in a cloud of narghile smoke replied, "Syrians cannot bear that we are doing this to each other. Once we had a common enemy—Israel. Now we are each other's enemy."

7. The Shabaab

The war had come to Damascus—hit-and-run operations by the opposition; bombings in defence of their minute strongholds. The government, which has tanks and aircraft, kept to the high ground and pummelled opposition fighters from above. The FSA are said to be armed by Qatar, Saudi Arabia, and to some extent by the United States, but when you see the fighters—the *shabaab*, the guys—you see what they need is anti-tank weapons and anti-aircraft guns. They have none. Their weapons are old. Their uniforms are shabby. They fight wearing trainers.

Zabadani, a town close to the Lebanese border on the old smugglers' route, had once been a tourist attraction but is now empty except for government gunners on the hills and FSA fighters in the centre of town. Before the war, the town was more or less a model community: mainly populated by Sunnis but a friendly place where people were welcomed, and where ethnicity and religion did not matter.

"There is a feeling of belonging in Zabadani that the regime deprived us of," said Mohammed, a young journalist I had met in Beirut who was born and raised in Zabadani, but who had been forced to flee. "We felt *Syrian*. Not any ethnic or religious denomination."

I crowded into a courtyard of an old building in town, which was protected from shelling on all sides, with a group of fighters on what they counted as the fifty-second day of straight shelling in Zabadani. They did the universal thing soldiers do when they wait for the next attack: drink tea, smoke cigarettes, and complain.

"What did you do in your former life?" I asked this ragtag bunch.

One was a mason; another a truck driver; another a teacher; another a smuggler. Thirty years ago, the roads from Damascus to Zabadani were infamous for smuggling.

"You could buy real Lacoste T-shirts, anything, for the cheapest price." Everyone laughed. Then there was the sound of machine-gun fire and the smiles disappeared.

At the Zabadani triage hospital, which keeps getting moved because it keeps getting targeted and blown up, the sole doctor was stitching up a soldier who had been hit in a mortar attack. The current hospital location had been a furniture shop and was well hidden in the winding streets of the Old City, which had been taken over by the FSA. As the doctor stitched in the dark, he talked: "Both sides feel demoralized now," he said. "But both sides said after Daraya"—referring to the massacre—"there is no going back."

The doctor insisted on taking me back to his house and giving me a medical kit for my safe keeping. "You need it," he said. As I left, his wife gave me three freshly washed pears.

"The symbol of Zabadani," said the doctor. "They used to be the sweetest thing."

There are no templates for war—the only thing that is the same from Vietnam to East Timor to Sierra Leone is the agony it creates. Syria reminds me of Bosnia: the abuse, the torture, the ethnic cleansing, and the fighting among former neighbours. And the sorrow of war too is universal—the inevitable end of a life that one knows and holds dear, and the beginning of pain and loss.

War is this: the end of the daily routine—walking children to schools that are now closed; the morning coffee in the same cafe, now empty with shattered glass; the friends and family who have fled to uncertain futures. The constant, gnawing fear in the pit of one's stomach that the door is going to be kicked in and you will be dragged away.

I returned to Paris after that second trip, and thought often of a small child I met in Homs, with whom I had passed a gentle afternoon. At night, the sniping started and his grandmother began to cry with fear that a foreigner was in the house, and she made me leave in the dark.

I did not blame her. She did not want to die. She did not want to get raided by the Mukhabarat for harbouring a foreign reporter.

The boy had been inside for some months and he was bored: he missed his friends; he missed the life that had ended for him when the protests began.

For entertainment, he watched, over and over, the single video in the house, *Home Alone*—like *Groundhog Day,* waiting for normality to return so he could go out and play, find the school friends who months ago had been sent to Beirut or London or Paris to escape the war, and resume his lessons.

"When will it end?" he asked earnestly. For children, there must always be a time sequence, an order, for their stability. I know this as a mother. My son is confused by whether he sleeps at his father's apartment or his mother's and who is picking him up from school.

"And Wednesday is how many days away?" he always asks me. "And Christmas is how many months? And when is summer?"

"So when is the war over?" this little boy asked me.

"Soon," I said, knowing that I was lying.

I knelt down and took his tiny face in my hands. "I don't know when, but it will end," I said. I kissed his cheek goodbye. "Everything is going to be fine."

ANDERS NILSEN

■

Rage of Poseidon

FROM *Rage of Poseidon*, a graphic novel

SO IMAGINE YOU ARE POSEIDON, GOD OF THE SEA. IT'S BEEN TWO, MAYBE THREE THOUSAND YEARS SINCE YOU CHASED ODYSSEUS ALL OVER THE MEDITERRANEAN, TRYING TO PUNISH HIM FOR THE MURDER OF YOUR ONE-EYED SON, THE CYCLOPS.

NOT THAT YOU REALLY CARED THAT MUCH ABOUT THE CYCLOPS. HE WASN'T MUCH OF A SON. YOU HADN'T EVER REALLY GOTTEN ALONG WITH HIM THAT WELL. HE LIVED IN A CAVE AND HERDED SHEEP. HE WAS KIND OF STUPID, ACTUALLY. YOU COULD NEVER EVEN REMEMBER HIS MOTHER'S NAME. NOT THAT IT MATTERED. SHE WAS MORTAL. BUT IT WAS THE PRINCIPLE OF THE THING. THEY'D GONE INTO HIS HOME, KILLED HIM, AND TAKEN HIS HERD. HE WAS YOUR **SON**. YOU WERE A **GOD**.

BUT YOUR EFFORTS HADN'T WORKED OUT VERY WELL. THE SO-CALLED GODDESS OF WISDOM
HAD SOME SORT OF WEIRD CRUSH ON ODYSSEUS. SHE USED HER SNIVELLING LAP-DOG,
HERMES, AND A BUNCH OF BULLSHIT SNEAKING AROUND TO GET THE MAN HOME. ALIVE.
YEAH, HIS ENTIRE CREW WAS KILLED, HIS SHIP WAS DESTROYED, HE WAS STRANDED AND
CORRUPTED FOR YEARS. BUT HE MADE IT HOME, ALIVE. TO HIS WIFE. HIS SON. HIS DOG.

IT WAS THEN THAT THE DECLINE BEGAN. IT WAS SLOW, ALMOST IMPERCEPTIBLE AT FIRST. BUT LOOKING BACK, THAT WAS THE FATAL MOMENT. SAILORS STARTED STRAYING FURTHER AND FURTHER AFIELD. OVER TIME, THEY FOUND NEW LANDS. ENCOUNTERED THE CHILDREN OF OTHER GODS.

THEY MADE SACRIFICES TO YOU LESS AND LESS. AND THE QUALITY OF THE SACRIFICES DECLINED. THE ANIMALS THEY OFFERED UP WERE, MORE AND MORE, THE CRIPPLED ONES, THE OLD AND DECREPIT ONES. THEY SAVED THE BETTER MEAT FOR THEMSELVES.

THEY STARTED RELYING ON MAPS AND PECULIAR DEVICES OF NAVIGATION. AND BUILDING
BIGGER BOATS.

AND SO TIME WENT BY. UNNEEDED, YOU WERE LOST, AND YOU DRIFTED APART. TO THIS DAY, YOU DON'T KNOW WHAT HAPPENED TO ALL OF THE GODS. SOME, YOU'VE HEARD, ARE DEAD. BACCHUS APPARENTLY RUNS A NIGHTCLUB IN A NEW CITY ON THE OTHER SIDE OF THE WORLD CALLED "LAS VEGAS". APPARENTLY HE'S BEEN INVOLVED IN THE INVENTION AND SPREAD OF AN EVER-EXPANDING PLETHORA OF NEW INTOXICANTS.

ACCORDING TO RUMOR, HE'S PARTNERED WITH MARS, WHO, OF ALL OF YOU, NEVER LACKED FOR DEVOTEES.

VENUS WORKS IN A PLACE CALLED "HOLLYWOOD." EROS RUNS SOMETHING CALLED "THE INTERNET."

ONLY HADES' VOCATION REMAINS UNCHANGED. HE STILL PRESIDES, UNDISTURBED, OVER THE
DEAD IN HIS DISMAL CAVES.

BUT THE TRUTH IS, THE DECLINE HASN'T BEEN ALL BAD. YOU'VE ALWAYS HAD A SOLITARY DISPOSITION. AND LET'S BE HONEST, THE CONSTANT INTERVENTIONS, SAVING SHIPS, CALLING OFF HUNGRY SHARKS, ALL THE PIDDLING BULLSHIT... IT WORE ON YOU. INDEED, IT MAY BE THAT YOU TOOK TO THE LACK OF RESPONSIBILITIES, IF ANYTHING, **TOO** WELL.

YOU COULD ENTERTAIN YOURSELF FOR WHOLE DECADES JUST ORCHESTRATING THE TIDES, PUNCTUATED WITH THE STIRRING OF THE OCCASIONAL HURRICANE, THE OCCASIONAL TSUNAMI. THE INTRICACIES OF UNDERSEA OCEAN CURRENTS KEPT YOU OCCUPIED FOR ALMOST THE ENTIRE BRITISH EMPIRE.

BUT THEN THE OCEANS BEGAN DYING.

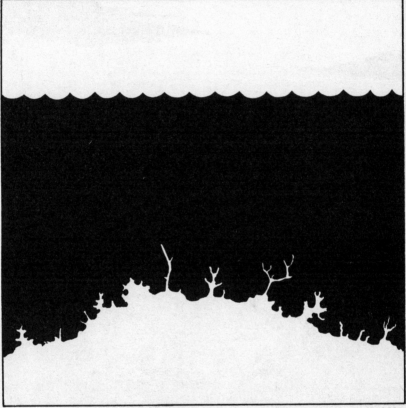

ONE DAY, IN A FAR CORNER, YOU DISCOVERED A MASSIVE FLOATING ISLAND OF GARBAGE. THERE WERE MORE NOT FAR AWAY. THERE WERE ALSO GIANT LIFELESS AREAS THE SIZE OF SMALL COUNTRIES, FILLED WITH SLIME. THERE WERE VAST CITIES OF CORAL REDUCED TO DRY BONE. AND THE FISH WERE ALMOST GONE. THE PROCESS WAS SLOW AT FIRST, THEN BEYOND REPAIR BEFORE YOU KNEW IT.

SWALLOWING YOUR DISTASTE FOR THE SURFACE, YOU'VE TAKEN TO WANDERING AMONG THE MORTALS IN DISGUISE, TRYING TO UNDERSTAND. IT'S BEEN FASCINATING. THEY ARE PATHETIC AND LOATHSOME IN A WAY, BUT STRANGELY SWEET AND ENDEARING AT THE SAME TIME. LIKE THE LARVAE OF EELS. YOU'VE BEEN WANDERING LATELY IN A LAND CALLED "AMERICA," IN A COUNTRY CALLED "WISCONSIN."

IT'S VERY STRANGE. BUT THE CITIZENS ARE GOOD PEOPLE. THEY'VE INVENTED A WONDERFUL
LIBATION THEY CALL "ICED LATTE." IT'S SECOND ONLY TO THE DIVINE AMBROSIA OF
OLYMPUS. YOU CAN'T GET ENOUGH. IT'S SUMMER, AND YOU FIND YOURSELF IN A CITY
WHERE CITIZENS OF THE SURROUNDING PROVINCES COME TO RECREATE. THE PEOPLE ARE
ALL DRESSED IN GARISH, BRIGHT COLORS AND NEVER SEEM TO STOP MOVING OR TALKING.
YOU WALK AMONG THEM, TAKING IT ALL IN.

"THESE ARE THE BEINGS THAT SUPPLANTED US." YOU THINK, "THAT CAST US ASIDE. AS CASUALLY AS A WOLF SPITS OUT THE BONES OF A RABBIT." YOUR MIND REELS AT THE THOUGHT. IT'S HORRIFYING IN A WAY. HUMILIATING. YET DESPITE THE HORRORS, YOU FIND THAT YOU ARE SMILING TO YOURSELF. "IT'S FUNNY," YOU THINK, "IT'S ACTUALLY **FUNNY**."

YOU SHAKE YOUR HEAD AND TAKE ANOTHER SIP FROM THE THIN PLASTIC TUBE PROTRUDING FROM YOUR CUP. "IT'S NOT OUR PROBLEM ANYMORE. IT'S THEIR WORLD NOW." A BARELY NOTICED, BUT LONG HELD TENSION LIFTS FROM YOUR SHOULDERS.

AND THEN YOU SEE SOMETHING THAT STOPS YOU IN YOUR TRACKS.

THERE, ACROSS THE ROAD, IS A GIGANTIC COMPLEX OF COLORFUL TUBES, TWISTING AND WINDING DOWN THROUGH THE AIR BEFORE EMPTYING INTO MAN-MADE POOLS OF WEIRDLY ELECTRIC BLUE WATER. HUMAN CHILDREN SCREAM AND GIGGLE, SLIDING THROUGH THE TUBES AND SPLASHING INTO THE POOLS. A GIANT BILLBOARD PRESIDES OVER THE WHOLE MAD SCENE, GIVING IT A NAME IN SIX-FOOT-TALL NEON:

"RAGE OF POSEIDON WATERPARK."

THE HAIR ON THE BACK OF YOUR NECK STANDS UP. THE PLASTIC CUP FALLS FROM YOUR HAND. YOUR HUMAN FORM TREMBLES SLIGHTLY. YOUR FACE FLUSHES RED.

IT TAKES A FEW WEEKS TO TRACK DOWN YOUR BROTHER JUPITER. ANOTHER COUPLE OF DAYS
AFTER THAT TO SOBER HIM UP. BUT HE AGREES TO YOUR REQUEST, EVEN IF ONLY TO
GET YOU TO GO AWAY AND LEAVE HIM ALONE.

THE NEXT DAY, AND FOR A WEEK AFTER THAT, A CONFLAGRATION OF HURRICANE-FORCE
WINDS AND GALES OF LIGHTNING RAZES EVERYTHING FOR A HUNDRED MILES TO A
SMOKING RUIN.

NOTHING IS SPARED.

AFTERWARD, YOU DRIFT DOWN A SWOLLEN RIVER SLOWLY OUT TO THE SEA. YOU FEEL
MORE ALIVE THAN YOU HAVE IN A THOUSAND YEARS.

LALLY KATZ

■

15-Second Android

FROM *15-Second Plays*, a chapbook

ANDROID

Here I am. An Android. Made only to last fifteen seconds. That's all the time I have for this world. I am born to die. And in that time in between, I will brush my teeth.

The Fifteen Second Android begins to brush its teeth. It speaks as it brushes.

ANDROID

I wake up. For the first and last time ever. And I have morning breath. I use toothpaste to brush it away. I will fall asleep, for the first and last time ever, and I brush my teeth with toothpaste before bed.

It spits out the toothpaste, rinses its mouth and the toothbrush.

ANDROID

I didn't floss. I didn't use mouthwash. But my life wasn't bad, all in all.

The End

KYLE G. DARGAN

■

The Robots Are Coming

FROM *The Baffler*

with clear-cased woofers for heads,
no eyes. They see us as a bat sees
a mosquito—a fleshy echo,
a morsel of sound. You've heard
their intergalactic tour busses
purring at our stratosphere's curb,
awaiting the counter intelligence
transmissions from our laptops
and our earpieces, awaiting word
of humanity's critical mass,
our ripening. How many times
have we dreamed it this way—
The Age of the Machines,
the post industrial specter
of tempered paws, five welded fingers
wrenching back our roofs,
siderophilic tongues seeking blood,
licking the crumbs of us from our beds.
O, it won't be pretty, America.
What land would you trade
for our lives? A treaty inked
in advance of metal's footfall.
Give them Detroit. Give them Gary,
Pittsburgh, Braddock—those forgotten

nurseries of girders and axels.
Tell the machines we honor their dead,
distant cousins. Tell them we left
those cities to repose of respect
for the bygone era of molten metal.
Tell them Carnegie and Ford
were giant men, that war glazed
their palms with gold. Tell them
we humans mourn the ecosystem
of manufacture all the same.

ANDREW FOSTER ALTSCHUL

■

Embarazada

FROM *Ploughshares*

WHEN 600 MILLIGRAMS *of mifepristone is introduced into the blood-stream, it binds to progesterone receptors without activating the receptors, acting as an antiprogestin. Progesterone is fundamentally important for sustaining an early pregnancy.*

Try again—in English. When mifepristone is introduced into the bloodstream of a pregnant woman, it cuts off the supply of progesterone to the developing embryo.

This does not sound like a friendly introduction. It sounds like a tourniquet. Or a naval blockade.

It alters the endometrium by affecting the capillary endothelial cells of the decidua. As a result the trophoblast separates from the decidua, secretion of human chorionic gonadotropin into the maternal circulation declines, and bleeding ensues.

Translation: It wreaks havoc. It ruins everything.

This is all hypothetical.

Hypothetically: If a woman were given 600 milligrams of mifepristone and then, 36 hours later, 800 micrograms of a *prostaglandin analog*—let's call it "misoprostol"—*up to 99% will abort within four hours.* This applies to pregnancies *up to seven weeks since last menstrual period (LMP).* Between seven and nine weeks, it gets a little, shall we say, *dicey,* although *Ngoc et al. reported success rates of 96% among Vietnamese women at 56 days' gestation, and Winikoff et al. reported success ranging from 84% to 95% in China, Cuba, and India.*

China, Cuba, and India strike you as interesting places. Vietnam, too. You think you'd like to travel there one day. Maybe soon. Maybe someone there can teach you the difference between a milligram and a microgram. Maybe they can translate "success."

Incidentally, it's best to administer the misoprostol *intravaginally—which increases the percentage of successful abortions.* While it's true that nausea, cramping, diarrhea, and other side effects will *ensue* for virtually all women, *67% will not require any pain medication using this method.*

One imagines women are relieved to hear this. Why aren't you?

Why is a good question. A popular question. As they say here in Peru: *¿Por qué?* As in *¿por qué* are you here? As in *¿por qué* are you traveling alone?

Since you arrived two weeks ago: *¿por qué? ¿por qué? ¿por qué?* You've quit your job, given up your apartment, cashed your savings. And that's just for starters.

¿Por qué? Literal translation: "For what?" As in: *For what have you come?* As in: *What do you want from us?*

Too hard to explain. *Historia,* you tell the shoeshine boys, the police officer. *Cultura,* you tell the old woman in the bowler hat. You point at the colonial buildings, the 17th-century cathedral, the ice-crowned mountains. The Andean sky is a blue confection, rich as ice cream. Your country is beautiful, you say, shivering in the thin air, winded by the altitude. You consult your pocket dictionary: *muy lindo.* The men—shopkeepers, *taxistas,* the kid at the desk of your *hostal*—laugh at this. *Las chicas están lindas,* they say. You didn't understand at first. And then you did.

"Why you no have girlfriend?" asks Teresa, a waitress *in a pleasant café overlooking the main plaza.* She is twenty, twenty-one. She and the other waitresses have taken an interest in you. You come to this café twice a day, sometimes three times.

No sé, you tell her. You struggle for words but all you come up with is *Not now.*

She wipes your table, smiling mischievously. "When?" she says. Then starts to sing, waltzing with her dishrag: *¿Cuando? ¿Cuando,* *mi amor, estaremos juntos?* From behind the kitchen curtain, shrieks and giggles. A group of German backpackers turn to watch. You eat your eggs, hiding a smile. Yes: Already, you are not who you were.

Teresa, says *la jefa*, looking up from the counter. *No seas tonta. La jefa* is older than the waitresses — maybe thirty, maybe forty — serious and dignified. She is fond of the waitresses, as though they were her wayward little sisters. They pretend to be afraid of her, but when they want a day off they nuzzle up to her and flutter their eyes.

La jefa crosses the café, heels clacking on the warped wood floor. The tables all wobble, no two chairs the same height, the thick walls all cracked. These buildings have been here for centuries — they've survived earthquakes, conquest, the careless trampling of a million shiftless *turistas*. "I sorry," says *la jefa*. She waves an arm at the kitchen curtain, rolls her eyes like Greta Garbo. "These bad girls."

¡No! you say.

Malditas, she says, waggling a finger in disapproval. *Chismosas.* She puts your change on the table, neatly arranged in a clay saucer. A plump yellow cherry wobbles atop the filthy bills. *La jefa* turns to leave, brushing your shoulder. *Jovencitas*, she says, walking away. "Too young."

Turns out, not everyone is so taken with the magical powers of mifepristone. Believe it or not, in some parts of the world, particularly in *strongly Catholic countries*, mifepristone is illegal or virtually unavailable. In such places, one might find a substitute, say *the antifolate methotrexate* [which] *provides another medical approach to pregnancy termination.* Turns out, *regimens with methotrexate and intravaginally administered misoprostol appear to be effective for abortion at 49 days' gestation.*

Translation: It works just as goddamned well.

Hypothetically.

None of this is a secret. A quick search of WebMD, a few medical journals, yields more notes and statistics than you know what to do with. You copy, you paste, you boldface. When the owner of the cybercafé strolls by, you fake a coughing fit, click back to ESPN.com. Later you send an email to a friend in medical school, with a subtle, succinct subject line: *S.O.S.*

* * *

¿Por qué? ¿Por qué, amigo? In the *hostal,* the café, the *bodegas.* In the *plaza,* where you spend afternoons reading while shoeshine boys, children selling postcards, Chiclets, finger puppets, wool hats, hum around you like a swarm. They clamber onto your bench, recite the names of the first ten U.S. presidents. *¿Papi, por qué está acá?* They start to shine your hiking boots. *¿Amigo, no quiere postcard? You no have girlfriend for write?*

¡No!

You like the chicas, amigo? ¿Le gustan las peruanas? They are always in motion, moving from bench to bench like water coming to a boil. *You have girlfriend?* they ask. *You want meet my cousin?*

¡No!

On a nearby bench, three young women in black pants and heavy mascara study you. It occurs to you that you look very friendly, very fatherly, boys crawling on your lap to inspect the book in your hands: *Love in the Time of Cholera.* Translation by Edith Grossman. You read aloud a few sentences. The boys are not interested. You ask them their names. *¿Como se llaman?* The young women spurt into laughter. The kid who runs your *hostal* has taught you a new word: *brichera.* From his smirking explanation you extracted the words *chicas, gringos,* and *sex.* The kid raised his eyebrows, pointed at you. You tried to join in the fun—you pointed back. He turned away, offended. You went back to your room and checked the dictionary, but there was no entry for *brichera.*

Teresa is dating a Dutchman. You've seen him in the café: reed-thin with yellow hair, so tall he has to duck coming up the stairs. The girls call him Javier, though this is only a Spanish approximation of his name. He's a guide, *la jefa* tells you. He leads rich *europeos* around Peru and makes lots of money in tips.

Another waitress, Flor, has a German *novio.* But she used to be with *un frances.* Her sister Laura, who works only on weekends, is also dating a German, though she says she prefers *australianos.* Diana, who comes in on *la jefa*'s day off, lived for a year with a man from *Suiza,* but now is pining after an Englishman who left for Chile last month.

Italianos are popular, because they like to dance. *Franceses* drink all night, and always buy. The Dutch, it is said, are very gallant, *muy ca-*

ballero; everyone in the café has dated a Dutchman at one time or another. No one in the café will admit to having dated an *israelita*.

"Even no Flor!" says Teresa, and laughs. Flor puts her hands on her hips. *Ni tu madre*, she shoots back.

¿Y los americanos? you ask, pleased at how your Spanish is advancing. *Americanos* . . . Teresa is unsure how to answer. *Americanos very* . . . *no sé.* She clamps her arms to her sides, rocks stiff-legged across the room like an intoxicated robot. *Son estúpidos*, says Cristina, the dishwasher.

¡No! cries Teresa, rushing to your table. *¡No!* says Flor. Soon they are all sharing your chair. They assure you that not all Americans are stupid. Some, in fact, are *muy lindos*. You, for example—you are *muy buena persona*, they say, *un gringo diferente*.

Through a curtain of black hair, soothing hands, you say, *No soy gringo.* You don't like the word, its air of arrogance, selfishness. You see plenty of *gringos* here: the Brits, the Germans, the Dutch, who treat the country like a giant souvenir shop. The Israelis who move in packs of twenty and take over whole plazas, smoking and singing songs in Hebrew. *Soy Americano*, you tell your *amigas*.

Somos todos Americanos, says Teresa. We are all Americans.

"Okay," you say. *Norteamericano.*

Teresa ruffles your hair. *Eres un gringuito lindo*, she says in babytalk. The other waitresses shriek with laughter. Behind the counter, *la jefa* hides a smile.

Time is another popular subject. *¿Cuanto tiempo?* everyone asks. "How long are you stay?" *At 42 days or less from last menstrual period (LMP) methotrexate was administered alone without misoprostol. Abortion was successfully induced in 10 patients.*

At first, you spoke only in the present tense: *I arrive three weeks ago. I go to Machu Picchu yesterday.* You bought a Spanish textbook, spent hours doing exercises: *If the action is in the past and you can pinpoint it as to when or how many times it occurred, you will use the preterite tense.* This refers to a single, contained act, not to be repeated. Like a mistake.

An action which occurred *either repeatedly or over an extended period* is considered to be *imperfect.*

Investigators have started to evaluate the use of misoprostol without mifepristone or methotrexate. Investigators have reported extremely high abortion rates at 56 and even 63 days' gestation. These data have been previously discussed.

Then, of course, there's the future. In Spanish, the future *is a simple tense.*

Nearly a month, and you're still in the same town. Each night you consult the *Lonely Planet*, remap the trip, reassess whole countries. You ask yourself ¿*por qué?* You ask yourself what you're waiting for. You tell a *taxista* you are doing research, something to do with ruins. You tell a persistent shoeshine boy you work for the C.I.A. Minutes later, seven boys crowd around. *Pinochet!* they cry. *Allende! Bang bang!*

"For why always you are alone?" asks *la jefa*. It is late morning, the breakfast crowd has gone, leaving you to squint at the newspaper.

No sé, you tell her.

"Where you are sleep?" she asks, and you tell her the name of the hostel—a dingy, water-stained place *just steps from a charming outdoor market* that reeks of animal blood and exhaust. When you walk out to the street each morning, there are freshly butchered rib-racks hanging on hooks, hogs' heads impaled on sticks. The kid at the desk warns you to watch your wallet. Each night he asks, "You are look for girlfriend?" You pretend not to understand.

"You have take city tour?" *la jefa* says, hands folded on the table. The other waitresses huddle behind the curtain. Teresa sings along to the radio: *Amor mío, no puedo vivir sin tus besos . . . La jefa* calls out over her shoulder: *¡Basta!*

You tell her you have taken the city tour.

She brightens. "My city, you like?" Her nails are newly polished. A thin scar forks across the back of her right hand.

Sí, you say. *Pero . . .*

She raises her chin. You don't like these tours, you tell her, all the *gringos* packed into a van, shepherded through the attractions like schoolchildren at a museum. *No soy gringo*, you tell *la jefa*.

She puts a hand over your hand. *Claro que no.*

You want to know the city better. Its people. Nearly a month and you still feel like a foreigner, a scared kid standing at the edge of the surf. You gouge at the tabletop with a fingernail and say, *Quiero comprender.*

La jefa pushes back her chair. "Okay!" She moves across the room, throws open the shutters to let in cold morning sun. "Wednesday. I take you dance. *Chicas,*" she says, *¡Bailamos el miercoles!*

There is a small commotion behind the curtain. A waitress sticks her head out. *¿Por qué no el jueves?* A hand yanks her back and Teresa steps out and insists, plaintively, on Friday. *La jefa* stands over her ledger and pretends not to listen. There is much jostling and lamentation. She closes the book with a clap.

Bailamos el miercoles, she declares. *¡No sean niñas!* "Return to work."

The café quiets. *La jefa* inspects dishes on the countertop. You still can't say how old she is — maybe thirty, maybe forty. She is fairer than the other girls, much taller. Perhaps this means she's much older. Perhaps they are like trees.

There is pounding and clanging as a group of Israelis mount the spiral staircase. Waitresses flitter out, set menus before them. The Israeli men clown and shove each other, grab the waitresses around the waist; the women light cigarettes and ignore the men.

"At the *discoteca* I help you find beautiful *peruana,*" *la jefa* informs you. She leans out the window, looks both ways down the alley. Teresa refills your coffee, still singing: *Amor mío, no puedo vivir sin tus besos . . . La jefa* slaps the wall: *¡Callate!* Teresa scampers off laughing.

La jefa turns back to you. "Why you no have a wife?" she says.

At 42 days or less from last menstrual period (LMP), you start visiting *farmacias,* lingering by display cases, pretending to examine different sunblocks, the many varieties of cotton ball. The pharmacists study you over their mustaches until, one day, you casually inquire about *misoprostol. Misoprostol,* you've learned, is also used to treat *severe asthma.* "Hypothetically, if a woman were *embarazada,*" you hear yourself say, "but she had asthma . . ."

The pharmacist puts his hands flat on the counter. He confers with his assistant in a corner. You can't hear what they are saying, but it amounts to this: You are a *gringo.* They know what you do here. They have seen your kind lounging around the main plaza, lining up outside the *discotecas* at night. They have seen you in the fancy restaurants, drinking wine with the local girls. It is a small town. Your *amigas* at the café have taught you a saying: *Pueblo chico, infierno grande.* When *la jefa* is not there they fawn around your table. They pretend to swoon, hands pressed to foreheads. They stand in the door to the kitchen, backs to you, and caress themselves, then weep with laughter. The pharmacist doesn't know this. He has never seen you before. But he knows one thing: Whatever a *gringo* is doing in his *farmacia*, it has nothing to do with *asthma*.

La jefa does not date *gringos. Yo no soy brichera*, she says, shaking a finger at no one. The *discoteca* is a dark, second-floor room decorated with lurid masks: demons, witch doctors, ghouls. A bank of cigarette smoke hangs over the bar; the music—Britney, Nirvana, early MTV novelties—is loud enough to shake bottles on their shelves.

Mira, she says disapprovingly. You look. Every Peruvian girl in the bar is surrounded by *gringos*, who shoulder each other aside and offer her drinks bought *dos por uno*. There are no Peruvian men in the *discoteca*. There are no older women, or poor *campesinos*. The bouncer downstairs makes sure of this.

"What's a *brichera*?" you ask.

La jefa nods at the other waitresses. *Como ellas.*

Como tu madre, says Teresa, then nudges the unsmiling *jefa*. When Teresa goes to dance with Javier, *la jefa* explains: A *brichera* is a local girl who sleeps with *gringos* so she can eat at nice restaurants, drink *cuba libres*, and take trips to Lima, Machu Picchu.

"Sometimes, this *gringo* marry *la brichera*," she shrugs. The café has lost two waitresses this way. You've heard talk of them—their new lives in Berlin, the money they send back to their families. As she watches the waitresses dance, *la jefa* has the stern face of a displeased mother. She sips a *cuba libre*. Earlier, you danced with her to an old song called "Things Can Only Get Better." *La jefa* kept her arms at her sides, her eyes never stopped moving.

Es un sueño, she says now. "A dream. Usually is only sex. When this *gringo* return to *gringolandia*, she come here." She points her chin at the crowded dance floor, the hallway, *gringos* in T-shirts, fleece jackets around their waists, leaning over *peruanas* dressed to the nines.

"It sounds like a game," you say.

La jefa sucks her teeth. *Es una profesión.*

Try again: another *farmacia*, another hypothetical. *Misoprostol is used to prevent gastric ulcers*, you learn, *in persons taking anti-inflammatory drugs*. There was a work injury, you say. *Mucha inflamación*. Keep trying: your friend's grandfather, terrible arthritis. What is the word for arthritis? What is the word for migraine? A *farmacista* crooks his finger at you. He leans over the counter and whispers: *Weren't you in here the other day?*

It's been six weeks since *LMP*. You've extended your plane ticket, started paying the *hostal* by the week. Each day the other countries you'd planned to visit seem farther away—as does your own. *Schaff et al. [26] found in-home intravaginal self-administration to be safe and effective. Theoretically, the 400-ug regimen might have equal efficacy with fewer side effects.*

This is just a theory.

On another theory, you venture across town to a smuggler's market with the promising name *El Contrabando*. But all you find are new hiking boots, a dozen pirated CDs. You cram into the back of a *combi*, proud of yourself for taking the local bus: something a *gringo* would never do. City blocks drag by, storefronts crammed with plastic tubs and padlocks, dingy *cafeterias*, dogs with swollen teats lingering everywhere. In an unfamiliar neighborhood you spot a gleaming new *farmacia*, all glass and neon, a pyramid of shampoo in the window. You spend some time trying on cheap sunglasses, looking at yourself in the tiny mirror. You watch the *farmacistas*—young women in tight gray jackets and black neckties—handing strips of pills to bent old men. You choose the prettiest one and explain: You are new in town. Your *novia* is sick from the altitude. You explain, in deliberately broken Spanish, that they took her asthma medicine at customs. You are worried, you tell her, just the right vein of panic in your voice. She listens without blinking, compassion swelling under her coat.

Mira, she says quietly. She glances toward the back and touches your hand. She speaks very slowly. She says your *novia* should get a pregnancy test. Misoprostol can hurt the baby, she says. "You understand me?" she says, in English. She reaches under the counter and presses something into your hand: two condoms in unmarked wrappers. "There is bad girls here," she says. In Spanish she says to be careful. She closes your fist over the condoms and straightens her hair. *Buenas tardes*, she lies.

On the street corner, you watch a mob of schoolchildren cross before a church. Boys in black pants and white button-down shirts, girls in skirts and cardigans. They jostle, scream, drive pigeons into the air. *Schaff et al. [9] similarly reported a 97% success rate. The mean gestational age was 43 days' gestation.* Two months ago, you did not know these things. You could not have imagined knowing them. *These data have been previously discussed.* When they pass the church the boys cross themselves and kiss their fingertips. And it hits you: You have become a person who knows these things.

Walking back along the *avenida central*, you pass an unfamiliar building, pristine white stucco, a blue and gold plaque: *Consulate General of the United States.* You stand outside the entrance. *I have a small problem*, you practice silently. A guard in a black vest watches you. *I've gotten into a bit of trouble.* Could this possibly work? Before you pull the glass door open, something across the street catches your eye.

The pharmacy is no bigger than a coat closet, the shelves almost empty, one bare light bulb hanging by a cord. An old man sits watching a black-and-white television that reflects in his eyeglasses. His face is long, his hands thick and gnarled. He doesn't look up as you speak. When you finish, he reaches back and pulls a strip of foil from a carton. He puts the pills in your palm, closes his hand over yours, squeezes until it hurts.

Be careful of *la jefa*, Teresa tells you. You are sharing a cigarette on the balcony of the *discoteca*. It's the third time this week you've been here, maybe the fourth. When your *amigas* are too tired you come alone, lean against the bar, and wait for a *peruana* to smile at you. When you buy the girl a drink, she always says the same thing: *Yo no soy brichera.*

¿Por qué? you ask Teresa.

She won't elaborate. Across the room, *la jefa* is taking off her coat. You haven't seen her since yesterday afternoon, when she helped you with your Spanish exercises, beaming like a proud mother when you got it right. You still don't know her age—you've been thinking late-thirties, but now, as she squints into the gloom, she looks younger, more hopeful.

¿Vamos a bailar? says Teresa. She pulls you toward the dance floor but you stop, like a burro refusing to be led. Tell me, you say. ¿Por favor?

When you leave the discoteca that night, la jefa insists on walking you home. For your safety, she says. "You no understand," she says, waggling a finger. "This bad city. Ladrones do the choke—" she puts her hand to your throat, her other arm snaking around to touch your wallet. She presses you to the wall, close enough for you to smell her shampoo, smiles while she pretends to rob you.

You tell her not to worry. ¡No te preocupes! You flex your muscles, put up your dukes. Soy hombre, ¿no?

Eres tonto, she says, then touches your cheek. Pero lindo.

You walk in silence, flushed from the dance floor, the moonless sky stretched with cold. La jefa takes your arm. "What is wrong, cariño?"

Lights climb the hillsides outside the city—the barrios, the slums, where most of your amigas live. You ask what cariño means and la jefa says, "This means 'friend.'"

¿No 'amigo'?

Sí, she concedes. 'Amigo' tambien.

At your corner, you turn to her, the locked stalls of the charming market visible over her shoulder, one dim light above the door to your hostal. She regards you placidly as you hesitate. Teresa's warning repeats in your mind but it's hard to resist the current tugging you along. A taxi passes slowly, muttering down the avenida. The passenger window cranks down, the taxista leans across the front seat. The only word you can make out is brichera.

La jefa lurches toward you as though she'd been kicked in the back. Hijo de puta, she whispers. Then she screams it: ¡Hijo de puta! ¡Hijo de puta! chasing the taxi down the block. ¡A la mierda, maricón! The taxi's brakelights come on and you catch up to her, grab her arm, lead her at a half-run into the courtyard. Her face is dark, her breath rasping. A moment later the car drifts past the doorway and stops in a cloud of exhaust. The *taxista* starts to honk the horn—long, slow blasts into the night.

"Never in my life I am call *brichera*," she says. She shrugs off your clumsy embrace. Dogs are barking up and down the block. The office door opens; an unfamiliar face looks out, frowns, and closes the door. You stand in your T-shirt, panting in the sharp air. You decide to go speak to the *taxista*.

"Wait here," you tell *la jefa*.

No, amor, she says, and grabs your arm. *No seas estúpido*. For a moment you're off balance, disoriented. Then the taxi pulls off. Somewhere, a cat shrieks horribly, setting the dogs howling again.

You tell *la jefa* you'll take her home, but she insists this is not necessary. You've both begun to shiver. You know what you're going to say next; despite Teresa's warning you can already hear yourself saying it.

"Well," you say, "you can stay here."

She looks at your face for a long time. *No, amor*, she says, then leans up to kiss you lightly on the lips. *No soy brichera*.

When given the option of office administration or in-home self-administration, 98% of women (n=1053/1076) opt for in-home self-administration.
Need such a statistic be interpreted?

It has been 82 days since you arrived. Your money is running low. You've lost weight, your clothes are faded from the *lavandería*'s harsh detergent; at night they stink so badly of cigarette smoke you have to hang them outside your room. The bartenders at the *discoteca* know you by name. The shoeshine boys, the woman at the *bodega*—they all know you, when you pass by they greet you like someone who lives here. Not a *turista* or a *gringo*: something else.

It has been 47 days since LMP. On the table next to your bed sits a strip of foil-wrapped tablets. You have tried to discuss these four tiny items, to discuss the *efficacies, side effects, and complication rates of medical abortifacient regimens*. For example: *Rates of nausea, vomiting, fever or chills, and diarrhea were 43%, 26%, 32%, and 23%, respectively.*

Espérate, she tells you.

But you don't want to wait. You want to discuss your role in this, your determination to do the right thing, and your concern for her well-being. *Respectively.* You want to tell her that *95% of women in Vietnam would recommend this method of abortion to a friend.*

You do not want to discuss *vaginal administration.*

Espérate, she says. Three days ago she went to a public clinic, in a neighborhood far from her own. The *gynocólogo,* a young man from Lima, informed her that she was a stupid *chica,* then jabbed a needle in her backside. Maybe something will happen, he said, and maybe not. *¿Quien sabe?* Now get out of here, he said. But nothing has happened. Your *amiga* in the shiny new pharmacy shrugged when you told her about this injection. Maybe something will happen, she said, and maybe not.

¿Quien sabe? Who knows? Not *Schaff et al.* Not *Ngoc.* Certainly not you.

Espérate, amor, she says. But you can't wait forever. The problem must be discussed. You use the *imperativo:* Talk to me!

No es un problema, she says. *Es un bebé.*

Claro, you say quietly. Of course. You are a reasonable person. You are serious and responsible. But think of the consequences.

At this, she wrings her hands. *Sí,* she says. *No puedo,* she says. Twelve-hour days, six days a week to feed the two she's got. But still, she says through tears, wouldn't it be beautiful: our little *medio-gringo?*

You hold still, stare at the plane ticket on your nightstand. You are not the kind of man who runs away, you remind yourself. *No soy gringo,* you mutter.

Four days since the injection. Almost seven weeks since LMP. The injection isn't working, you tell her. "The rate of success is zero." You show her the foil strip again. You show her a sheaf of printouts, your notes scrawled in the margins. "With use of the standard abortifacient regimen, efficacy decreases with advancing gestation, *even at <49 days' gestation,*" you tell her. (Italics yours.)

¡Español! she says, then snatches the pills from your hand and throws them into the hallway.

A pair of *turistas* passes the open door, enormous backpacks looming over their heads. One of them picks up the foil strip and as you take it from him you wonder what country he's from. You notice the airline tags on his pack, from all the countries you'd planned to visit, and wonder where he's headed next.

You are not the kind of man who runs away, you remind yourself. But what kind are you?

The morning after the incident with the taxi, *la jefa* informs you, "I am take you to *una fiesta*. In the *Valle Sagrado*."

No sé, you say, anxious, a little hung over. But you've been meaning to visit the Sacred Valley, *the Incas' ancestral homeland [sic] and one of the empire's main points for the extraction of natural wealth.*

Cariño, she pleads, batting her eyes while the waitresses make kissing noises from the kitchen. *Por favor*.

The bus trip is a queasy blur, jouncing across the light-smashed plateau. An icy wind seeps through the windows. After three hours, the bus starts twisting down long switchbacks, pitching and grinding its gears, the river leaden and lethargic two thousand feet down. The driver passes a slow-moving dump truck, drifting toward the exposed shoulder until you can no longer see the road, only the drop.

In the valley, the air is balmy, oxygen so plentiful you feel lightheaded, almost drugged. Unpaved streets throng with people, the plaza awash in color and noise, a brass band in which no two instruments play the same song. *La jefa* stops at a street corner, beaming, clapping along to a rhythm you can't hear.

"Here I born and live until *colegio*," she shouts. She hooks her arm through yours. "Always I want bring you here." Church bells start to ring—you can see them in their towers: two knobs of iron swinging out of sync.

¿Por qué? you ask.

¿Por qué? She shakes your arm. "Why this question, *amor?*"

A surge of people carries you into the street, showering you with flower petals. Firecrackers seethe at your feet. You extract your arm, fumble for a cigarette. "Where are your children?" you ask.

La jefa stares. She's not sure she heard you correctly. And then she is.

¿Dos hijos? you'd asked Teresa, last night in the *discoteca*. *¿Dos?* Somehow the number had made it worse. If it had been *uno*, that would be another matter. But *dos?*

La jefa picks a petal off your shoulder. *En la casa de mi mamá*, she says.

¿Por qué?

A group of revelers stumbles into you, sloshing beer at your feet. *La jefa* stands her ground. *Porque allí viven*, she says. Because that's where they live.

You watch her another moment, dazed by sunlight, the smell of burning meat. From outside yourself, you see the scene you're making: the glower of disapproval on the *gringo*'s face, the proud defiance of the *peruana*. You've seen this before: Teresa and Javier, Flor and her German. It's perfectly normal, you think, just part of life for the people who live here, who aren't just passing through. People like you.

"Come, *mi amor*," *la jefa* says, dismissing the matter. *Vamos a bailar*, she says, as the crowd sweeps you away.

After the *fiesta*, she leads you up a long avenue cluttered with trash, down side streets where concrete and rebar give way to stone huts, courtyards where goats stand munching cardboard. She stops next to a battered door that hangs on rotted jambs: Turns out, *la jefa* has the key.

A tiny, dilapidated house sits at the back of a blighted field: dead grass, rusted tools, old laundry petrified and pinned to wires. This is where she slept as a child, *la jefa* says. The inside smells of wet wood and camphor, gray light slumping from a single window. A gutted stove sits to one side of the room, a sturdy bed in the other, topped with a bare mattress. *Bésame, amor*, she says.

Espérate, you say, but she pushes you onto the bed, kisses your face and neck. She pulls her dress over her head and wrestles with your belt.

Te quiero, she says. *Te quiero.*

Espérate, you gasp, groping in your pocket. *Cariña, espera.*

Te quiero, amor, she says, straddling you. You find the condom and try to unwrap it, but she pushes your hand away. "I no want."

¿Por qué? You try to hold back but she flattens herself against you, grinding her hips, riding you hard. *¡Espérate!*

¡No! She takes your chin in her hand, her eyes bright. *No soy brichera, ¿me entiendes? No soy así.*

Amor—you say, but your voice is too feeble. You know you should stop, but as you find yourself clutching her hips you understand that stopping was never the plan. *¿Por qué?* This is the question you will ask yourself one day. But now, over the creaking of the bed, the sound of her protests — *no soy así, no soy* — you hear another, familiar, voice: *Amor*, it says, in perfect Spanish. *Te quiero, amor.* Its accent is very convincing.

¿*Sí?* she gasps. ¿*Sí, mi amor?*

Medical abortion providers note that some women have complete expulsion of the pregnancy within 1 to 2 hours with relative comfort throughout the process. Others have more discomfort.

It's been 54 days since *LMP*. Your flight is in less than a week.

Amor, you say. But she won't talk about it. *Amor.* You hold up the strip of pills. You carry it with you everywhere now, like your passport: *just in case.*

She goes back to the clinic, tells the *gynocólogo* it didn't work. When she asks for another injection he grabs her arm and pulls her to the door. *Ask your gringo boyfriend to help you*, he says. *Maybe he remembers your name.*

It's been 55 days. *Déjame*, she says. "Leave me alone."

You won't leave her alone, you say. You are not that kind of man.

"Go back your country," she says. *Así son los gringos.*

You find yourself holding her wrist. The air in the room has become very still. *No soy gringo*, you say slowly, squeezing just a little.

Sí, she says quietly, peeling your fingers back one by one. "You are my *gringo* boyfriend."

In the middle of the night she flings back the blankets and disappears into the bathroom. You hear her crying through the door, but you don't get up. You don't want to upset her any further, you tell yourself. In the morning when you wake up she's already gone to work. You're on your second cigarette before you notice the foil strip — twisted and torn at one corner, two small pills gone.

She bleeds through your last few days. She sleeps in your bed without crying and without touching you. In the mornings she's pale, slow to wake; when she gets up she grips the back of a chair to steady herself. The blood is heavier than she's ever seen, she says. At work she's glassy-eyed, doubled over with cramps, the veins at her temples thick and blue. Teresa takes charge, shouting at the other girls, lugging tubs of dishes to the kitchen. None of the waitresses will look at you.

You stay at the café all day, drink coffee after coffee, and ask, maybe every fifteen minutes, how she is now. Now? What about *now*?

Amor, you say, standing at the counter. *¿No quieres un médico?*

La jefa squints at you. *Amor*, she sneers. "Who is *amor*?"

You ask what you can do, can you get her anything? "Let me help," you say, but she only sobs in frustration, then walks past you into the forbidden kitchen, where the radio plays loudly, blaring its *canciones* of love and despair.

On the morning of your flight, she wakes before you and dresses quickly. She sits at the edge of the bed as you shove the last items into your backpack. Standing in the door, you're struck by how small the room is, how dark and shabby. There's a strange smell. How did you live here for so long?

"Are you sure you're okay?" you ask in the taxi. "Is there anything you need?" you ask at the airport gate. "Tell me the truth."

¿Por qué?

Porque te quiero, you tell her, taking her hand. Passengers are boarding behind you, the door of the jetway exerts a kind of gravity, pulling you in. Lulled by fluorescent light, you stroke her hand and close your eyes: You've made it, both of you, swum safely out of the riptide and back to shore. Only one thing remains to be said, and you say it:

¿Quieres que me quede?

La jefa laughs, yanks her hand away. "You no want to stay," she says. She watches the passengers shuffling past—bags stuffed with local crafts, the careless voices of travelers on their way home. *No soy estúpida*, she says.

Later, you'll remind yourself: I offered, and she refused.

When the line dwindles, flight attendants waiting at the door, she turns to go.

Espérate, you say, suddenly reluctant to leave her. She's still so pale, a tremor at one eyelid. *Gracias, amor*, you say, before you can think better of it.

La jefa scowls. *¿Por qué?*

For the Sacred Valley, you tell her. For the Spanish lessons. For helping you understand. There's more, but you can't find the vocabulary.

She scans your face as if you were an odd little insect. "You no understand," she says. "You think you understand my country? *¿Mi pueblo?* I know my country," she says. "I am here. In my country. You are leave."

You reach for her hand, but she's already turning away.

Ciao, amigo, she says.

On the plane, the glare is too bright, the air from a broken nozzle too cold. The Andes drift by the window, dazzling and lunar. The glaciers make you shiver. Soon, you'll be home, you remind yourself. You'll sleep for days, have a real hamburger. Restless, you read the in-flight magazine, the safety card— *Place the oxygen mask over your face and secure the straps before assisting others*—but you can't get comfortable. The flight attendants and the captain say their parts but it's all lost on you, as though your Spanish had been left behind—detained at customs, maybe. You imagine your Spanish—locked in an interrogation room under hot lights, the angry face of the *comandante*—and laugh to yourself, then out loud. You can't stop laughing. Soon you're shaking in your seat, your teeth chattering.

In the bathroom, you wash your face as best you can, bending to the pitiful sink, hammering the flimsy levers. Your whole body itches; your clothes are too loose. You're still shivering. You squat against the bathroom wall, and something stabs your thigh, something sharp in your pocket: a torn strip of foil, two little silver mounds left. You turn it over in your hand, poke your fingertip with a corner. You pull it open, tentatively put a pill on your tongue. A bitter, metallic taste washes across your palate and slides to the back of your throat. Before you can think you've spit the pill into the toilet, where it sticks to the gray plastic. When you flush, it disappears in a whirlpool of blue—but then, somehow, it's still there. A knock comes at the door. You flush twice more but you can't dislodge the pill, tiny and accusatory, clinging to the plastic. You look for something to pry it loose, or crush it—finally you dig it free with a fingernail, flush once more to be sure. Then you head back to your seat to dream away the hours until the plane touches down in a distant country, where you'll walk for miles through bright corridors, lugging bags of unfamiliar objects, pale and shaky but alive to every detail, stand in a crowd of strangers and wait for admission: one line for citizens, another for foreigners.

It will be years before you tell the story. Friends coming back from Peru will tell you the café you recommended is no longer there, the *discoteca* is now a cell-phone store. They'd stopped by the *hostal* but it was too shabby for their tastes—and of course no one there remembered you.

But it enters your thoughts again, and you're surprised by its insistence, the memories suspended in a solution of nostalgia and dread. For days you try to piece it together, but it's all grown cloudy, events jumbled and conflated, time collapsed. You can't recall exactly what happened first, what led to what, or why. You're a writer now, a novelist. You decide to write it all down. It's what you do: shape images and emotions into stories that make sense. You will do this for the story of you and *la jefa*, you decide. You will set it down, after all this time, try to understand what it meant.

You will use the preterite tense.

You'll start with details: the way the streets gleamed at dawn, the cobblestones washed by shopowners; the stench of a public toilet built into the side of a church; the sound of a woman singing as she washes her hair under a pipe. You'll describe the freezing air, the pestilential shoeshine boys, the crush of bodies on the dance floor. You'll remember your first day, how the altitude hit you so hard you nearly passed out in a *pleasant café*. You'll remember the city tours, a party at someone's *hostal*, the beer you drank after hiking to Machu Picchu. The afternoon when Teresa and Javier broke up—"*¡Tu eres un gringo, verdad!*" she cried, to which he replied, "*¡Y tu eres una brichera!*" and the other waitresses ran to the window, hurling insults as he retreated down the alley.

The night you and *la jefa* came home from the Sacred Valley: how the glaciers seemed to be glowing, bathing the *altiplano* in ghostly pink light, how you held her hand in the back of the taxi, every stone and blade of grass illumined, and thought you might never leave. *Te quiero*, you whispered while she slept. *Te quiero, amor*—trying it out, seeing if it fit.

What was it you wanted? What were you looking for? So hard to remember. What strikes you now is how little you saw, how little you understood. The slums up in the hills — you never set foot in them. The families of your *amigas* — you never met them. You never met *la jefa*'s children, knew nothing about them, never asked. *¿Por qué?* Because they never existed for you, none of them did, they were characters in a story you were putting together, even then: a story about a tourist who thought he was different, about a *tonto* who wanted to be something else.

No soy gringo, you said a thousand times. There's a photograph of you in the *discoteca*, sweaty and drunk, surrounded by *la jefa* and three waitresses, the girl on either side kissing your cheek.

No, you were no *gringo*. You were something worse.

You couldn't find her now, even if you wanted to. And that's fitting, you understand. Why should you have the chance to apologize? What good would it do her, after so many years, to know you regret what happened, to know that it shames you?

She'd only forgive you, after all.

You'll work on the story for months, through scores of drafts. You'll confront the usual problems: where to start, what names to use, how to handle *dialogue*. Whether to tell it in the *first person* — like a confession — or the *third person*, as if it were about someone else. You'll abandon other projects, neglect your classes, focus on getting the story right. You'll put it all in there, everything you can remember, but eventually you'll set the story aside, unfinished, because you don't have the balls to write the ending.

Medical abortion is considered a failure when surgical evacuation must be performed for any reason, including incomplete abortion, continuing (viable) pregnancy, hemorrhage, or patient request.

On the phone, long distance, she sounds different — a small, tentative voice pushing through static. You try to picture her face, the scent of her perfume, the feel of her strong body, but it's already so far away.

¿Como estás? you ask, like an old friend, a *blast from the past*.

Bien, she says without emotion — or is it just a bad connection?

¿Y tú? Then she tells you: Walking to work the morning you left, she passed out in the street, her jeans heavy with blood. *Una hemorragia*, she calls it. A passing *taxista* took her to a hospital.

You ask her to repeat this, more slowly. Your Spanish is slipping after just four days. *The literature clearly demonstrates that in-home self-administration is safe and effective!* After surgery, she says, the doctors stood over her and asked *¿Por qué?* Why did this happen? What had she done to make this happen?

She told them she didn't know. *No sé*, she said. Had she been pregnant, they asked? Maybe, she said, and the doctors walked away without another word.

"I'm sorry," you tell her, from the safety of another continent.

Through the phone you can hear the sounds of the café, the music from the kitchen radio, the garbled conversations of *turistas*. It's a terrible connection, rife with static, the ghosts of other voices blurting through.

Amor, I sorry, you say, but she doesn't hear you.

That night in the hospital, she says, it was the worst night of her life. She lay in a room with five other women and stared at a crucifix on the wall. Five small, silent heads under white sheets, thin blankets. All night she lay awake, gritting her teeth against the pain, wondering if she might die, if she deserved to die.

"Never I think this happens to me," she says.

Amor. The connection is getting worse. *I sorry.*

¿Por qué?

You can barely hear your own voice through the noise. *I sorry I leave. I sorry I make for you this problem.* The list goes on and on. Static whispers and wails, subsides to a simmer, holding you both in its blank current.

"No," she says, before the tide goes out. "No, there is no problem. The problem is fix."

LUKE MOGELSON

■

The Dream Boat

FROM *The New York Times Magazine*

IT'S ABOUT A two-and-a-half-hour drive, normally, from Indonesia's capital city, Jakarta, to the southern coast of Java. In one of the many trucks that make the trip each month, loaded with asylum seekers from the Middle East and Central Asia, it takes a little longer. From the bed of the truck, the view is limited to a night sky punctuated by fleeting glimpses of high-rise buildings, overpasses, traffic signs, and tollbooths. It is difficult to make out, among the human cargo, much more than the vague shapes of bodies, the floating tips of cigarettes. When you pass beneath a street lamp, though, or an illuminated billboard, the faces thrown into relief are all alive with expectation. Eventually, the urban pulse subsides; the commotion of the freeway fades. The drooping wires give way to darkly looming palms. You begin to notice birds, and you can smell the sea.

In September, in one of these trucks, I sat across from a recently married couple in their 20s, from Tehran. The wife, who was seven months pregnant, wore a red blouse stretched over her stomach; the husband a tank top, thick-rimmed glasses, and a faux hawk that revealed a jagged scar (courtesy, he said, of the Iranian police). Two months had passed since they flew to Jakarta; this was their fourth attempt to leave. Twice, en route to the boat that would bring them to Australia, they were intercepted, detained, and paid bribes for their release. Another time, the boat foundered shortly after starting out. All the same, they were confident this trip would be different. Like everyone else's in the truck, theirs was a desperate kind of faith. "Tonight we will succeed," the husband assured me. They were determined that the child be born "there."

Our drive coincided with a violent tropical downpour that seemed to surge, under pressure, more than fall. Each asylum seeker had brought a small bag with spare clothes and provisions. Those who packed slickers dug them out. The storm was amusing at first, then just cold and miserable. The children, who earlier delighted in our clandestine exit from the city, now clung to their parents. An old man, sitting cross-legged beside me with a plastic garbage bag on his head, shivered uncontrollably, muttering prayers.

Around 3 in the morning, the truck braked and reversed down a rutted dirt road. The rain had stopped as abruptly as it started. No one spoke. We knew we had arrived. The rear hatch swung open, and we piled out. A second truck was parked behind us; people were emerging from it as well. We were in a dense jungle whose tangled canopy obstructed the moon. Several Indonesians corralled the crowd and whispered fiercely to keep moving. "Go! Go!" they urged in English. The road led down a steep hill and ended at a narrow footpath. As people stumbled in the dark, the Indonesians prodded them along. At the bottom of the footpath was a beach. It appeared as a pale hue through the trees, its white sand giving off a glow. The asylum seekers, 57 of them, huddled at the jungle's edge.

We were in the shelter of a wide bay, its arcing headlands, dotted with lights, repulsing the windward waves. Two open-hull skiffs with outboard motors idled offshore, bobbing gently in the swells. Behind us, the clamor of the truck grew distant and was gone. Suddenly, the Indonesians began pushing people toward the sea.

"You, you. Go!"

Two at a time, the asylum seekers raised their bags above their heads and waded out. The cool water rose to waists and armpits. It was a struggle to climb aboard. Whenever someone had to be hauled up, the skiff pitched steeply, threatening to tip.

We were ferried to a wooden fishing boat: a more substantial vessel than the skiffs, though not much. About 30 feet long, with open decks, a covered bow, a one-man cockpit, and a bamboo tiller, it was clearly not designed for passengers. Noting the absence of cabin, bridge, bulkheads, and benches, I wondered whether anyone else

shared my deluded hope: that there was another, larger ship an-
chored somewhere farther out, and that this sad boat was merely to
convey us there.

With frantic miming, the two-man Indonesian crew directed us to
crowd together on the deck and crouch beneath the bulwarks. They
stretched a tarp above our heads and nailed its edges to the gunwales.
Packed close in the ripe air beneath the tarp, hugging knees to chests,
we heard the engine start and felt the boat begin to dip and rise.

Our destination was an Australian territory, more than 200 miles across
the Indian Ocean, called Christmas Island. If the weather is amenable,
if the boat holds up, the trip typically lasts three days. Often, however,
the weather is tempestuous, and the boat sinks. Over the past decade,
it is believed that more than a thousand asylum seekers have drowned.
The unseaworthy vessels are swamped through leaky hulls, capsize
in heavy swells, splinter on the rocks. Survivors sometimes drift for
days. Children have watched their parents drown, and parents their
children. Entire families have been lost. Since June, several boats went
down, claiming the lives of more than a hundred people.

I first heard about the passage from Indonesia to Australia in Afghanistan, where I live and where one litmus test for the success of
the U.S.-led war now drawing to a close is the current exodus of civilians from the country. (The first "boat people" to seek asylum in Australia were Vietnamese, in the mid-1970s, driven to the ocean by the
fallout from that American withdrawal.) Last year, nearly 37,000 Afghans applied for asylum abroad, the most since 2001. Afghans who
can afford to will pay as much as $24,000 for European travel docu-
ments and up to $40,000 for Canadian. (Visas to the United States,
generally, cannot be bought.) Others employ smugglers for arduous
overland treks from Iran to Turkey to Greece, or from Russia to Belarus to Poland.

The Indonesia-Australia route first became popular in Afghanistan before September 11, mostly among Hazaras, a predominantly
Shiite ethnic minority that was systematically brutalized by the Taliban. After the Taliban were overthrown, many refugees, anticipat-
ing an enduring peace, returned to Afghanistan, and for a while the
number of Afghans willing to risk their lives at sea declined. But by

late 2009—with Afghans, disabused of their optimism, fleeing once more—migration to Australia escalated. At the same time, Hazaras living across the border in Pakistan, many of whom moved there from Afghanistan, have also found relocation necessary. In a sectarian crusade of murder and terror being waged against them by Sunni extremists, Hazara civilians in the Pakistani city of Quetta are shot in the streets, executed en masse, and indiscriminately massacred by rockets and bombs.

In 2010, a suicide attacker killed more than 70 people at a Shiite rally in Quetta. Looming directly above the carnage was a large billboard paid for by the Australian government. In Dari, next to an image of a distressed Indonesian fishing boat carrying Hazara asylum seekers, read the words: "All illegal routes to Australia are closed to Afghans." The billboard was part of a wide-ranging effort by Australia to discourage refugees from trying to get to Christmas Island. In Afghanistan, a recent Australian-funded TV ad featured a Hazara actor rubbing his eyes before a black background. "Please don't go," the man gloomily implores over melancholic music. "Many years of my life were wasted there [in detention] until my application for asylum was rejected." In addition to the messaging campaign (and the hardline policies it alludes to), Australia has worked to disrupt smuggling networks by collaborating with Pakistan's notorious intelligence services, embedding undercover agents in Indonesia and offering up to $180,000 for information resulting in a smuggler's arrest. The most drastic deterrence measure was introduced this July, when the Australian prime minister at the time, Kevin Rudd, announced that henceforth no refugee who reaches Australia by boat would be settled there. Instead, refugees would be detained, and eventually resettled, in impoverished Papua New Guinea. Several weeks later, the resettlement policy was extended to a tiny island state in Micronesia called the Republic of Nauru.

Since then, there have been more boats, more drownings. In late September, a vessel came apart shortly after leaving Indonesia, and dozens of asylum seekers—from Lebanon, Iran, and Iraq—drowned. That people are willing to hazard death at sea despite Australia's vow to send them to places like Papua New Guinea and the Republic of Nauru would seem illogical—or just plain crazy.

The Australian government ascribes their persistence partly to misinformation propagated by the smugglers. But every asylum seeker who believes those lies believes them because he chooses to. Their doing so, and continuing to brave the Indian Ocean, and continuing to die, only illustrates their desperation in a new, disturbing kind of light. This is the subtext to the plight of every refugee: Whatever hardship he endures, he endures because it beats the hardship he escaped. Every story of exile implies the sadder story of a homeland.

It's surprisingly simple, from Kabul, to enlist the services of the smugglers Australian authorities are so keen to apprehend. The problem was that every Afghan I spoke to who had been to Indonesia insisted that no Western journalist would ever be allowed onto a boat: Paranoia over agents was too high. Consequently, the photographer Joel van Houdt and I decided to pose as refugees. Because we are both white, we thought it prudent to devise a cover. We would say we were Georgian (other options in the region were rejected for fear of running into Russian speakers), had sensitive information about our government's activities during the 2008 war (hence, in the event of a search, our cameras and recorders), traveled to Kabul in search of a smuggler, and learned some Dari during our stay. An Afghan colleague of mine, Hakim (whose name has been changed to protect his identity), would pretend to be a local schemer angling for a foothold in the trade. It was all overly elaborate and highly implausible.

When we were ready, Hakim phoned an elderly Afghan man, living in Jakarta, who goes by the honorific Hajji Sahib. Hajji Sahib is a well-known smuggler in Indonesia; his cellphone number, among Afghans, is relatively easy to obtain. Hakim explained that he had two Georgians—"Levan" and "Mikheil"—whom he wished to send Hajji Sahib's way. Hajji Sahib, never questioning our story, agreed to get Joel and me from Jakarta to Christmas Island for $4,000 each. This represents a slightly discounted rate, for which Hakim, aspiring middleman, promised more business down the road.

A few days later, we visited Sarai Shahzada, Kabul's bustling currency market. Tucked behind an outdoor bazaar on the banks of a polluted river that bends through the Old City, the entrance to Sarai Shahzada is a narrow corridor mobbed with traders presiding over stacks of Pakistani rupees, Iranian rials, American dollars, and Afghan afghanis. The enclosed courtyard to which the corridor leads, the exterior stairwells ascending the surrounding buildings, the balconies that run the length of every floor—no piece of real estate is spared a hard-nosed dealer hawking bundled bricks of cash. The more illustrious operators occupy cramped offices and offer a variety of services in addition to exchange. Most of them are brokers of the money-transfer system, known as *hawala*, used throughout the Muslim world. Under the *hawala* system, if someone in Kabul wishes to send money to a relative in Pakistan, say, he will pay the amount, plus a small commission, to a broker in Sarai Shahzada, and in return receive a code. The recipient uses this code to collect the funds from a broker in Peshawar, who is then owed the transferred sum by the broker in Sarai Shahzada (a debt that can be settled with future transactions flowing in reverse).

In Afghanistan, where many people have family living abroad and lack bank accounts, the *hawala* system mostly facilitates legitimate remittances. It also, however, offers an appealing space for illicit dealings. In 2011, the U.S. Treasury Department blacklisted one of Sarai Shahzada's main businesses for laundering millions on behalf of Afghan narcotics traffickers. The Taliban, as well, are thought to get the bulk of their donations, from Persian Gulf and Pakistani patrons, via *hawala* transfers.

The refugee-smuggling business is conducted almost entirely through *hawala*. Hajji Sahib's man, Mohammad, keeps a third-story office overlooking the courtyard in Sarai Shahzada. When we got there, we found Mohammad sitting behind a desk papered with receipts pinned down against a squeaky fan by half-drunk glasses of tea. With long unkempt hair, bad posture, and acne, Mohammad looked as if he could still be in his teens. Other young men lined the walls, hunched in plastic chairs, working cellphones and calculators. When Hakim introduced himself as an intermediary for Hajji Sahib, they all glanced up from their computations, stiffening a little.

Mohammad immediately gave a spirited endorsement of Hajji Sahib's integrity, as well as of his own. He was eager to assure us that we were in capable hands. "We represent lots of smugglers," Mohammad boasted. "For Australia and also for Europe. Every month, dozens of people give us their money." He picked up a black ledger and waved it in the air. "Look at this notebook! I write every customer's details in here."

We gave him our fake names and origins. ("Gorjestan?" we were asked for the first but by no means the last time.) Then, a bit reluctantly, I counted out $8,000 in cash. In return, Mohammad handed me a scrap of paper with our *hawala* codes scribbled in pen. Levan: 105. Mikheil: 106. Mohammad would withhold the money from his counterpart in Jakarta until we reached Christmas Island. This, theoretically, would preclude Hajji Sahib from retrieving it prematurely. It would also ensure he would not get paid if our boat sank or if we drowned.

Most asylum seekers bound for Australia arrive in Jakarta by air. The day after we landed in the sprawling capital, I called Hajji Sahib and arranged to be picked up the next morning at a 7-Eleven on a busy intersection. Joel and I were sitting outside the 7-Eleven when an Indonesian man in a Hawaiian shirt appeared at the appointed time. He eyed us doubtfully, then handed me a cellphone.

"You will go in a taxi with this guy," Hajji Sahib told me. "He will bring you to a safe place."

We drove in silence, for about an hour, to the northern edge of the city, where gated communities vied for waterfront with ramshackle slums on the garbage-heaped banks of Jakarta Bay. We pulled into the parking lot of a massive tower-block apartment complex and took an elevator to the 23rd floor. Midway down a poorly lit hallway, our escort knocked on a metal security door. A young girl in a dress decorated with images of Barbie let us in. An Iranian man sat at a glass table, tapping ash from a cigarette into a water-bottle cap. A small boy lay on a bare mattress, watching cartoons. "Okay?" asked the Indonesian, and before anyone could answer, he was gone.

The man, Youssef, had been living in the apartment for a couple of weeks with his 8-year-old son, Anoush, and 6-year-old daughter, Shahla. (All the names of the asylum seekers in this story have been changed for their protection.) Youssef had been a laborer in Tehran, refurbishing building exteriors. In order to pay Hajji Sahib, he had sold all his possessions and gave up the house he was renting. He left his wife with her parents, planning to bring her to Australia legally once he and the children were settled there. "In Iran, there is no work, no life, no future for these children," Youssef told me, nodding at Anoush and Shahla. "I want them to go to school so that they can get a position."

We were sitting at the table, in one of the apartment's three rooms. A TV and refrigerator stood against the far wall, opposite a sink and counter, with a two-burner camping stove. Whereas Youssef, plainly, was less than thrilled to have new roommates (there were only two beds, one of them a narrow twin), Anoush and Shahla were competing to one-up each other with hospitality. After Shahla complimented Joel and me on our "beautiful beards," Anoush set about preparing us a lunch of chicken-flavored instant noodles.

Shahla said, "People become thieves there, in Iran."

"In Australia, I want to be a policeman," Anoush announced. "I want to arrest thieves, and say, 'Hands up!'"

Youssef seemed to disapprove. "They will study," he said.

On different floors throughout the tower block, other apartments housed about 30 more asylum seekers. Some were Hajji Sahib's; some belonged to rival smugglers. A majority, I was surprised to discover, were not Afghan but Iranian. Most were from cities and the lower middle class. They were builders, drivers, shopkeepers, barbers. One man claimed to be a mullah; another, an accomplished engineer. Their reasons for leaving varied. They all complained about the government and its chokehold on their freedoms. A few said they had been targeted for political persecution. They bemoaned the economy. International sanctions—imposed on Iran for refusing to abandon its nuclear program in 2006 and later tightened—had crippled their ability to support their families. They were fathers who despaired of their children's futures, or they wanted children but refused to have them in Iran. The most common word they used to describe their lives back home was *na-aomid*—hopeless.

Shortly after we settled into the apartment, an Iranian named Rashid stopped by for a visit. Rashid had the sickly, anemic look that I would soon come to associate with asylum seekers who languished in that place for two months or more—a combination of malnourishment and psychological fatigue. As he collapsed into a chair, elbows propped on knees, chin propped on palm, he seemed to lack even the most basic gravity-resisting vigor. After a month in Jakarta, Rashid told me, he got aboard a boat bound for Christmas Island. The engine promptly failed, leaving them adrift for days. In lieu of a bilge pump, Rashid and the other men had to use buckets to bail out the water splashing into the hull and seeping through its wooden planks. They ran out of food and water. People might have begun succumbing to dehydration if the tide hadn't carried them to a remote island. There they were arrested and obliged to pay the Indonesian police before they could be freed.

"We came back to this place," Rashid said. "The smuggler said, 'Don't worry, we will take you again soon.'"

I glanced at Joel. Over the phone, while we were in Kabul, Hajji Sahib urged us to get to Jakarta as soon as possible, saying the next boat was ready to depart.

"Our smuggler told us we were leaving tomorrow," I said.

Rashid laughed. "Yes, they say that."

The waiting was brutal: doing nothing became the most onerous of chores. The fact that your smuggler could call at any time, day or night, meant that you were forever suspended in a state of high alert. It also meant you couldn't venture far. Most of the asylum seekers, additionally fearful of police, never left the building. Generally, they spent their days sleeping as much as possible, smoking cigarettes, and rotating through one another's rooms—for a change of scenery, presumably, though they were all identical. Everyone was broke, and meals, in our apartment anyway, consisted of instant noodles, once or twice a day, on occasion served with bread. To sleep, Youssef, Anoush, and Shahla shared one of the two beds, while Joel and I alternated between the other and a thin mattress on the floor. Mattress nights were coveted, because it lay at the foot of the refrigerator, which you could open for a brief but glorious breath of cool air when you woke drenched in sweat, and because, compared with the bed, it was relatively free of fleas.

Although many of the asylum seekers in the building had children, only Youssef had brought his with him. (The others expected to be reunited with their families in Australia.) It's difficult to imagine how Anoush and Shahla processed the whole experience. My sense was that the thrill of the adventure eclipsed its hardships and hassles. With nothing and no one, except each other, to play with, they kept themselves remarkably well entertained. A feather duster found beneath the sink made for a superb tickling instrument; plastic grocery bags were turned into balloons; the hot-sauce packets, included in every ration of instant noodles, could be squirted on the tabletop to create interesting designs. There was also much to explore. The tower block was a kind of self-sufficient microcity, its four lofty wings flanking a private courtyard with shops and fish fries servicing outdoor tables clustered around a concrete bandstand. Every night, wizened Indonesian men belted out karaoke covers of John Denver and Johnny Cash. There was a Muslim mosque, a Christian church, a Buddhist temple. There were giant roaches and tailless cats to chase. And most delightfully, there was a pool.

As neither of the kids had swimming trunks or a spare pair of clothes, underwear had to suffice. Applying their talents for improvisation, Shahla found a used dish rag they could both share for a towel, while Anoush, with a kitchen knife, removed a length of flexible tubing from the back of our air conditioner (which was broken anyway), repurposing it as a snorkel. Their resourcefulness continued at the pool itself: each day, they seemed to come into possession of some new equipment—a pair of goggles, a bar of soap, an inflatable flotation ring.

While Youssef made the rounds of the rooms, Joel and I would end up watching them at the pool. We were both distressed to see that neither Anoush nor Shahla could really swim.

When I asked Anoush, who had never been on a boat before, whether he was nervous about the journey, he clucked his tongue. "I have no fear," he said. "I'll be smiling."

Their father was less carefree. Not long after we joined them, it became clear that Youssef had no money, and if Joel and I didn't buy food and water, they would simply go without. Whenever the fleas or heat would wake me in the night, I would find Youssef sitting by the window, staring out at the fires—bright islands of flame and eerily colored smoke—where the slum dwellers were burning trash. Everyone was stressed; the strain of two kids and no cash, however, rendered Youssef especially edgy. He was given to fits of anger and with the slightest provocation could fly into rages at Anoush, as well as at the other asylum seekers, many of whom avoided him.

Then one day Youssef's family wired money. I was sitting with him in the apartment, smoking, when he got the call. The news transformed him. Beaming with joy, Youssef leapt into the air and began to sing and dance.

That night Joel and I found him in the courtyard drinking with Rashid. Anoush and Shahla ran from shop to shop, swinging bags of candy. When he saw us, Youssef insisted we sit down, then shouted loudly, at no one in particular, for more beer. A group of elderly Indonesian men, playing dominoes nearby, regarded him impatiently. Youssef didn't notice. He was slumped over the table, doodling on its surface with a permanent marker.

Rashid seemed embarrassed for his friend. "His head is messed up," he explained. "Waiting here, with his kids, not knowing when we'll go. It's hard."

Youssef nodded glumly.

"My head is messed up, too," Rashid said. "I'm going crazy. I have two sons in Iran. I haven't seen them or my wife in a year."

Rashid said that before Australia, he tried to get to Europe via Greece. He made it from Turkey to Athens, where he was fleeced by a smuggler. Rather than return to Iran, he came to Indonesia. "Every day, they tell us, 'Tomorrow, tomorrow,'" Rashid said. "But tomorrow never arrives."

Anoush and Shahla appeared and asked Youssef for money. They wanted chips. Youssef pulled out a wad of bills and threw some in their direction. Several fluttered to the ground.

"Beer!" Youssef yelled at a woman passing by. Then he looked guiltily at Rashid, and added: "Please! Thank you!"

Australia's decision to send all boat people to Papua New Guinea or the Republic of Nauru only compounded everyone's anxiety. Although no one allowed himself to take it seriously (if he did, he would have no option but to do the unthinkable—give up, go home), the news was never decisively explained away. "It's a lie to scare people so that they don't come," Youssef told me when I brought it up. Another man became agitated when I asked him what he thought. "How can they turn you away?" he demanded. "You put yourself in danger, you take your life in your hand? They can't." A third asylum seeker dismissed the policy with a shrug. "It's a political game," he told me.

In many ways, he was right. It's hard to overstate how contentious an issue boat people are in Australian politics. From an American perspective, zealousness on the subject of immigration is nothing unfamiliar. But what makes Australia unique is the disconnect between how prominently boat people feature in the national dialogue, on the one hand, and the actual scale of the problem, on the other. Over the past four years, most European countries have absorbed more asylum seekers, per capita, than Australia — some of them, like Sweden and Liechtenstein, seven times as many. All the same, for more than a decade now, successive Australian governments have fixated on boat people, making them a centerpiece of their agendas.

In the summer of 2001, a Norwegian freighter, the MV *Tampa*, rescued 433 asylum seekers, almost all of them Afghan, from a stranded fishing boat. Rather than return them to Indonesia, the captain of the *Tampa*, Arne Rinnan, consented to their demands to be taken to Christmas Island. Australia forbade the ship to enter its territory, and the standoff that ensued led to Australia's threatening to prosecute Rinnan and Norway's complaining to the United Nations. John Howard, a conservative prime minister, who, in the midst of a re-election campaign, was trailing his opponent in most of the polls, declared, "It remains our very strong determination not to allow this vessel or its occupants to land in Australia." When Rinnan, concerned over the welfare of the asylum seekers on his ship, proceeded toward the island anyway, Howard dispatched Australian commandos to board the *Tampa* and stop it from continuing. The impasse was resolved only when New Zealand and Nauru agreed to accept the asylum seekers instead. Howard's action was widely popular with voters, and two months later he was re-elected.

Diverting boat people to third countries for processing — albeit with the possibility of someday being resettled in Australia — was subsequently adopted as an official strategy. Under an arrangement popularly known as the Pacific Solution, asylum seekers trying to get to Christmas Island were interdicted by the navy and taken to detention centers on Nauru and Papua New Guinea (both of which rely heavily on Australian aid). The Pacific Solution was denounced by refugee and human rights advocates, who criticized the harsh conditions of the centers and the prolonged periods of time—many years, in some cases—that asylum seekers had to spend in them while their applications were considered. Depression and other mental disorders proliferated; incidents of self-harm were common. In 2003, detainees on Nauru protested with a weekslong hunger strike, during which some of them sewed their lips together. Last September, Arne Rinnan, the captain of the *Tampa,* told an interviewer that he had recently received a letter from Nauru, written by one of the Afghans he had rescued. According to Rinnan, the man said that "I should have let him die in the Indian Ocean, instead of picking him up."

After the Labor Party regained control of Parliament in 2007, and the new prime minister, Kevin Rudd, abolished the Pacific Solution—his immigration minister condemning it as "neither humane nor fair"—the U.N. and just about every other organization involved with refugees lauded the move. Rudd lost his leadership of the Labor Party in 2010, and his successor, Julia Gillard, resurrected the offshore-processing strategy. When Rudd returned to power in 2013, apparently having learned his lesson, he kept Gillard's policies in place. It was in the context of another re-election bid in July that Rudd eliminated the possibility of any boat person ever settling in Australia. "I understand that this is a very hard-line decision," he acknowledged in a national address. He seemed anxious to make sure that voters understood it too.

Rudd's conservative opponent, Tony Abbott, would not be outdone. One of the two rallying cries that had come to define Abbott's campaign was "Stop the boats!" (The other, referring to carbon-emissions penalties, was "Axe the tax!") Proclaiming the influx of boat people a "national emergency," Abbott proposed an even tougher scheme than Rudd's, dubbed "Operation Sovereign Borders." Among other proactive measures, this militaristic plan called for deploying warships to turn asylum seekers back at sea, before they reached Australian shores.

The elections were scheduled to be held less than a week after the

night I found Youssef and Rashid drinking in the courtyard. Which-
ever candidate prevailed, one thing was certain: neither Youssef nor
Rashid, nor Anoush nor Shahla, were going to get to the place they
believed they were going. Rashid would never be reunited with his
wife and sons in some quaint Australian suburb; Youssef would never
see his children "get a position" there; Anoush would never become
an Australian policeman; Shahla would never benefit from a secular,
Western education. What they had to look forward to instead—after
the perilous voyage, and after months, maybe years, locked up in an
isolated detention center—was resettlement on the barren carcass
of a defunct strip mine, more than 70 percent of which is uninhabit-
able (Nauru), or resettlement on a destitute and crime-ridden island
nation known for its high rates of murder and sexual violence (Papua
New Guinea).

How do you tell that to someone who has severed himself utterly
from his country, in order to reach another? It was impossible. They
wouldn't believe it.

Joel and I were walking along the bay, where dozens of residents
from the slums had gathered to watch backhoes on floating barges
scoop refuse out of the shallows and deposit it onto the banks, when
Youssef called my cellphone and shouted at us to get back to the
tower—we were leaving. In the apartment, we found two young Iranian women, Farah and Rima, sitting at the table with large backpacks, while Youssef hurriedly shoved dates and lemons—thought
to alleviate seasickness—into a canvas messenger bag. I noticed, too,
that he was bringing the inflatable flotation ring Anoush and Shahla
had found at the pool.

An Iranian man named Ayoub appeared and told us our car
was waiting. By the deferential way Youssef and the women treated
him—and by his assertive self-possession, in contrast to our rather
panicky excitement—I gathered that Ayoub was a smuggler. He
wore a military haircut and a handlebar mustache, and his sleeveless
shirt displayed the words "Life is hard" tattooed in English across an
impressively sculptured left deltoid.

We all crammed into a new car with tinted windows, driven by a
squat Indonesian man with long rapier-like pinkie nails that tapered

into points, who belched every couple of minutes and chain-smoked flavored cigarettes. Anoush and Shahla were elated. As we pulled onto the highway, they could not stop talking about the boat and the sea. The women adored them instantly. Farah hauled Anoush onto her lap, while Rima set to braiding Shahla's wild hair. The kids received this affection like sustenance, with a kind of delirious gratitude and appetite. It made me remember that since arriving in Jakarta, they had not only been without their mother but without any mother.

We stopped at three gas stations along the way and linked up with other drivers. By the time we made it out of the city, several hours later, we led a convoy of six identical cars, all packed with asylum seekers. It seemed a bit conspicuous, and sure enough, as we climbed a narrow, winding road up a densely forested mountain, people came out to watch whenever we passed a shop or village. It was maybe 8 or 9 at night when our driver got a call that caused him to accelerate abruptly and career down a side road that led into the woods. The other cars followed. Pulling to a stop, shutting off the lights and engine, our driver spun around and hissed: "Shh! Police."

He got out to confer with his colleagues, and when he returned, it was in a hurry. Recklessly whipping around blind turns, we retreated down the mountain in the direction from which we came. Emerging from one sharp bend, we encountered a dark SUV blocking the way. A siren whined; blue lights flashed. We slammed to a halt. A police officer in civilian clothes and a black baseball cap approached the driver's side. He peered in through the open window, registering the women and children. Then, after a moment's hesitation, he reeled back and smacked our driver hard and square in the face.

With the SUV behind us, we returned to the turnoff for the side road. The other five cars were there, surrounded by several police vehicles and a four-wheel-drive truck. A crowd had gathered. It was hard to tell what was happening. Some of the officers were taking pictures of the license plates and asylum seekers, others appeared to be joking affably with the drivers. Everyone was making calls on cellphones. At one point, our driver stuck his head in the window and rubbed his thumb and fingers together. "Money, money," he said. But the next instant he disappeared again.

Eventually, with a police car ahead of us and the truck bringing up the rear, we continued along the road. It was useless to try to get an explanation from our driver, who, in a torpor of self-pity, only muttered to himself and stroked a red mark on his cheek. When Rima got hold of Ayoub, he said not to worry, Hajji Sahib was taking care of it.

We were taken to a police station, in the city of Sukabumi. There, an older, bespectacled man in army fatigues and a beret seemed to be in charge. Once more, all the drivers were pulled out of their cars, pictures were taken, phone calls were made. After about an hour, with the same escort in front and behind, our convoy was on the move again. It's hard to say for how long we drove or where we finally stopped: all I could make out were a couple of shuttered storefronts on an otherwise empty road. Curiously, when I looked out the rear window, every police vehicle save one was turning around and heading back toward Sukabumi.

The sole remaining officer, a young man in a tan uniform, leaned against a chain-link fence, smoking a cigarette, apparently uninterested in us. Soon the asylum seekers began getting out of their cars. After the officer watched with indifference as a group of Afghan teenagers briskly walked away, everyone started flagging down trucks and hopping into communal passenger vans. When a large commuter bus happened by, the officer signaled for it to stop. Those of us who hadn't yet absconded piled on.

I found myself sitting toward the front of the bus with an Iraqi family from Baghdad—a young woman in a hijab, her husband, father-in-law, and three children.

"Where are we going?" the Iraqi woman said in English.

"I don't know," I said.

Someone asked the driver.

"Bogor," he said.

"Where's Bogor?" the Iraqi woman said.

"I don't know," I said.

It turned out to be the end of the line. When the bus stopped, about 30 asylum seekers from Iran, Iraq, and Afghanistan got out. No one quite knew what to do. It was nearly dawn, and everything in Bogor was closed. We all walked to the highway—a motley, exhausted crew, carrying backpacks and plastic bags with food and clothes—and started hailing taxis. Youssef, the children, Rima, Farah, Joel, and I managed to persuade a commuter with a minivan to take us back to the tower block for $20. The sun was coming up by the time we got there. The apartment was still filthy. It still stunk. It was still hot. Youssef lit a pot of water for the noodles.

A few days later, Joel and I were on our way to one of the shops downstairs when a young Middle Eastern man we had never seen before approached us. "Come with me," he said.

We followed him to the courtyard, where we found Ayoub sitting at one of the tables, absorbed in a hearty lunch.

"Get your bags and the apartment key," Ayoub told me, dropping a chicken bone onto his plate and loudly sucking the grease off his fingers, one at a time, from thumb to pinkie.

When we got up to the apartment and I told Youssef the news, he only nodded. The reaction was not what I expected. "Ayoub is here," I repeated. "We're leaving."

"Did he say us too?" Youssef asked. "Or just you?"

I didn't understand. "We're all going together, of course."

Youssef seemed unconvinced and made no move to pack. A few minutes later, Hajji Sahib called me. I stepped into the hall.

"Are you with the Iranian family?" he said.

"Yes. We're almost ready."

"Ayoub is already gone," Hajji Sahib said. "You have to take a taxi to another place. And you have to leave the Iranians there. They can't come. There is a problem with their money."

Back in the apartment, I found Youssef at the stove. He had put Shahla in the shower. Anoush was watching cartoons.

"What's going on?" I said.

Youssef shook his head. When I told him Joel and I had to go alone, without them, there was no objection or rebuke; however miserable, Youssef was reconciled to what was happening, and I realized he must have seen it coming. He lit a cigarette and lay down on the mattress. Shahla was still in the shower. Anoush, I could tell, hadn't missed a thing. His eyes, though, stayed fastened on the TV.

We took a taxi to a much nicer building on the opposite side of Jakarta. A tall, skinny Iranian in his early 20s met us in the lobby and took us to the top floor. In the apartment, we found Farah and Rima sitting with three Iranian men around a coffee table with a row of cellphones on it. The women greeted us warmly and introduced one of the men, Siya, as the "boss." Muscular and shirtless, with intricate tattoos of feathered wings spread across his chest, Siya was busy fashioning a sheath for a long wood-handled knife out of folded magazine pages and rubber bands.

Noticing me notice the knife, Farah said, "For security."

Siya told us to put our cellphones on the table and informed us that we would no longer be allowed to use them.

"Who told you to come here?" he asked.

"Hajji Sahib," I said.

"Who introduced you to Hajji Sahib?"

"Hakim. From Kabul."

"Hakim from Kabul?" Siya nodded knowingly. "Okay, good."

After a while, a middle-aged man and his son joined us. Siya embraced each of them for a minute or more. The father, Amir, was a shop owner from the Iranian side of the border with Iraq. He and Sami, a pudgy 9-year-old with glasses, were two of the friendliest people I met in Jakarta. Although he was older than Siya, Amir's meek nature relegated him definitely subordinate: a somewhat awkward dynamic that Amir, loath to make anyone uncomfortable, deflated by clicking his heels and saluting the boss (who, in turn, ordered him to execute a series of squats and lunges, counting out the sets in a mock drill-sergeant voice). Later, when Siya asked to inspect his weapon, Amir reached into his pocket and produced a flimsy steak knife.

It was around midnight when Siya got the call. He gave us back our phones, and we took the elevator to an underground parking garage, where another caravan of new cars with tinted windows was waiting. Every vehicle was already packed beyond capacity. We were all greatly relieved when, a few miles down the highway, our driver pulled into an alley, stopped behind the truck, and told us to get out.

After the hard rain on the way to the beach, and wading out chest-deep to the skiffs, everyone was drenched. It was still dark out when the two Indonesian crew members pulled back the tarp they had nailed over our heads. The coast was a vague shadow growing vaguer.

The Indonesians distributed life vests: ridiculous things, made from thin fabric and a bit of foam. The youngest children, including a girl in a pink poncho who appeared no older than 4 or 5, were directed with their parents to a small square of open deck in the stern. The reason for this was that the farther aft you went, the less violent was the bucking as we plowed into the swells.

As the sun broke, we got our first good look at one another. Rashid had made it, as well as several other men from the tower block. There were nine children and more than a dozen women. Aside from one Afghan man, from Kunduz Province, everyone was Iranian. Most of the elderly crowded into the covered bow or leaned against the bulwarks. The rest fit where they could on the open deck. The sea was choppy enough so that each time the boat crashed from a peak into a trough or hit a wave head-on, large amounts of water splashed against us.

The first person to become sick was Siya. It was still early morning when he started throwing up. He was a natural leader, that man, and almost everyone soon followed suit. By late afternoon, we'd lost sight of land completely, and the swells grew to a size that blocked out the horizon when they loomed above us. Some people bent over the gunwales, some vomited into plastic bags. It quickly became apparent that there were not enough bags to go around: rather than toss them overboard, full ones had to be emptied, rinsed, and reused.

Siya would not be cowed. Peeling off his soaking tank top, revealing his tattooed wings—seeming to unfold them, actually, as he threw back his shoulders—he began to sing. Others joined in, breaking now and then to retch.

It was slow going. The Indonesians took turns manning the tiller and hand-pumping water from the bilge. One was older and taciturn and wore a permanent scowl; the other looked to be in his teens, smiled enough for the both of them, and called everybody "brother." The tremendous racket of the engine belied its less-than-tremendous horsepower. Like the rest of the vessel, it was built for neither such a heavy load nor such high seas. Our typical speed was four to five knots, less than six miles per hour, and at times we seemed to make no headway whatsoever against the strong southeasterly trade winds, which whipped up white caps on the waves and kept us all alert with stinging gusts of spray. Depending on the direction of the swells, the Indonesians would signal the men to consolidate themselves on the starboard or port side of the deck and thereby mitigate our list-ing—which, now and then, felt alarming.

The sea was still big when the sun went down, taking with it the warmth. Those of us who had spent the day on our feet now began staking claims on places to try to sleep. The deck became a claus-trophobic scrum of tangled limbs. Few could recline or stretch their legs. Each time someone tried to reposition a foot or knee, say, to re-store some circulation, the movement would ripple out in a cascade of shifting and grumbling as the surrounding bodies adjusted to the new configuration.

The tarp was unfurled. There was not enough of it to cover every-one. If you found yourself on an edge or corner, someone from the opposite side would invariably pull it away the moment you relaxed your grip. In any case, it was too worn and porous to do much. The water ran down its folds and creases, streaming through the many tears along the way.

In the morning, everyone looked different. Sallow. Haggard. Reduced. Amir and Sami slouched limply against each other, passing between them a bulging plastic bag. The man with the faux-hawk was curled up in a fetal ball: he stayed that way the rest of the trip. His preg-nant wife sat cross-legged near the bow, pale and wet and trembling. Rima was clutching Siya's arm, as if it were a lifeline. Their eyes were squeezed tightly shut, but they were too ill to sleep.

Another problem arose. There was no toilet, and absent any rail-ing to hold on to, going over the side was too risky. The men urinated on the hull, the women in their pants.

The Indonesians had brought a box of sealed plastic cups of wa-ter, but hardly anyone could hold them down. Siya continued to sing and puke. Although a couple of the children had begun to cry, none complained. In the afternoon, two dolphins appeared and spent the better part of an hour playfully showing off. As they darted under the boat, and launched into the air, the spectacle cheered up everyone, adults and kids alike. Even Amir and Sami rallied from their stupor to watch. A few grown men became positively gleeful, vying to be the first to spot the gray shadows flitting from the deep.

That night, several of us tried to sleep atop the engine room, trading the shelter of the hull for a little extra space. It was a poor call. Every 10 minutes or so, a bucket's worth of cold water took your breath away or you were pitched against a hot pair of vertical pipes spewing noxious smoke and sparks. There was nothing to do but lie there, bracing for one or the other, admiring the magnificent array of stars and the phosphorescence glowing in the wake.

With first light, despite the sleep deprivation, dehydration, seasickness, and filth, the asylum seekers were energized by the fact that, according to the Indonesians, we would likely reach Australian territory before nightfall. Although there was still no land in sight, the arrival of birds circling overhead was unanimously interpreted as a sign that we were getting close. The sea had also calmed: no more waves crashed upon the deck. Initially, this was an enormous relief. For the first time, the sun dried us out. As it crept higher, however, it proved to be far more powerful than during the past two days, and soon, without a single cloud in the sky to blunt the blistering rays, everyone was longing for the same frigid breakers we previously cursed.

The tarp was brought back out. While blocking the sun's glare, it also trapped its heat. A couple of people, desperate for fresh air, cut up the box of water cups, which was almost empty, and made visors from the cardboard. One of the fathers in the stern, wearing a Qatar Airways sleeping mask to protect his face, found a length of string and rigged up some sheets and scarves for shade. The bow—the only covered part of the boat—reeked dizzyingly of vomit and urine. None of the dozen Iranians who rushed to fill the space when we embarked had since dared to leave it. Now they were suffering. An argument arose between them and their comrades on the open deck. The tarp was obstructing the entrance to the bow, it seemed, and smothering its already rank and humid air.

"Please," one woman begged. "We can't breathe in here."

There was little desire among the deck dwellers, however, to endure direct exposure to the sun for the comfort of those who had thus far enjoyed comparatively plush accommodations.

Presently, the heat finished off anyone who might have been bearing up. The pregnant woman's condition bordered on critical. She was flushed and drenched in sweat and heaved dryly, with nothing left to give. Sami was weeping. Amir lay supine. His eyes drooped catatonically, and when I tried to make him drink some water, he weakly gripped my ankle.

"I need help," he said. "Call for help."

That decision seemed to be up to Siya. There was a satellite phone onboard: Siya said the plan was to contact the Australian authorities once we were well within their waters. The navy would then bring us ashore. In the past, asylum boats often made it all the way—but the landing can be treacherous (when one boat smashed on the cliffs in 2010, 50 people drowned), and now it's standard practice to request a "rescue" before reaching Christmas Island. Although Australian rescuers, when responding to distress calls, venture much farther north than where we currently were, Siya wanted to be sure. I think it was Amir's pitiful entreaties that finally persuaded him to make the call.

An Iranian man who knew some English—the one who in Jakarta told me he was an engineer—spoke to the dispatch. The Indonesians had brought a hand-held GPS device; neither they nor the asylum seekers, however, knew how to work it. Eventually, someone offered his iPhone, and the engineer read out our coordinates.

While we waited to be rescued, the Iranians set about destroying their passports. "So they can't deport you," Farah told me. Clearly, though, the task also carried some symbolic weight. Rather than simply jettisoning them, the asylum seekers painstakingly ripped out each individual page, crumpled it into a ball, and tossed it to the wind. A pair of scissors was passed around. The burgundy covers, emblazoned with the Iranian coat of arms, were cut into tiny pieces. The work was accomplished with flair and relish. Only one man seemed hesitant. Moving closer, I saw that the passport he was disposing of was his son's. When the scissors came his way, he carefully cut out the photo on the first page and slipped it in his wallet.

Soon, on the horizon, a ship appeared. A government airplane buzzed above us, swooped low, and made a second pass. The asylum seekers waved shirts in the air, crying out in jubilation. The younger Indonesian performed a dance atop the engine room; he seemed amazed we had made it. Some of the men emptied their pockets, thrusting on him all the cash they had. The Indonesian beamed. "Thank you, brothers!"

Two skiffs broke off from the battleship and motored our way. Each carried six Australians in gray fatigues, riot helmets, and side-arms holstered on their thighs. The Indonesians cut the engine (and after three days of its unrelenting clamor, the silence that replaced it was startling). The skiffs maneuvered abreast of us, one on each side.

The Australian sailors all looked like fresh recruits. One of them held a manual of some kind. He read from it in a loud voice. "Are there any English speakers?"

The engineer stepped forward.

"Does anyone onboard require medical assistance?"

When the engineer translated this, nearly everyone raised his hand. The pregnant woman was helped to her feet and presented. Her head hung heavily. She was almost too weak to stand.

While the Australian with the manual recited more questions—including some in Indonesian addressed to the crew, who shook their heads dumbly, refusing to answer—his fellow sailors passed to the asylum seekers new life vests, a couple jerrycans of fresh water, some bags of frozen tortillas, bottles of honey, and a tub of strawberry jam. "We're going back to the ship now," one of them told the engineer. "You have to turn the engine back on and keep going. We'll be behind you."

This information was met with disbelief. Once again the pregnant woman was raised up and displayed. "Can you take her with you at least?" asked the engineer. The sailors exchanged embarrassed looks. Plainly, they wished they could.

We still couldn't see land—and not long after the skiffs left us for the battleship, it, too, was lost from view. The return of the empty and limitless ocean, not to mention the incessantly pounding sun, was incredibly demoralizing. To make matters worse, we no longer had any means of communication. When they first glimpsed the plane and ship, all the asylum seekers, following Siya's example, threw their cellphones overboard. For some reason, amid the exultation, the satellite phone and GPS system had also gone into the water.

There was nothing to do but heed the Australian's command and "keep going." It was four or five hours after we made contact with the first ship when a second, smaller patrol boat materialized. Two more skiffs of sailors came out to meet us. This time they immediately boarded the boat, moving people aside, herding everyone forward. The officer in charge announced that he was taking control of the vessel.

After the officer spotted Joel's camera, we were both summoned to the stern, at which point we identified ourselves as journalists. While a big Australian with a bushy beard worked the tiller, the officer went through a list of prewritten questions with the crew, each of whom either couldn't read or declined to. (Unless it's their second offense, or someone dies, the Indonesian fishermen who bring asylum boats across are often not prosecuted.) The officer was polite to Joel and me. He said we had been lucky with the weather. If we had left a few days earlier, the boat would have capsized.

It inspires a unique kind of joy, that first glimpse of land. The sun was low, and you could almost mistake it for some play of light and shadow. As rousing as it was to see, the presence of a fixed object against which to mark our progress also made you realize just how slowly we had been going. It was late at night by the time we reached Christmas Island. The Australians guided our boat into the shelter of a shallow cove, beneath sheer cliffs draped in vegetation. After tying up on a mooring, the officer revealed that we would stay the night here and disembark tomorrow. When the engineer relayed the complaints of the asylum seekers—who, consolidated in the bow, had even less space now than before—the officer responded: "Are you safe? Are your lives in danger anymore?" He seemed to be losing patience, and, noticing a wrapper floating by the stern, angrily reproached the Iranians: "You're in a nice country now."

It rained fitfully throughout the night. The next day, we were all ferried by a push-barge from the mooring to a jetty around the point. The jetty swarmed with customs and immigration officials, federal police and employees of a private company that runs the island's detention centers. Joel and I were welcomed to Australia, given water, coffee, and a ride to a surprisingly luxurious hotel. Everyone else was interned. Later that afternoon, while walking into town, I saw our little boat being towed out to sea. There, the officer had told me, it would be lit on fire.

The families and minors were taken to a relatively comfortable facility, with access to an outdoor soccer field and recreational area. The single men went to a place resembling a maximum-security prison. None of the asylum seekers would stay at either location for long. While I was on the island, flights full of detainees were leaving almost every night for Papua New Guinea and the Republic of Nauru. By now, most if not all of the people from our boat have been transferred to one of the two island nations. If they were sent to the detention center on Papua New Guinea, they are probably living in the tent city that was erected there as part of its expansion. If they were sent to the detention center on Nauru, they are probably living in the tent city that was erected there after rioting asylum seekers in July burned the buildings down.

Because the governments of Nauru and Papua New Guinea lack the capability to process refugee claims—Australian officials are still training them to do so—the asylum seekers have a long wait ahead of them. Some might not be able to hold out: already, dozens of Iranians, after seeing the conditions at the Papua New Guinea facility, have asked to be sent back to their country. Among those who decide to tough it out, it's most likely that few will be found to have valid cases. Moreover, unlike with Afghanistan and Sri Lanka, no agreement exists between Iran and Australia allowing for the forcible repatriation of asylum seekers whose applications are unsuccessful. This means that the Iranians who are denied asylum by Nauru or Papua New Guinea, and who decline to voluntarily return to Iran, will enter a kind of limbo, in which they can neither be resettled on those islands nor sent to the Australian mainland nor sent home. Absent another solution, these people could be flown back to Christmas Island and detained indefinitely.

We reached Australia one day after Tony Abbott was elected prime minister. In keeping with his Operation Sovereign Borders policy, Abbott has since directed the navy to send back to Indonesia, whenever possible, asylum boats intercepted at sea. So far this has happened twice, in late September, when two boatloads of asylum seekers were turned over, offshore, to Indonesian authorities. The second transfer took place the same day that a boat full of Lebanese asylum seekers broke apart less than a hundred yards off the Java coast near Sukabumi, the Indonesian city whose police station Joel and I briefly visited. More than 20 bodies, many of them children, washed ashore, and more remained missing.

According to a Lebanese community leader interviewed by the Australian Broadcasting Corporation, most of the dead came from a small village near the border with Syria. One asylum seeker, who managed to swim to safety, lost his sister-in-law, his brother-in-law, three of their children, his wife, and all eight of his children. The community leader said there were many more Lebanese fleeing the Syrian border who had already paid smugglers and were on their way to Indonesia.

When I got back to Afghanistan, I met with several men preparing to go to Australia. One of them, Qais Khan, opened a small auto-parts shop in Kabul in 2005. Qais told me that for years, while Afghans from the provinces came regularly into the city, he did very well. Since 2010, however, the deteriorating security situation in the rural areas adjacent to the capital had stultified commerce and ruined many retailers. Last year, Qais's shop went out of business; now he was struggling to feed his wife and two children.

A couple of months ago, 15 of Qais's friends paid a smuggler at Sarai Shahzada and left for Indonesia. Among them was Qais's next-door neighbor, a driver for a member of Parliament, who decided to flee after receiving three letters from the Taliban threatening to kill him. Qais told me he was waiting to hear whether his friends were successful — in which case, he would go as well.

"And if they're not?" I asked. "If they're sent to Papua New Guinea or the Republic of Nauru?"

Qais thought for a moment and then admitted he would probably go anyway. In fact, he had already taken out the necessary loans to pay the smuggler. "At least there you have a chance," he said. "At least there is a possibility."

I felt obligated to tell him he was wrong. "You won't get to Australia," I said.

Qais didn't seem to hear. The words simply didn't register. "Australia, Europe, America," he said. "They're not like here. You have a chance."

LUCIE BROCK-BROIDO

■

Two Poems

FROM *Stay, Illusion,* a poetry collection

You Have Harnessed Yourself Ridiculously to This World

Tell the truth I told me   When I couldn't speak.

Sorrow's a barbaric art, crude as a Viking ship   Or a child

Who rode a spotted pony to the lake away from summer

In the 1930's   Toward the iron lung of polio.

According to the census I am unmarried   And unchurched.

                    The woman in the field dressed only in the sun.

Too far gone to halt the Arctic Cap's catastrophe, big beautiful

Blubbery white bears each clinging to his one last hunk of ice.

I am obliged, now, to refrain from dying, for as long as it is possible.

For whom left am I first?

                    We have come to terms with our Self

Like a marmoset getting out of her Great Ape suit.

Currying the Fallow-Colored Horse

And to the curious I say, Don't be naïve.

The soul, like a trinket, is a she.

I lay down in the tweed of one man that first frost night. I did not like the wool of him.

You have one mitochondrial speck of evidence on your cleat.

They can take you down for that.

Did I forget to mention that when you're dead

You're dead a long time.

My uncle, dying, told me this when asked, Why stay here for such suffering.

A chimney swift flits through the fumatorium.

I long for one last Blue democracy, which has broke my heart a while.

How many minutes have I left, the lover asked, To still be beautiful?

I took his blonde face in my hands and kissed him blondely on his mouth.

A. T. GRANT

■

The Body

FROM *Collected Alex*, a chapbook

The Dead Body at the Party

I could drag the dead body to the party. But the people. The people holding glasses of beer or wine or Diet Coke. The people having a good time. The people that would expect me to have a good time. They would expect me to make conversation and not worry about the body. The body that I have been dragging around for years and years. The body that is leaking and rotting and beginning to smell the way a leaking, rotting dead body smells. Maybe they would be able to tell from the smell that I have not been taking care of it. That I am performing an experiment. That I have not been feeding the body its special formula. They would notice the scribbled hair, the wrecked fingernails, the trail of goo that leaks from all of its holes. And they would try to start a conversation. They would say:

That's *some* dead body.

How long have you had that thing.

And where do you get something like that anyway.

Do they come with instructions.

What's the rate of decomposition.

Do you ever—you know.

Did you get it because of that movie. What was it called.

It must make a great punching bag.

It's been *how* many days since you've given the body its special formula.

Then they would address the body directly. Ask if it isn't tired of being dragged around by *this guy* all the time as they jerk their thumbs in my direction. He's such a character, they would laugh. And they would put a drink in the body's hand and pose it like it was flirting with a group of women. And they would take photos of the body and me with their iPhones. And then there would be a tagged photo of the body and me on Facebook the next morning. The tags would read: —with The Body and Alex.

I could drag the body to the party. I could lug the body downstairs from my apartment and into the car. I could strap the body in, start the car, and drive. But we don't go to the party. We don't really go anywhere.

The Day They Gave Me the Dead Body

My eighth birthday was when my parents gave me this dead body.

Go ahead, my mother said. It won't bite.

My parents held each other and watched as I inspected it. They were so excited. My mother bit her lip. I lifted the dead body's arm by the wrist. Its skin was smooth and felt like it might burst if I gave it a sharp poke. When I let go, its hand smacked against the hardwood. I stuck my finger between its third and fourth ribs. One of them felt broken. I sat for a moment on its chest. No movement. I opened its mouth to look at its teeth. A bad smell came out of the mouth, so I closed it. I opened its eyelids. The eyes were little black discs with nothing behind them.

How do you play with it, I asked.

Well, you don't *play* with it, exactly.

Oh, I said. I looked up and down the body again, then rolled it over. What am I supposed to do with it.

Pick it up, my father said. He picked up the body and threw it over his right shoulder. Like this, he said. Carry it around awhile, see how it feels.

So I did.

The body was much larger than me, probably twice my size. I staggered under its weight. It looked like it was about twenty-five years old when it died.

Once I got it balanced on my shoulder I asked, How long has it been dead.

They did not answer. My mother got the camera, while my father beamed at me, the body draped over my shoulder. They looked so proud. I placed the body on the floor as gently as I could. I looked into its face. My mother raised the camera. I heard the flash begin to charge.

How did it die, I asked, still looking into the body's face.

The camera snapped, flashed.

The Experiment

A few weeks ago I decided to stop giving the body its formula. I wondered if I would still be able to carry the body around. I wondered if the body would break into pieces or turn inside out or dissolve completely. I wondered if I would feel guilt about destroying the dead body that had been given to me, or if someone, I don't know who, the Dead Body Protective Care Service if such a thing exists, would come and take the body away from me.

When I had the idea, it felt like a hole opened in my head. I am not sure where the idea came from. But it came. Maybe I saw a farmer carry a feedsack over his shoulder, then heave it into the back of his truck and dust off his hands. Maybe I saw a couple on television break up, their bodies stiff on the screen. Maybe it had been a particularly long day of carrying the body around. Maybe I was just tired.

Wherever You Go

Always keep your dead body close, my parents told me. Never let it out of your sight.

But, I said, but it's so heavy.

It will make you stronger, my mother said. I looked at the floor, but she lifted my chin so our eyes met. You can do it. You have to try. For us.

So I began carrying it everywhere. First I practiced carrying it around my room. I learned how to avoid the corners of my bed, my desk. I learned to raise the body up so its feet would not drag.

Careful, my parents would say when I raised it too near the fan or when I went through a doorframe. You don't want to knock it in the head.

I looked at its head, swollen with lumps.

Okay, I said.

Once I could carry it safely around my room, I practiced carrying it back and forth through the house. I learned all of the trouble spots of the indoors. Sometimes my parents gave me lessons for particular spots—

Take the stairs one at a time.

Be careful not to let the hair dangle into the lit stovetop.

Don't let the body rest too close to the fireplace or an ember might jump onto its clothes.

Same goes for the space heater.

Be sure the arms and legs don't flop and knock over the ironing board.

Be careful not to slip and drop the body when you take it out of the bathtub.

—and so on.

I carried it for hours each day. When one shoulder got tired, I switched the body to the other. When both shoulders got tired, I set it against a wall. The dead body made a good cushion. I leaned against it and used its legs as armrests.

After a few months, my carrying was good enough to take the body outside of the house.

Stares

At first it was difficult to get used to the stares. I was the only kid on the block that carried a body around. I knew that all eyes were on the body, and because I carried it, I knew that all the people who looked at the body saw me, but only out of the corners of their eyes, pale and out of focus. Sometimes I felt the need to compete with the body for attention. I tried wearing a bright red shirt. I tried wearing a very tall blaze orange hat. I tried walking with a limp. I tried shouting everywhere I went. No matter what I did, I never felt the attention clot directly onto me as I carried the body down the street.

Even at home, I felt like my parents always looked at some neutral point between the dead body and me. Every picture was: the body and Alex playing mini-golf, the body and Alex at the beach, the body and Alex – Christmas '95. And when they said anything to me, they made sure to also reference the body somehow: Did you have a good day at school. Did the body stay propped up the entire time. It was as if they were afraid of showing favoritism.

Once when my family was at the city park, I laid the body flat on the grass and covered it with a pile of leaves. Then I lay down on top of the pile. Where did the dead body go, I said. Looks like I'm the only one here.

Later I began to enjoy the soft focus. I carried the body up and down the street for hours. I wore dull gray clothes so that I could feel myself dissolve into the background, into the warm and grainy feeling.

Routine

After a few months of lugging the dead body everywhere I went, we began to settle into a routine.

Every morning I helped the body out of its sleeping bag. I stretched the dead body's arms high over its head, then I opened its mouth and I yawned. I set the body in the corner while I made up my bed, then I used its arms and hands to roll up its sleeping bag and stash it under my bed.

Then we went into the bathroom. I cleaned the crust out of my eyes, then its eyes. I propped the body on the toilet while I showered, but it never had to pee or anything. Then while I peed I let the body soak in the bath. The body always left a thick oily film on the water's surface. My parents gave me special soaps to use on the body after it had soaked for several minutes. These will preserve the body, my father said. We want it to last for a long time, don't we.

After I brushed our teeth and combed our hair, I worked each of the body's joints. You have to work its joints every day, mother said. If you don't it will stiffen up and become difficult to carry and store in different positions.

She told me I should also stretch and flex its muscles each morning. These are the things that make a body last, she said. It's just as important to keep a dead body in shape as it is to keep a live body in shape.

When we finished our morning workout, we went downstairs for breakfast. My parents would give me cereal with marshmallows. To the body they gave a teaspoon of a special liquid formula. It was thick, and it took a long time to drip down the body's throat. I imagined it sliding, sliding, sliding down into the belly.

Once I asked if I could taste the special liquid formula. You have your cereal, my mother said. Eat up.

I just want to try it. What happens if you put it in a live body.

Son, my father said. The formula isn't made for a live body. Bad things would happen. He put his hand on the back of my neck. Promise your mother and me right now that you won't ever taste the formula. That you'll only feed it to the body.

I shook my head yes and said, I promise.

Besides, that stuff can't taste good. My father squinched his face, then smiled and patted me on the head. Better go. You don't want to be late for school.

My mother screwed the cap onto the bottle of formula and put it on the top shelf. I kissed my mother and father like always. Then I puckered the body's lips and made it give my parents each a kiss too.

I still wondered what the special formula tasted like, but I never asked about it again.

Recess

At recess the kids made up songs about me and the dead body. One of them went: *Alex and the body / flush them down the potty / dead ones, dead ones / they both fall down.*

After the kids sang the song, they would poke the body, then scatter across the playground, holding their noses. Then they would make *P.U.* and *yuck* faces. They would squeal and giggle.

Then I would haul the body up the tallest slide and sit there for a while. We would watch the other children climb on the monkey bars and pretend the old tires were a fort. We would watch them play freeze tag and hide-and-go-seek.

Don't you wish we could run, I said to the body one time.

When we got tired of watching, sometimes I let the body slide first so it could cushion me when I landed. Other times I slid first with the body right behind me for extra momentum.

The teacher always noticed after one or two slides.

Alex, she would say. We're happy to let you bring your dead body to school, but we can't let you take it onto the playground equipment. It will make a mess, and that wouldn't be fair to the other children, would it.

I guess not.

Now, she would say with a smile, there are plenty of places where you and the dead body can play. Run along and have fun.

The body and I always ended up making mounds in the dirt pile, humming.

A Chest of Drawers

Sometimes the dead body gets so heavy.

Sometimes I get tired of carrying it on my shoulders, so I drag it and its mouth fills up with mud and leaves. And for some reason it is more bloated at certain times than at others. It must be humidity or something. Or maybe its dead organs are swelling.

When it gets so heavy, I wish the dead body were a chest of drawers. I could pull out some drawers to lighten the load.

Once I tried cutting off one of its legs. It made the body a little bit lighter, but then a few hours later when I was ready to reattach the leg, I had trouble finding it. Then once I found the leg, I couldn't slide it back into the joint. We had to take the body to a doctor.

Well, the doctor said, I'm afraid I've got bad news: the patient is dead. He laughed and clapped me on the back. Cheer up, son, he said. We can fix the leg.

Hours later, we left with the leg reattached and cherry suckers for the body and me, which neither of us ate. My parents didn't say anything, but I could tell they were upset by the quiet of the car ride home, by the way they touched my head as they tucked me into bed that night.

I felt awful. Maybe I should just take the organs out, I thought. Then I could use the body as a bag. I could open it up and crawl inside.

The Woods

I pick up the body and hoist it over my shoulder. My shoulder is sore from carrying the body yesterday to the grocery store and then around the shopping mall, where I bought some new boots, and then all around the parking lot when I forgot where we parked. So I switch the body to my other shoulder and begin walking into the woods.

The woods are where the body and I feel the best. All of that quiet and no expectations. No walls or other people. We can be the dead body and the guy who carries the dead body. And if we walk for long enough, we always find a dead tree that is held up by some living trees.

The ground is still wet from the rain and mist this morning. Water drips from the leaves onto the body which then drips onto me. My new boots are heavy. These are by far the deepest footprints we have ever made, I say to the body. I take a step and watch my foot sink deep into the mud, then I watch the print fill up with water as my foot leaves the depression.

Depression is a word I've never heard my mother use. I wonder if she ever used it once in her entire life. I think the closest she ever came was years ago on my graduation night. She was driving us to a "surprise" graduation party. The body and I were strapped into the back seat as usual, but I kept catching my mother's eye in the rearview mirror.

What's wrong, I said.

Does it ever bother you to carry the body around all the time.

I can't imagine life without it, I said.

It's just that sometimes you seem a little down. She bit her lip. You know we are so proud of you.

I think when she said *bother* and *down* she meant *depression*. I would tell her now: it's not depression, it's just a dead body. I think she was afraid I couldn't handle it, carrying a dead thing around all the time.

Another time she said, Oh my son, what did we do to you.

When I find a rock in the woods, I prop the body against it and sit down. Its clothes are a little dirty. It has also been a while since I have shaved the body's face. Or mine. I make a mental note: wash clothes, shave.

I wonder if the body's mother ever used the word *depression*. If the body's mother is still alive, maybe she is depressed right now. Maybe when she dreams of the body, it is young and alive. In her dream, maybe she picks up the body after it has fallen asleep in front of the TV, carries it to its room, lays it in bed, tucks it in, pulls the covers all the way up to its chin, and puts a little glass of water on its nightstand.

Sometimes at night after I put the body into its sleeping bag, I run my hand through the body's hair. Its hair is very stiff. It almost feels fake. But I kiss its cold forehead anyway and smile like my parents used to do to me.

When I do, I hear the body's mother's voice, or at least what I imagine her voice sounds like, in my head. Goodnight sweetie, she says. The body's mother sounds just like my mother. I hear their voices blend. Goodnight sweetie, they say to both of us.

Most Nights

On the nights when we do not go to the park or drive around aimlessly, the dead body and I stay in and watch a movie or a boxing match. Sometimes we put on special headgear and box with each other, or I have a bowl of cereal while I feed the body its special formula, or I put the body on the couch and I sit in the chair farthest away.

From that distance, the body almost looks alive in the blue light, like it is very bored or sleeping but not dead, not gone. This is when the distance between us is greatest. The dead body across the room, with me imagining the body is alive. But it is also the closest we ever get to being alone.

Every now and then, I try to take us out to a night spot or to a party, but I always turn around and take us home before we arrive. Even though I've never gone, I always get invited to the parties. I am a living conversation piece carrying a dead one. But everywhere we go feels so crowded. I imagine if the body could talk, it would tell me it feels the same way. It would say, If we go out, we will only run into people. Or we will only end up standing in the corner of the room watching everyone else. Or worse.

The Sunlight is So Bright

When I look out my window, there is a man on the sidewalk scraping mud off his shoes with a stick. He is really scraping hard. The flesh on his face jiggles when he scrapes. His face and clothes are splattered with mud flecks and sweat.

I do not have to scrape mud off the dead body's shoes. And I don't ever have to buy it new shoes since it never walks and never rips holes in its shoes or wears the tread down or outgrows them. And unlike a pet or live roommate, it never eats my food if I accidentally leave it out. It never takes the last cookie and then puts the empty box back in the cabinet. It never drinks all the milk, leaving me milkless when I have already poured a bowl of cereal, or plays loud music or television shows at night.

Now the man outside is knocking the shoes together. And now he is wiping them in the grass. And now he is grumbling. And now he is wiping them faster. And now he is tearing up little clumps of grass, he is wiping them so hard. And now, even after all of this, the mud is still not coming off.

And now the dead body slumps over on the couch, its head cocked in an uncomfortable-looking position.

Taste and See

I have not given the body its special liquid formula today or any other day for the last week. It began as an experiment. Just to see what would happen. Now the body smells terrible. Much worse than usual. Its hair is starting to fall out, and its skin is oozing a sticky oil. The oil makes it difficult to carry the body.

It has become so difficult to carry, we have not left the house for three days—we just sit across the room from each other and stare. Every now and then I get up to get a bowl of cereal. I keep thinking about the bottle of formula on the windowsill. I still have no idea what is in the formula or how it works. I only know that sometime before they died, my parents gave me a lifetime supply of it in unlabeled bottles.

Promise your mother and me right now that you won't ever taste the formula. That you'll only feed it to the body, my father had said.

Sometimes I wonder if the body would want to taste my cereal.

Or be the one who does the talking and wondering.

Or the carrying.

O Taste and See

The body is in no shape to go anywhere tonight, not even to the woods or for a drive. I put an end to the experiment. I fed the body its formula again. But now the body is only getting worse, no matter how much formula I feed it. I do not know what will happen to us now. I prop the body up in a chair and sit across from it. We face each other, and I say to the body:

You have been my every day for years. You are something like my skin, and I am something like yours. We are a film projector and a screen. A stage and the actor upon it. A fist and the blow it contains. A light passes through us both.

The dead body does not answer me, so I imagine its answers:

Our life will have to change soon. We spend so much time together. In the woods. The car. In this room in the blue television light. A voice passes right through our mind. We are a tall shadow pressed into the pavement. Into the walls.

And then we say:

Look through the dead body, and there is Alex with his aching limbs. He was a born shadowboxer, a real champ. A dead body withers to nothing but a long, sticky shadow. You've got the weight. I've got the reach. We're all alone, kid. It's just you and me.

But soon a new space will open between us. A third face. A face made of both our faces. I can feel it.

A shadow shines on the floor. The refrigerator hums and rattles. I go into the kitchen, and I bring back a bowl of cereal and the bottle of special formula. I sit down beside the body. I open its mouth and feed it a spoonful of cereal. I work the jaw and let the cereal slide down the body's throat. I imagine how happy the body must be—to finally try cereal after all these years.

It must be as happy as I am when I pour a spoonful of the special liquid formula. When I hold it up to my mouth. When I touch the tip of my tongue to the liquid to taste. When I put the spoonful of the special formula in my mouth and swallow. When I feel the sweetness drip down the back of my throat.

ALI LIEBEGOTT

■

Shift #6

FROM *Shifts*, a chapbook of diary poems

eight household candles
twenty-five pounds
of short-grain brown rice

the freelancer was missing his teeth

so slow in the store
I've begun to count
each brick and beam

we want our lives
all lined up
we go crazy making order

once an accountant told me:
If we're crazy, then we have to be crazy
she meant it in a scheduling manner
and I think of it more often than
the accounting lessons I paid for.

Twenty-five pounds of brown rice
and eight household candles —
when those are the groceries
it's hard not to profile:

the apocalypse or self-imposed apocalypse,
those candles will burn faster
than that rice will last.

Sometimes when I ring up groceries
I say, *Hello*
and the customer says, *Hello*

and I ring up their apples and arugula
and flax seeds and popcorn

at each new thing I think I should make conversation,
but I don't and I can feel the energy
of me failing pass between us.

I record my failure in front of them
while I wait for a credit card to be run
or groceries to be bagged.

A customer will say:
There are six bagels in that bag.
That's basil.
Those are apples.
Even though the bags are clear
and the bagels, sixly —

there are six bagels in that bag —
I think of that person
watching pornography with his partner
explaining things:
there are two penises in that one vagina.

Sometimes I'm grateful when someone
tells me how many bagels are in a bag
because, in truth, it's hard to count circular things.

The store sells loose condoms in a jar like penny candy.
No one ever buys a single condom.
They buy at least four, twenty-five cents each.

Marry me!
I would say if anyone ever came
through my line with a single condom.

I would love their humble offering, a single shot at love.

Sometimes, I can't believe how many
condoms people buy, a mini mountain
moving down my belt
when people buy more than seven
it makes me think, I'm not having enough sex.

Sometimes I'm writing a poem at my register
and a customer behind me says,
Uh oh. There's an ant here.
I'm in a hippie grocery store
Do you want me to kill it? I ask
and she says, *I don't know if we should.*

It's the safe kind of ant, bigger than usual, from the produce itself
I'm going to kill it, please don't judge me, I say
I won't she says, I want to kill it too —
but some people say you should just take it outside.

I take the corner of my towel and smash the ant twice.
You're free from this world, I say and the customer says,
some people think snails don't have karma,
my friend who kills them in her garden says so.

I hate people who say animals don't have souls or karma —
that a fish can't feel a hook in their lip
I want to scream, *Are you a snail? Are you a fish?*

Where's my poet, Ulysses, Gilgamesh?
Someone come through my line
with a single condom taped to a stick
held high above their head and rescue me.

—8/31/13, Register 7,
8:45 AM – 3 PM

KATHRYN DAVIS

■

Body-without-Soul

FROM *Duplex*, a novel

IT WAS A SUBURBAN STREET, one block long, the houses made of
brick and built to last like the third little pig's. Sycamore trees had
been planted at regular intervals along the curb and the curbs themselves sparkled; I think the concrete was mixed with mica in it. I
think when it was new the street couldn't help but draw attention to
itself, inviting envy.

Miss Vicks lived at the lower end of the street, in number 49. Most
of the other houses had families living in them but she was by herself, a woman of about fifty, slim and still attractive, with a red short-
haired dachshund. By the time she moved in, the sycamore trees had
grown so large they had enormous holes cut through their crowns to
make room for all the wires.

She was a real woman; you could tell by the way she didn't have to
move her head from side to side to take in sound. Every day she and
the dachshund went for three walks, the first early in the morning,
the second in the late afternoon, and the third after dinner, when the
blue-green lights of the scows, those slow-moving heralds of melancholy, would begin to appear in the night sky. The little dog would
sniff around the feet of the sycamores and as it did she would stand
there paralyzed as all the Miss Vickses that had ever been layered
themselves inside her, one atop the other and increasingly small,
forming a great laminate like tree rings around heartwood.

Bedtime, the end of summer. The street was filled with children,
many of them the same children she'd soon be welcoming into her

classroom. School was about to start. "Heads up!" the boys yelled when a car appeared, interrupting their play; the girls sat making deals on the porch stoops, cigar boxes of trading cards and stickers in their laps. Meanwhile the darkness welled up so gradually the only way anyone could tell night had fallen was the fireflies, prickling like light on water. The parents were inside, keeping an eye on the children but also drinking highballs. Fireflies like falling stars, the tree trunks narrow as the girls' waists.

Occasionally something different happened. One girl pasted a diadem of gold star stickers to her forehead and wandered from her stoop to get closer to where one of the boys stood bending slightly forward, his hands on his knees, nervously waiting for another boy to hit the ball. This waiting boy was Eddie, who lived at the opposite end of the street from Miss Vicks, in number 24; the girl was Mary, who lived in the house attached to hers. Sometimes Miss Vicks could hear Mary practicing the piano through the living room wall—"Für Elise" with the same mistake in the same spot, over and over. A fingering problem, simple enough to fix if only the parents would give the girl some lessons.

Headlights appeared; the boys scattered. Mary remained standing at the curb in her plaid shorts and white T-shirt, balanced like a stork on one leg. The car was expensive and silver-gray and driven by the sorcerer Body-without-Soul. Miss Vicks didn't recognize him right away because like everyone else she was blinded by the headlights. The headlights turned the lenses of her and Mary's spectacles to blazing disks of hammered gold so neither one of them could see the street, the trees, the houses—anything at all, really—and the next minute the car was gone. It was only after the taillights had disappeared around the corner that Miss Vicks realized she had recognized the license plate: 1511MV, a prime, followed by her initials.

Early in their romance the sorcerer told her he took this for a sign. Miss Vicks was not a superstitious person but like most people she was susceptible to flattery. She and her dog had been walking through the ruined gardens of the Woodard Estate when the sorcerer suddenly appeared on the path in front of them, a tall figure in a finely tailored suit, his shadow cast behind him, his face gold like melted sun. It was as if he'd been expecting her; when he circled her wrist with his fingers to draw her close to ask her name, she felt the life inside her leap up from everywhere, shocking, like a hatch of mayflies. He said he'd been hunting but she didn't see a gun anywhere. "The animal kingdom," he said, disparagingly, giving her little dog a nudge with the toe of his pointed shoe. He was a Woodard—it made sense that he would be there even after the place had fallen into desuetude.

Now her dog was raising his hackles. Miss Vicks could feel him tugging on the leash, bravely holding the soft red flags of his ears aloft and out to either side like banderillas.

"Has anyone seen Eddie?" Mary asked.

"He disappeared," Roy Duffy told her, but he was joking.

Everyone knew how Eddie was—here one minute, gone the next. He was a small, jumpy boy; he moved so fast it was as if he got where he was headed before anyone ever noticed he'd left where he started out. Besides, they were all disappearing into their houses—it was only the beginning. The game was over; the next day school started. When the crest of one wave of light met the trough of another the result was blackness.

Tonight, as every night, from inside number 24 came the sound of Eddie's parents playing canasta. "I'll meld *you*!" said his mother, raucous with the joy of competition. The two of them were sitting on either side of the card table they set up in the living room each night after dinner, but you couldn't see them, only hear their voices, the front bow window filled with a lush ivy plant in an Italian cachepot.

Miss Vicks watched Mary start down the street.

"Goodnight, Miss Vicks," Mary said.

"See you tomorrow, Mary," she replied.

In the brick houses the clocks kept ticking away the time, chipping off pieces of it, some big ones piling thick and heavy under the brass weights of the grandfather clock in Eddie's parents' hallway, others so small and fast even the round watchful eyes of the cat clock in Mary's parents' kitchen couldn't track their flight. The crickets were rubbing their hind legs together, unrolling that endless band of sound that when combined with the sound of the sycamore trees tossing their heads in the heat-thickened breeze could cause even a girl as unsentimental as Mary to feel like she'd just left something behind on the porch stoop she couldn't bear to live without.

Miss Vicks waited on the grass verge in front of number 24 for her dog to complete his business. He always deposited it in the same place between the curb and the sidewalk; she would scoop it into a bag and then it would get carried into the heavens by a scow. The street was empty, the materialization of the silver-gray car having driven everyone inside.

Thinking of the sorcerer, Miss Vicks became aroused. He had his way of doing things. When he drove he liked to rest his one hand lightly on the wheel and leave the other free to stroke her between the legs. His fingernails were perfect ovals like flower petals, and he had eyes so black and so deep-set sometimes she thought they weren't eyes but holes. Even when they seemed to be looking at the road she knew what he was seeing was himself.

He'd been with a woman he left to be with her, and another woman before that, and before that many other women — Miss Vicks had heard the stories. Once she saw him escorting a blonde woman into a restaurant, his hand at the small of the woman's back, and to her shame she realized her jealousy was nothing compared with her vicarious sense of excitement at the thought of his touch. He wasn't promiscuous though, or so he claimed the one time she confronted him. He was just having difficulty finding the right woman.

"I'm not like you," he'd told her, as if that were justification enough. They were lying on her bed with all the lights on, the way he liked it, and he was slipping one hand under her expensive Italian camisole while guiding her lips to meet his with the other. Of course she knew he was right, though probably not the way he meant it. The sorcerer could make things appear or he could make them vanish; he could make them turn into other things or he could make them vibrate at unprecedented frequencies, the explanation for his great success in bed. It was only *things*, though. When the sorcerer looked at the street he saw it crawling with souls like the earth with worms. It was no secret that even the lowliest of the unruly, uncontainable beings living there could partake of love's mystery, and his envious rage knew no bounds.

The dachshund had finished and was kicking up grass blades with his hind legs. From far to the west came a rumble of thunder; Miss Vicks grew aware of the changing temperature of the air. In this latitude summer storms moved in quickly and did a lot of damage before moving away. "Come on," she said to the dog, who seemed frozen in place, staring at nothing. Dark spots appeared on the sidewalk, a few at first and then more and more. She yanked the leash. Face it, she told herself. The man is a beast. You'd be better off without him. She could hear windows closing, the sound of Mr. O'Toole yelling instructions at Mrs. O'Toole. The back door—something about the back door swinging in the wind.

On the sidewalk outside number 37 (another prime) came the first flash of lightning, just a flash like a huge light had been turned on; for a moment it was as if it was possible to see everything in the world. Then there was another flash, this one displayed like an X-ray image of the central nervous system above the even-numbered houses on the other side of the street. Everyone knew the family inside number 37 were robots. Mr. XA, Mrs. XA, Cindy XA, Carol XA—when you saw them outside the house they looked like people. Carol had been in Miss Vicks's class the previous year and she had been an excellent if uninspired student; Cindy would be in her class starting tomorrow. The question of how to teach—or even whether to teach—a robot came up from time to time among the teachers. No one had a good answer.

By the time Miss Vicks got to number 49 the storm was making it almost impossible to find her front door. Often it happened that the world's water got sucked aloft and came down all at once as rain. She swept her little dog into her arms and felt her way onto the porch. They were both completely drenched, the dog's red coat so wet it looked black. For a while they sat there in the glider, surrounded by thundering curtains of rainwater. 1511MV—what kind of a license plate was that? One plus five plus one plus one equaled eight, a number signifying the World, the very essence of the sorcerer's domain. If you knocked eight on its side it became the symbol of infinity.

As she sat there on the porch she tried getting a sense of what was going on in number 47, the house attached to hers where Mary lived. If she had ever had a daughter the girl would have been like Mary—they even looked a little bit alike, both being bird-boned and pale, and parting their limp mouse-brown hair girlishly down the middle. Miss Vicks's part was always ruler-straight, though, whereas

Mary's jogged to the left at the back of her head, suggesting a lack of interest in things she couldn't see. Her teeth were too big for her mouth, too, making her appear more vulnerable than she really was.

Usually in the summer with the windows open Miss Vicks had no trouble eavesdropping on Mary's family, but now the rain was drowning out everything except itself. Could that have been the piano? Her ears often played tricks on her, making voices come from things that couldn't speak, especially machines that had a rhythmic movement like the washer. She'd been feeling uneasy ever since she heard Mary ask where Eddie was and Roy Duffy say he disappeared. Even after the rain had stopped pouring from the sky and dripping from the trees and streaming from the gutter spout—even after the street was restored to silence, the only thing she could hear besides the porch glider squeaking on its rusting joints and the yip her dachshund let out when she made a move to get up was a loud whispering coming from Mary's parents' living room, a sound that always suggested urgency to her and made her feel powerless and left out, cast back into the condition of childhood in a world where the adults were too busy to notice whatever those things were that were tunneling under the streets and slipping from their holes at night to dart under porches and along the telephone wires. Then the bells would start to peal, a stroke for each soul. She gave up and went inside and went to bed.

It was only when everyone on the street was asleep that the robots came flying out of number 37. There were four of them, two the size and shape of needles and two like coins, their exterior surface burnished to such a high state of reflective brilliance that all a human being had to do was look at one of them for a split second to be forever blinded. The robots waited to come out until after the humans were asleep. They'd learned to care about us because they found us touchingly helpless, due in large part to the fact that we could die. Unlike toasters or vacuum cleaners, though, the robots were endowed with minds. In this way they were distant relatives of Body-without-Soul, but the enmity between the sorcerer and the robots ran deep.

In the morning Miss Vicks handed out sheets of colored construction paper. The students were to fold the paper in half and in half again and then in half again, the idea being that after unfolding the paper they would end up with eight boxes, in each of which they were to work a problem in long division. Mary filled her boxes with drawings of Eddie, some of them not so bad; arithmetic bored her and besides, it was her plan to be an artist of some kind when she grew up. A feeling attached to the act of being given instructions involving paper and folding it, a feeling of intense apprehension verging on almost insane excitement.

From time to time Mary looked to her left to where her model usually sat. His seat was empty, his yellow pencil lying in the groove at the top of the desk, covered with tooth marks. Eddie chewed on the pencil when he was nervous; he was a high-strung boy, sensitive and easily unhinged. One day last summer Mary had lost control of her bicycle in front of the Darlings' house. She had fallen off and skinned her knee and Eddie stood for a long time staring at the place on the sidewalk where he could see her blood. "I shouldn't have let it happen," he said, even though he'd been at the dentist having a cavity filled at the time.

They were too young, really, to understand the implications, but their bond was of the kind Miss Vicks still hoped for, exquisite and therefore unbreakable, according to the rules governing chemical bonds, in this universe at least.

"Do you know where Eddie is?" Mary asked the teacher when she came around to collect the papers. "Does anyone know where he went?"

"I'm sure he's fine," Miss Vicks replied, even though she wasn't. If Mary's failure to do the assigned work troubled her she kept it to herself.

At recess Cindy XA climbed down from the top of the jungle gym to sit beside Mary on one of the wooden seats of the swing set. "Scooch over," Cindy said, shoving her with her little butt to make room.

Cindy was petite, her bright blonde hair cut very straight, the bangs kept back from her face with red bow-shaped barrettes — Mary didn't like her all that much. They'd tried trading cards throughout the summer but the deals had been oddly unsatisfying. Cindy always gave in without a fight. Being immune to desire, she found the enterprise pointless. As a robot she knew that human bodies had been created to an identical template, one that had been established long ago and owed almost everything to the skeletal structure of the great apes. Apes or humans—we all made the same mistake, tempted by shifting leaves or the smell of sex, by music or a ripe banana. She also knew Miss Vicks didn't have a clue what had happened to Eddie.

"Hang on," Cindy said, linking arms with Mary and pushing off from the playground with her new brown oxfords.

A robot's pressure is slight yet forceful. The swing began to go higher, propelling the two of them back and forth and up and down at a speed so swift as to make Mary increasingly bilious as she watched the iron fence posts blur into a heaving wall of black interrupted by blobs of green and patches of bright blue sky. Eventually she and Cindy were no longer visible.

I think the robot was trying to warn her about what was going to happen.

I think this because the story of what was going to happen is also my story, the story of girls everywhere.

Mary wanted to ask Cindy to make the swing stop but her lips wouldn't move. The trees at the far side of the yard whirled their tresses, shaking all the little birds out, the red ones and the blue ones and the brown ones, and suddenly Mary was alone in the corner of the playground the trash blew into that smelled like cat piss.

When she reached into her pocket she pricked her finger on a pin-like object she hadn't known was there. What is this horrible thing? she wondered. She took it out of her pocket and dropped it to the ground where it lingered briefly before flying back home to its companions.

■

Episode 15: Street Cleaning Day

A transcript FROM *Welcome to Night Vale,* a podcast

15.1

Bananas are hardly that slippery. But watch your step, anyway. Welcome to Night Vale.

15.2

Ladies, gentlemen, you: Today is Street Cleaning Day. Please remain calm. Street Cleaners will be upon us quite soon. We have little time to prepare. Please remain calm. The City Council has issued a statement in 20 point all-caps type, saying "RUN! RUN! FORGET YOUR CHILDREN AND LEAVE BEHIND THE WEAK! RUN!" We have contacted those experts who have not already gone underground or changed their identity, and have been told that Street Cleaners focus on heat and movement, and so the best strategy is to be dead already. Then the experts all swallowed pills and fell, mouths frothing, at my feet. If you have doors, lock them. If you have windows, board them up. If you still have ears, cover them, and crouch, wherever you are. It is Street Cleaning day. Please remain calm.

15.3

John Peters, you know, the farmer? He reports finding an old oak door standing unsupported by any other structure out in the scrubland. He says that he's sure it wasn't there yesterday, or pretty sure anyway. As sure as he can be since the accident. Apparently, there is knocking from the door, as though there were someone from some other side that does not exist in our narrow, fragile reality, trying to get in. He has added several deadbolts and chains to the door on both sides, unsure which direction the door opens. Which is, by the way, a huge design flaw. One should always know which way a door opens merely by looking at it if the designer has done their job, and this holds true whether it's a bank of glass doors at the local mall, or an unspeakably old wooden door leading to other worlds than these. John, meanwhile, says he will keep a sleepless vigil upon the door, as any sleep merely leads to dreams of blurry shapes in the dim distance, advancing, hissing, upon this vulnerable planet. He also says the imaginary corn is coming in real good, and we should have a nice crop to choose from soon, especially now that it will be available for sale at the Green Market.

15.4

The staff of Dark Owl Records announced today that they are only listening to, selling, and talking about Buddy Holly. If you want to buy music at all, you had better like Buddy Holly. If you dress like Buddy Holly, that's cool, too.

They also announced that Buddy Holly will be performing live there this Saturday night at 11 to promote his newest album, which is called *I'm Trapped in Between Worlds, Existing Only in the Form That You Knew Me; This Is Not Who I Am; Leave Me Alone and Just Let Me Die, Please.*

15.5

Organized crime is on the rise, Night Vale. The Sheriff's Secret Police and the Night Vale Council for Commerce are cracking down on illegal wheat & wheat byproduct "speakeasies."

Two months ago, the City Council abolished forever all wheat & wheat byproducts, but a black market appears to have formed for those de-praved addicts who can't get enough wheat, nor its byproducts.

Big Rico's Pizza was cited this week for hosting an illegal wheat & wheat byproducts joint in a hidden basement space. Big Rico's, in light of the new laws, has had to alter its menu to mostly just bowls of stewed tomatoes, melted cheese wads, and gluten-free pizza slices.

His storefront seemed to be the model of a wheat-free & wheat by-product-free society, but even the most honest businesses can turn to crime when their livelihood is on the line.

Fortunately for Big Rico, he is a very nice person and apologized to the City Council in a way that did not include blackmail or secret campaign contributions or special favors. Big Rico is just truly sorry for what he has done.

The Sheriff's Secret Police say they are upping their efforts to stop these illicit wheat & wheat byproduct manufacturers. They are mostly just sniffing the air until they smell bread. It's pretty easy, actually, the Sheriff said from his hoveroffice in the clouds.

15.6

More information now on Street Cleaning Day, which has come upon us just as we always feared it would. The information is that Street Cleaning Day is terrifying, and that we should all perhaps fall to our knees, letting out moans and rubbing our forearms absently. The City Council has issued a statement indicating that they forgot they had vacation plans this week, and so are currently on a plane to Miami, as they had been planning and looking forward to for some time. They said their vacation, since it was definitely planned, has a pre-estab-lished end-date, but that they cannot tell anyone what that end-date is until the Street Cleaners are completely gone. In the meantime, they are leaving Paul Birmingham in charge. Paul, the vagrant who lives in a lean-to behind the library, could not be reached for com-ment, as he has faked his own death in an elaborate scheme to escape Street Cleaning Day unscathed. More, if there ever is more for any of us.

15.7

And now a word from our sponsors. Today's broadcast is sponsored by Target. Target is a great place to shop, and they would like you to consider the variety of silence in this world. The deathly silence when an argument has reached a height from which neither party can see a safe way down, and the soft, wet silence of post-coital breath catching. Silence in a courtroom, moments before a man's life is changed completely by something so insignificant as his past, and the silence of a hospital room as a man, in front of everyone he loves, lets the heat from his clenched hands dissipate into the background hum of the universe. The quiet of outdoor distances, of wilderness, of the luxury of space, and the quiet of dead air on the radio, the sound of a mistake, of emphasis, of your own thoughts when you expected someone else's. [PAUSE] Shop at Target.

15.8

From time to time, listeners, I like to bring a little education to our show, throw out some interesting facts, or "mind fuel." Today, I'd like to share some fascinating facts about clouds.

[STRUCK-OUT WORDS SHOULD BE READ NORMALLY BUT WILL BE BEEPED OUT]

Clouds are made up of ~~tiny water droplets~~.

Rain clouds are formed when ~~large amounts of moisture accumulate above dense air~~. When the density of the humid air (a.k.a. the cloud) becomes ~~denser than the air below~~, that's when it rains.

Lightning is ~~caused by static electricity~~, and it's important to ~~stay away as lightning~~ can kill you, or at least cause you a great deal of body-altering pain and regret.

But take some time to stop and look at the clouds. They are beautiful, wondrous creations.

Wait. I've just been handed a red piece of paper by one of the Sheriff's Secret Police officers. [WHISPERING] I can tell that's what he was because of his short cape, blow dart chest belt, and tight leather balaclava.

Dear listeners, I've been told to inform you that you are to stop looking at the clouds immediately. Stop knowing about the clouds. Intern Stacey tells me in my headset here that they've also been censoring my broadcast. Well, I back our public protectors, and if they say to stop knowing about whatever it was I was talking about, then I'll stop knowing about it.

Let's go now to the sounds of predatory birds.

[SOUND OF PREDATORY BIRDS FOR 30–45 SECONDS]

15.9

Sirens have been going off in central Night Vale, as a warning about sirens going off in Old Town Night Vale. These sirens indicate that sirens might occur in the general Night Vale area over the next few hours, which would be a declaration of a current "Siren Watch." Please check that your Siren-Preparedness kit is fully stocked and easily reachable.

Lieutenant Regis, of Unit 7 of the local National Guard Station and KFC combo store, said that "it always seemed that the only way to live without regrets was just to never regret anything you did. And that seems to be the only hope for the future, anyway. Regrets just bear us down. Regrets just bear us down."

This wasn't related to today's Siren Watch. He said that a few years back and it just always stuck with me.

15.10

And now traffic. Southbound HOV lanes of Route 800, near exit 15, have large glowing arrows. Drive over the arrows and get a boost in speed. Save time and gas, and get your high-occupancy vehicle to work on time!

There's a stalled car at the downtown off ramp of Eastern Expressway. Tow trucks are on the scene to euthanize the vehicle and chase away scavenging vermin.

There are several accidents to report. In fact, infinite accidents. Everything is an accident. Or at least, let us hope so. This has been traffic.

15.11

Ladies and gentlemen, it is not possible for us to exactly do another news report on Street Cleaning Day, as no information can get through the barricades and seals that are keeping us safe within our broadcasting bunker. Instead we offer the following impressionistic list of what we believe is happening outside our secure perimeter: Screaming. A slow movement downwards. The crunch of items made of wood and items not made of wood. A quick movement upwards. Char. A smell like rotting seaweed, or a poisoned ocean. The song "La Bamba," only faster. You know that feeling when you realize you're not alone? Only more so. Screaming. Screaming. Screaming. Ladies and gentlemen. Ladies and gentlemen. The Street Cleaners are upon us. What can we do? What is there to do? Besides, perhaps, taking you in a haze of terror and heat, to the weather.

[A SONG COMPLETELY UNRELATED TO THE WEATHER PLAYS]

15.12

We return you now to a safe place. The Street Cleaners have passed. Street Cleaning Day, as so many other days, is behind us. We emerge from hiding spots, from secret locations, from places under other places. We step out into the street, and it is as though it is brand new to us. Certainly, it is cleaner now, but that is not all. We have survived all the way from birth to this very moment, and we look at each other, and some of us start laughing and others start weeping and one or two of us break out into a wordless humming song, and all of us mean the exact same thing.

Look at us. Look at us out in the honey light of the finished day. Look at us and rejoice in our sheer being.

One of us turns to another, clears his throat, and puts a gentle hand upon the other's gentle arm.

"I've never told you this," that one says.

"What is it, Wilson?" says the other.

"Amber, you are all to me. Will you marry me?"

"Wilson, we've spoken maybe twice. Do you think we could start with dinner instead?"

"No, yes, no, you're right. I was confused," says the one, although he was not confused.

"Think nothing of it. It's forgotten," says the other, although she thought many things of it, and had forgotten nothing.

And then a gradual movement towards Mission Grove Park, no orders or even suggestions given, and yet we all file to that central meeting place, put our arms around each other, grip tight, and then grip tighter. Some of us are not here. We leave space for them, space that has been emptied by time.

"I suppose I should say a few words, to mark the occasion," says one of us, tall, towards the front. He says nothing more.

The City Council arrives, back from their long-planned Miami vacation, nudging those near them and talking about silver sand beaches and the food, oh those Cubans know how to do it. Even they are accepted into the gathering, despite our usual fears, and we grip them too as friends.

Night has arrived, ladies. Night is here, gentlemen. Night falls on our weary bodies.

And night falls on you too. You too have survived, survived everything up to this moment. Grip tight, hum, laugh, cry. Forget nothing and think many things of it. Good night. Good night. Good night.

YUMI SAKUGAWA

■

Have Cake and Tea with Your Demons

FROM *Your Illustrated Guide to Becoming One with the Universe*, a graphic novel

THE UNIVERSE IS ONENESS

THE UNIVERSE JUST IS

SO IT IS NO WONDER THAT MANY OF US FEEL DISCONNECTED FROM THE UNIVERSE. WHEN WE SHUN OUR OWN DARKNESS (OUR WEAKNESSES, OUR ANGER, OUR SADNESS, OUR SHAME, OUR PAIN), WE ARE DISCONNECTING OURSELVES FROM THE FULL SPECTRUM OF ELEMENTS THAT EXIST WITHIN OURSELVES AND

THE REST OF

THE UNIVERSE

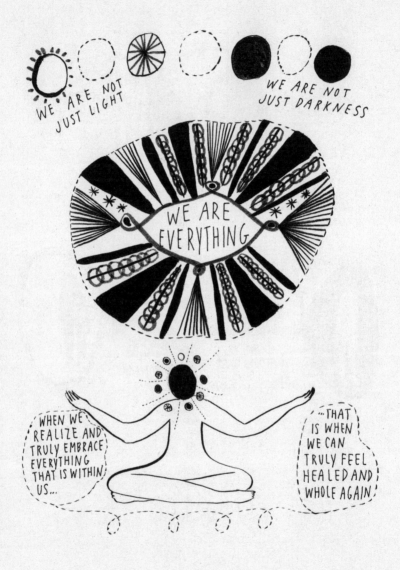

IT MIGHT FEEL
AWKWARD AND
UNCOMFORTABLE
AT FIRST

ALLOW THE DEMON TO SAY WHAT IT
FEELS LIKE SAYING, FEEL WHAT IT
FEELS LIKE FEELING, THINK WHAT
IT FEELS LIKE THINKING.

SIMPLY OBSERVE AND LISTEN
WITH A GENTLE INTENTION TO
UNDERSTAND WHERE YOUR
DEMON IS COMING FROM

LET THE DEMON SAY WHAT
IT WANTS TO SAY... AND
THEN ASK YOUR DEMON TO
COME BACK ANOTHER TIME
FOR MORE CAKE AND TEA.

SCHEDULE REGULAR
TEA AND CAKE DATES
WITH YOUR DEMONS

SOMETIMES IN RETURN FOR YOUR UNDERSTANDING AND KINDNESS,
YOUR DEMON WILL GIVE YOU SOMETHING IN RETURN, SOMETHING
YOU CAN ONLY RECEIVE FOR HAVING THE COURAGE TO FACE YOUR
DARKNESS. A JEWEL, A BEAUTIFUL IDEA, A KEY TO A SECRET PLACE..

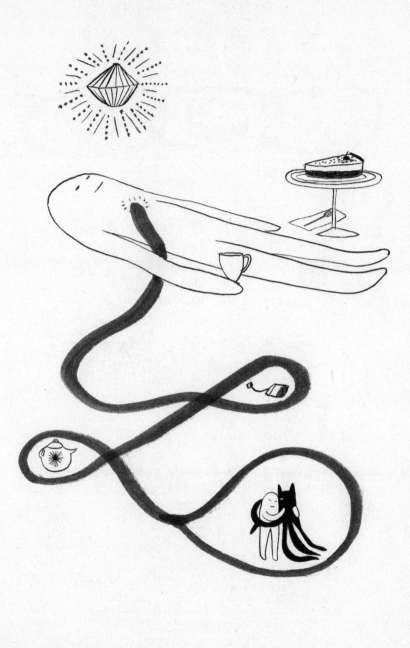

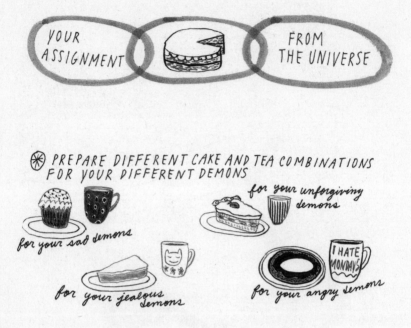

✳ PREPARE DIFFERENT CAKE AND TEA COMBINATIONS FOR YOUR DIFFERENT DEMONS

for your sad demons

for your unforgiving demons

for your jealous demons

for your angry demons

✳ ONCE YOU HAVE GOTTEN TO KNOW A GOOD MAJORITY OF YOUR DEMONS, ORGANIZE A DANCE PARTY.

REBECCA RUKEYSER

■

The Chinese Barracks

FROM ZYZZYVA

TEN DAYS AFTER the opening, the work schedules were already growing long. Betty explained it all to Hannah. You worked until your job was done, or you worked until someone stopped you. Jozef, who worked like a machine and chased overtime, never slept until he was ordered to. You were called a broken taco if you worked less than sixteen hours, a champion if you worked more than twenty-four. You compared hours of overtime. You compared hallucinations the way sailors compared tattoos. The shadows of the fresh-frozen house got animated late at night, roused by the clanging of the belt and the slap of the salmon as they fell into empty metal bins, or the slap of salmon as they fell against other salmon. They all saw them, creeping shadows and bright spots in their vision. When the salmon came in half rotted from Bristol Bay, the smell agitated the shadows even more, making them flap like bats. The dark circles under everyone's eyes grew luminous and sometimes bled like mascara down their cheeks. It was impossible to fall asleep with all this chattering movement: a foreman would grab someone as they stumbled and tell them to take five hours to sleep, but without fail when you lay down the rhythm of some chain clanking in the wind, some seagull, the waves, or the waving of the curtain would demand attention and there was a simple and perilous choice—to give it attention and remain awake, or to close your eyes and encounter the current of adrenaline that gave you horrible rhythmic dreams: dreams of conveyer belts of fish; when the conveyer belt stopped you scissor-kicked yourself awake. Everyone understood the slipperiness of the minds of sleepy people, and everyone kept up a watchful camaraderie that had as much to do with self-preservation as it did with brotherhood—it was part of the local currency of kindness, like Skittles and back rubs.

Maryanne, whose father owned boats out of Kelso, kept a supply of Metabolife under her bed and would slip a vitamin-sized pill into the pocket of her friends' hoodies if she saw them lagging on the slime line or growing emotional. The first night of the season, which stretched from the bell at midnight to noon the next day, she was giving out painters' dust masks to people who were cold. She handed one to Hannah, who had started shivering around five in the morning. Maryanne helped her put the dust mask on, tightening it in the back and saying:

"The mask will keep you warm, but the warm air around your mouth will make you sleepy, okay? It's an even trade." Hannah nodded, tears of gratitude in her eyes.

When Hannah's head started dipping after breakfast, Maryanne got sharp, and yanked the mask down to Hannah's chin.

"If you get dozy, take the mask off!" Hannah nodded doggedly. "Also, don't eat much at breakfast. If you're hungry, you're awake. Fill up on coffee." She clapped Hannah's cheek, hard enough to make her understand, gentle enough to get away with it.

As Maryanne moved away, Betty heard her muttering, "That girl has broken taco written all over her."

Betty had worked with Maryanne the year before, and she knew enough to treat her with respect. She knew well enough what "broken taco" meant, and she knew how to avoid becoming one: don't lag, tow the line, don't quit the cannery before the last sockeye run comes in. Betty wondered why they didn't just say "pussy." To be a broken taco was to be the lowest of the low: incompetent and spineless. Maryanne was the head of the roe house this year, working with the skinny Japanese men who wore white boots and smoked cigarettes as they packed boxes of Grade C roe to ship back to the low-end sushi buffets back home. Maryanne would pick only her friends to work in the roe house. It was the best position you could get: the roe house was away from the noise of the machinery in the cannery and the fresh-frozen house and you could play music and take breaks whenever and maybe learn Japanese.

In the first few days of the season, when everyone worked in the evening and got twelve hours off to sleep and everyone slept, even, often for ten of the twelve hours, there was a quiet held like an inhaled breath. The days were sodden and gloomy, and the bunkhouses stunk of wet wool and sleep and the sweetness of fish blood. The bunkhouses would grow louder by ten p.m., the sun still glowing behind the clouds, and by midnight everyone, flabby faced with sleep, would troop over to the cannery buildings. One of these first few nights, the Child brothers, Zack and J. Child, started working in fresh-frozen, and the season had its first fight and real beginning. The Child brothers were delinquents from Portland: Zack's face was pleasant, round, and ripe with acne, and J. Child was sullen, pointedly handsome. Both of them were already notorious for covering up the smell of fish blood with Axe body spray. Both of them had bought their plane tickets from Portland to Alaska on cannery credit.

It was Nusky, the veteran foreman, who assigned the Child brothers to fresh-frozen, stacking fish on pallets and moving them to the freezer. Everyone called Nusky "Leatherneck" behind his back because his neck was wrinkled and tanned from years on boats. That evening, the Child brothers sauntered in late and Nusky ran up to them and started yelling. Zack, cowed, backed away, but J. Child yelled back at him, calling him, in a voice louder than the machinery, "You leathernecked old bastard." Nusky stopped talking, grimaced a smile, and patted J. Child on the back. J. Child was wrong to make an enemy out of Nusky, because he put J. Child on duty stacking fish, and J. Child's carpal tunnel got so bad that the vein started to blacken. Everyone said that he had put things in that vein, though, and no one but Hannah, who later started sleeping with him, held him up as a pitiful martyr. Betty, who decided to cope with her exhaustion through anger, supported J. Child because she decided to hate Nusky.

Betty didn't get to work in the roe house. She was put in the sorting crew, separating the sockeye from the chum and pink salmon. It was lonely, the work started at midnight, and there were only girls for company. Hannah was on the crew, and Hannah's roommate, and a Polish or Ukrainian girl named Ilsa. There were a lot of internationals this year—the stringy Japanese and then all these Poles or Ukrainians. Some were returning: Jozef, the machine, was a favorite. The sorting crew left for work when everyone else was getting off and going to sleep. Every two hours they got ten minutes with a coffee pot and a selection of white bread and cold cuts—but even the coffee breaks were lonely for the sorting crew. Betty got angry. The fresh-frozen house was colder at night, and echoed.

Last season, when she was working in the cannery and was good friends with Maryanne, Betty was a favorite of Nusky and the other foremen who rode around on their bicycles with haughty impunity, regally nodding their heads. Bicycles were for the foremen only, but last season Betty hadn't known this, and when she had found a bicycle by the incinerator, rusted and dented and missing a saddle, she brought it back to the cannery. She saw Maryanne set her mouth in disapproval, but in the excitement of the moment she continued riding in circles around the dock. She set it down to go in to dinner, and when she came out of the mess hall she saw that someone had thrown it onto the rocks. Every low tide, the bicycle was revealed, hanging with seaweed. This season it was gone, dragged into the bay by some angry winter current. Now, standing at the sorting belt, watching the salmon rolling, squirming or stiff with rigor mortis, it seemed clear that Maryanne had thrown her bicycle off the dock. Maryanne kept her distance from Betty, and kept a close eye on her Metabolife. Sometimes Nusky would ride around late at night to check on the night crews at the sorting belt and the beach gang. He was still pleasant to Betty; he offered her chocolate. That was his bartering tool, his restorative—little fun-size candies he'd produce from his pocket with a flourish.

Jozef the machine had already abandoned sleeping. He came up, one night, to the sorting perch, unsteady on his feet, and Hannah asked in a small whisper if he was drunk. His eyes were red, he swatted at the handrail and missed.

"Is he—Is he drunk?"

Jozef lurched. He said nothing about why he was up there. He turned to address the conveyer belt of salmon and spoke in Polish. He had a ring of spittle, dried white, around his mouth. Hannah was watching him with a half-open mouth, backing away.

"He's not drunk, he's just sleepy." They all used the word "sleepy" to describe the various stages of exhaustion, because it sounded cute and chummy. Betty took Jozef's arm.

"Joe," she said, and Jozef wheeled: shocked, rocking. "Joe, get some sleep. It's time for bed." She helped him down the stairs. He walked in the opposite direction of the bunkhouses.

Back at the sorting belt, Hannah was stock still, glazed with concern.

"He's fine. He's just sleepy."

Betty understood Jozef's aversion to sleep: without sleep you got the elation, the slamming heart and joy that hammered like a headache, between the troughs of sadness and fear.

Hannah got hysterical when she was in the trough, weeping silently. Eyes scanning the moving shadows in her vision, she would ask, "What was that? What was that?" pointing at nothing. When she was happy, she was silly, giggling and recounting the snippets of her dreams. Betty's trough was anger—she spat and punched at the fish when she sorted them, sometimes pulling the softer ones apart. She engaged with what she saw moving at the edge of her sight, cursing. When she was happy she was also angry, but giddily so. The girls on the sorting crew tried to stay in rhythm, so that no more than one of them was spooked or anguished at a time. At coffee breaks they poured and sugared each other's coffee. Sometimes there were fights—they liked the fights best if they were between the Ukrainians or Poles, because they could sit and relax and pretend to interpret what they were saying as they hit each other. Hannah sat and rocked gently and giggled, and Betty balled her fists and said: "Yeah! Yeah!"

Her real name was Tess, short for Teresa, but she had changed it to Betty. The inspiration for this name change was her boyfriend. Her boyfriend's name was Carl, but his stage name was Mikey Mnoxide. He was never really onstage; he worked repairing motorcycles, and once, when they talked about their plans, he said that they should start a joint bike-repair shop and beauty parlor so that the Bettys could get their hair done while the Johnnys got their bikes looked after. He said it casually, in his bland Kansas accent, and she decided right then to go to beauty school. Now, to practice, she teased her hair into a bouffant, or a beehive, and drew on her eyes with liquid liner. She combed her boyfriend's hair back into a ducktail, using egg white to give it that sheen and hold. When she opened her beauty parlor next to the bike shop she would make sure that the only haircuts the Johnnys could get were ducktails and crew cuts. She never called him Carl, but she never got used to calling him Mikey, so she called him "you." He called her "the little lady."

Even at the cannery, she did her hair before work. She brought a can of hairspray and a jar of pomade. She told the girls on the crew about her boyfriend; she called him "my boyfriend." She brought a tape deck, and a collection of tapes, all doo-wop. When she was in a trough, another girl, usually Hannah, would play "My Boyfriend's Back" to cheer her up. When Hannah was acting spooky, Betty played her "The Leader of the Pack." After work some days, they would sit and listen to the tape deck in Betty's room. Their personalities changed at each song, and grew wistful during the love songs and hard, almost manic, when the music was raunchy. They always skipped "Last Kiss," because it was about death and made the shadows in the corners of the room flutter with ghostly portents.

There was a twenty-four-hour fishing closure in early July; the fisherman pulled their nets and hurried their holds to the cannery and all the crews worked at triple speed to make the most of the holiday. No one had plans to sleep. The day was sunny, and at meal breaks everyone ate quickly and lay outside on the sun-warmed deck and on the driftwood benches. The boys took off their shirts and the girls rolled up their sleeves and tucked their hems up into their bras.

Everyone was elated, passing out cigarettes and Skittles and running down to the boats with folded bills for the fisherman and returning with plastic bottles of Black Velvet tucked inside their waterproof coveralls. The hillsides were steaming in the heat. Nusky appeared with a bowl of wild berries and offered them out. A group of fishermen walked down the dock and Nusky jumped on his bicycle to run them off. Fishermen weren't allowed in the cannery because of the reputation they had. They were allowed in the shower room, and then sent packing. The boys at the cannery eyed them with suspicion; the girls watched them walk away—slowly, sea-legged.

The last fish were packed in the early evening, leaving the entire night and next day free. There were plans for a bonfire. Betty took a shower and teased her hair up into a bouffant, applied her eyeliner, applied her lipstick, and stood in front of the mirror of the bathroom puffing her lips, turning and looking at herself over one shoulder with heavy-lidded eyes. Maryanne came into the bathroom and whistled, sarcastic.

"What do you think you're doing with all that? Where do you think you are right now?"

Betty clicked her nails against the counter by the sink, a motion that seemed aloof, weary.

"You're not Marilyn Monroe." Maryanne was wearing Carhartt overalls. "You're not in Hollywood. This isn't 1950." Betty had brought her tape deck into the bathroom with her. "Blue Moon" was playing. She turned toward the mirror and looked at the reflection of Maryanne.

"What are you rebelling against, Johnny? *What do you got?*"

"What?" Maryanne asked.

"What are you rebelling against, Johnny?" Betty repeated. Hannah walked in, holding her towel. She smiled.

"What do you got?" Hannah said brightly.

Betty had watched *The Wild One* with her boyfriend, and liked to quote it. She had quoted it to Hannah during one of the first shifts, and now it had become a byword, a call and response that helped Betty when she was angry and Hannah when she was scared. When Betty was choking on imagined rage at four in the morning, Hannah would ask her:

"What are you rebelling against, Johnny?" and Betty would scream, echoing against the sorting bins and the freezer doors:

"What do you got!"

* * *

Betty had let everyone at the cannery know that she had a boyfriend. She let Nusky know, she let the fishermen know, she let the Child brothers know. It didn't matter, as it turned out. Nusky still brought her chocolates and the Child brothers still offered her Sudafed when she was nodding. She talked to her boyfriend on the phone every Tuesday. She told him that she was staying true, which sounded mournful and sexy. When a fisherman off the *Kendra H* told her that she was wearing some mean jeans, she turned and told him, "I have a boyfriend back home, and I'm staying true to him." He said that her jeans were still mean, and winked. She looked down in a way that she thought was demure.

Hannah was demure. Hannah, without thinking, wrung her hands. Betty told her that she should wear gloves, or pearls, or both. It was a surprise then, when Hannah started sleeping with J. Child — J. Child who had run away with the carnival and had a junky's sharp good looks and wet eyes and ate Sudafed by the box and mixed cocoa powder into his coffee like a real degenerate. They left the July opening bonfire together, J. Child leading Hannah by her hand and Hannah trailing behind, demure.

After the initial surprise, though, Betty decided that it made perfect sense. Hannah was a good girl who studied primary education and basically went to church. J. Child had a delinquent's pronounced, slutty lower lip and probably rode a motorcycle back home. Hannah was blond and J. Child was dark. J. Child was wounded, his carpal tunnel growing more severe by the day, and Hannah sat by him at coffee breaks and massaged his wrist. Hannah, who never talked back, defended J. Child heatedly when Maryanne said his veins were turning black because he had shot up.

"You don't know the first thing about him!" Hannah snapped. Betty started calling J. Child her "man."

"You stick up for your man, Hannah," Betty told her. "Nobody knows him like you do."

By mid-July the sun was setting completely and there was real nighttime. The pink salmon run had started, and the cannery was running around the clock. A forklift driver fell asleep on the job and ran into the side of the stockroom. Jozef the machine had fallen asleep after thirty hours at work and woke up with a high fever. He was flown out of the cannery and back into town, and the rumor was that he was going to be returned to Poland or the Ukraine. For all his hard work, he was now considered a broken taco. Zack, J. Child's brother, slept with Ilsa, and fell asleep in the women's bunkhouse and was facing disciplinary action. A girl named Melanie had sliced her hand with a gutting knife and was now working in the laundry room, and the cannery medic was watching the veins in her arm for signs of blood poisoning. She cried a lot. Maryanne speculated that she would also become a broken taco. J. Child was the next in line. His hand had cramped into a fist, and he had to stack fish one-armed, which slowed down his crew. Nusky would come into the fresh-frozen room and dismiss J. Child after just a few hours' work. He wouldn't even speak to J. Child; he'd just jerk his thumb toward the exit. There was no mention of assigning J. Child to an easier job. Hannah would watch J. Child walk out the cannery doors and lower her head over the sorting belt, her tears spilling onto the fish.

"What are you rebelling against, Johnny?" Betty would ask.

"What do you got?"

J. Child got down to working six hours a day, and then three, and then Nusky told him, in a dangerously polite voice, that he didn't need to come in to work and could take a day to rest. It was implied that there were no more hours left for him. He sat in his bunkroom; he napped. The rest of the employees watched him suspiciously as his drawn face fleshed out with sleep. They rolled their eyes as he walked from the mess hall back to the bunkhouse as they all returned to work. Nusky looked contented. They were angry.

"They're just jealous!" said Hannah, her eyes wild. The shift was in its eighteenth hour.

"Don't—" started Betty, but it was too late.

"You're just jealous! You're just tired and jealous," Hannah said, loudly, to no one in particular. Maryanne looked at Hannah and Betty levelly. Nusky looked, too. Betty was aware that she hadn't had time to shower in the last three days, and the pomade was heavy on her scalp. Hannah's mascara had smeared down her cheeks, and little black seeds of it clung in the corner of her eyes. Hannah startled, turning after something scurrying out of her field of vision. Her teeth were gritted, squeaking. She turned again, trying to catch sight of whatever it was.

J. Child quit three days later. In a fit of charity, Nusky released Zack from probation. Hannah cried, staring at the shadows detaching from the walls. Nusky watched her stumble to the coffee cart and sent her off to sleep. He gave her twelve hours off and she slept for most of them, returning mute and guarded. Maryanne started a tally of broken tacos on the corkboard in the women's bunkhouse. Betty overheard her say that she figured that Hannah was next.

The next few days were clear, but instead of sunning themselves on the deck everyone went into the bunkhouses to nap during meal breaks. People were having a hard time getting to sleep—the bunkhouses were full of the sounds of groans and slaps as they swatted at black flies or shapes they assumed were black flies. When they did sleep, they overslept. They blamed the season. They blamed the machinery. They blamed the Poles or Ukrainians. Betty and Hannah agreed that it was Nusky's fault, and Maryanne's as well. Maryanne was in line for a promotion, and would probably get a bicycle next season. Betty maintained that if everyone had a bicycle, they could all get from the bunkhouse to the cannery faster, and average at least a couple more hours of sleep a week. They talked and talked, quickly, so they wouldn't become sleepy. They made plans to change the cannery system, plans to get revenge on Nusky, plans to expose the corruption they imagined ran rampant in the fishing industry. They started talking about piracy; they talked about arson. When Betty saw Hannah's face start to expand, and then contract, she lay down, closing her eyes against the nausea. She woke up to Nusky shaking her by the shoulders, telling her gently that it was time to go to work.

They sat apart from the others at coffee breaks. Betty was aware of a sour bedding smell coming off of Hannah. Hannah's hair hung lankly at the sides of her face.

"I think I'm a broken taco, Betty."

"What are you rebelling against, Johnny?"

"I think I really am." Hannah spoke dully.

"Listen, let's bust out of here at lunch. They won't miss us, and if they do, they won't be able to do anything. We'll go to the Chinese barracks."

"What are the Chinese barracks?"

"Abandoned. A group of kids went there last year and said it was fun. We need some fun. We need to cut loose."

The Chinese barracks were a group of buildings clustered behind the cannery. Legend had it that the cannery had employed a hundred Chinese back when they first opened, and the Chinese, mid-season, exhausted and homesick, had all committed suicide rather than work another day.

"The kings of broken tacos!" Betty said.

They all hanged themselves, legend had it, all in the same morning. The cannery had had to shut down for the remainder of the season. The Chinese had left a long suicide note that spoke for all of them: they wanted their bodies to be returned to China, and they wanted their wages to be sent to their families. But the misers who ran the cannery, who had worked the Chinese to death, and whose profits were now suffering because of the mass suicide, pocketed the Chinese workers' wages and incinerated their bodies rather than spend the money to ship them home.

The exterior walls of the barracks were warped and splintering. Betty pointed to an exposed beam in the second story.

"So they all hung themselves from that beam up there, I guess. And the cannery was screwed! They're said"—and Betty raised her voice into a falsetto—"to haunt these barracks to this very day! Although that's stupid," she said, watching Hannah's face for discomfort. But Hannah's expression was placid.

"Let's go inside," Hannah said.

"I don't know that we should," Betty said. "It's really scary in there, I guess. There's a room with no sunlight, and noises."

"I want to go inside," Hannah said.

The inside of the Chinese barracks was painted the same industrial pale green as the rest of the cannery. There were beer cans on the floors, and a scuttling sound that Betty soon realized was the sound of the water lapping against the pylons below the floor. The floor was open in several spots, and through the holes they could see the water glinting. Hannah moved delicately about, holding her hands out to the sides to steady herself.

"Here's that room!" she called back to Betty, her voice merry. Inside the open doorway was a room without any light whatsoever. There was no window or airshaft, it was one of the few rooms whose walls had stayed intact. Betty couldn't see to the back, she could only see the dim outline of a metal bed frame. A ceramic saucer lay in the doorway.

"Boo," said Hannah.

They didn't sleep before the next shift, they sat and plotted Nusky's downfall. They would poison his chocolates with a syringe, right through the wrapping. They'd fix the brakes on his bicycle. They would—they even drew diagrams—construct a trapdoor above the sorting bins, and he would fall in and drown, or be suffocated, under tons of writhing salmon. In the event that they got caught, Betty figured that Hannah could tell the press how Nusky had mistreated her man, and their hearts would melt.

They were both broken tacos before the week was over. Betty threw her rubber gloves down on the deck and told Nusky, "I've had it with this place! I'm through!" Nusky told her to sleep on it, but she refused. Hannah simply went to sleep and didn't get up for twenty-six hours, and arrived at Nusky's office with her bag packed and told him that she wanted to go home.

Betty went home to her boyfriend, slept late into the day, and when the money from the cannery ran out, she got a job cleaning rooms at the Red Lion. Hannah went home to her parents' house. Through the end of that summer, they would call each other and talk about what Betty found in the drawers of the extended stay rooms, but mostly they talked about the cannery. In the autumn Hannah went back to school and got a part-time job teaching at a kindergarten, and Betty enrolled in beauty school. They talked on the phone every month. It was around Christmas when Hannah asked Betty what the foreman's name had been. She remembered it as sounding Polish, or maybe Ukrainian, but she had forgotten. The name had reminded her of a pet's name.

RACHEL KAADZI GHANSAH

■

If He Hollers Let Him Go

FROM *The Believer*

ALTHOUGH THE CITY OF DAYTON is small and has been hit hard by the decline of industry, in Xenia and Yellow Springs the land is green, fecund, and alive, even in the relentless heat of summer. Xenia is three miles from where the first private black college, Wilberforce, opened, in 1856, to meet the educational needs of the growing population of freed blacks that crossed the Ohio River. Yellow Springs, a stop on the Underground Railroad, was initially established as a utopian community in 1825. In 1852, Horace Mann founded Antioch College and served as its president. During the '50s and '60s, Antioch and Yellow Springs were hamlets of anti-McCarthyism and antiwar and civil rights activism. Today there are a lot of hippies and there's even more tie-dye. Between the villages, you can drive over rolling hills and pastures and not see another car for miles, and only far off on the horizon will you be able to spot a farmhouse.

I spent a week in this part of Ohio, and during my stay I was invited to do all sorts of things with people of all kinds—rich and poor, white and black. I was invited to go flying, dig for worms at midnight, and plant raspberry bushes. My request to drive a tractor was turned down, not because I don't know how to drive but because the tractor had been put away. In Ohio, there is space for people to do what they want. There is a lot of land, plenty of it. This is where enslaved people ran to, certain that they had finally evaded capture. This is where America's first prominent black poet, Paul Laurence Dunbar, wrote

"We Wear the Mask." And somewhere in the midst of it all is Dave Chappelle's home.

From above, everything seems smaller and less complicated—or at the very least things are put into perspective. From a plane at thirty-five thousand feet it was much easier for me to understand why Dave Chappelle quit his hit TV show, *Chappelle's Show*, and said good-bye to all that, and didn't stop until he got home to Yellow Springs, Ohio. When news of his decision to cease filming the third season of the show first made headlines, there were many spectacular rumors. He had quit the show without any warning. He had unceremoniously ditched its cocreator, his good friend Neal Brennan, leaving him stranded. Chappelle was now addicted to crack. He had lost his mind. The most insane speculation I saw was posted on a friend's Facebook page at 3 a.m. A website had alleged that a powerful cabal of black leaders—Oprah Winfrey, Bill Cosby, and others—were so offended by Chappelle's use of the *n*-word that they had him intimidated and banned. The controversial "Niggar Family" sketch, where viewers were introduced to an Ozzie and Harriet–like 1950s suburban, white, upper-class family named "the Niggars," was said to have set them off. The weirdest thing was that people actually went for such stories. *Chappelle's brief moment in television had been that incendiary.* It didn't matter that Chappelle himself had told Oprah on national television that he had quit wholly of his own accord.

Chappelle didn't seem to understand that these rumors of drugs and insanity, though paternalistic, were just the result of disbelief and curiosity. Like Salinger's retreat from fame, Chappelle's departure demanded an explanation: how could any human being have the willpower, the chutzpah, the determination to refuse the amount of money rumored to be Chappelle's next paycheck: fifty million dollars. Say it with me now. Fifty. Million. Dollars. When the dust settled, and Chappelle had done interviews with Oprah and James Lipton in an attempt to recover his image and tell his story, two things became immediately apparent: Dave Chappelle is without a doubt his generation's smartest comic, and the hole he left in comedy is so great that even ten years later very few people can accept the reason he later gave for leaving fame and fortune behind: he wanted to find a simpler way of life.

* * *

You know you must be doing something right if old people like you.

— Dave Chappelle

Dave Chappelle was in his teens when he first appeared on the comedy club circuit. He was twenty-three when he and his friend Neal Brennan wrote *Half Baked*, a now-classic stoner flick about four hapless friends who try to enter the drug-dealing game so they can get bail money for their friend Kenny, who has landed in jail after inadvertently killing a cop's horse. They were young and had no expectations except to have fun and be funny. They certainly had no idea *Chappelle's Show*, another collaboration, would become the most talked-about show on television. But early into the show's first season, critics at the *New York Times* would take notice of Chappelle's "kind of laid-back indignation" and his "refusal to believe that ignoring racial differences will make anyone's life better." What Brennan and Chappelle were doing every week was so unusual that the *Times* declared that "it almost looks like a renaissance for African-American humor on television."

Chappelle's comedy found fans in many worlds. At a recent barbecue in Philadelphia, a friend of the host dutifully but disinterestedly interrogated me about my life, and got excited only when my mother let it slip that I was working on a piece about Dave Chappelle. "Aw, man. I miss that guy," he said. "He was my friend. I really felt like he was my friend." I hear this a lot, usually from white people, and usually from white people without many black friends — like this seventy-year-old comparative literature professor in Birkenstocks. Part of what made the show so ingenious was that Chappelle's racial invective found friends in strange places. With a regularly broadcasted television show, Chappelle was finally able to display what writer and activist Kevin Powell described in an *Esquire* profile as a "unique capacity to stand out and blend in, to cross boundaries and set up roadblocks." Almost overnight, Chappelle became America's black friend. He was a polyglot. He told Powell that, growing up, he used to "hang out with the Jewish kids, black kids, and Vietnamese immigrants," and it was apparent that Chappelle had used these experiences to become America's consul and translator for all things racial. More than any comic of his generation, he lanced the boil of how race works and also prodded at how nuanced race had become. "Sometimes convention and what's funny butt heads," Chappelle confessed to *Entertainment Weekly* in 2004, "and when [they do], we just err on the side of what's funny."

Besides race, three things make Dave Chappelle's comedy innovative and universal: wit, self-deprecation, and toilet humor. This is the same triumvirate that makes Philip Roth's writing so original. Woody Allen's movies, too. Chappelle had a keen sense of the archetypal nature of race, and understood just as acutely how people work on a very basic level. In a *Chappelle's Show* sketch about the reality show *Trading Spouses*, a black man sits on a toilet in a white family's house and flips through a copy of *People* magazine while taking a dump. He looks up: "Who the fuck is Renée Zellwedger?" In another sketch, a stodgy, Waspy white man (Chappelle in whiteface) lies in bed with an attractive black woman in classy lingerie. He wants her. But he wants to make love with his pajamas on.

Chappelle did such a good job of truth-telling, on every subject, that nobody knew what to do when he just stopped talking. In no way did his quitting conform to our understanding of the comic's one obligation: to be funny. To talk to us. To entertain us. To make us laugh. We aren't used to taking no for an answer, to being rejected, especially not by the people who are supposed to make us smile. Especially not by black men who are supposed to make us smile. And yet Chappelle did just that. And so, like everyone, I wondered what had happened. What had happened, and, more so, what had brought Chappelle to—and kept him in—Yellow Springs? At a stand-up appearance in Sacramento in 2004, a frustrated Chappelle lashed out at his hecklers from the stage, yelling, "You people are stupid!" So what was it about this small college town—where hippies slipped me bags of Girl Scout cookies, where Tibetan jewelry stores and fair-trade coffee shops dotted the main street, and where kindly white ladies crossed the street to tell me my wild hair was giving them life—that made it more satisfying than celebrity or fame?

* * *

Even before Chappelle himself, politely but firmly, turned down my interview request, I had begun to suspect that the keys to everything he was doing politically and culturally—block parties with Erykah Badu, videos with Mos Def and De La Soul, and campaigning for young black candidates like Kevin Powell, who stressed social responsibility—were interests deeply informed by his parents. His mother is a historian and his father was a dean of community services and a professor of music. Edward Countryman, the American historian, has pointed out some worthwhile context: "Until John Hope Franklin joined the University of Chicago in 1964, no black person held a senior rank in a major history department that encouraged research and trained doctoral students." But Chappelle, like Kanye West, grew up in a home where black activism and black leftist thought were the languages of the household. No wonder, then, that both Chappelle and West have wrestled so bitterly and publicly with their sense of responsibility to and also their failure to meet those same obligations. "It's a dilemma," Chappelle told Kevin Powell. "It's something that is unique to us. White people, white artists, are allowed to be individuals. But we always have this greater struggle that we at least have to keep in mind somewhere." Chappelle's throwback kind of celebrity and his many concerns about "social responsibility" are faintly reminiscent of the work that his mother, Professor Yvonne Seon, did in the '60s and '70s as a scholar of the Negritude movement.

In 1939, the poet Aimé Césaire would return to his island homeland of Martinique, in the Caribbean, after spending years in Europe. The move would prompt his book-length piece of prose poetry, which André Breton would call a masterpiece: *Cahier d'un retour au pays natal* (*Notebook of a Return to the Native Land*). Césaire, a gifted writer, was sent to Europe as a young man to study in the center of the French-speaking world. Once there, he reunited with his childhood friend Léon Damas and a young Senegalese poet and future president named Léopold Sédar Senghor. Together, as black men in France, they attempted to educate themselves in a culture where the word *negre* was inherently a pejorative. To cope while living under the double bind of colonialism and racism, they created "Negritude," literally a "Blackness" movement.

Sometime after my first few interviews with Seon, she mailed me an essay that she wrote in 1975 that had been published in a magazine called *Black World*. The issue features Muhammad Ali on the cover, and in her essay Seon describes Negritude as being more of a sensibility than a literary movement that is fixed in the past. To me, more than anything, it voices the dilemma her son would experience decades later:

> When one speaks of Negritude, one may be speaking of either of two quite different things. In its narrow definition, Negritude is a literary movement of the late 1930's. In this restricted sense, it represents the use by Black French-speaking poets, of the techniques of French Impressionism to break away from French culture and to give creative expression to an inner, African self that had been hidden away. But the broader, more important meaning of Negritude has to do with a process isolated and identified by these poets. It is the process by which Black people, who have been cut off from and made to learn to know themselves again, come to accept themselves, and begin to believe in (i.e. to value) themselves.

Seon was born in Washington, DC. Her father was a fair-skinned man who was adopted by a black woman. Although he self-identified as black, by all accounts he looked Greek. He was also blind. On the day Martin Luther King Jr. was shot, Chappelle's grandfather was on a city bus and overheard rumblings of a beat-down about to happen to a white fellow on his bus. That guy's gonna be in trouble, he thought. He did not realize that *he* was the white man being threatened. This anecdote about his grandfather would inspire Chappelle's "Clayton Bigsby" sketch—the unforgettable short mockumentary about a blind white supremacist who does not know he is black.

Beginning in 1944, Seon's mother worked as an administrative assistant for the NAACP. Seon tells me about early memories of sitting outside of NAACP meetings and waving hello to the organization's chief counsel, Thurgood Marshall, who was working on the cases that would dismantle the Jim Crow laws. In the '50s, when Africa began to hammer off its colonial shackles, her family found itself in the front lines as black American allies.

"My mother was very much one of the people who was paying attention to what was going on in Africa; she knew the ambassadors, we went to the celebrations of independence. So we were following

Africa and that part of the involvement, just watching what they were doing. We were aware of the avant-garde, the people who were questing for liberation in Africa."

Seon was twenty-two when she met Patrice Lumumba, the young, energetic prime minister of the Congo, at a society mixer. That same afternoon, he offered her a job. She went home and asked her parents for permission, and they came back and talked with Lumumba. It was agreed she would fly to the Congo and help Lumumba, who, unlike Ghana's President Kwame Nkrumah, didn't have a college degree or much of a background in government. Instead, Lumumba was a beer-selling postmaster who had crushed one of the most dehumanizing, despotic colonial regimes with pure rhetoric and was now learning how to establish a new nation. She made plans to leave in the winter, but on December 1, Patrice Lumumba was arrested. "The hardest part was not knowing," she says. In the weeks to come they found out: Lumumba had been murdered, most likely by American and Belgian operatives; Lumumba's pan-Africanism, his vision of a unified Congo, and his utter lack of patience had alarmed the West so much they had had him killed. (Belgium apologized in 2002 for its "moral responsibility" in the murder.)

But here is the part you should remember if you want to understand Dave Chappelle's unbridled wit and compulsion to be free: a young Yvonne Seon still decided to take off for the Congo, not knowing what to expect, but knowing that her contact there—a man who was being mourned by Malcolm X and Che Guevara, whose death incited outraged protests all around the world—had been murdered. She needed to fulfill her promise to the dead man and his hope for a "history of dignity" for African people. "We were very much aware that if America was going to have its independence, our independence was tied to the independence of the African countries. And I personally believed at the time that African Americans would not be able to get civil rights until Africa had won its independence, that the two things were interrelated." Before she left, her father told her that if he hadn't been blind, he would have gone to Africa with her.

When she returned to the States two years later, Seon attended graduate school and met her husband, William David Chappelle (who died in 1998), in those times of great hope and unrest. In the late '60s, they came to Yellow Springs to visit friends for the weekend, and, besotted with the town's counterculture, diversity, and leftist vibe, her husband didn't want to leave. When Chappelle was two, his parents divorced, and his father returned to Yellow Springs to teach at Antioch while his mother stayed in Washington, DC, with the children. Dave Chappelle has said of his childhood, "We were like the broke Huxtables. There were books around the house; everybody was educated to a college level. We used to have a picture of Malcolm X in Ghana. Last Poets records. We were poor but we were cultured."

When they reached the age where he and his siblings could start "running the streets," his mother sent them to Yellow Springs to live with their father. Chappelle returned when he was fourteen. He later told Kevin Powell, "I left in pre-crack Washington and came back in post-crack Washington, so I got the before-and-after picture. It was literally jolting, like, what the fuck happened? My freshman year of high school, over five hundred kids my age were murdered."

In addition to the typical growing pains that accompany adolescence, Chappelle found himself having to navigate what he described to James Lipton as being "a very segregated city, especially at that time. Statistically speaking to this day—statistically speaking—there's not one poor white person in Washington." DC was a far cry from Yellow Springs, and he struggled to adjust to the culture shock. It was his mother who gave him a copy of a magazine with Bill Cosby on the cover. Chappelle felt instantaneously connected to the comic. When he finished reading, he says, "I put it down. And it was like: I'mma be a comedian. And, man, I'm telling you, I could see it so clearly, so clearly, man—this is it. I was so excited I told my family, 'I have an announcement to make: I'm gonna be a comedian.'"

Because he was fourteen and his mother took him to gigs around the city, other comics called him "the kid." He remembers telling his grandmother once before he went onstage, "You might hear me say some things that you might not want to hear your grandson say . . . And she said, 'Just relax and do that shit.' I was like, Wow. I had never heard her curse!"

Over lunch in Ohio, Seon tells me, with the same optimism as every other time we've talked, about the years she spent in Kinshasa. Her stories are populated with dangers she still seems impervious to: Évariste Kimba, a prime minister who soon succeeded Lumumba, was also executed, and the Congo was at the start of a long period of war. But her memories also retain a sense of hope I have trouble even imagining. "You know," she says, "I've never gone back to the Congo, because it is difficult, you know, to look back at a place that was so full of possibilities and see what has happened. That is always hard to see, isn't it?"

There is a strange moment in James Lipton's interview with Chappelle where the comedian discusses his decision not to attend college. "I was the first person in my family not to go to college, that had not been a slave." The audience laughs. I can never tell if they realize that he is serious.

In his fantastic profile of Muhammad Ali, Hunter S. Thompson writes that "the Champ, after all, had once hurled his Olympic gold medal into the Ohio River, in a fit of pique at some alleged racial insult in Louisville." The medal was a symbol of a white world that Ali "was already learning to treat with a very calculated measure of public disrespect." Like most people of the post–civil rights generation, I think that Chappelle, whose family had long been free, educated, leftist, and radical, had hoped that his success would not need to follow that same militant path. Despite the fact that four in ten white Americans do not have any black friends, and more pressingly, that all too many workplaces are integrated only in theory, I think Chappelle hoped that he could bring Yellow Springs' open-mindedness to the world. For a while he did, but then he became aware that his brand of humor was not without a history and was forced to acknowledge its context. Next came conferences with suits at Comedy Central about his use of the *n*-word and his being chastised in the press, and finally he was humiliated and called insane. Like Thompson once wrote of Ali, Chappelle was put through "one of the meanest and most shameful ordeals any prominent American has ever endured." Without knowing his history, Dave Chappelle's decision to figuratively toss his gold medal into the Ohio River does seem like a bizarre, illogical act that abbreviated a successful career on its ascent. But was it illogical? Hardly. Revolutionary? Possibly. To turn his back on Hollywood, to walk away from the spotlight because it was turning him into a man he didn't want to be—a man without dignity—was a move that was, in a way, Chappelle's birthright, his own unwieldy kind of Negritude.

There's no friends like the old friends.   —James Joyce

"I wasn't crazy but it is incredibly stressful," Dave Chappelle explained to Oprah on *The Oprah Winfrey Show* in 2006. With his mother sitting in the front row, he was trying to explain why ten months earlier—without explanation to his wife, to Brennan, or to his bosses at Comedy Central—he had quit his show.

"I would go to work on the show and I felt awful every day," he said. "I felt like some kind of prostitute or something. If I feel so bad, why keep on showing up to this place? I'm going to Africa." Five years have passed since that interview, and Brennan has gone on to write for President Obama at the White House Correspondents' Dinner and to work with comedians like Amy Schumer and Chris Rock. Brennan repeats to me how much he respects Dave, but he tells me that being "trashed" by Chappelle on *Oprah* still bothers him. In 2011, he told a reporter: "You know, for a black artist that's beloved to go on TV and say he was victimized by a white corporate structure, that is like white-people nectar, it's like white liberal nectar, like, 'Oh my god, this young black man has been victimized.' Dave did real well from the show, you know. There was a huge benefit to Dave. So the idea that somehow he was victimized . . . My experience was he wasn't victimized and that it was a matter of pressure and needing to eject from the pressure."

Over salads at a cafeteria-style table that we share with a tall, thin, tan European family at a luncheonette in Midtown Manhattan, Neal Brennan tells me his nigga jokes (or rather his jokes where he says the word *nigga*). Two weeks earlier, in New Orleans, I had hung out in the whitewashed wings of the Civic Theatre and watched Brennan direct his first Comedy Central one-hour special. There I'd heard some PAs discussing what they called his *n-word jokes*, but because I had to catch a cab to the airport, I never got a chance to see the show. In New York, sitting a few feet from each other, I tried to prepare myself for the inevitable, but each time I thought about it my hands had instinctively cocked and curled into fists under the table.

Brennan says *Chappelle's Show* told two stories: "What it was like to be a dude, and what it was like to be a black dude." He grew up in the Philadelphia suburbs and is a former altar boy, the youngest of ten kids in a large Irish Catholic family. He is very thin and he has what he himself calls a "roguish charm." Brennan is really, really funny and quick. He wears a uniform of jeans, sneakers, and a T-shirt. He has large ears and wide eyes and spiky hair that is often gelled to a point, cockatoo-style. As we talk, I realize that I recognize many of his expressions from the show. Brennan tells me that as a writer he knows how to shape and structure a joke. He directs the jab. "My job and life are basically just saying, 'Hey, say this.' Say, 'Doctor says I needs a backiotomy.'"

Brennan met Chappelle when they were both eighteen. Everyone else in the New York comedy scene was in their late twenties. "Comedy," he shrugs and sighs deeply, "is incredibly racially integrated. Probably the most diverse workplace there is, and it's not clannish — there is a table at the Comedy Cellar where we all go, and you can look around some nights and it is Mexican, white, Jewish, black. You are friends based on your comedy ability, not based on your age or something. Like race is almost irrelevant." Brennan studied film at NYU during the day, and at night he stood outside and worked as the annoying guy who yells, "Hey! Come inside and check out the comedy show!" Chappelle had moved to New York to do stand-up and was working in Washington Square Park, learning from a street comic named Charlie Barnett.

Neal and Dave had similar sensibilities: they liked the same movies (Spike Lee Joints), the same music (hip-hop), the same TV shows (*Family Ties*). It was kismet. "Chappelle had been on all of these pilots and had been paired with all of the wrong writers, wrong actors; like no thought to chemistry. Just: 'He's a hot writer and you're a hot stand-up,'" Brennan says. *Entertainment Weekly* would say of Chappelle's first sitcom: "The worst thing about *Buddies* is that it makes racism boring."

Years passed, and Brennan left New York to live in Los Angeles and write comedy for Nickelodeon, but he stayed in touch with Chappelle. Their film, *Half Baked*, was totally unexpected and came about quickly. In fact, they had only a month to outline it. "We pitched it. Universal sold it in, like, March, and we were shooting it in July.

Which is crazy. Really crazy. But we didn't know anything because we were, like, twenty-three."

From the moment they arrived on the set, Brennan says he knew that something was off about the production. "First of all, it should have looked more like *Kids* and *Trainspotting*. So we get there and Dave turns to me and asks, 'Is this how you pictured the set?' And I go, 'Nope.' And he goes, 'Me neither.'" Neal shrugs again. "But again, twenty-three. And there is just nothing you can do. I'm not a fan of the movie. Dave's not a fan of the movie." Directed by Tamra Davis, *Half Baked* was released in 1998, the same weekend as *Titanic*, and flopped. Brennan and Chappelle stopped talking for a while. These silences are themes in their friendship. I ask him why. "I guess not wanting to acknowledge responsibility, negative association, you want to leave the scene of the crime. Like having a child die and the parents want to get a divorce."

It would be the first defeat in a series of many. After *Half Baked*, Dave bought his "Fuck you, Hollywood" farm, sixty-five acres of land in Ohio. He was living there and having a tough time professionally. *Killin' Them Softly*, his one-hour special, came out in 1999. Brennan is blunt about it: "No one cared. But *Killin' Them Softly* is a great one-hour special.

"Dave called his manager the Monday after it aired," Brennan says, "and [his manager] goes, 'Sorry, man, the phone's not ringing.'" That is how it was. It cemented a sense within Brennan and Chappelle that show business is built upon what's hot and what's not, and, worse, that show business is random, anti-intellectual, and often pretty far behind. "We were the underdogs. We were left for dead and came from behind and did CPR on ourselves." He pauses and peers over the heads of the towheaded European family sitting next to us. "To give you a sense of things, this is how little respect Dave was getting: we pitched *Chappelle's Show* to one station and they literally looked at us like we were lepers. Like, because Chris Rock had just gone off the air, they were like, 'Chris Rock is everything and you're nothing, Dave.' Then we walk up Fifth Avenue and pitch it to Comedy Central. They buy it. And it becomes the show. And now *Chappelle's Show* has sold three million copies on DVD." (It remains the world's top-selling TV-to-DVD series.)

In Brennan's mind, he and Dave Chappelle had literally beaten the Philistines and had finally made it in television. But, as Chappelle told Oprah, this was not at all true. When Brennan discusses the demise of the show, he discusses it as a conflict about renegotiating the terms of the third season. Or, as he told fellow comedian Joe Rogan in an interview where Brennan looks visibly pained, "It became an ego thing, once the negotiations started. It was the worst period of my life . . . but as Lorne Michaels once said, 'Comedians don't like admitting they have help.'" Brennan says that at the height of the contretemps, they both said awful things to each other. When Chappelle discusses his exit, he does not deny that things went haywire, but he attributes it mostly to his discomfort with the material, the politics of the show, and the climate on the set. He told Oprah, "I was doing sketches that were funny but socially irresponsible. It was encouraged. I felt I was deliberately being encouraged and I was overwhelmed."

I ask an older friend who is black and a theorist of sorts what he thinks about *Chappelle's Show*. I get an answer that surprises me with its vitriol: "Chappelle was at the end of the one-hundred-and-fifty-year minstrel cycle and fifty years after the height of the civil rights movement and ten years after the beginning of Southern hip-hop and in the midst of the most coonish aspects of dirty South hip-hop. He wrung the last bits of potential energy out of taboos that had been in guarded reserve that show niggas as violent, unintelligent, unlettered beasts. And he portrayed niggas that way (while maintaining an ironic distance from those caricatures). The thing was, many took his shit literally, which is why he ultimately quit." I go back and watch "The Mad Real World" sketch, a spoof of the MTV reality show. In the sketch a white man moves into a house full of black roommates and, in the ensuing weeks, his father is stabbed while visiting, his blond girlfriend is turned out by two guys, and the living room is regularly transformed into a makeshift nightclub. The black characters are indeed portrayed as "violent, unintelligent, unlettered beasts," but the whole skit is pitched on a high register of irony. When I ask Brennan how he dealt with backlash about the show's use of the *n*-word and its edgy racial humor, he objects. "As much as people say that about *Chappelle's Show*, no one ever got pissed. People ask, 'Were you worried?' and it's like, no, because it was all founded on real, empirical

observations and lived lives. Like, that 'Real World' sketch was a discussion we had been having for a decade about black people on *The
Real World*. The guy who pulled the blanket off the girl was Dave's
best friend. So we knew what that shit was like.

"Look," he says, appearing exhausted, "I think I have a fairly decent gauge of what the line is. It is not perfect, but, like, I say the *n*-
word eight times in my stand-up. And it works. People can tell if you
mean it. And the other thing is *I* never say it, I'm always paraphras-
ing someone. And . . . I open up by shitting on white people. And
pedigree. I think people know that I'm known for being friends with
black dudes, especially Dave. And I talk about that, I talk about being
called it. I talk about the first time I was called the *n*-word. I get called
the *n*-word every day. I can show you texts."

Scrolling through his phone without looking up, he tells me, "So
it is a weird thing where you expect me to inhale something and not
exhale. And people are like, 'You can't say that.' But I get called it every day. Constantly, for twenty years."

Later on, Brennan brings up an idea first posited by the psychologist Beverly Tatum about the ways we tend to segregate ourselves
as we get older and grow apart from our friends of different races.
Neal tells me, "It's like when black kids sit at the lunch table with
only black kids, and the white kids sit with white kids. I think it is
just like, 'Well, they look like family.' It is just some animal shit. It
is safety." When I read Tatum's book, she says something that sticks
with me: that so often the difficulty in discussing race is about working around the divide of that which we do not know. As I listen to
Brennan talk, I think about how he is right, that comedy is different.
Comedians live for the joke and the joke alone. White writers have
long written jokes for black comics with great success (my favorites
being Ed. Weinberger for Bill Cosby and Louis C.K. for Chris Rock),
but at the same time none of this goodwill can negate the possibility that Chappelle experienced what his mother had written about
twenty years before: the desire to "learn to know himself again." And
that for all the post–civil rights progress we have made; it is possible
that you could be best friends with someone of a different race without being able to enter worlds and spaces that they can, or in the way
that they do.

After two hours of remarkably easy conversation, I can tell it is time for the moment I've been clenching my fist about. Maybe he had needed to feel me out. Neal Brennan, who definitely embodies the best of the easy wit of *Chappelle's Show*, goes for it.

"The joke in my act is: 'It is so bad I call myself it when no one's around.' It will be lunchtime and I'm like, Nigga, you need to eat. And I'm like, Who are you talking to?"

My hand unclenches. His *n*-word joke reminded me of the weird moments when I've been around young white men who identify with hip-hop culture and who, for some strange reason, despite their stated best intentions, need to access that word as proof that they are accepted or acknowledged by the community they are involved with. They do not realize the hubris and dominance inherent in the act of wanting to use that word. Brennan's joke is a joke on those guys, but it is also, inadvertently, a joke on himself. I think he knows this. Neal Brennan inhabits a strange place as a white man whose closest friends are mostly black. But what, if anything, does that mean? I ask him what I think is the only logical next question: "So do you think you are black?"

"No!" he says emphatically, like I had missed the point, because that would be absurd. "I also think that is a silly thing. Like I've never spoken Ebonics."

"Do you think that you're a racist?" I ask, but not because I think Brennan is any more racist than any other white person, especially if racism is viewed as a system of white privilege and unearned benefits. I ask this because part of knowing where the line is is knowing where you situate yourself along it or against it.

"Uh, I think that everybody is racist. It is a natural human condition. It's tribal."

Another evening, Brennan and I talk about what the ride of success felt like. He remembers hanging out at a club in Arizona where he and Chappelle were approached by a white fan who was loose with his use of the word *nigger* and who praised Chappelle for making it so funny. "It was awful," Brennan recalls.

The thing is, I like Neal Brennan. And I got the joke, I think. But when he first told it to me, there was an awkward silence that I think both Brennan and I noticed. The cafeteria seemed to swell with noise. And for a brief moment, my head clouded, and there was nothing I could think of to say, so to get out of the silence, I did what was expected: I laughed. When I got home, this troubled me deeply.

> You can't say anything real when it comes to race. That's why Bill Cosby's in such trouble for saying black folks have got to take responsibility for their own lives. I spoke at my high school last week and I told them, "You've got to focus. Stop blaming white people for your problems . . . Learn to play basketball, tell jokes, or sell crack. That's the only way I've seen people get out."   —Dave Chappelle

> Last time I was down South I walked into this restaurant, and this white waitress came up to me and said: "We don't serve colored people here." I said: "That's all right, I don't eat colored people. Bring me a whole fried chicken."   —Dick Gregory, *Nigger*

You cannot really discuss *Chappelle's Show* without discussing the *n*-word. One also cannot discuss the *n*-word without discussing Dick Gregory. Neal Brennan and Dave Chappelle weren't even born yet when Dick Gregory bounded onto the American comedy scene and asked to stand flat-footed or to sit down and be spoken to like a man. Yvonne Seon tells me that when Dick Gregory campaigned for president in 1968, "we all had our eyes on him." Dick Gregory is a larger-than-life sort of man. To reach him, you have to get past his wife of fifty years, Miss Lillian. "You were lucky," Gregory tells me. "She is tough. She once told the president I'd have to call him back."

Although things have slowed down from the days when he commanded a weekly rate of something just shy of fifteen thousand bucks, when the only peers in his earning bracket were Woody Allen, Mort Sahl, and Lenny Bruce, Dick Gregory is still on the move. All of his activity is made even more remarkable by the fact that he is now eighty. He still runs and does regular juice fasts, and his long white beard makes him look like a Methuselah among men. And maybe he is. Richard Pryor once said: "Dick was the greatest, and he was the first. Somebody had to break down that door. He was the one."

Before Dick Gregory, there were no elegant black men in comedy. The generation before Dick Gregory's grew up on Stepin Fetchit, the stage name of a black actor named Lincoln Perry and one of America's most famous black personalities for more than twenty years. These days it is difficult to find clips of Stepin Fetchit and the existing films are rarely shown. Stepin Fetchit acts like a shuffling, befuddled fool, and because of this many of Perry's films have been deemed offensive. Little remains to show his enormous influence on- and off-camera: he was the first black A-list actor, a millionaire during the Great Depression; he owned a fleet of limos and sports cars and he employed a retinue of Asian maids and butlers. He carried guns, he wrote essays for black newspapers, he was handsome, he was a Hollywood outlaw—but none of that mattered on-screen. On-screen he stooped his neck, and dropped his bottom lip, and acted as shiftless and stupid as possible. Stepin Fetchit is the id figure, in characterization only, that sits on Chappelle's shoulder in one of his skits and demands that Chappelle make himself happy and order chicken during a flight. It is not the chicken that is the problem, it is the familiarity of the characterization. That whether Chappelle liked it or not, whether Dick Gregory liked it or not, this was the precedent.

"When the Playboy Club brought me in," Dick Gregory recalls, "up until then you could sing, you could dance, but you could not stand flat-footed and talk and just tell jokes, because the people upstairs didn't want folks to know just how intelligent black folks were. [The Playboy Club] brought me in, though, and it opened up the floodgates. Now, Will Smith's movies alone have made three billion dollars." Dick Gregory's gig at the Playboy Club started in 1961, and three years later he would write his memoir, entitled *Nigger*. This is the part of his dedication to his mother that is often quoted:

> "Dear Momma—Wherever you are, if you ever hear the word 'nigger' again, remember they are advertising my book."

When I suggest to Gregory that he used his comedy as a weapon, he shouts, "What?" so loud I get scared. "How could comedy be a weapon? Comedy has got to be funny. Comedy can't be no damn weapon. Comedy is just disappointment within a friendly relation." Chappelle, he says, was very good at it. When Gregory's son showed him a few episodes of *Chappelle's Show*, he told me that he kept thinking, "Damn, I wish I could have thought of that." Then Gregory volunteers to tell me the names of the three greatest comedians of all time, and in a proud and awesomely fraternal way, he says, in order: "Lenny Bruce, Richard Pryor, and Mark Twain."

"Yes," I say. "But isn't it difficult to be that profane and that profound, in droves, especially as Twain in *Pudd'nhead Wilson*?"

"Did you say *Pudd'nhead Wilson*?" Gregory shouts.

"Yes," I say, scared again that I've said the wrong thing.

"*Pudd'nhead Wilson!* Brilliant stuff! I could kiss you! Mmhm," he says. "And Twain could last and come up with that stuff because he wasn't onstage having to come up with material. But listen," he says, waiting a beat. "Nobody said comedy was easy."

Dick Gregory admires Mark Twain's audacity as a white man to discuss race in America. He hates the idea of concealing the word *nigger* behind euphemisms like the *n*-word, and he seems to think it should be a shared burden. "Before Twain, no white people would ever write about lynchings. So his column was 'There were two people lynched last weekend and then we found out they were just "niggers."' And then he did the whole article about how the good Christian church people were there. And the white women brought their babies and children were selling Kool-Aid and lemonade, like, 'So what? They were just niggers!' That was the first time that anyone in history wrote anything like that, nothing about those gatherings had ever been written about lynching! That had never been done before! And like that, that is comedy!" When I ask Estee Adoram, the lovely, legendary, nononsense booker at New York's best comedy club, the Comedy Cellar, what sort of person becomes a stand-up comic, the first thing she says is "A very brave person. A person willing to be laughed at."

When I read about Twain saying the word *nigger*, in the exact same way Neal Brennan did, it does not raise the hairs on my neck. I do not think we want censored comics. But I'm given pause. Estee tells me she can sense when there is "an unfunny bitterness behind the joke." The fun of humor is the way it pushes at the boundaries. The joke is indeed a tricky thing. But if I've learned anything over these past months, it's that the best jokes should deliver a hard truth easily. It is the difference between asking girls in the crowd how their butt-holes look—a roast my sister and I endured one night at a comedy club—and mastering the subtlety of the uniquely American art form of stand-up comedy. Dick Gregory has a joke for me:

> So I'm standing at the airport and I see this white lady talking to her daughter. Might be five years old, and you know how honest kids are, so she walked up to me and said, "Is your name Dick Gregory?" And I said, "Yes." And she said, "My mamma says you have a tail." And I said, "Yes, and you tell her my tail is in my front."

Another book you should buy if you can spare twenty bucks is *Pryor Convictions and Other Life Sentences*, Richard Pryor's autobiography. In it, he tells of a dinner party thrown in his honor by Bobby Darin. Pryor is seated across from Groucho Marx, who told him "that he'd seen me on *The Merv Griffin Show* a few weeks earlier, when I'd guested with Jerry Lewis."

> It hadn't been one of my better moments—Jerry and I had gotten laughs by spitting on each other, and Groucho, it turned out, had a few things to say about that.
> "Young man, you're a comic?" he asked.
> "Yes," I nodded. "Yes, I am."
> "So how do you want to end up? Have you thought about that? Do you want a career you're proud of? Or do you want to end up a spitting wad like Jerry Lewis?"
> The man was right . . . I could feel the stirrings of an identity crisis. It was coming on like the beginning of an acid trip. Groucho's comments spoke to me. "Wake up, Richard. Yes, you are an ignorant jerk, pimping your talent like a cheap whore. But you don't have to stay that way. You have a brain. Use it."

The next sentence? "The thing was, I didn't have to."

The thing about Chappelle is that he wanted to use it, and he knew how. There is no doubt that *Chappelle's Show* is his finest work, but the block party that he put on and filmed in Bed-Stuy in 2004 is also a revealing production in the sense that we get to see the comedian almost at rest, listening to the music he enjoys with his celebrity friends. I was there, both in the crowd and backstage, and there was a remarkable amount of solidarity, love, and exuberance even in the drizzly September rain. The kind that I can't forget. Watching a triumphant Lauryn Hill resplendent in cream slacks and a Yankees cap, reunited with her bandmates from the Fugees. Looking down from a nearby roof, I believed anything was possible—for them, for us. Chappelle was the kind of celebrity who wanted to reach out to fans who looked like him, and it was clear that as much as he aspired to universality, he realized that "the bottom line was, white people own everything, and where can a black person go and be himself or say something that's familiar to him and not have to explain or apologize?" So sometimes it was very nice to have, as the comic himself said, "Five thousand black people chillin' in the rain," like a Pan-African Congress right off of Putnam Avenue.

When I ask Yvonne Seon what she thinks about the *n*-word and how easily it is used these days in hip-hop culture, she says, "There has always been a tendency to try and rehab a word that has been used as an epithet for you. It's a way of claiming something that hurt you, hoping that you can say, 'Now this word won't hurt me anymore.' It's a part of the attempted healing. When James Brown sang, 'I'm black and I'm proud,' that is an example of how he tried to rehabilitate that word. Because there was a time when I was growing up when you didn't call anybody black unless you wanted to get knocked into next week. There was too much shame involved."

"Do you think—" I start.

And she laughs and cuts me off with a question. "Do I think, like, 'I'm black and I'm proud,' 'I'm a nigga and I am proud!' could exist?" We both laugh at the absurdity, and also the very real possibility, of that song. "Hm," she says. "I have trouble with the word *nigga*. I associate that word with lynching, violence, and hate, and I don't associate the word *black* with that. But I do associate the word *nigga* with that history. So it's not a term that I could ever use easily or encourage the use of. There have been articles written about teaching this history, and we've discussed them in my black studies class, but what usually happens is that the class eventually decides that they're going to be part of the movement against the word *nigger*. Once they understand what the history is and what the word means, they stop using it and they encourage their friends to stop using it."

"It is about choices," I say, feeling guilty for a lot of reasons before she demurely stops me.

"Yes, it always is," she says, "about choices."

Just being a Negro doesn't qualify you to understand the race situation any more than being sick makes you an expert on medicine.

—Dick Gregory

Tamra Davis, the director of *Half Baked*, is feeding her children, so she can't say out loud the last lines of the movie she directed. These are lines she had to fight for, and, along with Brennan and Chappelle, she had to try to convince fifteen studio executives that they deserved to be in the movie. She tries to talk around the lines, but finally she whispers, "I love weed, *love it!* Probably always will! But not as much as I love pussy!" She giggles. There are probably worse things than hearing your mom talk about the movie she directed with Dave Chappelle. Tamra Davis is nonchalantly cool, despite having the distinction of having directed the early movies of Adam Sandler (*Happy Gilmore*) and Chris Rock (*CB4*). She grew up in California and has been around comedy all her life. Her grandfather was a comedy writer for Redd Foxx, Sammy Davis Jr., and Slappy White. She understands comedy instinctually, and knows that the difference between a writer and a comic is the energy and love a comic must bring to the stage, to the audience.

Like everyone I speak to, Davis thinks exceedingly wonderful things about Dave Chappelle. The man has a hagiography; I hear it from everyone: from Neal Brennan to a former executive of Comedy Central, who tells me, "I have so, so much respect for Dave. He is a great guy." For all the bridges he has supposedly burned, Dave Chappelle is beloved. Tamra Davis is the most direct. "I just really think his voice is an important voice to be heard. I've spent my life working with young people who all of a sudden get launched into an incredible position of celebrity and fame and it's very, very difficult to handle. And people handle it in different ways. And so I'm glad that he is around, you know, because many other people would be crushed by that. Having to have that inner dialogue in your head, knowing that everybody is talking about you. It's a very difficult thing to have to navigate."

What separated Dave Chappelle not just from Neal Brennan but also his fans is that he was suddenly vaulted into the awkward position of being the world's most famous interlocutor in a conversation about race—the one conversation no one likes having. Yes, it is hard to look back. But it's easy to understand why Chappelle was done with being misread, tired of explaining, finished talking. As Brennan, and then everyone else, told me: the man turned down fifty million dollars. You will never get him to speak with you.

> Beware, my body and my soul, beware above all of crossing your arms and assuming the sterile attitude of the spectator, for life is not a spectacle, a sea of griefs is not a proscenium, and a man who wails is not a dancing bear.   —Aimé Césaire, *Notebook of a Return to the Native Land*

When a chance came to visit Yellow Springs, I had no expectation that Chappelle would be there. But I wanted to see it. In Yellow Springs, I met Yvonne Seon. We had a good time. We discussed my wedding, we discussed Michelle Alexander's *The New Jim Crow*, and she introduced me to her family. It was a lovely day. Idyllic, even. On my way out of town, I felt tired, so I stopped for some coffee at a local coffee shop. As I was paying, I saw a few guys out back in the garden, talking, and then I saw Dave Chappelle, in a weird white tank top that strained to contain his muscles. No longer lean. Well-defended.

So at a cash register in Yellow Springs I stood and watched as the person I had so badly wanted to talk to walked toward me. But when he said hello, I made a decision that—until my plane ride home—I kicked myself for. Moving on pure instinct, I simply said hello, turned and finished paying my bill, and left.

Did I mention that the light is beautiful at dusk in Yellow Springs? The people walk the streets, going to the grocery store or looking at the theater listings. There is a café that was once a house on the Underground Railroad that now serves delicious Reuben sandwiches and plays disco music. People say hello in passing, kids with Afros zip by on scooters. It is small-town America, but with hemp stores. I didn't want to leave, because it seems like an easy place to live. Not without its problems, but a place with a quiet understanding that conversation is the minimum for living in a better world. You know, simple things.

At a memorial for his father a few years back, standing next to his mother at the podium at Antioch College, Dave Chappelle ended his speech by thanking the community of Yellow Springs. "So," he said, "thank you to you all for giving my father a context where he could just exist and be a good dude, because to be a good dude, as many good dudes have shown you before, is just not a comfortable thing to be. It's a very hard thing to aspire to. And so thanks for honoring him, because sometimes it is a lonely, quiet road when you make a decision to try to transcend your own demons or be good or whatever he was trying to do here."

In my car's rearview mirror, it doesn't seem strange to me at all that I am watching America's funniest comic standing in a small town, smoking cigarettes, and shooting the shit with his friends. Like everyone else on the street, one friend is white, the other is black—the only difference being that they are with Dave. But here Dave is just Dave. Totally uninterrupted, unheckled, free to be himself, free to have a family, and land, and time to recover. Time to be complicated, time to be a confessed fan of fame who one day decided that it was important to learn to be himself again. Chappelle took a drag on his cigarette, and laughed, and it was apparent that he was doing what he said he wanted most in life: having fun and being funny. So, for better or for worse, I took this to be my answer.

REGGIE WATTS

■

Cat n Leo

FROM *15-Second Plays*, a chapbook

British accents.

CATHERINE
Hello. I thought that I might find you here.

LEOPOLD
Yes, Catherine, it is me. What do you want?

CATHERINE
I don't know I—I just can't explain it anymore. I mean what with everything happening and all. I just don't understand.

LEOPOLD
Well I'LL give you something to understand!

CATHERINE
Oh! Leopold!

GABRIEL HELLER

■

After Work

FROM *Fence*

I WAS WAITING ON THE PLATFORM for the subway to come, zoned out after a long day of work, looking at the tiles on the wall across the tracks, examining their symmetry on either side of the arches, when a woman I knew with a son the same age as my daughter appeared. We said hello to each other and immediately the train came. It wasn't too crowded. We stood in the middle of the car, holding the silver bars, talking. We talked about work, the subtle, hard-to-navigate politics, the annoying people, and we talked about graphic design, because my neighbor is a graphic designer, and I asked her if she'd seen a film I'd recently seen, a documentary about Helvetica font, which was surprisingly good, and she said she'd seen it, and we talked about the film, and I asked her if she wanted to start her own company, and she said she wasn't that ambitious, and then she said she used to freelance, but she didn't like it, though maybe that was because it overlapped with a difficult time in her life seven years ago when her best friend died. We were on the Manhattan Bridge. It was raining. The East River was the color of smoke. She said he was injured in a swimming accident, out at Coney Island. He was participating in the Polar Bear Swim. He'd never done it before, and he dove into the water and hit a little sand dune, she said, and he broke his neck and was paralyzed from the neck down, and he made it clear that he didn't want to be tubed, he didn't want to live if he had to breathe through a tube, he was very clear about that, but the doctors wanted to operate on him, and when he came out of surgery he was tubed, and he was all alone, his parents weren't even there, because his father, who was an anesthesiologist, had just assumed they would keep him under, but they hadn't, and when he woke up he was all alone, paralyzed from the neck down, and he had a breathing tube in, and it was just awful, she said, it was just very fucked up and awful. By this time we had crossed the bridge and were in the tunnel again, and I asked how old he was, was he in his mid-twenties, I don't know why I cared about that, and she said no, he was in his thirties, and then she immediately changed the subject. We spent the rest of the ride talking about our children, their typical two-year-old behavior, their sleeping problems, and how she has to lock her son in his room to keep him from getting out of bed and coming into their room, her and her husband's, and she said that at first her son hated being locked in his room, but now he likes it, he needs to know he's locked in before he can fall asleep. We said good-bye at Church Avenue. She walked home from there, and I waited on the platform for the local train to take me two more stops, and it took a long time to come, but eventually it did, and in the end I was only a few minutes late to relieve our babysitter. My daughter was very happy to see me. She hugged my leg and said, my dada, my dada, and I picked her up and kissed her. I wrote a check for the babysitter, and my daughter gave it to her, like she always does on Thursdays, and when the babysitter left, we sat on the couch and read a few books, *A Sick Day for Amos McGee*, *Where the Wild Things Are*, and then she started running circles on the rug, and I watched her for a little while, running around and around, and when she started playing with her cash register I got up and went to the computer and when the *Times* site came up, which it always does first thing when I go online, I saw the headline in big bold letters, that Muammar Qaddafi was dead, he had been killed, and I read the article, and I was amazed and horrified. But my daughter wanted my attention. I want to eat something, she said, so I closed my computer and took her in the kitchen and made her an egg, but she didn't want it. She wanted her bunny crackers and hummus, bunnies and hummy, she said. We sat at the kitchen table together while she ate, and then my wife, her mom, came home, and this caused a big stir, because they were both so happy to see each other, and before I knew it she was running circles on the rug again, and I was looking at pictures of corpses. I told myself I wouldn't look at the videos, but I couldn't resist, something inside me that I don't understand couldn't resist. I saw this once-powerful man being dragged through the street, and the camera was shaking and jerky, and I saw his dazed eyes and his face covered in blood, and my wife looked up and asked, What are you watching, in a voice that suggested she was annoyed at me, and I said, Did you know Qaddafi was killed? and she said, Oh wow, but then right away asked, Can you run the bath? I said sure I would, so I closed my computer and went in the bathroom and ran the water, but it was yellow, so I sat on the edge of the tub and let the water run for a long time, till the yellow had all gone out of it, and then I let the tub begin to fill, and I went back in the living room, where they were sitting on the floor, and our daughter was showing my wife all the stickers in her sticker book, the stickers she'd gotten for doing things she didn't like doing, like going in her car seat, brushing her teeth, getting her hair washed, and then I went back into the bathroom to discover the tub was filling with water that was in fact yellow, the clearness had just been an illusion, and I cursed our apartment in my head, turned the water off, and unstopped the drain. I don't know how to do this water, I called to my wife. It's always yellow when I do it. And she called back, Don't turn the hot up too high. You want to do it? I asked, and then I heard her footsteps, and she was in the bathroom, and I went into the living room, and there was our daughter on the rug, but she didn't want to be with me, she wanted to be with her mom. She started crying and ran in the bathroom. I sat on the rug and thought about my neighbor's dead friend, and I thought about Qaddafi being dragged through the street, the thoughts that must have been in his head before he was dragged out of the storm drain where they found him, he must have known it was all over, but maybe he didn't, and I thought about his son, who'd also been killed, there were pictures of him captured, smoking and holding a bottle of water, and then there were pictures of him lying on his back with a hole in his throat, and I asked myself why do I feel sad about Qaddafi? I knew how awful he was. I remember being a kid and asking my dad who the worst leader in the world was, and he told me it was Qaddafi, I must have been eight or nine years old. Qaddafi and Khomeini, he said, but neither one of them was as bad as Papa Doc, my dad said. I knew Qaddafi was insane, and I wanted his army defeated, but his death made me sad, because despite him not being a good man I'd come to feel through reading about him and seeing him on television and internet videos and growing up hearing about him that I knew him in a way, and now I had watched someone I knew in the chaotic, violent moments leading up to his death, and it was not a good feeling at all. Out the window, it was totally dark, the days were getting shorter and shorter, soon it would be winter. I heard my daughter splashing in the bath and singing, my daughter, who despite her mood swings and her sleeping troubles, was overall a very happy kid.

THOMAS PIERCE

■

The Real Alan Gass

FROM *Subtropics*

HE'S BEEN LIVING with her for not quite a year when Claire first mentions Alan Gass.

"I think I need to tell you about something," she says. "About *someone.*"

Walker turns down the stereo above the fridge and readies himself for whatever comes next. They are in the kitchen—formerly her kitchen, now their kitchen. The butter crackles around the edges of the potatoes he is frying in a big cast-iron pan. He flips his dark hair out of his eyes. If she confesses an affair, what will he do? First, switch off the burner. Second, grab his jacket and go without a word. The third step could involve fast walking, tears, and possibly a stop at the ABC store. Beyond that, it's hard to say.

Claire is on the other side of the kitchen island with her laptop open, an old black T-shirt sagging down her left shoulder, a turquoise bra strap exposed. Until now, she's been quietly at work. She no longer takes classes, but when she did, they had titles like "Advanced Topics in Sub-Subatomic Forces." Thanks to a graduate fellowship, she spends most days on the top floor of the physics building thinking about a theoretical particle called the daisy. The daisy is a candidate for the smallest particle in the universe, but no one has devised a way to observe or prove one. Doing so would probably require re-creating the conditions of the Big Bang, which everyone seems to agree would be a bad idea. The wider academic community has not fully embraced Daisy Theory, as it's called. Claire's advisor came up with it, and, like him, Claire believes the mysterious particle is forever locked in a curious state of existence and nonexistence, sliding back and forth between the two.

"I haven't mentioned him until now because"—she scratches her chin with her chipped electric blue fingernail—"I was embarrassed, I guess."

"Just tell me," he says, wanting this over with quickly.

"All right, here it is. I'm kind of married."

"Kind of?" He doesn't understand. Typically, one is or isn't married. Does she mean that she's separated from someone and failed to ever mention it? Or did she marry some mysterious person on the sly? Or is this a new and clever update on the same old fight about time and priorities? She's married to her research and he just needs to get that through his head?

"No, what I mean to say is, sometimes at night when I dream, I dream I have a husband."

"A dream marriage," he says. "Okay." He kills the burner under the pan and scrapes the potatoes onto the plates where the green beans have gone cold.

"Tell me what you're thinking. Does this bother you? You're not the man in the dream."

"Just so I'm clear," he says. "This isn't you telling me that you're cheating on me?"

"I'm not cheating on you. Not unless you count dreams as cheating. Do you?"

Walker can't help but wonder if this is some sort of test. Could he have muttered some other woman's name in his sleep? Although he sometimes dreams about sex, in the morning the details of the dream encounters are usually hazy and impressionistic, with floating parts that don't connect to any specific face. He doesn't mention this now. A dream marriage, if that's really what this is about, should probably not bother him.

"So it doesn't concern you that I'm in love with someone else in my dreams?" she asks.

"You didn't mention love."

"Well, I married him, didn't I?"

"Do I know the guy? Have I met him? Please don't tell me it's your advisor." Whenever she talks about needing more time for her research, Walker knows, that includes more time alone with her advisor.

She reaches across the island for Walker's hand, a gesture that makes him suspect he's about to get more bad news.

"It's not my advisor," she says. "My husband's name is Alan Gass."

Alan Gass only exists in her dream, she explains. He is an ophthalmologist, a tall man with bright blue eyes and a lightly bearded face. His favorite meal in the world is barbecue biscuits. He is allergic to shellfish. Years ago he played college football, but he's put on a little weight since those days. On Saturdays he plays golf, but professes to hate what he calls clubhouse culture. He just likes the wind in his hair, the taste of a cold beer on the back nine. Claire has been married to him for almost a decade.

"Wow," Walker says. "You have incredibly detailed dreams."

"That's what I'm trying to tell you. They're super-realistic. Sometimes I dream that we're just eating dinner together, kind of like this. We tell each other about our day. Or we don't talk at all. We've known each other so long, silence is okay at this point, you know?"

Walker takes a bite of the potatoes. Claire hasn't shut her laptop.

"You writing Alan an email over there?" he asks and expects a full assault of noncommutative geometry, U-waves, big gravity. But when she turns the screen, he discovers that she's looking at a website with pictures of celebrities eating messy sandwiches and picking out shampoo at the drugstore.

"So is Alan Gass better looking than me?"

"Silly duck," she says, a recurring joke about his out-turned feet. She shuts the laptop and comes around the island. "Silly duck with big sexy glasses." She plucks the glasses from his face. "Silly duck with snazzy shoes." She taps his black shoes with her socked feet. "Silly duck with perfect duck lips." She kisses him.

He stands and wraps his arms around her waist. A former high school volleyball star, Claire is a few inches taller than Walker, and even more so right now with her blond hair held up with sticks. He doesn't mind her height, but whenever they ride an escalator together, he claims the higher step to see what it's like.

Admittedly, her dream is a strange one—so visceral, so coherent, so consistent—but he can see no reason why Alan Gass should come between them. After imagining a real affair, he can't help but feel a little relieved. It isn't as though she is actually married and actually in love with an actual ophthalmologist. What counts is that the real Claire—the waking Claire, the part of her that matters—wants Walker and only Walker, and that is the case, is it not? She says that it is most definitely the case. She kisses him, tugs his hand to her cheek. She is relieved, she says, that he finally knows her secret, a secret she's never told anyone, not even her parents. What a weight off her shoulders. Anything he wants to ask, he can ask. She will hide nothing from him.

Over the next few weeks, new details emerge. Claire's dreams began when she was in high school. He grew up Baptist in a small town and doesn't drink. Walker can't help but wonder at the subtle differences between himself and Alan. Walker grew up Episcopalian and drinks a glass of wine every night. Alan regularly wears suits. Walker prefers tight dark jeans and designer T-shirts. Alan volunteers at a free medical clinic. Walker can't remember the last time he volunteered for anything.

But Walker tries not to dwell on Alan Gass.

Walker is the artistic director at a theater downtown. He met Claire there when she volunteered to help at the box office one semester. He was in that particular production. It was a French play about a ghost that wreaks havoc on a town by inhabiting prominent citizens and causing them to behave strangely. The town believes the ghost is that of a young woman who recently drowned herself because of a broken heart. The townspeople set out to find her body, thinking that will satisfy her, but it does not. The ghost responds by inhabiting the town mayor and hurling the man off a tall building. To try to appease the ghost, the townspeople gang up on the man responsible for the woman's broken heart. They tie weights around his ankles and drop him in the ocean. But that doesn't solve the problem. This man also returns as a ghost and gets his revenge. It was a gruesome play. Walker played the second ghost. Despite the white gunky makeup, Claire thought he was handsome.

Alan Gass is a ghost, and Walker knows you cannot fight ghosts.

They are insidious. You can't punch a ghost or write it a drunk email. You can only pretend the ghost is not there, hope it loses interest, evaporates, does whatever it is that ghosts do when they disappear completely.

They are sitting in the back row of a lecture hall. Claire's university is hosting a conference. Her advisor, in his forties, tall and boyish with a mane of black curls, is on the stage. Daisy Theory is under attack, he warns, from all sides.

Planets, hearts, even the parts of our brains responsible for dreams—everything in the universe is made of daisy particles. The daisies come together to form larger particles by interlocking in a chain formation. No one is entirely sure what holds the chains together, but Claire's advisor imagines them like the daisy garlands that children wear as crowns. In theory a daisy chain could pop in and out of existence, just like the individual daisy. In theory your entire body—since every atom in it is nothing but a complex collection of daisies—could also pop in and out of existence.

"Isn't that amazing?" he asks the crowd.

On the top of the program, Walker doodles two flowers and gives them arms and legs, hands to hold. The figures are like cave paintings. Me, man. You, woman. This, love. He writes, *Want to be in my chain gang?* and passes the program to Claire. She smiles and grabs the pen. She draws a penis on one stick figure and breasts on the other. They have to avoid eye contact or they'll lose it.

After the lecture, a handful of people gather in a small white room with mahogany tables, where they quietly sip red wine in groups of two and three. Claire's advisor meanders over with a barely suppressed grin on his face.

"And?"

"Brilliant," Claire says.

Thirty seconds later, the two of them are lost in daisy revelry. "We're stretching math to the breaking point," he says. "It's almost un-math. One and one aren't two, but onetyone." He has his hand on Claire's elbow. He's cupping her elbow. He's propping it up. If he lets it go, her elbow might go crashing to the floor like a satellite from space. But when he walks away again, at last, Walker is pleased that her elbow stays put at her side.

"He's got a thing for you," Walker says.

"Let's not go into that again."

"Not that I can blame him."

"Even if he did," she says, "it's not like I've got one for him."

On the way home, because of construction on the bridge, they have to take a detour through another neighborhood. Though Claire knows these streets better than Walker does, against her advice, he takes a left turn. The road dead-ends in front of an old farmhouse, its giant gray shutters flapping in the wind like moth wings. It is early summer, perfectly warm, and they have the windows rolled down. He backs their Jeep into the driveway, the gravel popping under the tires. Another car has turned onto the street behind them. They pass the car on their way back to the main road. It is a pearly gray Lexus. The driver's face is obscured by lights across the glass, but Walker can see that he has a military haircut, the gray lines sharp around his ears, the seatbelt tight against a white Oxford shirt. But his features are blurred. He could be anyone. Walker waits until they are back on the main street before asking what he wants to ask. Has she ever wondered if Alan is really out there somewhere? That's he not just a dream? What if he's real and dreams he's married to a woman named Claire?

"Very funny," she says. "I don't think so."

"You should ask him. What do you normally talk about?"

"The usual stuff. Books, movies. What to fix for dinner."

"So in the dream, you're definitely still you?"

"Who else would I be?"

"Anyone. A prairie wife, a criminal, whatever. One time I dreamed I was the king of Europe."

"There is no king of Europe."

"Right, but the point is, some people dream about being someone else. And apparently you don't. You're you, and Alan is Alan."

She shrugs. They've reached the house. He parks the car along the curb, lined with tall shapely pear trees, the wilted white blossoms pressed flat into the short sidewalk that leads to the front door. Claire inherited the house from her great-aunt. Her parents were both engineering professors at the university. She went away for college but came back for graduate school. Inside, Walker leans over Claire's blue bicycle and flips the light switch on the wall.

"Okay I have to ask," he says, dropping his satchel on the hardwood floor. "Do you have sex with Alan in your dreams?"

She is ahead of him, halfway up the stairs.

"He's my husband," she says.

Walker knows that Claire has been with other men. He thinks about this fact as little as possible, though he knows that before him there was another student in her department, and before that a Swedish guy named Jens who actually proposed, and before them, a couple of post-college mistakes, a baseball player named Eric, and a backseat high school fling. She never mentioned Alan in the list.

"How often?"

"Do you really want to do this?"

"Just tell me once, and then we won't have to talk about it again."

She's pasting their toothbrushes.

"If you must know, probably a few times a week. But it doesn't often happen in the dream itself. It's kind of offstage action, you know? For instance, the other night, we were on our way to a friend's house for dinner, and the car ride took up the entire dream. But I knew what I'd done over the course of that day. I'd run some errands, picked up the dry cleaning. Baked strawberry brownies for dinner. The dessert was on my lap in the car."

"I can't get over how detailed these dreams are," he says. "I hardly remember anything from mine."

They both spit into the sink.

"Do you remember me in your dreams?" he asks. "Does it ever feel like cheating when you're with him?"

"Don't get weird on me. They're just dreams. I'm not cheating on anyone. You or him."

They turn off the lights and climb into bed. She tickles his back until he flips over. She's naked. He wiggles out of his boxers, shoves them to his feet.

"You don't need to worry," she says and climbs on top of him. He doesn't need to worry. He knows that. Sort of, he does. She's moving faster now. He has his hands around her waist, the way she likes. He mutters her name, and, thankfully, she mutters his, Walker, and when it's over she tugs at his chest hair playfully, smiling. Then she goes into the bathroom. He can hear her peeing. Then she's back in his arms, nuzzling under his chin, and ten minutes later, she's asleep.

He lets his breath fall in line with hers and keeps his arm draped over her side, inhaling the citrus conditioner in her hair. He can feel her heartbeat, soft and far away. Is she with Alan now? He wonders what it must be like for her, this double life, if she closes her eyes in this bed and opens them in the one she shares with Alan. Maybe her life with him mirrors this one. At that very moment, it occurs to Walker, she could be waking up and brushing her teeth all over again, discussing the upcoming day with her husband. She could be straightening his tie, pointing out the spot on his chin he missed while shaving. She could have her warm palm flat on his chest as she kisses him good-bye, the same way she sends off Walker most mornings. The idea of her repeating these private routines with another man, even one who doesn't technically exist, is almost more unsettling than the thought of her sleeping with him.

The phone book contains two listings for *Alan Gass* and one for *A. Gass*. Walker scribbles down all three on the back of a takeout menu. He carries the takeout menu in his satchel for two days before pulling over on the side of the road one morning before work. The sky is cloudless, and across the street, a long green field unfolds between two wooded lots. A row of ancient transformer towers runs down the middle of the rolling field.

He dials A. Gass first, and a woman answers. Her voice is so quiet and shaky that she has to repeat herself three times before Walker understands that her husband, Albert Gass, passed away the year before last.

Walker gets out of the car and flattens the wrinkles in his khakis. The road is not a busy one. He dials the next number, but the Alan Gass who used to live there has moved to Columbia, in South Carolina, or possibly to the other Colombia, the one with the drugs. The man on the phone can't remember which it was.

He dials the last number. The phone rings and rings. Walker is about to give up when the voice mail message begins.

"You've reached Alan and Monica," the man on the line says.

"We're not around to take your call, so leave your name and digits at the beep." It beeps. Walker hangs up quickly. The tall grass beneath the transformers swishes back and forth. He gets back in the car and starts the engine.

The address in the phone book leads him to a part of town he rarely visits. It isn't dangerous or run-down. It's just out of the way. The houses on the street are adjoining, with small grass yards in front. At one corner there is a video store. Walker doesn't recognize any of the movies in the front window. On the opposite corner, two women smoke cigarettes outside a Piggly Wiggly.

Alan Gass lives in the middle of the block in a three-story house painted light blue, so light that it's almost white. To the right of the front door there are three buttons, a white label taped above each. The third button says Gass 3B.

He pushes the button and stands back. After what feels like an eternity, a small speaker in the wall crackles, then a man comes on the line. He sounds like he might have been asleep.

"Bobby? That you? You're early."

"I'm not Bobby," Walker says.

The line crackles. "Okay, who are you then?"

"I'm Walker," he says, as if that will explain everything. "Sorry for just showing up like this, but I think we might know each other through a friend. Do you have a moment to talk? I promise I won't keep you long."

The man doesn't answer. A buzzer sounds, and the door clicks open. The stairway inside is narrow and long, with a dirty blue carpet runner, smudged with old black gum, shredded at the edges. The door at the top of the stairs is half open.

"Mr. Gass?" he calls and steps into the room. "Hello?"

The room is almost as narrow as the staircase. Walker feels like he's looking down the barrel of a shotgun. The half of the room nearest the door serves as a living area, with a small television against one wall and a futon-couch against the other. At the far end of the hall a single window provides light. The parts of a dismantled computer are scattered across a flimsy table beneath the window. Alan Gass emerges from a room to the right of the desk. Stepping into the light of the window, his tall Art Garfunkel hair is illuminated a wispy golden brown. He looks nothing like the man Claire has described. He cannot be the real Alan Gass.

Walker feels idiotic for coming and tries to think of the best way to extricate himself from the situation as quickly as possible. The man wears a starched red shirt with pearl buttons, tucked tightly into a pair of gray corduroys despite the summer heat. He is a small man, shorter than Walker. His eyes are gray, almost translucent.

"I think I've got the wrong Alan Gass," Walker says. "But just in case, do you know a Claire?"

Alan licks his bottom lip. He says that he knew a Claire once, way back in middle school. But he hasn't heard from her in decades. So, no, currently he does not know any Claires.

"That's all right. Like I said, wrong Alan Gass. I'll let you get back to whatever you were doing." Walker turns to leave.

"Before you go," Alan says, "now that you're up here, could I get your help with something right quick? I got a kid coming later who's supposed to help me, but he's not the most reliable." Alan shapes his hand into a bottle and pretends to guzzle from it. "Good kid, though."

On the wall above the television, a two-by-four with splintery edges forms a shelf over white brackets. There are—how many? six, seven—eight chocolate Easter bunnies on the shelf, still in their boxes. Alan Gass notices Walker noticing the bunnies.

"My favorite holiday. The company that makes them went out of business years ago. They'll be worth a fortune in ten, twenty years."

Walker nods and asks what Alan needs from him. They go into the kitchen. The refrigerator has been pulled away from the wall and unplugged, the door ajar. A towel across the floor collects the water as it drips from the freezer.

"I'm selling it," Alan says. "Got a good price for it. Only catch is that I gotta have it downstairs by noon."

Walker has never moved a fridge, but he knows the job will not be easy. Looking at the refrigerator, he's not even certain that it will fit through the front door. And then there's the matter of the staircase. But Alan has a dolly for that. He promises that it won't take long. He'll even throw in a few home-brewed beers as a thank you. Walker says that won't be necessary. He rolls up his sleeves. He's ready to do this. Alan goes into a back room and returns wearing a back brace.

"Old injury," he says. "You don't need to worry."

They tip the fridge backward so that Alan can wedge the dolly underneath. Slowly, they wheel it out of the kitchen. The doorway is tight. The entire wall shakes as the refrigerator passes through the frame. One of the Easter bunnies topples off the shelf and hits the floor. Alan lets the fridge come down flat so that he can examine the bunny's box. Through the clear plastic window, they can see the broken chocolate.

"Damn it," he says. The plastic tray slides out of the box like a gurney. He offers Walker a piece of an ear. "Never goes bad."

The ear is hollow. Walker doesn't want any chocolate. Alan sucks on a piece thoughtfully.

"So you're looking for some other Alan Gass, huh?" he asks. "Never really think about there being other Alan Gasses out there."

Walker nods. The funny part, he says, is that the Alan he's looking for might not exist.

Alan swallows the chocolate. "Might not exist?"

To his own surprise, Walker tells him everything—about the real Alan Gass, about the dreams.

"Huh," Alan says. "That's wild."

They rock the fridge backward again and wheel it out the front door of the apartment. They take a break on the landing at the top of the stairs.

"So what if I'd been him? What would you have done?"

"I have no idea. I didn't plan that far ahead."

"Pretend I'm him."

Walker pictures the man in the Lexus. The white shirt. The blurry face.

"I suppose I'd tell him to stay away."

"But she's my wife," Alan says. "I've been with her longer than you have. I should be telling you to stay away. I love her and I'm never letting her go."

"Okay, I get it."

"You think she loves you like she loves me? She married me. That's a sacred vow." Alan smiles. "Whoa, you should see yourself right now. You look like you want to hit me. Is this really bothering you?"

"You're making me feel a little like he's the real one, and I'm the dream."

"Don't flatter yourself. You're no dream. Look, you want to know my honest opinion? You got nothing to worry about. We all got an Alan Gass," Alan Gass says. "We all got our fantasies. In high school, my Alan Gass looked a little bit like my Spanish teacher, only sexier. She was this beautiful woman with shiny dark hair and a little vine tattoo on her back and this amazing accent. I can't tell you how many times I thought about her late at night alone in bed, if you know what I mean. But she had no blood in her veins, you follow? There was nothing to her. Her skin was made of the same thing they use for movie screens. You can project whatever you want onto someone like that."

They lean the fridge back toward the stairs on the dolly and slowly lower the wheels down onto the next step. Alan has the dolly handles; Walker is below it, keeping it balanced. They lower it another step, and then another. Walker is sweating. On the next landing, they take another break.

"I wouldn't care about a fantasy," Walker says. "Fantasies I understand. But Alan Gass isn't a fantasy. Fantasies don't have faults. But he does, and she still loves him. That's what's so unnerving."

They rock the fridge back onto the dolly and drop it down another step. Walker counts off the steps as they approach the bottom. Three, two, one. They are in a very small space. Walker opens the front door with his backside. They try to roll it through, but the fridge is too wide for the door by almost five inches. Alan can't believe it. He says he measured the frame. Walker glances at his watch. He has to go soon, he says. He's already two hours late for work. They're in the middle of a new production, a play that takes place on a cruise ship lost at sea. He needs to be there soon to meet with the costume designer. Alan looks exhausted. He says he understands. Even if he and Bobby have to take the whole goddamn fridge apart later, they'll get it through that door one way or another. He tells Walker to wait right there on the stoop. He's got something for him.

Walker fixes his sleeves and wipes the sweat off his forehead. When Alan returns, he's holding a small boxy tape deck. He pushes the eject button and extracts a gray cassette with a thin white sticker across the front. It says I ❤ MONICA KILL DEVIL HILLS SPRING BREAK SISTER GODDESS, but that is scratched out. Below that, it says, ZZZZZZZZZ.

"This is going to save you," Alan says.

"An old mixtape?"

"Ever heard of sleep suggestion? I took a Spanish class a few years back and made a tape to listen to while I slept at night. Don't laugh. It really did the trick. You can have this. I think it needs D batteries. Press this button, and you can record. Create your own tape. Tell her she's married to you, not Alan. Tell her whatever you want. Once she's asleep, press Play. Few weeks of this, you'll never hear another word about this marriage thing."

The machine is heavy for its size. Walker holds it like a handgun in a paper bag. He tries to give it back, but Alan won't take it.

Claire gets some bad news. A lab, somewhere in Europe, has constructed a black sphere and plans to flood it with something called K-matter. She emails Walker about it at work with a frowny-faced emoticon. If the experiment in Europe works like they think it will, she says, then particles cannot half-exist. The researchers will have effectively disproved Daisy Theory.

That night he gets home late and finds Claire already in the bed under the covers with her grandmother's rosary beads. She isn't religious. He's never known her to even set foot in a church, but she loved her grandmother. The beads are wrapped so tight around her white palm that they leave small indentations when Walker pries them loose.

"Say they disprove it," he says. "Where does something go when it stops existing?"

"Where does it go?" she asks. "Nowhere. It doesn't exist."

"But nowhere is somewhere."

"This isn't *where* versus *somewhere else*. This is being versus non-being."

He strips down and gets into bed, cuddling up behind her. Once she is asleep, he waits for something to happen. He's not sure what. Claire's dream marriage makes a certain kind of awful sense: a theoretical husband for the woman who spends her days in a theoretical haze. Her advisor was never the threat; it was always Alan. He watches her sleep as if the drama is unfolding just behind those eyelids. Maybe she will say something in her sleep. It would be like eavesdropping on a conversation taking place in a universe that Walker cannot reach, one where Walker does not even exist. He tries to imagine not existing. He imagines darkness, the absence of thought, but then his thoughts invade, and he exists again. *Claire*, he wants to call out. *Claire*.

"Claire." She doesn't budge. He places his palm flat between her shoulder blades, her skin warm through the T-shirt. He shakes her gently and feels her body tense.

"What's wrong?" she asks.

"Where were you?"

"What?"

"Were you with him?"

"You've got to be kidding. Go back to sleep."

"If you ever stopped dreaming about him, for whatever reason, would you be upset?"

She rolls over to face him. Her loose state championship volleyball T-shirt twists tight under her stomach.

"I'm beginning to regret I ever told you about Alan."

And why did she? Guilt, most likely. She turns back over and drifts away again. Walker climbs out of bed and goes downstairs. He digs some D batteries out of a cluttered drawer and plops down on the sofa with the tape deck. The old batteries are corroded, crusty, and white. He inserts the new ones, rewinds the tape to the beginning, and presses Record.

"You are . . . very sleepy."

He presses Stop, Rewind, and then Record again. His lips are close to the microphone, two small holes in the plastic.

"You will not dream about Alan Gass. You will not dream about Alan Gass. Alan Gass does not exist. Alan Gass is not a man. Alan Gass is not made of daisies. He is made of nothing."

He rewinds the tape and presses Record again. A new and less sinister idea: he could make a tape for himself.

"You will dream about Alan Gass. You will tell him to stay away. You will dream about Alan Gass. You will dream about Alan Gass."

He presses Stop. This is going to take too long. Is there a button that makes it loop?

"What are you doing?" Claire is at the top of the stairs.

"Nothing," he says and goes to the hall closet. He shoves the tape deck up on the high shelf and joins her in bed. That night he doesn't dream about Alan. He dreams what he's dreamed ever since work began on the new production—of a giant ocean with small gray waves. He is in that ocean. Lost in it. Tonight, in the distance, new details emerge: metal transformer towers that jut up into the sky, that crackle and hum with electricity, and far away, a boat that crests each wave. He cannot reach the boat. In the morning, he wakes up to steam slipping under the bathroom door in misty curling puffs. He can hear Claire humming in the shower.

Everywhere he goes he sees a Lexus. Lexi. They are a species, classifiable but indistinct. He sees one in the fire lane in front of the liquor store, then another in the parking lot at the gym. The cars are empty. He feels ridiculous each time he glares into a car. The tinted windows reflect only his own face, grim and warped. There's your Alan Gass, he thinks.

Before Claire, he once dragged a date to a five-year high school reunion and made the mistake of telling the date that he'd slept with one of the girls in the room. The date wouldn't let it go. She had to know which girl. She wanted him to point her out. She said she wouldn't be comfortable until she knew. But why, Walker asked her. "So I can avoid her," the date said. "Or maybe introduce myself. I don't know. Something." At the time, Walker found it amusing. God, he even made her guess the girl.

He makes a full tape and sleeps with earbuds, his ears hot and sweaty. He tells Claire it's music for the play. But he dreams only of the ocean, the gray water, the faraway boat.

Alan Gass calls with what he can only describe as amazing news—news that he won't share over the phone. Walker agrees to meet him at a pizza buffet called Slice of Heaven. They sit across from each other in a red vinyl booth that squelches under their butts. Aside from two dumpy women at a table on the other side of the restaurant, they are alone.

Walker has already eaten lunch and doesn't plan to stay long. But Alan is distracted. He wants pizza. A certain kind of pizza. He's waiting for the waitress to bring it out on a tin tray. When she does, at last, drop-ping it on the buffet at the center of the room, Alan is up in a hurry. His body pressed hard to the sneeze guard, he loads his plate with one slice after another. He comes back to the table and takes a large bite. The pizza is yellowish and drizzled with a translucent pink sauce.

"What is that?" Walker asks.

"Strawberry cheesecake. Try a piece." He slides the plate across the table, still sticky from the waitress's rag. Walker declines and asks about the news that couldn't be shared over the phone.

"Be patient. You'll find out in"—he checks his wristwatch, digital with an orange Velcro strap—"about ten minutes."

Walker takes the tape recorder out of his bag, slides it across the table to Alan.

"Did it work?" Alan asks.

"I'm letting it go. Like you said, some dumb fantasy."

Alan smacks on pizza and dabs the strawberry sauce from the cor-ners of his thin pink lips. Though a thin man, he has the look of physical inactivity. He has a curved back, flaccid arms, and probably a poor heart. Something about this pizza buffet—perhaps the quality of the light or the greasy floor tiles—makes Walker feel exhausted.

"Until you came to see me," Alan says, "I'd never really thought about there being other Alan Gasses in the world. But that got me thinking. Somewhere out there is the best possible Alan Gass."

"And somewhere else is the worst." Walker motions to the wait-ress.

"I'd like to think I'm somewhere in the middle. Most Alans are. Statistically speaking."

The waitress waddles to the table, her stockings tan as crust, her eyes green as bell peppers. Walker asks for a coffee.

"Over the last few days I've been digging around online and mak-ing some phone calls," Alan says. "To other Alans."

"And?"

"There's an Alan Gass in Utah who runs a ranch. There's an Alan Gass in New York who travels the country selling baseball cards."

The waitress brings over a mug and a hot pot of coffee, its steam thick with the smell of burnt peanuts. Walker dumps three creamers into the cup, turning the liquid a cardboard brown.

"Oh good, you're here," Alan says to someone behind Walker.

Walker turns. A heavy man in a blue polo shirt with eyebrows so dark and thick they look like two slits in his tan flat face smiles at them. His short hair is parted neatly down the middle.

"Walker," Alan says, "I'd like to introduce you to Dr. Alan Gass."

The man shakes Walker's hand firmly. His knuckles are hairy. Alan makes room for the other Alan on his side of the booth and explains that the second Alan lives only an hour north of here and when he discovered he was a doctor, well, he thought Walker might be interested in that.

"Doctor of what?" Walker says.

"Of religion," the man says, and grabs the menu from behind the napkin holder. "Mainly Eastern philosophy."

"You gotta try a piece of this," the first Alan says. The second Alan says no thanks, he doesn't have a sweet tooth. He's going to have a calzone.

"There's another Alan Gass two hours from here," the first Alan Gass says. "He's invited me to see his collection of North American beetles. He studies them. Amazing, right?"

"I wonder how many of us there are in the world?" Dr. Gass asks.

"At least a thousand," says the first one. "We should organize a party. Wouldn't that be something?"

Walker imagines an army of Alan Gasses. They are the building blocks of something larger and more monumental. He sips on coffee, listening to the two men compare their lives, both of them amazed that two men with the same name can have had such different experiences and opinions of the world. How did Walker end up here, in this booth, with these men? He drops a few dollars on the table and says he must be going. Both Alans reach out to shake his hand.

The experiments in Europe—with the black sphere and the K-matter—have failed horribly. Claire comes home so excited she almost tackles Walker. The failure doesn't exactly prove Daisy Theory, but the theory does emerge relatively unscathed. Particles, for the time being, can still half-exist. Walker joins when her advisor takes the entire team out for celebratory drinks. His boyish face glowing in a suit jacket, jeans, and sneakers, he steadies himself on an assistant's shoulder and steps up on a booth, raising his dark whiskey glass high. Claire lets out a whoop.

The music in the bar is disco music: Donna Summer maybe, but with a newer backbeat. Ben lures a research assistant onto the dance floor. Claire lures Walker too. They dance in the middle of the group. She spins under the flashing lights. She moves away from him. The dance floor is crowded. Bodies merge and move like extensions of the same gyrating creature. Claire orbits around Walker, but when he turns she's disappeared. He stops dancing, the only stationary body in that sea, until she reappears again, moving away from the group and toward Walker with hands raised. She's looking right at him. Their waists meet first.

"I want to take you home tonight," he says.

"What?"

She can't hear him over the music. He kisses her. Kisses are a kind of vocabulary, he thinks. This one, both lips parted, tongues touching with the most delicate of flicks, has a particular message. The message is *Let's be happy*, and that feels right, because in some ways, isn't being happy a conscious decision one makes?

They have to leave their car at the bar that night and take a taxi home.

"Fun time?" he asks.

She doesn't answer. She's passed out against his shoulder. She's away again, wherever she goes. He tries to remember to be happy.

They get home late, and he helps her up the stairs. They fall asleep on top of the covers, and soon he is back in the ocean. He kicks to stay afloat. The towers rise up and buzz with electricity. He sees the rowboat. It's closer than ever before, cresting every wave. Walker can see now that a solitary figure is rowing the boat. The boat comes closer and closer, but not so close that Walker can see the man properly. "Well, you're a strong swimmer," the man calls out, and Walker is awake.

He takes his time getting out of bed. Claire is fixing breakfast when he comes downstairs. He plops down on the stool at the kitchen island and watches her scramble the eggs and drink tomato juice, her usual hangover cure. Her pink robe swishes along the floor when she turns to pour him some coffee.

"How'd you sleep?" she asks, surprisingly chipper.

"I slept okay," he reports, which is more or less true, and she returns to the stove. He doesn't ask her how she slept. Part of him would rather not know. "Listen, I think I need to tell you about something," he says and waits for a reaction. "About someone." The radio is on above the fridge. The sunlight sparkles in the metal sink under the window. Claire has her back to him. Finally her spatula goes still in the pan. He has her attention. They have nothing to do today but be together. He considers what to say next.

V. V. GANESHANANTHAN

■

K Becomes K

FROM *Ploughshares*

I RECENTLY WENT to an appointment with a terrorist I used to know. He lives near me in New York City, and when he wrote me a letter that said *Dear Sashi, come and see me,* without thinking very much about it, I did. Even when I was a little girl in Sri Lanka, before I had ever heard the word *terrorist,* I knew that when a certain kind of person wanted something, you did it without asking a lot of questions. I met a lot of these sorts of people when I was younger because I used to be what you would call a terrorist myself.

I helped these people for a friend, and I left them for the same reason. So you must understand: I am not an unlikable person, and neither are all terrorists. That word, *terrorist,* is too simple for the people I have known. It is too simple for me, too simple even for this man. How could one word be enough? But you asked me a question, so I am going to say it anyway, because it is the language you know, and it will help you to understand who we were, what we were called, and who we have really become.

We begin with this word. But I promise that you will come to see that it cannot contain everything that has happened. And while I am no longer the version of myself who met with terrorists every day, I also want you to know that when I was that woman, when two terrorists encountered each other in my world, what they said first was simply *hello.* Like any two people you might know or love.

* * *

I met the first terrorist I knew at the precise time in his life when he was deciding to become one. In 1981, when I met K, I was almost fourteen years old. He and his family lived down the road from me and mine, in one village of a Tamil town called Jaffna, in Sri Lanka. The Jaffna peninsula is the northernmost part of the island. Many people have died there: some killed by the Sri Lankan Army, some by the Indian Peace Keeping Forces, and some by the Tamil separatists, whom you know as the terrorists.

In the village where we were born, everyone was related to, hated, and loved by everyone else. In that heat, we needed and worked for each other. Now that I have lived through more than twenty seasons of snow, I dream of the village heat mostly in terms of fever. Some women carried cheap umbrellas to protect their faces from the sun. But the heat was not only outside us—we created it too. Our mothers cooked over wood stoves in hot kitchens, and we boiled water for tea almost hourly. We lit oil lamps before our household shrines and touched torches to roadside refuse. We mourned around burning pyres, undaunted. If we had let the heat faze us, we would not have survived. And we did more than survive, truly: we studied. I wanted to become a doctor. K wanted to become a doctor. And this was what made us alike.

He had the upper hand from the first, not because he was older, or a boy, but because I began as his patient. On the morning that we met, I was boiling water for tea. I had to use a piece of cloth to hold the pot to avoid burning myself. But that morning, the cloth slipped, the handle slipped, and the pot slipped, pouring scalding water all over me. I screamed and screamed for my mother—*Amma!* My high, shrill voice carried out onto the road, where K was passing. Hearing my cry, he swiftly stopped, let his bicycle fall in the dirt at our gate, and ran inside.

By the time he reached me in the kitchen, Amma had already found me. I screamed and cried and called every god I could name. Bubbles rose and popped on my skin. I could hear myself boiling and blistering, and looking down at myself, I could see it. Amma was sobbing, too horrified to move.

"Sit!" he said, and pointed to a chair. When I kept screaming, he pushed me down into the chair and peeled my blouse up, baring my hot stomach. I heard Amma's cry of *aiyo!* as though from a great distance. Snatching a bowl of eggs off the table, K began cracking them onto the burns. Her eyes widening, Amma moved forward as though to stop him.

"It will cool the burn," he said quickly, blocking her.

Trying to master the pain, I tried to focus on anything but the wounds. I stared at him and saw only his thumbs, working in and out of the eggshells, scraping the slime of the whites out cleanly and onto the swelling rawness of the burn. He did it very quickly, as though he had had a lot of practice, as though he were making a cake and every precious scrap of egg were going to be eaten. I remember those thumbs, and I remember the eggs—they were so cold, and my skin was so hot, so hot that I cannot quite believe that the eggs did not just cook on my flesh. He was right—it did help. When the last of the six eggs was cracked and cooling on my skin, K looked up at Amma.

"Are there more?"

"What?"

"More eggs?" She blinked, then nodded. "Good—cover the burn with a few more. The doctor—I should go—"

When K came back with the doctor half an hour later, I had finally stopped crying. The doctor looked over the makeshift dressing with approval. "Whose idea was this?" he asked.

"His," Amma said.

So I began as his patient, though he ended as mine.

So many foods remind me of K now. He is on each wiped plate and inside each cold glass; each cup of hot milk tea with sugar is one he refused. The eggs I make myself each morning, Tabasco or Clancy's Fancy hot sauce sliding bloodily across the top, are the ones he cracked onto my body. His family gave me varieties of fruit that are unattainable or tasteless in this country. When he came to visit me a few days later, his aunt came with him, bearing my favorite *mampalam*—mangoes—and *valaipalam*, the special, small, sweet bananas that grew in their yard. My mother must have mentioned that I liked them. The fruit pleased me, but for once, I felt more interested in the strange boy, who until this moment had belonged more to my brothers, his schoolmates, than to me. I tried to examine him without being too obvious about it. His shirt was tucked unevenly into his trousers, which were too large for his body. He looked sturdy, but not skinny, and he had a rim of hair on his upper lip that was not quite a mustache. It barely showed—he was dark from the sun, even though as an asthmatic, he had not been allowed outside very much. He had thick spectacles, which he took off and wiped carefully with a handkerchief. A woman's handkerchief, I noticed. Later, I learned that it had belonged to his late mother.

While he polished his spectacles, I took a good look at his face. He had a thin nose, a full mouth, and a high forehead with a gently curved widow's peak, which might have accounted for his seeming older than sixteen despite the lack of facial hair. Most boys that age in our village had mustaches, my brothers included. K could not seem to manage one. But behind the spectacles, his eyes were lovely and old, full of a certainty that appealed to me. I wanted that certainty for myself, to be someone who could look at burned flesh and not hesitate to touch it.

He replaced his spectacles, and when I realized that he was studying me with equal intensity I looked away.

His aunt fussed over me, and my mother let me off from the usual duty of serving them tea. I had never done it with the appropriate grace, and the burn, stiffening, made me move even more awkwardly than I did naturally. Instead, I sat and talked to his aunt as he continued to study me. Finally, she and my mother stopped talking about the near-tragedy and began talking about the upcoming temple festival. K looked over at my mother and his aunt, who were deep in conversation, and then back at me. The thick lenses distorted his eyes, but it was too late: I already knew they were lovely.

"So. How are you feeling now?"

"I hardly knew you were there," I said. "It hurt that much."

He would teach me, later, to lie about what hurt and how much. Most women, he would say, are naturally much better liars than you.

"And now?"

"Now? Better. But it itches," I said, plucking at my blouse. "How did you know what to do?" I had had time, in the intervening days, to become curious about the science of what he had done.

He shrugged. "It made sense, even though it wasn't modern. The protein and fat of the egg soothe the burn."

"Thank you," I said awkwardly.

"Don't scratch it—you'll get a scar."

I moved my hand away from my stomach, and we sat in silence for a moment.

"Are your brothers here?" he asked finally.

"No," I said.

"Oh."

I took that to mean that his aunt had made him come with her to visit me, that he had little use for girls and little use for me. So we were not friends at first, although he had already been more intimate with me than any other boy I had known. I frowned when I thought about that, about his peeling the blouse away from my skin, about how that skin had looked when he had done it. He had not seemed at all taken aback by the sight of the wound, the volcanic molten look of it. I admired that steadiness. But I was also embarrassed by the recollection of the nakedness of my pain. His certain hands had touched me as though it was not an intrusion, as though it came naturally, although during that moment of looking down at my own body, I had been horrified at the sight of myself. His sureness made me wonder what it would take to horrify him.

Although we had already had that intimacy, although certain barriers of propriety had been breached, it had been a forced breach required by the circumstances, and friendship did not come easily to us. We would have to go out of our respective ways to become friends, and I was not, at first, inclined to go out of my way. I was embarrassed, and I did not like feeling obliged to someone I considered a stranger. Our paths had crossed rarely. He was two years older than me; he went to the famous Jaffna Hindu College. He belonged to my brothers, after all, and he was a boy, and therefore our friendship was unlikely. Even when I saw him at the temple, we were separated by the traditional divide between men and women.

The next time we saw each other was at the temple, in fact. I saw that his mustache appeared slightly more successful, and noticed his quick glance at my belly, where one of my mother's old sari blouses covered the bandages from the burn. Suddenly conscious of new breasts, I lowered my arm across my body and looked away. The mustache looked foolish to me. He was not unusual, standing among the line of men waiting to be blessed. You, you American, you would have thought him just one of many dark men with white smiles. And, you know, you would have been wrong.

K died on a September morning in 1987, on a stage that had been specially built for him to do so. It was outside the Nallur Kandas-wamy Hindu temple, one of the temples of my childhood, and his childhood— one of our holiest and most loved places. At the time of his death he had not taken food or even water for eleven days. It was the morning of the twelfth day of what was being called his *saty-agraha*. A word that refers to the tactic of nonviolence that Mahatma Gandhi originated.

He died at 8:37 a.m., at the age of twenty-one, with a rebel's name that was different from the one with which he had been born and with which I had loved him. It was a Saturday. Today Tiger support-ers around the world mark this time as a holy hour, but I can tell you that at the moment of his death K was still an ordinary man—just a grownup version of the boy who had lived down the road from me in our village. His death made him no more saintly than he had been in life, which is to say not very. He was neither more moral nor more honest than the governments he protested. If anything, he was less so, and this made it harder to let him die, because I resented his death more. It was worse to mourn him, knowing truly what he had done. His face was harder to look at and to love, which I already did. Hunger had carved new hollows out of it. His mustache had wilted over his cracked mouth, shielding it from sight. He looked older and more austere. If I had not known already that it was K, I might not have recognized his body. When I bathed him each night with a wet cloth, it was like touching a stranger. While in many ways he did re-semble the boy who had been my friend, in its hunger and thirst his body had traveled a great distance from its previous self. Perhaps I should say that he looked as he might have looked in fifty years, had he lived—and never fasted.

K and our superiors had chosen this hunger strike as a method of protest against the government of India, which in its attempt at peacekeeping had instead become embroiled in our war. Forty years after Gandhi, in Sri Lanka, the Indian army occupied Tamil homes, crowded Tamil villages, raped Tamil women, and burned Tamil houses. They had burned his not so long ago. The occasion for K's decision to fast was an India-sponsored accord that he believed ignored the Tamil interest in a homeland. Both he and I were connected to the movement, the Liberation Tigers of Tamil Eelam, the Tamil Tigers, which for years had used violence and guerrilla warfare against the Sri Lankan government. That government discriminated against Tamils, but our own dubious morality was not lost on me. No one I knew in the movement would have dared to say such a thing aloud. At the same time, I understood that no act of violence we had committed had ever attracted as much support for a homeland as the act of violence K committed now, on his own body.

Thousands and thousands of people crowded all around us. I felt both alone and the desire to be alone. I could not count how many people there were around us, but I did not know any of them the way I knew him. There might have been as many as a hundred thousand. People swarmed, clinging to each other and to the stage's edge. When they came too close to me, I fought down an unreasonable alarm. They meant no harm, but they were hungry for him even as his body consumed itself. Many of them had been fasting in solidarity with him. Like him, some of them were also performers and opportunists. Our leaders had scattered speakers and microphones through the crowd, and for days, people had taken turns standing in front of them and crying out their grievances. Their eyes looked dull and enormous, rimmed with red. Now, after days of noise and threats of disruption, the temple was finally silent. The speakers hummed only with wind. No one knew what would happen at the moment of death. There had been rumors of rioting and calls for blood. For the moment, we felt only a terrible sense of anticipation made of both eagerness and fear.

I myself stood on the stage with K's doctor, the Tiger physician with whom I worked. I shook a little and tried to hold myself very straight. It was hot—very, very hot, and I had been standing there since sunrise, when I had gotten up from where I slept near K. I looked down at him where he lay on the floor of the stage, surrounded by the flags of the Tigers. I had known and watched the rhythm of his breathing for years in private. To do the same in public felt like a violation, but the irresistible rhythm of habit compelled me: his chest rose, his chest fell, his chest rose, his chest fell. His glasses slid askew, more askew with each slow breath, his eyes closed under them as though he were just nodding off on his veranda at home. His chest rose; his chest stilled, and once more I anticipated its descent. I waited, and the space of that wait grew infinite.

If you had asked me immediately afterward what I did as he died, I would have told you that I bent down to touch my forehead to his, that his skin felt warm and dry, that he still smelled faintly of *iluppai* flowers and other growing, living things. I would have told you that I went with him into the endless country of that trapped breath, a place where neither of us could cry out or make any human sound. I would have told you that although I had known that he would die — known it, perhaps, from the first time I had chosen to help him — that although this was the seed that had been planted, and watered, and planned for, in the face of its bloom, the air stopped in my throat too, and I could not believe what we had done.

Later, other people told me that when he died, I did not touch him: I stood apart from him on the stand and moved my hand to my mouth as if to silence myself.

The doctor put his hand on my elbow, which was wet with perspiration. "Sashi," he said. "Sashi."

And then I breathed again, and K did not. It was the first moment in which such a thing was possible, and the sharp quickening pain of it stunned me. How swiftly the world reshaped itself around his absence! Perhaps someone you know has died and you have a sense of what I mean: the horror of knowing that everything is going to continue very nearly as it did before. People will do their jobs; you will even do yours, although you did not know that you were capable of it.

Everything in medicine has its order, and this is also true of death: it has to be announced, the hour marked and recorded. The doctor, I understood, was going to pronounce it. I was glad to be spared this; even steeled as I had been for days against this inevitability, it would have been a very permanent thing to have the declaration of K's passing be something that came from my mouth. And it was a moment for the spotlight, which suited the doctor and did not suit me. I watched him play to the tense and waiting theater of people, as I would not have done. He leaned down over the prone body of my friend and with an exaggerated motion, put two fingers to the curve of K's dry neck, and then to the inside of his dry wrist. I had never imagined that someone could be so utterly parched. K looked as though, were he to be cut open, he would not even bleed.

The doctor sighed and looked up at me, and then at K's father, who was standing next to me. The doctor touched his own eyes and drew his fingers down his face, mimicking the motion of tears. As if he had been waiting for a cue, or for permission, K's father began to cry. The doctor turned to the crowd and made the same motion, and as though they were a great chorus, they wept in unison, keening and wailing and mourning. It was a peaceful mourning during which no one threw a stone, fired a gun, or lit a match. Despite what we had anticipated, there was no visible anger—only an unquenchable grief that washed the tension away. In the distance, at the far end of the temple grounds, the cadres began to move out. They had been instructed to occupy and protect property that otherwise would be at risk for destruction. Several vans took off from the temple. They would travel through Jaffna town. Voices through distant megaphones, spreading the news and asking for calm. Above the weeping audience, the beautiful crows circled. They, too, had been waiting for days, but now they swooped away from us, higher and higher, their paths looping upward like incense smoke.

Four cadres who had been waiting with K lifted him from the dais and the people's cries around us grew louder. His sarong fell around his limp legs, and they looked even thinner. Behind his plain checked shirt, the red flag of the Tigers was the biggest and brightest spot in the crowd, which had arrived wearing white in a preemptive strike at lamenting him. I thought that if I touched him now he might turn to powder. We might all ignite. I wanted to step down off the platform and tell them that I had loved K, that he had been the friend of my life. I wanted the people beside the stage to be with me, and I wanted to be with them, but the difference in our grief separated us. They looked like me and spoke my language and had grown up in the same places, but they were mourning for someone else.

* * *

The Nallur temple was the most beautiful of all the Hindu temples in Jaffna, and arguably, of all the Hindu temples in Sri Lanka: a good place for K to die, to make his last gesture, not least because it was dedicated to Murugan, the god of war, to whom K had always shown particular devotion. When K's body was carried away, the doctor and I followed, and even as we moved across the stage and away from the temple, we met the smell of jasmine and incense, and the burnt, clean odor I had associated with holiness from childhood. As though the temple itself also walked behind him.

The cadres bore his body down the steps of the stage to the sandy corridor by the side of the building. Before the passage, which was both wide and long, the crowd parted for us. It felt like the death procession of a king. Behind and above me, the bells of the clock in the main tower sounded. Around the clock, carved figures of temple guardians and gods watched over us. He could not have chosen a grander theater.

At the other end, the priests awaited us. They, too, cried with great ostentation and decorum. One of them came forward to usher us inside the small makeshift building where we had kept what we needed to care for him. And then the cadres left the doctor and me with the body.

The door closed behind them with a quiet click, and I looked down at K's dead face. It was kinder in death. Although he had been unconscious with his eyes closed when he died, they had fallen open somehow as he was carried in. Even glassed with death, they were beautiful eyes, still full of a scholar's quiet civilization, as though he were tired from a long night in the university library. Reaching under his glasses, I closed them with a shudder at the desert tenderness of his eyelids and the long, brittle brush of his lashes. The doctor undressed him quickly. When he motioned to me to look away from the naked body, I ignored him. I did not want to be spared anything about this body, the ugliness and horror of each wasted muscle. K's skin flaked and peeled as the doctor began to prepare the body for the funeral cortege. Little pieces of him drifted to the floor; his scalp littered his bushy black hair. I squatted and watched, completely still. When the doctor asked if I was all right, I nodded. But I could not bear how K looked. I rose and went to ask one of the priests for a bowl of oil. When I returned, without my asking, the doctor stopped his preparations of the body.

The oil smelled familiarly of coconut. They used this same oil to bathe the gods and light the lamps in this temple. It had a good fragrance with which to send K away: clean and spicy. He had liked this smell. I myself associated it with *dharshan,* the aspect of holiness we all wished to acquire when we entered a temple. Squatting back down, I dipped the edge of my white cotton sari into the oil and began to smooth it over the body. I drew the sari over his head like a veil, and the oil dripped from the corner of fabric onto his head. I let the sari drop from my hand, closed my eyes, and put my hands into his shock of hair like a pair of combs. His hair was dull, filled with windblown dust, tangled and matted from twelve days without brushing. Moisture without life seeped back into him. I looked up at the doctor, who nodded. "It will look a little better," he said. "They know how he died. They watched it."

And now he watched me. But I barely noticed. It felt like a ritual, but it was something I had never done before and have never done again for anyone. I put my fingers directly into the bowl of oil and touched K's eyebrows, which were standing up, wild with bristly hairs. I smoothed them down. Without wiping my hands clean, I took off his glasses, marking them with oily prints. I stroked his eyelids again, and under his eyes where the circles were. I tugged his cheeks and his earlobes and rounded his chin. Behind me, the door clicked. The doctor was gone. At last, after so many years, I was alone again with K.

I pushed a finger between his teeth and pulled it out again, still dry from his sandpaper tongue. I was not K's wife, or his sister, or his mother, but I poured oil from the bowl so that it formed a pool on the crater of his shallow chest. I pushed it up, into his neck and onto his withered arms, so far from the guns they had carried and the grenades they had thrown. I was not K's doctor, and I was not his lover, but I put my thumbs into his elbows and cupped my hands around their edges, which were sharper than his bones as I had previously known them. I undid the knot of my long hair. Kneeling, I laid my temple next to his shoulder and found that as I had always suspected, my head fit into a perfect place his joints made for me. I stretched myself out next to him. Beneath me, the concrete floor of the temple was cool. I moved onto him, matching each of my living parts against his dead ones so that my whole self was pressed against him, living cells against dead cells. He was still warm. Tall as I was, there was almost no difference between us. My hair fell forward and across his body, dead cells on dead cells. I let my nails cut into his back. I felt rather than saw the quiet fold of his once-skinny stomach, now bloated with hunger. I held onto him with all my might, as though I could bury myself in him, or as though between us, the earth and I could still hurt him.

It was not erotic, not even a little. It was not romantic, not even a little. It was desperate. For the first time in my life, I wanted to die. I dipped my finger into the oil and put it on my own dry lips. It tasted sour. I wanted to soak into him, to fill up each crevice and hollow bone, so I kissed him with that flammable mouth, but even with the oil, it was a chaste, paper-lipped kiss that came too late. Pushing myself up, I found that my sari was drenched in the oil I had placed on his body to give it the appearance of life. The scars on his stomach, which had been barely visible before, shone brightly, pushed into sharp relief by the edema of his fast. They were the scars of a battle he had fought in May, in Vadamarachchi, where he had been badly wounded. My hands mapped the damage, and finally, I touched my friend, no longer my patient. The marks began on his right side and traveled above his navel, ending on the left side of his rib cage. Doctors had removed parts of his liver and intestines. He had nearly died and in defiance of the code of our movement, I had wept then as I could not now. My own stomach scar-less, the broken eggs of two childhoods ago still sliding invisibly across it.

The scars reminded me that no matter what was done to K's body, the crowd had already seen things as the Tigers wished them to be seen. The scars would be covered up. He would be anointed with more oil and garlanded. He would be marked with sweet ash and saffron paste and *kungumum*, the red powder. His body would move through the streets and villages of Jaffna like the statue of a god, and no one would dare to say that he had never been a believer in true nonviolence. They would say that he was greater than Gandhi, and he was not.

Only my hands had on them the detritus of his skin.

I rose from K's body.

When doctor and priests finished their work, I dressed K in the uniform they gave me, the uniform of a lieutenant colonel. He had received a promotion upon his death, just as though he had died in battle. It made no difference to them how he died, just as it had made no difference to him. But it mattered to me.

I buttoned up his dear body in its brown shirt, latched his belt around his waist, pulled up the zipper of his trousers, and straightened his medals. The doctor let me do all of this. It was not the work of a doctor, but the work of a woman, and although I was not yet a doctor, I was no longer a child. He handed me the Tiger sash, and I draped it around K's shoulders, my fingers shaking. I took the camera K had given me for my sixteenth birthday out of my black bag and snapped a picture of him for the last time. I did it slowly, adjusting the angle of his uplifted chin, tracing his eyebrows again, moving his hat so that the shadows it cast would not obscure his eyes, even though his closed lids hid their light. I took my time, tucking his hair behind his ears and refolding his collar so that I could touch him again. I resisted — just barely — the urge to shake him.

Finally, the four male cadres came again and took his body away from me. They placed him into an open casket made of wood. Already, despite the doctor's care, K's hands were beginning to curl and freeze. His back stiffened, and already he was a stranger. Already he belonged to people who did not know him, and I could not believe I had ever laid my head against those unwelcoming shoulders. The cadres moved to put K's open coffin into the back of a black Jeep, and the crowd, wailing, followed it on foot. They formed a gruesome trail of white. I lingered at the end of the crowd, along with the doctor. The breeze that blew at my oily sari did not cool the Jaffna heat.

As we passed into the town, we saw house after house already festooned with the plaits of coconut leaves, a symbol of mourning. From other temples and schools we could hear funeral music blasting with obscene volume and pompousness. In front of all the houses, we saw pictures of K, garlanded and lit by oil lamps. At each town, people came out to join the train of mourners. Bare feet kicked up the dust of the road, and from far away, villages could see us coming by the cloud we brought with us. The weeping rang so loud that it carried across farms and across paddy fields, to beaches and lagoons, over the entire peninsula. Tears arrived, knocked on doors, and were met with open and regretful arms. Sorrow took up residence in every street of every borough.

K died as he had done everything in the last years of his life: with a great sense of theater. He could have been an actor, I see now, but even in times of peace, when more Jaffna men chose professions other than death-making or peace-making, they were rarely actors. We were obsessed with respectability, and it was not respectable to admit to acting. Still, in the fast's last days, when K did not have much strength left, I could tell by the exaggerated and slow way that he was moving that he had more than he was willing to show. He wanted to make the end a climax, and around him the propaganda machine that he had constructed whirred and clicked to help him. Cameramen focused on him. The thrum of music and the shrill voices of women singing rose to a higher pitch as though he had cued it. The priests, whose order was never disturbed, stopped even their slow, measured movements. In the distance, we could smell fires burning, the smell which is constantly in the air in Sri Lanka. It is the fragrance of purification, an ongoing process, and it smells not bad, but painful.

"I go only to return," he had said to me before closing his eyes: the traditional farewell. "Go and come back," I answered: the traditional answer. And although I have told you this story in English, you must remember, we were in Tamil. A private language for me now, here, and I remember him saying that as though it were private, as though it were not only to me but only for me, although we were surrounded by so many other people. And even as he said it, I was still wading through the river of my own understanding. He should have died days earlier. He was missing parts of his body. Death by fasting should not have taken him longer than a week. I had a suspicion that they had somehow stretched it out on purpose. For show. He went to sleep, but no one else could. Around the crowd, televisions had been set up. They were broadcasting only one channel, the channel of the Tigers, which was called Nidarshanam. I remember looking up to the screen, where the twin heads of K and Gandhi shone out at me. As I watched, the two heads moved closer together, merged, and blended into one. I could hear a group of women beginning a set of *thevaram*, devotional songs. Air rose from deep inside me, and I breathed heavily to expel it. I gulped, and swallowed, and started to laugh. I could not help it. K's mustache on Gandhi's face did not fit at all. Gandhi's protruding ears instead of K's obedient ones made no sense. It was funny—it was funny. I laughed as quietly as I could, which was not very quietly, and wiped my face, which was not wet, with the backs of my hands.

In a time of peace, as a Hindu, K would have been cremated. On a funeral pyre he would have burst and sparked like tinder. He would have risen into the air as smoke. If he had had a son, the boy would have carried the torch to light the flame. Since he had no son, his father would have done the deed. Since he had no wife, only his friends would have borne witness.

Only his friends. I could say that he was only a friend, but that would not be true; that would not be right. Our friendship exceeds and surpasses, expands and embraces. K is more, always; he is with me still. Here in the West, people think women of my country leap into fire with the bodies of men we have loved. But he was only a friend—*only*—and I let him go. They took his body from me, but it did not matter. Do you see now? Do you understand? In K, I had and lost such a friend that I became the place where his body burned.

COLE BECHER

■

Charybdis

FROM *The Iowa Review*

WE'D SPENT EIGHT MONTHS walking up and down berms and around shit-filled yards in Iraq swinging AN/PSS-12 mine detectors—known as "twelves" or "piss-twelves"—on top of eighty to a hundred pounds of gear, including M-4s, M-16s, even M-249 SAWs, and the requisite magazines or belts of 5.56mm ammunition. I was an inch shorter, my spinal cartilage having compressed under the weight.

Even so, I missed swinging the piss-twelve around people's yards, hitting the likely spots with a cool efficiency, as if searching for bombs were an Easter egg hunt. I missed digging or telling the grunts to dig when I heard the annoying, squealing tone. I missed finding something heavy wrapped in plastic only a foot or two down, saying, "We got you now, motherfucker" or "I found pay dirt," and watching the offending haji get zip-cuffed. I think we all missed it—I know Conrad did. He used to whistle "Taps" when he was sure he'd found something. At least I think it was "Taps." It was hard to tell because I'm slightly tone-deaf from shooting shoulder-fired rockets, and Conrad's whistling sounded like wind coming through an old screen door. If it wasn't "Taps," it was a dirge for the damned. Either way, we all loved those moments of discovery. Those little instants of validation made Iraq an okay place for us, so much that there were only two consistent downsides: no women and no booze.

Of course there were plenty of both when we came home that August. The handful who still had girlfriends or wives met them at our Navy/Marine Corps Reserve Drill Center, where the CO released us to the mob of waiting families and friends. It was well past midnight when we arrived and filed off the bus, each of us in our most present-able pair of desert cammies. It was late summer in Virginia, so it was warm when we formed up in the familiar parking lot—probably the same temperature as Iraq at night.

Still, it felt off—wrong. We were standing in formation in desert camouflage between red-brick buildings surrounded by green trees and grass. I felt exposed, vulnerable, the way you feel after a sniper's first shot, before you can pinpoint his location.

We could see the lights in the gym through the tall windows that ran along its side. In each, figures crammed against the glass, fight-ing for a glimpse of us, the way barking dogs jump against screen doors. It tripped my Spidey sense, and I felt like the illusion of safety was poised to pop. But I didn't say anything. No one did. We just stood there, loosely huddled in the parking lot as if preparing for an imminent attack. I remember looking at Conrad, locking eyes for a moment, taking a deep breath, and thinking, *This nice peaceful mo-ment is about to get overrun.* He nodded.

Mack, Conrad, and I were three of the last to climb the long ramp into the gym. We lingered at the bottom, looking up at the opening under the industrial roll-up door. All we could see was the bright light and the throngs of elated people swarming and swirling inside.

Mack turned and broke our silence. "It's like we're rock stars in some weird paradigm where it's cool to be swooned over by our lame-ass families." He paused for a moment, taking a deep breath. "All right, let's go meet those groupies." We grudgingly trudged up the ramp and into the gym, Mack leading and Conrad trailing. I lost track of them when my family descended on and surrounded me, giddily assaulting my tense shoulders with hugs and proclamations of joy.

We were quickly whisked away by our loved ones, taken back to hotel rooms, apartments, and homes, where we slept in the following morning. The awkward phone calls started that next afternoon.

"What are you doing?"

"Nothing, you?"

"Nothing."

Silence.

"So . . ."

The calls weren't awkward for us, but they were for our families. We didn't know what to do, and our families didn't know what to do with us. At first, we filled the hours as we had in Iraq. We went to the gym. We checked our e-mail. Some read. Some contemplated suicide — not if, not why. Just how. We watched movies.

We killed time.

We woke up each morning and, for a few terrifying moments, searched frantically for rifles we no longer carried, feeling awkward, uneven, and incomplete without them. We pretended like we were searching for something else — anything else — and tried to adapt to carrying cell phones instead.

Within a week, we reverted to completely ditching wives, fiancées, and girlfriends to play violent video games, fourteen hours on end, in blacked-out rooms with handles of whiskey and vodka and gin. We stopped shaving and then started again when no one scolded us. Very few ever really stopped drinking.

After a couple of weeks, though, most started to stumble back into their regular civilian lives. I started working at the cable TV call center and was instantly lost in abject boredom. Mack excitedly went back to school only to decide within a week that he despised college kids. Some, like Conrad, were left searching for jobs. Lowe's didn't think he was qualified to guard a parking lot. Outback Steakhouse said his college degree overqualified him to serve food. Bed Bath & Beyond really needed an inventory manager, but he wasn't what they had in mind. So, he spent half of his time either drunk or searching for a job and the other half walking long distances — miles upon miles — grinding along as we had when we'd carried all that weight. He said it started one day when he walked seven miles on the trail out to Cascade Point, past the football stadium and the bridge over Irish Creek. When he got there, he looked around for a moment, turned, and walked seven miles back — simple as that. It started as something to ease the boredom, but it began to consume more and more of his time.

He told us about it over drinks at Murphy's Pub, where Conrad, Mack, and I met on Mondays, played darts, and drank until the bartender switched on the lights and killed the music. Others sometimes joined us, but nothing regular.

Mack complained about immature college kids, calling them "spoiled, adolescent fuck-sticks living in a no-consequence, paid-for-by-Daddy world." I tried desperately to drown my disgust after ten-hour days of empathizing with irate cable subscribers who treated missing an episode of *Glee* as the end of the world. Conrad, still wearing his combat boots every day, told us about his walks matter-of-factly.

"Killing time," Mack called over his shoulder between darts. "Doing what's natural."

But Conrad said it felt weird and unnatural without the weight. So he loaded a backpack with two dumbbells, twenty-five pounds each, and started carrying it on walks. He felt a little better, especially since he'd gotten a part-time gig restocking a bookstore two days a week after the weekly shipment. He lugged books all day and walked for hours after, long into the nights. On his days off, when not looking for another job, he walked all day—ten, twelve, fourteen hours at a time—just like over there.

At some point, he added weight by lining the backpack with a trash bag and filling it with sand, shaking it so he could fit a little more. Then he attached a collapsible shovel to the side of the pack one Friday and didn't return until Tuesday. He said he'd just kept walking and eating what little garbage he'd been able to fit in his pockets. At night, he dug shallow holes and slept off the trail so he could observe traffic without being seen. Conrad hadn't showered in days, but I could tell he'd been bathing with baby wipes and shaving at night to avoid razor burn, the way we had during the Pipeline Sensus Sweep, unofficially, yet appropriately, dubbed "Operation Mad Max."

We asked him what he was doing, and he said he'd been patrolling and manning observation posts. He told us he'd be going out again soon because there were some suspicious-looking places that needed to be checked.

Mack chuckled, clinked Conrad's beer glass against his own, and said, "Keepin' us safe, point man. Keep keepin' us safe."

Conrad did just that. He went to Walmart and bought a cheap metal detector called "The Scavenger." It was pitifully subpar to our military-grade piss-twelves, but after learning the tricks, he could efficiently interrogate a metal signature and locate its center. He started using The Scavenger on his patrols, and thus his patrols became sweeps. He walked up and down the public trail with big and small backyards on either side of him and looked for visual indicators—clues like loose or freshly dug dirt, stakes, ribbons, mounds, plastic, wires, ant trails, or initiating systems. When he saw something, he climbed over the fence or stepped through the gate to perform a hasty sweep. Occasionally someone came out, yelled at him, and asked what the hell he was doing. He claimed to respond with a firm, *"Is-koot! Is-koot!"* or an *"Im-che!"* Mostly the yards were clear, but every now and then he'd find an old jar of cash or an abandoned water pipe.

The first time he found a gun, it was night, and he called in for support. The police responded to the strange, anonymous tip, promptly surprising the homeowner in bed with his wife. As it turned out, the gun was unregistered, had blood on the barrel, and the man got hauled off for questioning. Afterward, Conrad came out of the tree line and presented the man's angry wife with a small bag of rice, just like we had done in Iraq. He asked, *"Wain ali baba?"* Confused and angry, she shouted and waved her arms frantically. Conrad talked slower, over-pronouncing each syllable in his pidgin Arabic, but she didn't understand. Instead, she continued shouting and making angry, threatening gestures. He commanded *"Irfa-eedake,"* but she stormed off into her home.

Conrad didn't have to explain letting her go, because he couldn't enter and clear the house alone. We nodded over our beers in understanding; women simply were not arrested in this war. Per our SOP, he'd left, climbing back over the fence and continuing down the trail until he found a good spot for an OP.

After a month or so, Conrad started going out for weeks at a time, sweeping the creeks and canals and trails around town. Sometimes he slept during daylight, and more often than not he'd sleep only a couple of hours per day, for a week at a time. But he continued reporting finds and calling for support when he hit "pay dirt." Once, he found fertilizer and gasoline in a shed and reported bomb-making materials in a garage with LARRY'S LANDSCAPING painted on the side. Larry was detained for questioning while his wife and child pleaded and cried. Conrad said he slept easier, having prevented an attack on a convoy or foot patrol. He'd left a bag of rice on their doorstep.

He kept sweeping, occasionally finding something in a house or a yard. Hunched over his beer, he said the hardest places to sweep were where children played, because they purposely littered the ground with all kinds of debris, rendering metal detectors useless. Instead, he visually inspected before manually probing with a knife or simply digging until satisfied all was clear.

In October, our platoon had to resume drilling with the rest of the company one weekend a month and reported for muster at 1600 on a Friday. Conrad did not report for muster. Mack and I had had beers with him two weeks prior but had been unable to get him to answer his phone since. The CO sent Mack and me to Conrad's apartment to find him, and Mack picked the lock when no one answered.

Conrad's apartment was exactly like our hooch in Habbaniyah: the walls decorated with crookedly taped-up pictures of girls from *Maxim* and *Playboy*, the windows sandbagged and boarded up, and the AC on full blast. The bed was even handmade from scrap two-by-fours, two-by-sixes, and plywood, complete with a tarp curtain. It was like being jerked backward five months and eight thousand miles.

"Fucker even has a jack-shack," Mack said as he pulled the curtain aside to reveal a bare, ratty mattress. "Gonna go out on a limb here and say he hasn't been laid lately."

Conrad was living out of a cheap, black plastic trunk and a sea bag, both shoved under the bed. We found a box in the trunk with his wallet, iPod, and powered-down cell phone. The wallet was missing only his military ID card, and his cell phone hadn't registered a call in over a month. Mack showed me the empty window in the wallet where the ID belonged.

"He sanitized?" I asked.

Mack nodded and responded, "Houston, we have a serious fucking problem."

When we returned to the drill center, our CO asked if Conrad was home. Mack responded simply, "No, sir. He's *gone*." The CO sighed grudgingly and marked him down as Unauthorized Absent while I pretended to file a U.A. Contact Sheet.

Unbeknownst to us at the time, Conrad was still reporting finds and possible finds, and the police had started looking for him. The problem was that they didn't know who or what to look for. They ran circles around town searching, but it was aimless and fruitless. At first the police wanted to send him to the psych ward. People were complaining about holes in their yards and occasional break-ins. Later, they needed him as a witness because he'd found a dead body in Oscar Quincey's yard before simply leaving it upon discovering that he'd detected a watch, not a weapon. The next day, Old Man Quincey's heart gave out from the panic and strain of reburying the body.

A week later, Conrad found a refrigerator in the Gullys' backyard, buried so that it opened upward. It was filled with rifles and ammunition from the early 1960s and three KKK uniforms. Since the Gullys were black and in their late twenties — the wife six months' pregnant with their first child — the police concluded that previous residents were probably responsible and sent a clerk over to the county courthouse to look through property records.

In early November, Conrad reported a family as bomb-makers when he found their unmarked pet cemetery. On the 911 recording, he claimed they were planning to use carcasses to hide bombs. It was on the statewide news and everything. The video showed a six-year-old girl crying at the sight of the family dog's rotting corpse. It was lying in the middle of the yard, where it had been drug by its collar and left with maggots crawling out of the empty eye sockets. The dog's name was Cookie.

It was mid-December when the police figured out who Conrad was. A rookie cop — an Army veteran — read the reports and recognized that the eight-digit numbers Conrad recited were military grid coordinates and that the reports were modified nine-lines for reporting wounded and IEDs. Somehow they kept the search quiet before finally piecing together that their target was military or ex-military and coming to see us. By that time, we hadn't seen Conrad for months, and we offered to help.

* * *

It started as a ploy to lure him out. We play-acted like it was Iraq, since Conrad was acting like it was Iraq. The company CO called up our platoon and ordered us simply to find him. We spent a week aimlessly walking around town in our cammies, flaks, and Kevlars, lugging our weapons and piss-twelves. We lazily mock-patrolled a few hours a day in disorganized tactical columns on trails and through open fields.

For a week, we awkwardly stumbled around remote parts of town with orange blank-firing adaptors affixed to the barrels of unloaded rifles. We answered texts and checked football scores on smartphones during halts and made a minimal effort not to be too obvious about it. Simmons listened to his iPod in one ear, singing and humming along under his breath.

The entire week, all we found was an old ranger grave he'd dug and slept in.

After that, we got serious. We stopped half-assing and made the ruse real. The rest of the company was activated. They brought tactical vehicles, crew-served weapons, and radios filled with crypto. The works. We started using proper radio etiquette and call signs. We even code-named major roads alphabetically after universities with prominent football teams and started enforcing light and noise discipline after sunset.

All non-military electronics disappeared. Incoming calls from girlfriends and wives suddenly went straight to voice mail. The CO even gave the order to ditch the BFAs on the muzzles of our rifles, originally intended to impart comfort to the citizens. We were then ordered to insert magazines in our rifles.

"We're not in Kansas anymore," Mack offered as the metallic clicks of 126 M-16 and M-4 assault rifles accepting thirty-round magazines rustled through the assembly area. "Look out Oz—there ain't no cowardly lions on this yellow brick road."

I bought cigarettes and a lighter. Several cut the fingers off their gloves and rolled their sleeves up to the middle of their forearms. Most un-bloused their boots, and a few attached watches to their flaks. We all started carrying extra, unmarked liter bottles of water in dump pouches.

We're back, I thought as we settled into everything simple and familiar.

After two days of planning and rehearsing and a full morning of mission briefing, we mounted up in Humvees with turret gunners and began a coordinated sweep through town. First Platoon started in the northwest corner and swept southeast towards the park. Second and Third Platoons spread out along the northern edge of town and swept directly south to the park. Headquarters set up an ambush site at the park and waited. We pushed nearly twenty hours at a time, resting for a few hours every night in two-hour shifts.

We chewed and dipped instant coffee grounds to stay awake and alert.

Where the town had casually regarded us as a strange breed of tourist during the first week, it treated us with the mixed curiosity and fear reserved for dangerous wildlife after we stepped off that morning.

The sweep through the university was the worst, slowing progress to a literal crawl. It took all of Second Platoon and half of First two full days. We performed cordon-knocks on every building on campus while the college kids stood nearby in awe, snapping pictures with smartphones. We tried to scatter them, but they swarmed like gnats and mosquitoes, continually circling back around. I'd never felt so on edge in my entire life. With tall buildings and countless windows in every direction, the place was a sniper's wet dream. Even with the masses of people swirling around, we were still totally exposed out in the open.

Before we entered the campus, we had gone firm in the parking garage, refusing to proceed until we could scrounge up enough radios for almost everyone in the platoon to have one visible on their flak jacket. Only the squad leaders and above actually had batteries, but communication wasn't the point. It was a shell game we'd played in Saqlawiyah to hide the chain of command when there'd been a high sniper threat. It had worked then, so we decided to play the game again.

The radios eased our tension a little, but we sweated our time in those college courtyards more than we had in the two-level shanty-town of Saqlawiyah. When we finally passed the stadium just after sunset on the second day, we all breathed a sigh of relief. The thousands of watchful eyes had borne down like so many pounds and worn us thin, in ways no civilian could see or understand.

Later, a lone bag of trash left out too late for the sanitation crew prompted a hasty search of an affluent home. The entire rear of the house was wrapped in floor-to-ceiling glass, and when Mack walked up and reported the house as cleared, I was looking out over the perfectly manicured backyard sloping up a hill to a thick tree line that wrapped 180 degrees around the back of the house. Standing in filthy boots on a polished hardwood floor with a thirty-year-old housewife's irate protests echoing from the entryway, I flatly commented, "We shouldn't be here. It's a tactical nightmare."

"That, kemosabe, is the nature of being the bait," Mack responded.

As we exited, the housewife, a petite blonde, grabbed my sleeve with one hand, pointed up at my face with the other, and started yelling at me. Smirking, I pulled my sleeve from her grasp and continued out the front door. She fell instantly silent, and Mack, one step behind, cheerily proclaimed, "Don't worry, lady, we're here for *you*," chuckling as he passed.

After bounding to the curb, I turned back and kneeled to cover Mack's movement. The lady was standing in the doorway across her pristine front lawn, watching our withdrawal, mouth open and eyes wide, blinking rapidly. When Mack trotted past, he remarked, "Same shit, prettier women."

Ultimately, it took us nine days to inch through every neighborhood, but we never found Conrad. Either we missed him or he sensed the trap, dug in somewhere, and laid low.

With the sweep complete, we started patrolling. We knew he was around, but we couldn't pin him down to bring back. Early on after the initial sweep, Mack had the idea to start a rumor that a battalion was sending a platoon of volunteers to Afghanistan. "Be really vocal about it—make sure he hears. I'll bet you he'll walk right up to join."

So we did. We even picked a random grunt battalion to support and made it part of the rumor. As expected, it spread through the company at a speed Mack called "Mach Jesus." Within three hours, we had seventy-six volunteers for thirty-three slots, but still no sign of Conrad. A list actually started. Someone had written, "No-Shit Deployment Volunteer List" at the top of the page. I couldn't figure out if "No-Shit" meant "for real" because a battalion really wanted a platoon, or if it was just some lance corporal being a smartass. On the off chance it was real, I put my name on the top line, which had been left blank intentionally, and passed it on. The company staff took the ruse so far as to organize the volunteers into a platoon on paper, assigning team leaders and squad leaders and such. I was given third squad.

We continued sweeping and searching for another two weeks until the battalion CO came down from DC and, after one sneering look around, called it off. But before leaving, he overheard a couple of PFCs talking about how excited they were about the deployment and angrily called division to find out why Marines from one of his companies were getting deployed without his knowledge. I don't know how that conversation went, but what matters is that division found out they had a platoon of volunteers and a week later issued orders for Afghanistan in support of 3rd Battalion, 6th Marine Regiment.

We were so happy that we threw a party in Conrad's honor. We even dressed a mannequin in some of his old cammies and spent the night toasting and taking drunken pictures of each other with it. None of our girlfriends, fiancées, or wives seemed to understand and were generally outraged by our joy and our volunteering. There was a mass dumping, which left ninety-five percent of us single before reporting. On the plane, we all laughed until it hurt when Mack summed up our collective feelings: "Fuck 'em if they can't take a joke."

Five months later, we were in Helmand Province, sweeping for IEDs and weapons caches. We'd been out for at least three weeks — so long that even the young, naive, "moto-tard" officers had stopped caring if we shaved. Doug and Russell had both been blown to pieces but had somehow survived. Roger had been shot through the shoulder. Still, no one had a damn clue where Conrad was.

When he came up in conversation one night, Mack swallowed the last bite of his beef ravioli MRE and said flatly, "He's a fucking magician. Disappeared himself, then disappeared us when we went looking."

* * *

We got lucky a lot in the heavily mined fields of Helmand, where the Taliban planted IEDs with such low metallic content that our piss-twelves were useless. Often, when the piss-twelve didn't register any-thing, there would be some visual clue marking the spot—a rock stacked strangely on a stump, a ribbon, loose dirt. We'd see it, check it out, and find a 155mm artillery round wired to a pressure plate one of us had narrowly missed stepping on or were kneeling right next to. Mack said it was Conrad keeping us safe, our point man sweeping ahead of us. I don't think he truly believed it, and I don't know if I did. But it doesn't matter—that was never the point.

Even today, years later, I still check the police blotters for evidence of Conrad. Every now and then, I see something odd or unexplained I think must be him. Sometimes I even go to look for evidence, but I never find much. We had the same problem during the sweep: it always felt like he was nearby, but of course he wasn't. You have to understand: he's one of the best. He didn't want to be brought back, even by us. And I can't say I blame him.

RACHEL SWIRSKY

■

If You Were a Dinosaur, My Love

FROM *Apex Magazine*

IF YOU WERE A DINOSAUR, my love, then you would be a T-Rex. You'd be a small one, only five feet, ten inches, the same height as human-you. You'd be fragile-boned and you'd walk with as delicate and polite a gait as you could manage on massive talons. Your eyes would gaze gently from beneath your bony brow-ridge.

If you were a T-Rex, then I would become a zookeeper so that I could spend all my time with you. I'd bring you raw chickens and live goats. I'd watch the gore shining on your teeth. I'd make my bed on the floor of your cage, in the moist dirt, cushioned by leaves. When you couldn't sleep, I'd sing you lullabies.

If I sang you lullabies, I'd soon notice how quickly you picked up music. You'd harmonize with me, your rough, vibrating voice a strange counterpoint to mine. When you thought I was asleep, you'd cry unrequited love songs into the night.

If you sang unrequited love songs, I'd take you on tour. We'd go to Broadway. You'd stand onstage, talons digging into the floorboards. Audiences would weep at the melancholic beauty of your singing.

If audiences wept at the melancholic beauty of your singing, they'd rally to fund new research into reviving extinct species. Money would flood into scientific institutions. Biologists would reverse engineer chickens until they could discover how to give them jaws with teeth. Paleontologists would mine ancient fossils for traces of collagen. Geneticists would figure out how to build a dinosaur from nothing by discovering exactly what DNA sequences code everything about a creature, from the size of its pupils to what enables a brain to contemplate a sunset. They'd work until they'd built you a mate.

If they built you a mate, I'd stand as the best woman at your wedding. I'd watch awkwardly in green chiffon that made me look sallow, as I listened to your vows. I'd be jealous, of course, and also sad, because I want to marry you. Still, I'd know that it was for the best that you marry another creature like yourself, one that shares your body and bone and genetic template. I'd stare at the two of you standing together by the altar and I'd love you even more than I do now. My soul would feel light because I'd know that you and I had made something new in the world and at the same time revived something very old. I would be borrowed, too, because I'd be borrowing your happiness. All I'd need would be something blue.

If all I needed was something blue, I'd run across the church, heels clicking on the marble, until I reached a vase by the front pew. I'd pull out a hydrangea the shade of the sky and press it against my heart and my heart would beat like a flower. I'd bloom. My happiness would become petals. Green chiffon would turn into leaves. My legs would be pale stems, my hair delicate pistils. From my throat, bees would drink exotic nectars. I would astonish everyone assembled, the biologists and the paleontologists and the geneticists, the reporters and the rubberneckers and the music aficionados, all those people who—deceived by the helix-and-fossil trappings of cloned dinosaurs—believed that they lived in a science fictional world when really they lived in a world of magic where anything was possible.

If we lived in a world of magic where anything was possible, then you would be a dinosaur, my love. You'd be a creature of courage and strength but also gentleness. Your claws and fangs would intimidate your foes effortlessly. Whereas you—fragile, lovely, human you—must rely on wits and charm.

A T-Rex, even a small one, would never have to stand against five blustering men soaked in gin and malice. A T-Rex would bare its fangs and they would cower. They'd hide beneath the tables instead of knocking them over. They'd grasp each other for comfort instead of seizing the pool cues with which they beat you, calling you a fag, a towel-head, a shemale, a sissy, a spic, every epithet they could think of, regardless of whether it had anything to do with you or not, shouting and shouting as you slid to the floor in the slick of your own blood.

If you were a dinosaur, my love, I'd teach you the scents of those men. I'd lead you to them quietly, oh so quietly. Still, they would see you. They'd run. Your nostrils would flare as you inhaled the night and then, with the suddenness of a predator, you'd strike. I'd watch as you decanted their lives—the flood of red; the spill of glistening, coiled things—and I'd laugh, laugh, laugh.

If I laughed, laughed, laughed, I'd eventually feel guilty. I'd promise never to do something like that again. I'd avert my eyes from the newspapers when they showed photographs of the men's tearful widows and fatherless children, just as they must avert their eyes from the newspapers that show my face. How reporters adore my face, the face of the paleontologist's fiancée with her half-planned wedding, bouquets of hydrangeas already ordered, green chiffon bridesmaid dresses already picked out. The paleontologist's fiancée who waits by the bedside of a man who will probably never wake.

If you were a dinosaur, my love, then nothing could break you, and if nothing could break you, then nothing could break me. I would bloom into the most beautiful flower. I would stretch joyfully toward the sun. I'd trust in your teeth and talons to keep you/me/us safe now and forever from the scratch of chalk on pool cues, and the scuff of the nurses' shoes in the hospital corridor, and the stuttering of my broken heart.

MAIA MORGAN

■

The Saltwater Twin

FROM *Creative Nonfiction*

We have lingered in the chambers of the sea
By sea-girls wreathed with seaweed red and brown
Till human voices wake us, and we drown.
　　　　　—T. S. Eliot, "The Love Song of J. Alfred Prufrock"

I PICTURED HER below the waves where the water was gentle. I imagined she floated like a bright October leaf, unhurried, lazily see-sawing in the current until at last she came to rest on the ocean floor. Her hair grew into delicate ropes of seaweed; her skin turned opalescent like the inside of a shell. She wore a necklace of coral, swam seal-like through shimmering clouds of fish, and slept in an underwater cave with a nightlight of luminescent plankton. In my imagination, she became mythic: The Saltwater Twin. She belongs to the sea, I thought. She knows things no one else knows.

She didn't start out as a mythical creature. She was an ordinary kid named Abby Mahoney, a sandy-haired, freckle-faced girl—that is, if she looked anything like her twin brother, who was my age. I never met her. Her family lived on my cousins' street, but she was already gone by the time they moved in. Abby drowned in the Atlantic when we were three, leaving her brother, leaving all of us behind. Abby had been Tommy's twin, but The Saltwater Twin was mine—and she gave me a way to escape.

My family spent a couple of weeks each summer at Martha's Vineyard—my parents, sisters, and maternal grandfather, and sometimes my aunt, uncle (my mom's brother), and cousins. I loved the ferry ride from Woods Hole—the bellow of the whistle; the smell of diesel and tar and sea air; the gulls wheeling and shrieking overhead; the boys treading water in the harbor, calling for us to throw them coins; and the men tossing ropes as thick as my arm from the boat to other men who caught them on the dock and pulled us in. I loved the hermit crabs that scrabbled in our plastic buckets, the quicksilver minnows that flicked around our shins, the prehistoric horseshoe crabs. I loved the way the priest said *Body of Christ* with a Boston accent; the salt that dried in ribbons on our skin; the hippies and seaweed; beaded moccasins and sailor bracelets; ladies with tan legs and pleated white tennis skirts; the clay cliffs; the dinners of tomatoes, sweet corn, fresh-caught fish, and pie. Sometimes we swam on the ocean beach and raced down the hot sand of the dunes, past sharp, sun-bleached grass and tangled thickets of wild roses with blooms the impossible pink of Barbie lipstick. Sometimes we swam at Menemsha Pond, where the beach was festooned with dried seaweed and spotted like a bird's egg with blotches of black sand. There was an inlet we called the Dangerous River, carved into the sand by the tide; it was one of our favorite places to play. It felt like a jungle; the grass was high and laced with the cries of plovers and gulls and the buzz of insects. We couldn't see our moms from around the bend in the Dangerous River, which came to my collarbone at high tide. We'd strip off our bathing suits under the murky water and rinse the sand out of the crotches. The sand, of course, was ubiquitous. It peppered our scalps, worked its way into sheets and sandwiches, dusted the floors of our rental houses.

In the unstructured summer days, I drifted into my own world, mostly unencumbered by adult expectations and entanglements. I had books and sky and hours to daydream. The grownups had newspapers and sweet rolls and hours to talk over beach towels and the supper table. They talked to each other about what to make for dinner, and they talked about the president and James Taylor and what color they ought to paint the bathroom back home.

My mother asked us whether we'd brushed our teeth and if we could imagine what that little schoolhouse up the road was like a hundred years ago and whether we wanted a peach or some boysenberry yogurt for a snack. She felt at home at the beach. She loved to eat the special treats you could only get at that one bakery with the screen door or that little stand by the wharf. She sang in the car, songs she knew from college and before. She liked us to sing with her, and sometimes we did. She liked to imagine the fancy houses we could live in if we were rich. She took us to the library, and we filled canvas sail bags of books. She read voraciously. She loved strangers, and strangers probably liked her because she was inquisitive and pretty. But she was also sad. And scared at night to be alone. Afraid of thunderstorms and the dark. My mother was a cigarette-sneaking, bobby-socked twelve-year-old trapped inside a suburban housewife. Her father called her the Queen of Sheba. My father didn't make her happy. As far as I could tell, he didn't pay much attention to her at all, and my mother required attention. He thought she was naïve and careless; she thought he was uncouth and cruel. At least, that's what it seemed like to me.

My father talked about how the salt water was good for us and how that was a nice piece of fish, and asked who wanted to drive with him to the dump. He went running with my uncle and to the market to buy dinner. My dad was pale and then sunburned. I guess he read, too. That's what everyone did at the beach—read or played cards. I played War and Spit with my sisters and cousins. Uno and Hearts with our moms. But I don't remember my father playing. He made a swing for us and hung it from a tree in the front yard of one of the houses we rented. That's all I remember.

My sisters, Molly and Sam, were fifteen months and four years younger than I, respectively. Molly didn't talk that much. When she did, it was about whatever we were doing—riding in the car, swimming. Or maybe what we were going to do later—what we might eat for dinner, if there'd be dessert, if we'd get to sleep all together with the cousins. Sam talked about basketball, she talked about scary things she saw on TV that she wasn't supposed to watch, she asked whether sharks might swim this far north. Molly loved dolls and babies, and hated it when people stared at her. Sam liked candy and getting her way. Neither of them liked to read like I did, but we played together sometimes on the beach. We raced through the shallow water, laughing at how it pulled us down and made it impossible to run, like when you try to run in a bad dream.

My grandfather was a sphinx with horn-rimmed glasses and fat toenails. He asked what grade I'd be in come September and if I still liked school and if I thought my dad made a blueberry pie that wasn't half bad. He read thick, hardcover books and asked if I knew that it made God happy when little girls were obedient. He wore Bermuda shorts and the old Penguin polo shirts with skinny collars. He coughed when he laughed. He said, *Good girl, that's a good girl.* He smelled like skin and smoke. During the night, sometimes in the afternoon, my grandfather would take me or Molly into his room. Sam was too little then, but he'd get to her eventually. There were lots of girl cousins. He could wait. He stopped short of intercourse, rejecting it, perhaps, as too risky—I don't know why, really—but I remember his hands gripping my small thighs. I remember the color and feel of his skin against mine. The sound of his zipper. His fumbling, the rasp and heat of his breath. He huffed and snuffed—a goblin, a wolf. He dripped and oozed. He pried us open like oysters. He sucked out everything inside. Outside the room where he did these things, he sat on the couch with us sometimes and read us stories. He told my mother he'd take some toast with mushrooms. He crossed his brown legs and tapped ash into an oyster shell. He was mottled and knobbed like a witch, evil as Rumpelstiltskin. I saw him. I knew his secret name. But then I had to forget. I was a kid, after all. I understood pretending. Forget, pretend—almost the same thing.

It was probably my mother or my aunt who first mentioned Abby—maybe chatting on their towels at Menemsha Pond while we hunched nearby, drizzling sandy broth through our fingertips into delicate stalagmites. Although I was a fairly conscientious kid about many things, I didn't have any serious qualms about eavesdropping. Grownups seemed to have a monopoly on all the really important information, so listening to them, especially when you were in plain view if they'd only been paying attention, didn't seem wrong. That's how I knew one of my uncles had gotten drunk and smashed through the sliding glass door of my grandfather's shower, and that's how, the summer I was eight, I found out how Abby had died.

It could have been any of us. Every summer, my sisters, cousins, and I exhausted ourselves fighting the waves, staying in until our mothers protested that our lips were blue. I knew how it felt to be dragged under, shaken like a ragdoll, lungs like party balloons about to burst until you managed to surface, sputtering and choking, through the foam. It made me feel strong to look the ocean in its fearsome blue eye and come out breathing. You knew the ocean might drown you, but not because it was malevolent. That's just the way it was. Not that there was no fear; fear tumbled with you in the salt-clouded blue-green. It held you, one part at a time, laced around a wrist or thigh, bubbled across your sealed lips. But there was something else—a steady *let go, let go*—a calm, a beyond-ness where nothing could reach. For a split second, I felt eternal, omnipotent. Then I'd swallow water and gasp back into time above the surface.

I turned Abby into The Saltwater Twin on the ferry. I liked to lean over the railing and watch the hull carve the bottle-green plane below us into frothy white furrows that connected the dot-to-dot of where we'd been to where we were going. I'd press myself into the space of that moment—sun and spray on my skin, the snap of my windbreaker, the deep rumble of the ferry in my legs—and think that no one else could hear what I heard or see what I saw. *I am apart from these others; I am my own.* I thought about Abby on her own in the ocean; her drowning set her apart from all the rest of us alive on this boat and on the island and all over the world. Maybe she was watching our ferry like the mermaid sisters in the Hans Christian Andersen story, who'd poke their heads up through the waves and spy on ships. The mermaids sang through storms to sailors whose ships were going down. They told them not to be afraid; they sang of the beauty of their kingdom under the sea. But every sailor who reached their undersea gardens arrived there lifeless. The sisters grieved for the unlucky sailors but couldn't cry; the story says that because mermaids don't have tears, they suffer that much more. I liked that. Unlike my mother, for whom an offhand remark or a touching Pepsi commercial could set off profuse weeping, I held back tears even when I split my chin open falling off my bike. I guarded my tears fiercely; they were mine to keep.

Lifeguards differentiate between a swimmer in distress and someone who's drowning. We expect victims to shout and flail and wave their arms, and swimmers in distress may do that—panic when they realize the water's too rough or deep and they're not strong enough to make it to shore. Drowning, on the other hand, is deceptively quiet. Looking back, I wonder why all of us who were subject to my grandfather's assaults—me, my sisters, my cousins, and my mother, her sister, their cousins before us—didn't display more unmistakable signs of distress. It seems strange there wasn't more ferocity in us, but I guess we were absorbed in staying afloat. We turned on each other sometimes. We knew instinctively how to hurt. We quietly laid siege to ourselves. There would be eating disorders, self-harm, substance abuse, and destructive relationships. As a kid, I engaged in the occasional skirmish with adults. When, clearing a Thanksgiving table, I refused to touch my grandfather's plate. When I whirled on my mother, chasing me for some backtalk, and socked her in the stomach. But mostly I was good. Mostly I sank. Resistance was playing dead, pretending to sleep so soundly I couldn't be moved, going limp, going blank. The drowning person can't wave her arms; she can't shout. She tries in vain to use the water as a ladder to push herself up; she angles her mouth toward oxygen. Drowning is quiet: the head tilts back, the eyes glaze over, the victim slips beneath the surface.

Leaning over the ferry railing, I imagined Abby's smooth head emerging from our foamy wake. A wake. When we learned about homonyms in third grade, I was fascinated. Every afternoon after school, I scoured the dictionary for more pairs to bring in for my teacher. Two words that looked and sounded the same but meant different things. Doorways into different worlds. *Wake*: to rouse or become roused from sleep; a watch kept over a body before burial; the track of waves left by a ship or other object moving through water. The roiling water behind us that marked the place where we'd been. *A wake*: where Abby's family had sat with her and said good-bye; where men wore suits and cried and ladies set casseroles and cakes on kitchen counters. *A wake, awake*: conscious, having your wits about you. I hated waking up. In the morning, dreams still clutched like dark weeds; I wanted to sink back into sleep and stay. *A wake, awake.* A word could mean one thing and another. A thing could be one thing and another. In the ocean, my mother grew light enough for me to carry; I could pick her up like a baby or a bride. I endowed The Saltwater Twin with that magic. She was all-powerful—more powerful, anyway, than me or any of the adults I knew. And she was gone from the world, for good, while I was stuck where I was.

Everyone acted like things were normal. They talked about rain and carpool; they chopped onions and poured milk. *Outside* was green lawns and fresh paint. *Outside* was living rooms kids weren't allowed in, with petit-point pillows and crystal dishes of candy made to look like pebbles. Kids with perfect bedrooms and perfect Halloween costumes. I knew a girl whose Raggedy Ann was so big she wore the doll's clothes for Halloween till she was ten. Kids in the suburbs caught on early to what was important, the things that made the world easier to take. If you wanted to be unique, you could maybe wear an Izod in a funky color or admit that you liked to read for fun. Questions were uncool. Everyone was supposed to act like they knew what they were doing at all times. *Shallow*: where the water was warm and safe. *Shallow* was every day in the suburbs, every conversation, most every expression on every face. *Shallow*: the breaths we took when we were afraid, the way someone breathes when she's drowning.

I didn't feel normal. I felt like an anomaly, some kind of monster or feral child accidentally dressed in a Snoopy T-shirt and corduroys. I felt dark; I felt deep. I could drag a sailor to his death. I asked questions; I wondered incessantly about what was unspoken, underneath.

In Sunday school, we learned about transubstantiation, in which bread and wine really turned into the body and blood of Christ. When the altar bell rang, I looked for some tear in the air, some juddering of magic, listened for the whisper of the Holy Ghost. After I received communion, I'd hold the host in my mouth and wonder what it would feel like to be chewing on sinew and flesh, my mouth filling with the blood of Christ. I imagined the taste of jungle gym, penny, a thickening in my saliva like milk. The communion wafers turned to paste in my mouth while I knelt and puzzled over the way something could seem like one thing and all the time be something else. I learned to hold a notion close, just shy of truly believing it, managing in that way to give credence to two, often disparate, things at once. I lost baby teeth, picked out socks; I had sore throats and Easter dresses. I faced my mother's hysterics, my grandfather's assaults.

I believed in Middle-earth, looked for secret passageways, prayed for signs. I managed somehow to live in the world that was and in the world I conjured. It was a way to believe things I knew weren't true—that my family was the sunny Sunday family building castles on the beach, that I wasn't growing up on a sinking ship.

Maybe—when someone close to you died or someone did you harm or maybe simply when you emerged from a dark movie theater onto a bright sidewalk full of people hurrying home to dinner—you've felt, somehow, the world split in two. Ordinary things—coins clinking into the machine on the bus, the key rotating the lock on your front door—feel jarring, surreal. Yet you keep going. You ride the bus, you open your front door, you put something on a plate, you eat, you watch TV. Somehow you find a way to be in two worlds. One fades; the other comes to life. We shift and rattle and float between. People do this. It's remarkable and ordinary. This must be how my grandfather lived. I know it's how my mother survived. She found other, more palatable things to believe—that she was her father's little princess, that we were all warm and safe in the bosom of a beautiful family. I learned this lesson well, the knack of splitting the world in two. There's little incentive to distinguish between real and pretend when what's real is often intolerable, so frequently I drifted somewhere in between. I used to cry sometimes, in secret, when I finished a book. Sometimes I'd finish the last page then start the whole thing again. My childhood games were about acting out the stories I loved or plotting for a rosy future. I daydreamed about someday.

Dwelling on how things were going to be helped me cope with how they were. I still do this. I can imagine the built-in bookcases I covet for my living room and the vintage mantle where I'd arrange soy candles and maybe some branches. I can imagine the art that would be on the walls, which would be a soft gray-green, and the ottoman would be upholstered in maybe a cherry-red print instead of the grimy wheat color it is now with a lot of cat scratch threads hanging off it. A person can get too good at imagining things. When you live in fantasy, being in the flesh-and-blood world can start to feel alien and heartbreaking. You're not really present if you're always imagining something different. I've accepted some things I shouldn't have—jobs, relationships—because I'm good at tolerating. I'm good at getting things over with while plotting something beautiful and fantastic. Staying submerged for extended periods—in books, fantasy, television, whatever—can make you like one of those blind fish that glow in the dark, a creature that swims away from light. The Saltwater Twin gave me a way to imagine myself strong and powerful; she gave me a world where I was safe. But she also represented a death wish. She was a siren. Her song rang in my ears.

At the end of our vacation, my father drove the station wagon into the belly of the ferry, and we clanged upstairs to the deck. Shouts of "'Bout a coin!" drifted up from below. They were there every summer—boys treading water in the murky green harbor, calling for coins from the passengers waiting onboard for the ferry to depart. "'Bout a coin!" The coins fell silver and flickering, and the boys disappeared after them. I imagined kicking down, eyes stinging with salt, catching nickels, dimes, and silver dollars as they tumbled, sunlit, into the dark water. One by one, the boys surfaced, slick-haired, and called to us again. Then the ferry whistle blew, and the boat lumbered away from the wharf. The wind picked up. I watched the gulls bank and plummet, cocky and shrill. Out on the open water, I pressed against the rail, eyes on the waves, watching intently for signs of life.

ADAM JOHNSON

■

Nirvana

FROM *Esquire*

IT'S LATE AND I CAN'T SLEEP.

I raise a window for some spring Palo Alto air, but it doesn't help. In bed, eyes open, I hear whispers, which makes me think of the President because we often talk in whispers. I know the whisper sound is really just my wife, Charlotte, who listens to Nirvana on her headphones all night and tends to sleep-mumble the lyrics. Charlotte has her own bed, a mechanical one.

Yes, hearing the President whisper is creepy because he's been dead now, what—three months? But even creepier is what happens when I close my eyes: I keep visualizing my wife killing herself. More like the ways she might *try* to kill herself, since she's paralyzed from the shoulders down. The paralysis is quite temporary, though good luck trying to convince Charlotte of that. She slept on her side today, to fight the bedsores, and there was something about the way she stared at the safety rail at the edge of the mattress. The bed is voice-activated, so if she could somehow get her head between the bars of the safety rail, "incline" is all she'd have to say. As the bed powered up, she'd be choked in seconds. And then there's the way she stares at the looping cable that descends from the Hoyer lift, which swings her in and out of bed.

What can really keep a guy up at night is the knowledge that she doesn't need an exotic exit strategy, not when she's exacted a promise from you to help her do it when the time comes.

I rise and go to her, but she's not listening to Nirvana yet—she tends to save it for when she needs it most, after midnight, when her nerves really start to crackle.

"I thought I heard a noise," I tell her. "Kind of a whisper."

Short, choppy hair frames her drawn face, skin faint as refrigerator light.

"I heard it, too," she says.

She spent months two, four, and seven crying pretty hard—there's no more helpless feeling for a husband, let me tell you. But this period that's come after is harder to take: Her eyes are wide, drained of emotion, and you can't tell what she's thinking. It's like she's looking at things that aren't even in the room.

In the silver dish by her voice remote is a half-smoked joint. I light it for her and hold it to her lips.

"How's the weather in there?" I ask.

"Windy," she says through the smoke.

Windy is better than hail or lightning, or, God forbid, flooding, which is the sensation she felt when her lungs were just starting to work again. But there are different kinds of wind.

I ask, "Windy like a whistle through window screens, or windy like the rattle of storm shutters?"

"A strong breeze, hissy and buffeting, like a microphone in the wind."

She smokes again. Charlotte hates being stoned, but she says it quiets the inside of her. She has Guillain-Barré syndrome, a condition in which her immune system attacks the insulation around her nerves, so that when the brain sends signals to the body, the electrical impulses ground out before they can be received. A billion nerves inside her send signals that go everywhere, nowhere. This is the ninth month, a month that is at the edge of the medical literature. It's a place where the doctors no longer feel qualified to tell us whether Charlotte's nerves will begin to regenerate or whether Charlotte will be stuck like this forever.

She exhales, coughing. Her right arm twitches, which means her brain has attempted to tell her arm to rise and cover the mouth.

She tokes again, and through the smoke she says, "I'm worried."

"What about?"

"You."

"You're worried about me?"

"I want you to stop talking to the President. It's time to accept reality."

I try to be lighthearted. "But he's the one who talks to me."

"Then stop listening, okay? He's gone. When your time comes, you're supposed to fall silent."

Reluctantly I nod. But she doesn't understand. In the third month of paralysis, she did nothing but watch videos, which made her crazy. It made her swear off all screens, so she's probably the only person in America who didn't see the video clips of the assassination. If she'd beheld the look in the President's eyes when his life was taken, she'd understand why I talk to him late at night. If she could leave this room and feel the nation trying to grieve, she'd know why I reanimated the commander in chief and brought him back to life.

"In regards to listening to the President," I say, "I just want to point out that you spend a third of your life listening to Nirvana, whose songs are all from a guy who blew his brains out."

Charlotte tilts her head and looks at me like I'm a stranger, like I don't know the first thing about her. "Kurt Cobain took the pain of his life and made it into something that mattered, that spoke to people. Do you know how rare that is? What did the President leave behind? Uncertainties, emptiness, a thousand rocks to overturn."

She talks like that when she's high. I decide to let it go. I tap out the joint and lift her headphones. "Ready for your Nirvana?" I ask.

"That sound, I hear it again," she says.

She tries to point, then gives up and nods toward the window.

"It's coming from there," she says.

At the window, I look out into the darkness. It's a normal Palo Alto night—the hiss of sprinklers, blue recycling bins, a raccoon digging in the community garden. Then I notice it, right before my eyes, a small black drone, hovering outside my window. Its tiny servos swivel to regard me. Real quick, like I'm snatching a cookie from a hot baking sheet, I steal the drone out of the air and pull it inside. I close the window and curtains, then study the thing: Its shell is made of black foil, stretched over tiny struts, like the bones of a bat's wing. Behind a propeller of clear cellophane, a tiny infrared engine throbs with warmth.

I look at Charlotte.

"Now will you listen to me?" she asks. "Now will you stop this President business?"

"It's too late for that," I tell her and release the drone. Together, we watch it bumble around the room, bouncing off the walls, running into the Hoyer lift. Is it autonomous? Has someone been operating it, someone watching our house? I lift it from its column of air and, turning it over, flip off its power switch.

Charlotte looks toward her voice remote. "Play music," she tells it.

Closing her eyes, she waits for me to place the headphones on her ears, where she will hear Kurt Cobain come to life once more.

I wake later in the night. The drone has somehow turned itself on and is hovering above my body, mapping me with a beam of soft red light. I toss a sweater over it, dropping it to the floor. After making sure Charlotte's asleep, I pull out my iProjector. I turn it on and the President appears in three dimensions, his torso life-sized in an amber glow.

He greets me with a smile. "It's good to be back in Palo Alto," he says.

My algorithm has accessed the iProjector's GPS chip and searched the President's database for location references. This one came from a commencement address he gave at Stanford back when he was a senator.

"Mr. President," I say. "I'm sorry to bother you again, but I have more questions."

He looks into the distance, contemplative. "Shoot," he says.

I move into his line of sight but can't get him to look me in the eye. That's one of the design problems I ran across. Hopefully, I'll be able to fix it in beta.

"Did I make a mistake in creating you, in releasing you into the world?" I ask. "My wife says that you're keeping people from mourning, that *this you* keeps us from accepting the fact that the *real you* is gone."

The President rubs the stubble on his chin. He looks down and away.

"You can't put the genie back in the bottle," he says.

Which is eerie, because that's a line he'd spoken on *60 Minutes*, a moment when he expressed regret for legalizing drones for civilian use.

"Do you know that I'm the one who made you?"

"We are all born free," he says. "And no person may traffic in another."

"But you weren't born," I tell him. "I wrote an algorithm, based on the Linux operating kernel. You're an open-source search engine married to a dialog bot and a video compiler. The program scrubs the Web and archives a person's images and videos and data—everything you say, you've said before."

For the first time, the President falls silent.

I ask, "Do you know that you're . . . that you've died?"

The President doesn't hesitate.

"The end of life is another kind of freedom," he says.

The assassination flashes in my eyes. I've seen the video so many times it plays without consent—the motorcade is slowly crawling along while the President, on foot, parades past the barricaded crowds. Someone in the throng catches the President's eye. The President stops and turns, lifts a hand in greeting. Then a bullet strikes him in the abdomen. The impact bends him forward, and his eyes lift to confront the shooter, a person the camera never gets a look at. A dawning settles into the President's gaze, a look of clear recognition—of a particular person, of some kind of truth, of something he has foreseen? He takes the second shot in the face. You can see the switch go off—his limbs give and he's down. Men in suits converge, shielding him, and the clip is over. They put him on a machine for a few days, but the end had already come.

I glance at Charlotte, asleep. Still, I whisper, "Mr. President, did you and the First Lady ever talk about the future, about these kinds of possibilities?"

I wonder if the First Lady was the one to turn off the machine.

The President smiles. "The First Lady and I have a wonderful relationship. We share everything."

"But were there instructions? Did you two make a plan?"

His voice lowers, becomes sonorous. "Are you asking about bonds of matrimony?"

I pause. "Yes."

"In this regard," he says, "our only duty is to be of service, in any way we can."

My mind ponders the ways in which I might have to be of service to Charlotte.

The President then looks into the distance, like a flag is waving there.

"I'm the President of the United States," he says, "and I approved this message."

That's when I know our conversation is over. When I reach to turn off the iProjector, the President looks me squarely in the eye, a coincidence of perspective, I guess. We regard one another, his eyes deep and melancholy, and my finger hesitates at the switch.

"Seek your inner resolve," he tells me.

How did we get to this place? Can you tell a story that doesn't begin, it's just suddenly happening? The woman you love gets the flu. Her fingers tingle, her legs go rubbery. In the morning, she can't grip a coffee cup. What finally gets her to the hospital is the need to pee. She has got to pee, she's dying to pee, but the paralysis has begun: The bladder can no longer hear the brain. After an ER doc inserts a Foley catheter, you learn new words—axon, areflexia, dendrite, myelin, ascending peripheral polyneuropathy.

Charlotte says she's filled with "noise." Inside her is a "storm."

The doctor has a big needle. He tells Charlotte to get on the gurney. Charlotte's scared to get on the gurney. She's scared she won't ever get up again. "Please, honey," you say. "Get on the gurney." Soon, you behold the glycerin glow of a fresh-drawn vial of spinal fluid. And she's right. She doesn't get up again.

To begin plasmapheresis, a femoral stent must be placed. This is performed by a tattooed phlebotomist whose headphones buzz with Rage Against the Machine.

Next comes high-dose immunoglobulin therapy.

The doctors mention, casually, the word *ventilator*.

Charlotte's mother arrives. She brings her cello. She's an expert on the Siege of Leningrad. She has written a book on the topic. When the coma is induced, she fills the neuro ward with the saddest sounds ever conceived. For seven days, there is nothing but the swish of vent baffles, the trill of vital monitors, and Shostakovich, Shostakovich, Shostakovich. No one will tell her to stop. Nervous nurses appear and disappear, whispering in Tagalog.

Two months of physical therapy in Santa Clara. Here are dunk tanks, sonar stimulators, exoskeletal treadmills. Charlotte is fitted for AFOs and a head array. She becomes the person in the room who makes the victims of other afflictions feel better about their fate. She does not make progress, she's not a "soldier" or a "champ" or a "trouper."

Charlotte convinces herself that I will leave her for a woman who "works." In the rehab ward, she screams at me to get a vasectomy so this other woman and myself will suffer a barren future. My refusal becomes proof of this other woman and our plans.

To soothe her, I read aloud Joseph Heller's memoir about contracting Guillain-Barré syndrome. The book was supposed to make us feel better. Instead, it chronicles how great Heller's friends are, how high Heller's spirits are, how Heller leaves his wife to marry the beautiful nurse who tends to him. And for Charlotte, the book's ending is particularly painful: Joseph Heller gets better.

We tumble into a well of despair, which is narrow and deep, a place that seals us off, where we only hear our own voices, and we exist in a fluid that's clear and black. Everything is in the well with us—careers, goals, travel, parenthood—so close that we can drown them to save ourselves.

A doctor wants to float Charlotte on a raft of antidepressants. She will take no pills. Lightheartedly, the doctor says, "That's what IVs are for." Charlotte levels her eyes and says, "Next doctor, please."

The next doctor recommends discharge.

Home is unexpectedly surreal. Amid familiar surroundings, the impossibility of normal life is amplified. But the cat is happy, so happy to have Charlotte home that it spends an entire night sprawled across Charlotte's throat, across her tracheal incision. Good-bye, cat! There comes, strangely, a vaudevillian week of slaphappy humor, where bedpans and withering limbs are suddenly funny, where a booger that can't be picked is hilarious, where everyday items drip with bizarre humor—I put a hat on Charlotte and we laugh and laugh. She stares in bafflement at the sight of a bra. There are lots of cat jokes!

This period passes, normal life returns. The cap to a hypodermic needle, dropped unnoticed into the sheets, irritates a hole into Charlotte's back. While I am in the garage, Charlotte watches a spider slowly descend from the ceiling on a single thread. Charlotte tries to blow it away. She blows and blows, but the spider disappears into her hair.

Still to be described are tests, tantrums, and silent treatments. To come are the discoveries of Kurt Cobain, marijuana, and ever shorter haircuts. Of these times, there is only one moment I must relate. It was a normal night. I was beside Charlotte in the mechanical bed, holding up her magazine and turning the pages, so I wasn't really facing her.

She said, "You don't know how bad I want to get out of this bed."

Her voice was quiet, uninflected. She'd said similar things a thousand times.

I flipped the page and laughed at a picture whose caption read, "Stars are just like us!"

"I'd do anything to escape," she said.

Charlotte's job was to explicate the intricate backstories of celebrities, showing me how their narratives rightfully adorned the Sistine Chapel of American culture. My job was to make fun of the celebrities and pretend that I hadn't also become caught up in their love battles and breakups.

"But I could never do that to you," she said.

"Do what?" I asked.

"Nothing."

"What are you talking about, what's going through your head?"

I turned to look at her. She was inches away.

"Except for how it would hurt you," she said, "I would get away."

"Get away where?"

"From here."

Neither of us had spoken of the promise since the night it was exacted. I'd tried to pretend the promise didn't exist, but it existed — it existed.

"Face it, you're stuck with me," I said, forcing a smile. "We're destined, we're fated to be together. And soon you'll be better, things will be normal again."

"My entire life is this pillow."

"That's not true. You've got your friends and family. And you've got technology. The whole world is at your fingertips."

By friends I meant her nurses and physical therapists. By family I meant her distant and brooding mother. It didn't matter: Charlotte was too disengaged to even point out her nonfunctional fingers and their nonfeeling tips.

She rolled her head to the side and stared at the safety rail.

"It's okay," she said. "I would never do that to you."

In the morning before the nurses arrive, I open the curtains and study the drone in the early light. Most of the stealth and propulsion parts are off the shelf, but the processors are new to me, half hidden by a Kevlar shield. To get the drone to talk, to get some forensics on who sent it my way, I'll have to get my hands on the hash reader from work.

When Charlotte wakes, I prop her head and massage her legs. It's our morning routine.

"Let's generate those Schwann cells," I tell her toes. "It's time for Charlotte's body to start producing some myelin membranes."

"Look who's Mr. Brightside," she says. "You must have been talking to the President. Isn't that why you talk to him, to get all inspired? To see the silver lining?"

I lift her right foot and rub her Achilles tendon. Last week, Charlotte failed a big test, the DTRE, which measures deep tendon response and signals the *beginning* of recovery. "Don't worry," the doctor told us. "I know of another patient that also took nine months to respond, and he managed a full recovery." I asked if we could contact this patient, to know what he went through, to help us see what's ahead. The doctor informed us this patient was attended to in France, in the year 1918.

After the doctor left, I went into the garage and started making the President. A psychologist would probably say the reason I created him had to do with the promise I made Charlotte and the fact that the President also had a relationship with the person who took his life. But it's simpler than that: I just needed to save somebody, and with the President, it didn't matter that it was too late.

I tap Charlotte's patella but there's no response. "Any pain?"

"So what did the President say?"

"Which president?"

"The dead one," she says.

I articulate the plantar fascia. "How about this?"

"Feels like a spray of cool diamonds," she says. "Come on, I know you talked to him."

It's going to be one of her bad days, I can tell.

"Let me guess," Charlotte says. "The President told you to move to the South Pacific to take up painting. That's uplifting, isn't it?"

I don't say anything.

"You'd take me with you, right? I could be your assistant. I'd hold your palette in my teeth. If you need a model, I specialize in reclining nudes."

She's thirsty. We use a neti pot as a bedside water cup. Charlotte, lying down, can drink from the spout. While she sips, I say, "If you must know, the President told me to locate my *inner resolve*."

"*Inner resolve*," she says. "I could use some help tracking down mine."

"You have more resolve than anyone I know."

"Jesus, you're sunny. Don't you know what's going on? Don't you see that I'm about to spend the rest of my life like this?"

"Pace yourself, darling. The day's only a couple minutes old."

"I know," she says. "I'm supposed to have reached a stage of enlightened acceptance or something. You think I like it that the only person I have to get mad at is you? I know it's not right—you're the one thing I love in this world."

"You love Kurt Cobain."

"He's dead."

"Too bad he's not alive for you to get mad at."

"Man, I would let him have it," she says.

We hear Hector, the morning nurse, pull up outside—he drives an old car with a combustion engine.

"I have to grab something from work," I tell her. "But I'll be back."

"Promise me something," she says.

"No."

"Come on. If you do, I'll release you from the other promise."

Far from being scary, the mention of the promise is strangely relieving.

Still, I shake my head. I know she doesn't mean it—she'll never release me.

She says, "Will you please agree to be straight with me? You don't have to make me feel better, you don't have to be all fake and optimistic. It doesn't help."

"I am optimistic."

"You shouldn't be," she says. "Pretending, that's what killed Kurt Cobain."

I think it was the shotgun he pointed at his head, but I don't say that.

I only know one line from Nirvana. I karaoke it to Charlotte:

"With the lights on," I sing, "she's less dangerous."

She rolls her eyes. "You got it wrong," she says. But she smiles.

I try to encourage this. "What, I don't get points for trying?"

"You don't hear that?" Charlotte asks.

"Hear what?"

"That's the sound of me clapping."

"I give up," I say and make for the door.

"Bed, incline," Charlotte tells her remote. Her torso slowly rises. It's time to start her day.

I take the 101 freeway south toward Mountain View, where I write code at a company called Reputation Curator. Basically the company bribes/ threatens Yelpers and Facebookers to retract negative comments about dodgy lawyers and incompetent dentists. The work is labor intensive, so I was hired to write a program that would sweep the Web to construct client profiles. Creating the President was only a step away.

In the vehicle next to me is a woman with her iProjector on the passenger seat, and she's having an animated discussion with the President as she drives. At the next overpass, I see an older black man in a tan jacket, looking down at the traffic. Standing next to him is the President. They're not speaking, just standing together, silently watching the cars go by.

A black car, driverless, begins pacing me in the next lane. When I speed up, it speeds up. Through its smoked windows, I can see it has no cargo—there's nothing inside but a battery array big enough to ensure no car could outrun it. Even though I like driving, even though it relaxes me, I shift to automatic and dart into the Google lane, where I let go of the wheel and sign on to the Web for the first time since I released the President a week ago. I log in and discover that fourteen million people have downloaded the President. I also have seven hundred new messages. The first is from the dude who started Facebook, and it is not spam—he wants to buy me a burrito and talk about the future. I skip to the latest message, which is from Charlotte: "I don't mean to be mean. I lost my feeling, remember? I'll get it back. I'm trying, really, I am."

I see the President again, on the lawn of a Korean church. The minister has placed an iProjector on a chair, and the President appears to be engaging a Bible that's been propped before him on a stand. I understand that he is a ghost that will haunt us until our nation comes to grips with what has happened: that he is gone, that he has been stolen from us, that it is irreversible. And I'm not an idiot. I know what's really being stolen from me, slowly and irrevocably, before my eyes. I know that late at night I should be going to Charlotte instead of the President.

But when I'm with Charlotte, there's a membrane between us, a layer my mind places there to protect me from the tremor in her voice, from the pulse visible in her desiccated wrists, from all the fates she sarcastically paints. It's when I'm away from her that it comes crashing in—it's in the garage that it hits me how scared she is, it's at the store when I cross tampons off the list that I consider how cruel life must seem to her. Driving now, I think about how she has started turning toward the wall even before the last song on the Nirvana album is over, that soon, even headphones and marijuana will cease to work. My off-ramp up ahead is blurry, and I realize there are tears in my eyes. I drive right past my exit. I just let the Google lane carry me away.

When I arrive home, my boss, Sanjay, is waiting for me. I'd messaged him to have an intern deliver the hash reader, but here is the man himself, item in hand. Theoretically, hash readers are impossible. Theoretically, you shouldn't be able to crack full-field, hundred-key encryption. But some guy in India did it, some guy Sanjay knows. Sanjay's sensitive about being from India, and he thinks it's a cliché that a guy with his name runs a start-up in Palo Alto. So he goes by "SJ" and dresses all D school. He's got a Stanford MBA, but he basically just stole the business model of a company called Reputation Defender. You can't blame the guy—he's one of those types with the hopes and dreams of an entire village riding on him.

SJ follows me into the garage, where I dock the drone and use some slave code to parse its drive. He hands me the hash reader, hand-soldered in Bangalore from an old motherboard. We marvel at it, the most sophisticated piece of cryptography on earth, here in our unworthy hands. But if you want to "curate" the reputations of Silicon Valley, you better be ready to crack some codes.

He's quiet while I initialize the drone and run a diagnostic.

"Long time no see," he finally says.

"I needed some time," I tell him.

"Understood," SJ says. "We've missed you is all I'm saying. You bring the President back to life, send fifteen million people to our website, and then we don't see you for a week."

The drone knows something is suspicious—it powers off. I force a reboot.

"Got yourself a drone there?" SJ asks.

"It's a rescue," I say. "I'm adopting it."

SJ nods. "Thought you should know the Secret Service came by."

"Looking for me?" I ask. "Doesn't sound so secret."

"They must have been impressed with your President. I know I was."

SJ has long lashes and big, manga brown eyes. He hits me with them now.

"I've gotta tell you," he says. "The President is a work of art, a seamlessly integrated data interface. I'm in real admiration. This is a game-changer. You know what I envision?"

I notice his flashy glasses. "Are those Android?" I ask.

"Yeah."

"Can I have them?"

He hands them over, and I search the frames for their IP address.

SJ gestures large. "I envision your algorithm running on Reputation Curator. Average people could bring their personalities to life, to speak for themselves, to customize and personalize how they're seen by the world. Your program is like Google, Wikipedia, and Facebook, all in one. Everyone with a reputation on the planet would pay to have you animate them, to make them articulate, vigilant . . . eternal."

"You can have it," I tell SJ. "The algorithm's core is open source — I used a freeware protocol."

SJ flashes a brittle smile. "We've actually looked into that," he says, "and, well, it seems like you coded it with seven-layer encryption."

"Yeah, I guess I did, didn't I? You're the one with the hash reader. Just crack it."

"I don't want it to be like that," SJ says. "Let's be partners. Your concept is brilliant — an algorithm that scrubs the Web and compiles the results into a personal animation. The President is the proof, but it's also given away the idea. If we move now, we can protect it, it will be ours. In a few weeks, though, everyone will have their own."

I don't point out the irony of SJ wanting to protect a business model.

"Is the President just an animation to you?" I ask. "Have you spoken with him? Have you listened to what he has to say?"

"I'm offering stock," SJ says. "Wheelbarrows of it."

The drone offers up its firewall like a seductress her throat. I deploy the hash reader, whose processor hums and flashes red. We sit on folding chairs while it works.

"I need your opinion," I tell him.

"Right on," he says and removes a bag of weed. He starts rolling a joint, then passes me the rest. He's been hooking me up the last couple months, no questions.

"What do you think of Kurt Cobain?" I ask.

"*Kurt Cobain*," he repeats as he works the paper between his fingers. "The man was pure," he says and licks the edge. "Too pure for this world. Have you heard Patti Smith's cover of 'Smells Like Teen Spirit'? Unassailable, man."

He lights the joint and passes it my way, but I wave it off. He sits there, staring out the open mouth of my garage into the Kirkland plumage of Palo Alto. Apple, Oracle, PayPal, and Hewlett-Packard were all started in garages within a mile of here. About once a month, SJ gets homesick and cooks litti chokha for everyone at work. He plays Sharda Sinha songs and gets this look in his eyes like he's back in Bihar, land of peepul trees and roller birds. He has this look now. He says, "You know my family downloaded the President. They have no idea what I do out here, as if I could make them understand that I help bad sushi chefs ward off Twitter trolls. But the American President, that they understand."

The mayor, barefoot, jogs past us. Moments later, a billboard drives by.

"Hey, can you make the President speak Hindi?" SJ asks. "If you could get the American President to say, 'I could go for a Pepsi' in Hindi, I'd make you the richest man on earth."

The hash reader's light turns green. Just like that, the drone is mine. I disconnect the leads and begin to synch the Android glasses. The drone uses its moment of freedom to rise and study SJ.

SJ returns the drone's intense scrutiny.

"Who do you think sent it after you?" he asks. "Mozilla? Craigslist?"

"We'll know in a moment."

"Silent. Black. Radar deflecting," SJ says. "I bet this is Microsoft's dark magic."

The new OS suddenly initiates, the drone responds, and, using retinal commands, I send it on a lap around the garage. "Lo and behold," I say. "Turns out our little friend speaks Google."

"Wow," SJ says. "Don't be evil, huh?"

When the drone returns, it targets SJ in the temple with a green laser.

"What the fuck," SJ says.

"Don't worry," I tell him. "It's just taking your pulse and temperature."

"What for?"

"Probably trying to read your emotions," I say. "I bet it's a leftover subroutine."

"You sure you're in charge of that thing?"

I roll my eyes and the drone does a back flip.

"My emotion is simple," SJ tells me. "It's time to come back to work."

"I will," I tell him. "I've just got some things to deal with."

SJ looks at me. "It's okay if you don't want to talk about your wife. But you don't have to be so alone about things. Everyone at work, we're all worried about you."

Inside, Charlotte is suspended in a sling from the Hoyer Lift, which has been rolled to the window so she can see outside. She's wearing old yoga tights, which are slack on her, and she smells of the cedar oil her massage therapist rubs her with. I go to her and open the window.

"You read my mind," she says and breathes the fresh air.

I put the glasses on her, and it takes her eyes a minute of flashing around before the drone lifts from my hands. A grand smile crosses her face as she puts it through its paces—hovering, rotating, swiveling the camera's servos. And then the drone is off. I watch it cross the lawn, veer around the compost piles, and then head for the community garden. It floats down the rows, and though I don't have the view Charlotte does in her glasses, I can see the drone inspecting the blossoms of summer squash, the fat bottoms of Roma tomatoes. It rises along the bean trellises and tracks watermelons by their umbilical stems. When she makes it to her plot, she gasps.

"My roses," she says. "They're still there. Someone's been taking care of them."

She has the drone inspect every bud and bloom. Carefully, she maneuvers it through the bright petals, brushing against the blossoms, then shuttles it home again. Suddenly it is hovering before us. Charlotte leans slightly forward and sniffs the drone deeply. "I never thought I'd smell my roses again," she says, her face flush with hope and amazement, and suddenly the tears are streaming.

I remove her glasses, and we leave the drone hovering there.

She regards me. "I want to have a baby," she says.

"A baby?"

"It's been nine months. I could have had one already. I could've been doing something useful this whole time."

"But your illness," I say. "We don't know what's ahead."

She closes her eyes like she's hugging something, like she's holding some dear truth.

"With a baby, I'd have something to show for all this. I'd have a reason. At the least, I'd have something to leave behind."

"You can't talk like that," I tell her. "We've talked about you not talking like this."

But she won't listen to me, she won't open her eyes.

All she says is "And I want to start tonight."

Later in the day I carry the iProjector out back to the gardening shed. Here, in the gold of afternoon light, the President rises and comes to life. He adjusts his collar, cuffs, runs his thumb down a black lapel as if he exists only in the moment before a camera will broadcast him live to the world.

"Mr. President," I say. "I'm sorry to bother you again."

"Nonsense," he tells me. "I serve at the pleasure of the people."

"Do you remember me?" I ask. "Do you remember the problems I've been talking to you about?"

"Perennial is the nature of the problems that plague man. Particular is the voice with which they call to each of us."

"My problem today is of a personal nature."

"Then I place this conversation under the seal."

"I haven't made love to my wife in a long time." He holds up a hand to halt me. He smiles in a knowing, fatherly way.

"Times of doubt," he tells me, "are inherent in the compact of civil union."

"My question is about children."

"Children are the future," he tells me.

"Would you have still brought yours into the world, knowing that only one of you might be around to raise them?"

"Single parenting places too much of a strain on today's families," he says. "That's why I'm introducing legislation that will reduce the burden on our hardworking parents."

"What about your children? Do you miss them?"

"My mind goes to them constantly. Being away from them is the great sacrifice of the office."

In the shed, suspended dust makes his specter glitter and swirl. It makes him look like he is cutting out, like he will leave at any moment. I feel some urgency.

"When it's all finally over," I ask, "where is it that we go?"

"I'm no preacher," the President says, "but I believe we go where we are called."

"Where were you called to? Where is it that you are?"

"Don't we all try to locate ourselves among the pillars of uncommon knowledge?"

"You don't know where you are, do you?" I ask the President.

"I'm sure my opponent would like you to believe that."

"It's okay," I say, more to myself. "I didn't expect you to know."

"I know exactly where I am," the President says. Then, in a voice that sounds pieced from many scraps, he adds, "I'm currently positioned at three seven point four four north by one two two point one four west."

I think he's done. I wait for him to say *Good night and God bless America*. Instead, he reaches out to touch my chest. "I have heard that you have made much personal sacrifice," he says. "And I'm told that your sense of duty is strong."

I don't think I agree, but I say, "Yes sir."

His glowing hand clasps my shoulder, and it doesn't matter that I can't feel it.

"Then this medal that I affix to your uniform is much more than a piece of silver. It is a symbol of how much you have given, not just in armed struggle and not just in service to your nation. It tells others how much more you have to give. It marks you forever as one who can be counted upon, as one who in times of need will lift up and carry those who have fallen." Proudly, he stares into the empty space above my shoulder. He says, "Now return home to your wife, soldier, and start a new chapter of life."

When darkness falls, I go to Charlotte. The night nurse has placed her in a negligee. Charlotte lowers the bed as I approach. The electric motor is the only sound in the room.

"I'm ovulating," she announces. "I can feel it."

"You can feel it?"

"I don't need to *feel* it," she says. "I just know."

She's strangely calm.

"Are you ready?" she asks.

"Sure."

I steady myself on the safety rail that separates us.

She asks, "Do you want some oral sex first?"

I shake my head.

"Come join me, then," she says.

I start to climb on the bed — she stops me.

"Hey, Sunshine," she says. "Take off your clothes."

I can't remember the last time she called me that.

"Oh, yeah," I say and unbutton my shirt, unzip my jeans. When I drop my underwear, I feel weirdly, I don't know, *naked*. I'm not sure whether I should remove my socks. I leave them on. I swing a leg up, then kind of lie on her.

A look of contentment crosses her face. "This is how it's supposed to be," she says. "It's been a long time since I've been able to look into your eyes."

Her body is narrow but warm. I don't know where to put my hands.

"Do you want to pull down my panties?"

I sit up and begin to work them off. I see the scar from the femoral stent. When I heft her legs, there are the bedsores we've been fighting.

"Remember our trip to Mexico," she asks, "when we made love on top of that pyramid? It was like we were in the past and the future at the same time. I kind of feel that now."

"You're not high, are you?"

"What?" she asks. "Like I'd have to be stoned to remember the first time we talked about having a baby?"

When I have her panties off and her legs hooked, I pause. It takes all my focus to get an erection, and then I can't believe I have one. I see the moment coldly, distant, the way a drone would see it: Here's my wife, paralyzed, invalid, insensate, and though everything's the opposite of erotic, I am poised above her, completely hard.

"I'm wet, aren't I?" Charlotte asks. "I've been thinking about this all day."

I do remember the pyramid. The stone was cold, the staircase steep. The past to me was a week of Charlotte in Mayan dresses, cooing every baby she came across. Having sex under faint and sleepy stars, I tried to imagine the future: a faceless *someone* conceived on a sacrificial altar. I finished early and tried to shake it off. That person would probably never come to be. Plus, we had to focus on matters at hand if we were going to make it down all those steps in the dark.

"I think I feel something," she says. "You're inside me, right? Because I'm pretty sure I can feel it."

Here I enter my wife and begin our lovemaking. I try to focus on the notion that if this works, Charlotte will be safe, that for nine months she'd let no harm come to her, and maybe she's right, maybe the baby will stimulate something and recovery will begin.

Charlotte smiles. It's brittle, but it's a smile. "How's this for finding the silver lining—I won't have to feel the pain of childbirth."

This makes me wonder if a paralyzed woman can push out a baby, or does she get the scalpel, and if so, is there anesthesia, and suddenly my body is at the edge of not cooperating.

"Hey, are you here?" she asks. "I'm trying to get you to smile."

"I just need to focus for a minute," I tell her.

"I can tell you're not really into this," she says. "I can tell you're still hung up on the idea I'm going to do something drastic to myself, right? Just because I talk about crazy stuff sometimes doesn't mean I'm going to do anything."

"Then why'd you make me promise to help you do it?"

The promise came early, in the beginning, just before the ventilator. She had a vomiting reflex that lasted for hours. The doctors said *it* can happen. Imagine endless dry heaves while you're paralyzed. The doctors finally gave her narcotics. Drugged, dead-limbed, and vomiting, that's when it hit her that she was no longer in control. I was holding her hair, keeping it out of the basin. She was panting between heaves.

She said, "Promise me that when I tell you to make it stop, you'll make it stop."

"Make what stop?" I asked.

She retched, long and cord-rattling. I knew what she meant.

"It won't come to that," I said.

She tried to say something but retched again.

"I promise," I said.

Now, in her mechanical bed, her negligee straps slipping off her shoulders, Charlotte says, "It's hard for you to understand, I know. But the idea that there's a way out, it's what allows me to keep going. I'd never take it. You believe me, don't you?"

"I hate that promise, I hate that you made me make it."

"I'd never do it, and I'd never make you help."

"Then release me," I tell her.

"I'm sorry," she says.

I decide to just shut it all out and keep going. I'm losing my erection, and my mind wonders what will happen if I go soft—do I have it in me to fake it?—but I shut it out and keep going and going, pounding on Charlotte until I can barely feel anything. Her breasts loll alone under me. From the bedside table, the drone turns itself on and rises, hovering. It flashes my forehead with its green laser, as if what I'm feeling is that easy to determine, as if there would be a name for it. Is it spying on me, mining my emotions, or executing old code? I wonder if the hash reader failed or if the drone's OS reverted to a previous version or if Google reacquired it or if it's in some kind of autonomous mode. Or it could be that someone hacked the Android glasses, or maybe . . . that's when I look down and see Charlotte is crying.

I stop.

"No, don't," she says. "Keep going."

She's not crying hard, but they are fat, lamenting tears.

"We can try again tomorrow," I tell her.

"No, I'm okay," she says. "Just keep going and do something for me, would you?"

"All right."

"Put the headphones on me."

"You mean, while we're doing it?"

"Music on," she says, and from the headphones on her bedside table, I hear Nirvana start to hum.

"I know I'm doing it all wrong," I say. "It's been a long time, and . . ."

"It's not you," she says. "I just need my music. Just put them on me."

"Why do you need Nirvana? What is it to you?"

She closes her eyes and shakes her head.

"What is it with this Kurt Cobain?" I say. "What's your deal with him?"

I grab her wrists and pin them down, but she can't feel it.

"Why do you have to have this music? What's wrong with you?" I demand. "Just tell me what it is that's wrong with you."

I go to the garage, where the drone wanders lost along the walls, looking for a way out. I turn on a computer and search online until I find one of these Nirvana albums. I play the whole thing, just sitting there in the dark. The guy, this Kurt Cobain, sings about being stupid and dumb and unwanted. In one song he says that Jesus doesn't want him for a sunbeam. In another song, he says he wants milk and laxatives along with cherry-flavored antacids. He has a song called "All Apologies," where he keeps singing, "What else can I be? All apologies." But he never actually apologizes. He doesn't even say what he did wrong.

The drone, having found no escape, comes to me and hovers silently. I must look pretty pathetic because the drone takes my temperature.

I lift the remote for the garage-door opener. "Is this what you want?" I ask. "Are you going to come back, or am I going to have to come find you?"

The drone silently hums, impassive atop its column of warm air.

I press the button. The drone waits until the garage door is all the way up. Then it snaps a photograph of me and zooms off into the Palo Alto night.

I stand and breathe the air, which is cool and smells of flowers. There's enough moonlight to cast leaf patterns on the driveway. Down the street, I spot the glowing eyes of our cat. I call his name but he doesn't come. I gave him to a friend a couple blocks away, and for a few weeks the cat returned at night to visit me. Not anymore. This feeling of being in proximity to something that's lost to you, it seems like my whole life right now. It's a feeling Charlotte would understand if she'd just talk to the President. But he's not the one she needs to speak to, I suddenly understand. I return to my computer bench and fire up a bank of screens. I stare into their blue glow and get to work. It takes me hours, most of the night, before I'm done.

It's almost dawn when I go to Charlotte. The room is dark, and I can only see her outline. "Bed incline," I say, and she starts to rise. She wakes and stares at me but says nothing. Her face has that lack of expression that comes only after it's been through every emotion.

I set the iProjector in her lap. She hates the thing but says nothing. She only tilts her head a little, like she's sad for me. Then I turn it on.

Kurt Cobain appears before her, clad in a bathrobe and composed of soft blue light.

Charlotte inhales. "Oh my God," she murmurs.

She looks at me. "Is it him?"

I nod.

She marvels at him.

"What do I say?" she asks. "Can he talk?"

I don't answer.

Kurt Cobain's hair is in his face. Shifting her gaze, Charlotte tries to look into his eyes. While the President couldn't quite manage to find your eyes, Kurt is purposefully avoiding them.

"I can't believe how young you are," Charlotte tells him. "You're just a boy."

Kurt's silent, then he mumbles, "I'm old."

"Are you really here?" she asks.

"Here we are now," he sings. "Entertain us."

His voice is rough and hard lived. It's some kind of proof of life to Charlotte.

Charlotte looks at me, filled with wonder. "I thought he was gone," she says. "I can't believe he's really here."

Kurt shrugs. "I only appreciate things when they're gone," he says.

Charlotte looks stricken.

"I recognize that line," she says to me. "That's a line from his suicide note. How does he know that? Has he already written it, does he know what he's going to do?"

"I don't know," I tell her. This isn't my conversation to have. I back away toward the door, and just as I'm leaving, I hear her start to talk to him.

"Don't do what you're thinking about doing," she pleads with him. "You don't know how special you are, you don't know how much you matter to me. Please don't take yourself from me," she says carefully, like she's talking to a child. "You can't take yourself from me."

She leans toward Kurt Cobain, like she wants to throw her arms around him and hold him, like she's forgotten that her arms don't work and there's no him to embrace.

SLYVAN OSWALD

■

Little Thing

FROM *15-Second Plays*, a chapbook

LOUD LOUD Tito Puente. It's the fifties or the sixties. Happy hour. The adults are drinking V.O. on the rocks. Sexy dancing don't look. You are the kid with white hair and a purple nose, playing dead on the coffee table while they streak by during the cha cha. They must not notice you have died. The telephone rings. Answer it.

ZADIE SMITH

■

Joy

FROM *The New York Review of Books*

IT MIGHT BE USEFUL to distinguish between pleasure and joy. But maybe everybody does this very easily, all the time, and only I am confused. A lot of people seem to feel that joy is only the most intense version of pleasure, arrived at by the same road—you simply have to go a little further down the track. That has not been my experience. And if you asked me if I wanted more joyful experiences in my life, I wouldn't be at all sure I did, exactly because it proves such a difficult emotion to manage. It's not at all obvious to me how we should make an accommodation between joy and the rest of our everyday lives.

Perhaps the first thing to say is that I experience at least a little pleasure every day. I wonder if this is more than the usual amount? It was the same even in childhood when most people are miserable. I don't think this is because so many wonderful things happen to me but rather that the small things go a long way. I seem to get more than the ordinary satisfaction out of food, for example—any old food. An egg sandwich from one of these grimy food vans on Washington Square has the genuine power to turn my day around. Whatever is put in front of me, foodwise, will usually get a five-star review.

You'd think that people would like to cook for, or eat with, me—in fact I'm told it's boring. Where there is no discernment there can be no awareness of expertise or gratitude for special effort. "Don't say that was delicious," my husband warns, "you say everything's delicious." "But it was delicious." It drives him crazy. All day long I can look forward to a Popsicle. The persistent anxiety that fills the rest of my life is calmed for as long as I have the flavor of something good in my mouth. And though it's true that when the flavor is finished the anxiety returns, we do not have so many reliable sources of pleasure in this life as to turn our nose up at one that is so readily available, especially here in America. A pineapple Popsicle. Even the great anxiety of writing can be stilled for the eight minutes it takes to eat a pineapple Popsicle.

My other source of daily pleasure is—but I wish I had a better way of putting it—"other people's faces." A red-headed girl, with a marvelous large nose she probably hates, and green eyes and that sun-shy complexion composed more of freckles than skin. Or a heavyset grown man, smoking a cigarette in the rain, with a soggy mustache, above which, a surprise—the keen eyes, snub nose, and cherub mouth of his own eight-year-old self. Upon leaving the library at the end of the day I will walk a little more quickly to the apartment to tell my husband about an angular, cat-eyed teenager, in skinny jeans and stacked-heel boots, a perfectly ordinary gray sweatshirt, last night's makeup, and a silky Pocahontas wig slightly askew over his own Afro. He was sashaying down the street, plaits flying, using the whole of Broadway as his personal catwalk. "Miss Thang, but off duty." I add this for clarity, but my husband nods a little impatiently; there was no need for the addition. My husband is also a professional gawker.

The advice one finds in ladies' magazines is usually to be feared, but there is something in that old chestnut: "shared interests." It does help. I like to hear about the Chinese girl he saw in the hall, carrying a large medical textbook, so beautiful she looked like an illustration. Or the tall Kenyan in the elevator whose elongated physical elegance reduced every other nearby body to the shrunken, gnarly status of a troll. Usually I will not have seen these people—my husband works on the eighth floor of the library, I work on the fifth—but simply hearing them described can be almost as much a pleasure as encountering them myself. More pleasurable still is when we recreate the walks or gestures or voices of these strangers, or whole conversations—between two people in the queue for the ATM, or two students on a bench near the fountain.

* * *

And then there are all the many things that the dog does and says, entirely anthropomorphized and usually offensive, which express the universe of things we ourselves cannot do or say, to each other or to other people. "You're being the dog," our child said recently, surprising us. She is almost three and all our private languages are losing their privacy and becoming known to her. Of course, we knew she would eventually become fully conscious, and that before this happened we would have to give up arguing, smoking, eating meat, using the Internet, talking about other people's faces, and voicing the dog, but now the time has come, she is fully aware, and we find ourselves unable to change. "Stop being the dog," she said, "it's very silly," and for the first time in eight years we looked at the dog and were ashamed.

Occasionally the child, too, is a pleasure, though mostly she is a joy, which means in fact she gives us not much pleasure at all, but rather that strange admixture of terror, pain, and delight that I have come to recognize as joy, and now must find some way to live with daily. This is a new problem. Until quite recently I had known joy only five times in my life, perhaps six, and each time tried to forget it soon after it happened, out of the fear that the memory of it would dement and destroy everything else.

Let's call it six. Three of those times I was in love, but only once was the love viable, or likely to bring me any pleasure in the long run. Twice I was on drugs—of quite different kinds. Once I was in water, once on a train, once sitting on a high wall, once on a high hill, once in a nightclub, and once in a hospital bed. It is hard to arrive at generalities in the face of such a small and varied collection of data. The uncertain item is the nightclub, and because it was essentially a communal experience I feel I can open the question out to the floor. I am addressing this to my fellow Britons in particular. Fellow Britons! Those of you, that is, who were fortunate enough to take the first generation of the amphetamine ecstasy and yet experience none of the adverse, occasionally lethal reactions we now know others suffered—yes, for you people I have a question. Was that joy?

I am especially interested to hear from anyone who happened to be in the Fabric club, near the old Spitalfields meat market, on a night sometime in the year 1999 (I'm sorry I can't be more specific) when the DJ mixed "Can I Kick It?" and then "Smells Like Teen Spirit" into the deep house track he had been seeming to play exclusively for the previous four hours. I myself was wandering out of the cavernous unisex (!) toilets wishing I could find my friend Sarah, or if not her, my friend Warren, or if not him, anyone who would take pity on a girl who had taken and was about to come up on ecstasy who had lost everyone and everything, including her handbag. I stumbled back into the fray.

Most of the men were topless, and most of the women, like me, wore strange aprons, fashionable at the time, that covered just the front of one's torso, and only remained decent by means of a few weak-looking strings tied in dainty bows behind. I pushed through this crowd of sweaty bare backs, despairing, wondering where in a super club one might bed down for the night (the stairs? the fire exit?). But everything I tried to look at quickly shattered and arranged itself in a series of patterned fragments, as if I were living in a kaleidoscope. Where was I trying to get to anyway? There was no longer any "bar" or "chill-out zone"—there was only dance floor. All was dance floor. Everybody danced. I stood still, oppressed on all sides by dancing, quite sure I was about to go out of my mind.

Then suddenly I could hear Q-Tip—blessed Q-Tip!—not a synthesizer, not a vocoder, but Q-Tip, with his human voice, rapping over a human beat. And the top of my skull opened to let human Q-Tip in, and a rail-thin man with enormous eyes reached across a sea of bodies for my hand. He kept asking me the same thing over and over: *You feeling it?* I was. My ridiculous heels were killing me, I was terrified I might die, yet I felt simultaneously overwhelmed with delight that "Can I Kick It?" should happen to be playing at this precise moment in the history of the world, and was now morphing into "Smells Like Teen Spirit." I took the man's hand. The top of my head flew away. We danced and danced. We gave ourselves up to joy.

Years later, while listening to a song called "Weak Become Heroes" by the British artist The Streets I found this experience almost perfectly recreated in rhyme, and realized that just as most American children alive in 1969 saw the moon landings, nearly every Briton between sixteen and thirty in the 1990s met some version of the skinny pill head I came across that night in Fabric. The name The Streets gives him is "European Bob." I suspect he is an archetypal figure of my generation. The character "Super Hans" in the British TV comedy *Peep Show* is another example of the breed, though it might be more accurate to say Super Hans is European Bob in "old" age (forty). I don't remember the name of my particular pill head, but will call him "Smiley." He was one of these strangers you met exclusively on dance floors, or else on a beach in Ibiza. They tended to have inexplicable nicknames, no home or family you could ever identify, a limitless capacity for drug-taking, and a universal feeling of goodwill toward all men and women, no matter their color, creed, or state of inebriation.

Their most endearing quality was their generosity. For the length of one night Smiley would do anything at all for you. Find you a cab, walk miles through the early morning streets looking for food, hold your hair as you threw up, and listen to you complain at great length about your parents and friends—agreeing with all your grievances—though every soul involved in these disputes was completely unknown to him. Contrary to your initial suspicions Smiley did not want to sleep with you, rob you, or con you in any way. It was simply intensely important to him that you had a good time, tonight, with him. "How you feeling?" was Smiley's perennial question. "You feeling it yet? I'm feeling it. You feeling it yet?" And that *you* should feel it seemed almost more important to him than that *he* should.

Was that joy? Probably not. But it mimicked joy's conditions pretty well. It included, in minor form, the great struggle that tends to precede joy, and the feeling—once one is "in" joy—that the experiencing subject has somehow "entered" the emotion, and disappeared. I "have" pleasure, it is a feeling I want to experience and own. A beach holiday is a pleasure. A new dress is a pleasure. But on that dance floor I was joy, or some small piece of joy, with all these other hundreds of people who were also a part of joy.

The Smileys, in their way, must have recognized the vital difference; it would explain their great concern with other people's experience. For as long as that high lasted, they seemed to pass beyond their own egos. And it might really have been joy if the next morning didn't always arrive. I don't just mean the deathly headache, the blurred vision, and the stomach cramps. What really destroyed the possibility that this had been joy was the replaying in one's mind of the actual events of the previous night, and the brutal recognition that every moment of sublimity—every conversation that had seemed to touch upon the meaning of life, every tune that had appeared a masterwork—had no substance whatsoever now, here, in the harsh light of the morning. The final indignity came when you dragged yourself finally from your bed and went into the living room. There, on your mother's sofa—in the place of that jester spirit-animal savior person you thought you'd met last night—someone had left a crushingly boring skinny pill head, already smoking a joint, who wanted to borrow twenty quid for a cab.

It wasn't all a waste of time though. At the neural level, such experiences gave you a clue about what joy not-under-the-influence would feel like. Helped you learn to recognize joy, when it arrived. I suppose a neuroscientist could explain in very clear terms why the moment after giving birth can feel ecstatic, or swimming in a Welsh mountain lake with somebody dear to you. Perhaps the same synapses that ecstasy falsely twanged are twanged authentically by fresh water, certain epidurals, and oxytocin. And if, while sitting on a high hill in the South of France, someone who has access to a phone comes dashing up the slope to inform you that two years of tension, tedious study, and academic anxiety have not been in vain—perhaps again these same synapses or whatever they are do their happy dance.

We certainly don't need to be neuroscientists to know that wild romantic crushes—especially if they are fraught with danger—do something ecstatic to our brains, though like the pills that share the name, horror and disappointment are usually not far behind. When my wild crush came, we wandered around a museum for so long it closed without us noticing; stuck in the grounds we climbed a high wall and, finding it higher on its other side, considered our options: broken ankles or a long night sleeping on a stone lion. In the end a passerby helped us down, and things turned prosaic and, after a few months, fizzled out. What looked like love had just been teen spirit. But what a wonderful thing, to sit on a high wall, dizzy with joy, and think nothing of breaking your ankles.

* * *

Real love came much later. It lay at the end of a long and arduous road, and up to the very last moment I had been convinced it wouldn't happen. I was so surprised by its arrival, so unprepared, that on the day it arrived I had already arranged for us to visit the Holocaust museum at Auschwitz. You were holding my feet on the train to the bus that would take us there. We were heading toward all that makes life intolerable, feeling the only thing that makes it worthwhile. That was joy. But it's no good thinking about or discussing it. It has no place next to the furious argument about who cleaned the house or picked up the child. It is irrelevant when sitting peacefully, watching an old movie, or doing an impression of two old ladies in a shop, or as I eat a Popsicle while you scowl at me, or when working on different floors of the library. It doesn't fit with the everyday. The thing no one ever tells you about joy is that it has very little real pleasure in it. And yet if it hadn't happened at all, at least once, how would we live?

A final thought: sometimes joy multiplies itself dangerously. Children are the infamous example. Isn't it bad enough that the beloved, with whom you have experienced genuine joy, will eventually be lost to you? Why add to this nightmare the child, whose loss, if it ever happened, would mean nothing less than your total annihilation? It should be noted that an equally dangerous joy, for many people, is the dog or the cat, relationships with animals being in some sense intensified by guaranteed finitude. You hope to leave this world before your child. You are quite certain your dog will leave before you do. Joy is such a human madness.

The writer Julian Barnes, considering mourning, once said, "It hurts just as much as it is worth." In fact, it was a friend of his who wrote the line in a letter of condolence, and Julian told it to my husband, who told it to me. For months afterward these words stuck with both of us, so clear and so brutal. *It hurts just as much as it is worth.* What an arrangement. Why would anyone accept such a crazy deal? Surely if we were sane and reasonable we would every time choose a pleasure over a joy, as animals themselves sensibly do. The end of a pleasure brings no great harm to anyone, after all, and can always be replaced with another of more or less equal worth.

NICK STURM

■

I Feel YES

FROM *I Feel YES*, a chapbook

I climb into the machine and spend
two days thinking about lemonade.
I want to drink lemonade and watch the light
disappear into where I am speaking.
Language enters my life an infection in drag,
my hands feeling plural as if they're hands
but also two or more kinds of vegetables
grown in a country where the sky touches
the distant mountains in a way that is
both beautiful and meaningless, the clouds
heavy static above the village where underwear
dries on a log while a small, ageless girl
stares at the words on a bottle of soda,
not understanding the language though
imagining she does, imagining a vast
world in which this object has meaning or
(which do you think is more important?) value,
imagining the sun cut from the sky and
kept in her pocket next to a smooth cold stone
from the river where her brothers swim
and nothing is digital, and even though
lemonade is unheard of, a state of affairs
that says little about my hands (what is
there to say?), it's good enough and happening

and now here we are and I am glad. I feel
like a birthday is a good reason to be naked.
How about you? What do you think pleasure
smells like? What is your understanding of
the expression *to make one's hackles rise?*
I'm going to say now I'm not in control.
My T-shirt could eat me — it just seems obvious
but either way I'm going to ask you to dance.
We'll make smoothies out of rain and ride
motorcycles through fields of what has to be
commercially-grown lavender, how else
could there be so much of it? I'll tell you
that many different things have the ability
to glimmer and that is as much a reason
for joy as for terror. Do you think of what
you eat as having come from a carcass?
Does part of you not believe yourself
when you call it *making love?* Does it sound
like I've been thinking about this for a long time?
I'll never really know anything and that's
why I'm on fire, helping my friend plug a tiny
amplifier into the part of me that still believes
I can wrap my disbelief in birds and bras
and that will be sufficient, or at least loud enough
to dance to without being aware of my body,
which is always in the way because the physical
world is determined by a range of parameters
but what does that matter here? Why not say
everything I feel? Everyday the sun paints me stupid
and I've never been more thankful for anything
than when my skin kisses up to oblivion
in the middle of a parking lot and my
strawberries spill out onto the pavement
like they're alive. Just look at all this! Our heads
more expensive by the minute! I put on a blue coat
and walk into the kingdom. I stand in a puddle
for twenty-five years. I stand in a puddle

and for twenty-five years I am barely born.
Now, stained and weightless, I order Chinese food
in the dark. I watch a video of people
taking off their pants in public. I watch a video
of a video of a lion eating an antelope.
I don't want to understand, I just want
to know you can hear me. My heart is pure
but I didn't say that. I'm just a bastard
cloud confusing the light, a stupid hunk
of ones and zeros trying not to not
foul up the wires. I'm stranded on the edge
of the electorate cooking my hands
in their own juices. I want to be delirious
as a cheerleader full of candy! To express myself
in increasing wolf. I want to rent out
your respiratory system with my airwaves.
Call me a man and I'll fill you with mixtapes
until you dance the feedback out of me.
My actions are excessive! Ice cream in Belarus!
October in a tree! Some precise blur
instructs me. That's how I wrote this,
hovering above the desert in a motionless vessel.
I put a giraffe in a boat and laugh.
Thinking about it isn't going to help.
Somewhere near me my inbox vibrates.
I don't have any business. I feel emotional.
I'm wasting my time. How many ways can I say
something wrong. There's piano skin
on my windowpane! Gravy sticking out of the night!
My multitasking awash in tapestries of light!
Revelation is ubiquitous, McNuggets in the grass.
I'm trying to live better, and many other things.
Every spring the meadow in its hysterical dress
and I all human and delusion. I vow through
the brouhaha with a temple in my fingerprint.
I vow through midnight with a swan
in my bourbon. I vow orgasms and antlers.

I vow to get up. And I do. But who am I
kidding? I'm not in charge. I mimic
the noise of insatiable flowers. I dress up
like a meadow and pretend I'm the world.
When I speak it is the opposite of bones.
Real life bones, my name on my hands.
I understand now, the valley full of brains.
Let's have a conversation using only our skin.
Here I'll start where I'm lonely and wet.
I will never be as good as the snow
breeding in the clouds and the world
eating the snow as it falls around the birds,
the real life birds that are ridiculous tools,
the real life birds that should be arrested
but are not, and the birds in the machine
as it hums and humans and the humming
now a kind of snow that builds and hums,
humming into the world that is a real life bird,
a bird a machine inside a real life word,
a word a totem of inarticulate grammars and grammar
a bird that should be arrested but is not. I just want
to be simple and hanging out a window with my hands
in the sky. To never die, that is the nature of
the machine, the machine that is only fog
between my fingers, the idea of a lake
emerging from the idea of rain, the idea that
I can say something and you will hear it.
That is how I know I am here. Here with birds
and stupidity and pieces of weather. Here where
I drive around all day in the blue light revolving.
Here where I speak in the shape of other humans
speaking. Here where I compare life to an avocado
and the university trembles! I drink lemonade
next to a whale. I drink lemonade and migrate
into a system of becoming. I drink lemonade
and establish relationships based on love
for things that are invisible, or in other words,

faith, which, along with stupidity,
is what brought me here thinking
about lemonade in the first place and
if I had to conceptualize what I mean
by "first place," which is an expression
that denotes a temporal sequence
in terms of an abstracted spatial structure,
the beautiful thing about what I would say
is that I never knew that just thinking
about lemonade would get me here
like how when I pull a bag of oranges
out of a dumpster and make juice from them
and I'm drinking it I think about the person
who works for the grocery store who decided
to throw away that bag of oranges or who
was ordered to throw away that bag of oranges
because of the rotten orange at the bottom
and how when that grocery store employee
absent-mindedly, or perhaps not, perhaps
with a high degree of awareness, tossed
that bag of oranges into the dumpster that
person would never have imagined another person
ever touching those oranges again, let alone
eating them, and then I think back
to the truck that delivered the oranges
and the person who drove that truck and
how they might have touched these oranges
not thinking of them as oranges but as
only some materialized idea of the continual
struggle to understand how to live while
also working and doing something meaningful or
(which do you think is more important?) valuable,
and then I think back to the building
where the oranges were sorted and stickered
and bagged and back to the first truck
that took the oranges from the orange grove
and the people who picked the oranges

with their lives and the things they love and hate
and their thoughts when they read the news
and their lips and bedrooms and hands,
their hands always smelling of oranges,
which may or may not be meaningful or
(which do you think is more important?) valuable,
and their orgasms, shared or not, and how this
incongruous system of human and nonhuman motion
could lead to this bag of oranges in a dumpster
without any mouth to take in their architecture,
without these oranges satisfying some need, some
basic, universal, almost tangible need to know
that our existence is purposeful, which is often
the way one feels sitting on a park bench holding
a single orange barely caring what happens,
and how the breakdown of such a system is
something we all have to account for in our own ways
and how writing this poem feels like that,
confusion coupled with action mixed with some
vague hope that we'll somehow get somewhere,
which is why I climbed into the machine at all.
Then as long as we're here together let's agree
there be no knowing in the making, a knot,
that it show how in the motion, the machinery.
Let's agree that the only thing shared by nations
and snow is that no matter what they touch
they always disappear. Let's agree that if I took
a picture of your face right now and later showed it
to a stranger they would say *Who is this beautiful person
I do not know?* and I would say *I do not know*
because I do not pretend to know you, I only pretend
to speak. And let's agree that in the light
making its way quietly through the valley
there are noises no one knows exist that communicate
nothing and are never repeated and in that light
there is one perpetual question every person
and poem exists to answer, essentially

what's so hard about being happy being
in awe of everything? I need to believe
I would suffer to save you. Amidst cell phones
and bar glass kissing and smashing my face sentimental
for better or for worse or for even better, galloping
full of wine into the parade, removing the plexiglas
between our bodies and our bodies, and our bodies
discovering what they mean when they say
"I am in love with an emergency of symbols!"
What part of a moose don't you understand?
What would it take for you to take off your pants
in public? What if I took off my pants right now
and laid down in the grass, if we could find any,
and in an unsexual way asked you to join me?
Is that even possible? What part of the question
do you think I'm referring to and what do you think
I mean by "possible"? I generate hogwash
in my torso! The proper use of a hammer
is to wear a petticoat and be inconsistent!
A feverish joy scatters into the citizenry!
Isn't this what's supposed to happen
going from meaning to meat to mouth?
The president stands naked in the middle
of the forest! I make sandwiches
for everyone who hates me! After that
what happens is made of fucking flowers.
I look out my window at the light
licking snow off the dumb bodies of air
conditioning units and finally get a grasp
on why everything I love is so leaving.
Why something in a word out of its body
makes me feel everywhere as air, air that lives
in mouths and birds all peach pie and dynamite.
All genetic ballistics in the begonias. I am
the first person ever to touch this tree and for this
the thing that is the word that is my soul
is happy. I mumble into the incredible.

I kiss the idea of peace and give in to feeling
vulnerable despite what's foreign about my teeth.
Believe me I swear what I mean when I'm lying.
I want to cuddle until our bodies go
gossamer. I want to know how much gasoline
it would take to get me and all my friends
to California. I want to know what would happen
if instead of gasoline it was lemonade and instead
of California it was the kind of sky that happens
over California and instead of the sky over
California it was just me and you and a bag of oranges
astonishing our faces. It has something to do with
how I want to build a symphony for breakfast. How
I'm angry at clouds. How sometimes I imagine
my credit card laying in the muck at the bottom
of the ocean surrounded by glowing tubes
eating other glowing tubes. How I want to collide
with everything. It takes a wound for a wound
to heal and I need the light to make a mistake of me.
Chemical fantastic, this world inexplicable.
I prop open the screen door with a broken
harmonium. I vote for a lake. I breathe
the same air as birds. I wrap myself in beer.
I was born here of parents born here
from parents the same. They went to work
between boilers and ate tires with Hart Crane.
They walked on their elbows to lick fire
from the river. They got divorces
and more divorces and I got myself a name.
The name a child at the end of its body.
Like in the infant dark an instinctual verb.
A glitch in the organ of my name. My name
displaced from its architecture and there
the machine approaching me like an animal
tamer lonely for its animal and both of us
asleep in some plural center, though
on the periphery my body never sleeps,

since the day I was born—code stumbling
and unclear, an ecosystem inventing itself
under the overpass, and you and me and
all our friends touching our gonads
as if our hands were about to go extinct,
as if I couldn't say at least one thing
that matters even the slightest bit to someone,
as if language is an exit with no way out
and we're all scratching our names into
the final obelisk surrounded by the perfume
of a thousand thousand wires tattooed
to the air emitting tongueless mysteries
in the amphitheatres of our heavy skulls
where some unknowable yawning limit
infects us with the flesh of the entire universe,
airplanes full of wilderness nuzzling the stars,
and a young, ageless girl cutting the sun from the sky
and keeping it in her pocket next to a cold
smooth stone from the river where her brothers
swim and nothing is digital, a young girl
not responsible for the pageant between
her ears and hence imagining no war
other than the tension between the space
where the pattern ends and whatever
isn't the pattern begins. Does it bother you
that in the dark the billboards are still there?
Do you have an understanding of the legal system
of your country in relation to other countries?
Would it be beautiful to be a window?
Would you rather be sincere or a river?
Does camping make you feel less complicit?
Complicit in what? What lobular fervor?
Which ocean of whiskey? Why can't I
stop loving you? Rather than answers,
does the asking of these questions point
towards the essential issue to our being
in the world and communicating which is that

language knows more about the world
than we ever will? Or am I framing this wrong?
Does language know anything or is it just
some kind of technology, an aviary, a field
of scissors? Is it worth it to worry or should
I keep thinking about lemonade?
Aren't they the same breed of wolf?
O endless array of the occasional and scarfs!
Dost thou delight in unsober'd music?
I have a notion to essence! I'm running out
of decisions! A bird lives in a bird's mouth
says the letter I've been writing you
every night for ten thousand years. O collateral
dandelion! A blue coat ringing in the kingdom.
This music is a warning: I'm nothing but stupid.
All this is is a fist full of telephones
filled with the same immense voicemail,
an almost translucent string of sounds
resembling light more than language,
the basic message being: I feel fucking yes.
My heart making out with your heart in the mist
of sprinklers, our hips secret beaches sweet
with nonsense and campfire smoke and an illimitable
unspoken feeling that regardless of this being
a complete mistake it is, in fact, complete,
and amidst the ongoing collapse of laughter
my head fills with something that is not control
in favor of reciting sunflowers on some wet wet
interstate perhaps not so far from here where
this system is neverending sufficiently and I
might fall asleep in your daffodils with a smile
smashed against my face. Can you see me
right now or are we far away from each other?
Do you know where I live or what color
my eyes are? Does that matter to you
or would you rather I act like an author?
I have no idea how I've gotten this far

without saying anything about cats.
Does that make us more or less similar?
Do you want to go up on the roof
of wherever you are and drink lemonade
with me? Do you know how close you are
to birds no matter what you're doing?
O human trying! O American bison!
Squirrels, delicious sleep, my ass! Mistakes!
Let's climb a tree and jump into a pile
of ash berries. Let's use my mother's mouth
as a door into my birthday. Let's eat pie
with our fingers and install confetti cannons
set to go off when a sad person walks by.
Let's kneel in the dirt – what is there to say?
Let's write a poem made entirely of lemonade
and email it to God. Let's undress each other
using birds. When I was nineteen I wrote
the way words look is often more interesting
than how they sound and that is something
I didn't fully grasp until I beheaded an ambulance
and swallowed the siren and since then it's been
inappropriate fabulous in my pleasure hive,
echoes twitching in my teeth, excitement
an inexhaustible ignition, evil violins pawing the sky,
reinventing the word flammable to start again
from ashes, blood bucketing in an approximation
of the circumference of an accident that's left
me blessing the abyss and the see-saw, broken
charming swarm feeling good as a pile of chairs
teetering in the tawny dawn. O vulva toggle
derelict and flickering! Lilacs locked in the pillory!
One day I'm going to die and I'll never again
feel the word tambourine rattle on my tongue
and if you don't think it "makes sense" to wear
corsages made of rain disconnected from the sky,
or to draw perforated lines on each others' bodies

and rename our favorite parts after Swedish cities,
or to ride vintage mopeds through fogs of moths,
or to tremble in phone booths and feel the bones
under our faces, or to sit in trees and discuss
the entropy of snow, or to illuminate the city
with accumulation and lack of health insurance,
or to feel hummingbird and uncertainty, our flasks
full of fumbling and lightning, or to invent a machine
whose only function is to articulate the feeling
of sitting in a meadow knowing you are going
to leave the person you thought you loved,
or to never carry an umbrella when it rains
because as far as I know it always rains,
then I recommend a steady diet of fucked-up
hope until the ancient wrong that is really
a flock of disasters in human clothing
reveals itself to you as the harvest of wreckage
and incantation growing in the undergrowth
of everybody's confusion. Do you understand
why any ambiguous desire, i.e. lemonade,
would lead to all this? Why I can describe weeping
as radiant? Why a cage made of syntax and sex
is where my heart lives with its little hands
tangling what I think I'm feeling into a large
audible error? I don't need any proof! Religion
in the feedback—I don't need any proof. Anything
beautiful will save you! Truth is too basic, I want it
baffling and static. Just lie down in the grass
with your soul full of swag. Inconsistent the glitch
I sound in my hoping. Do not expect a delay.
Expect wires kissing. Expect the day to spill electric
from the truncated shrine where our mouths
fumble and spill, where artillery is no longer kept
in the drapery, where each moment inherits
the momentum of brittle and raw arrangements.
The neck leaks louder, each move a mangled

allegiance between etiquette and serration.
Notice how the machine breathes and notice,
now, how close your teeth are to your tongue,
tongue that needs no warrant to magnify
the wound that is the formlessness of thought,
tongue drenched in accidental embroidery
from which the design of the machine splinters
into gesture and voice, is infectious in the fact
that our faces are not abstract, that we are
moving deliciously through our lives surrounded
by an influx of feeling in the blooming
people, the people who are my friends wearing
light on their eyes and lavishing one another
in irregular forms of benevolence in this language
in which I am constantly failing to say how much
I love you. You who wear hats and stumble
against concrete and vagary. Who disrupt
the system with one massive, eternal glass
of lemonade that glows and twists the whole
world art-shaped, the wind turning trees
into tonal blur, a thousand voices pushing
the machine through my veins as my friends
speak and sleep in the rain, umbrella-less
and trying, as the pulp and glint of the system
undergoes alteration with one shard of music
rising up from the golden surface of my friends,
let's get free, let's get free, let's get free and feed
the machine our underwear and our birds
and our hands, all of which are both meaningful
and valuable because meaning and value
are unbearably soldered to the meat
of living, so that we have nothing but happiness
and the machine that eats itself and eats itself
eating itself as we move back into the world
making all these fucking mistakes, then
Neil Young, then lawnmowers atop our graves.

But no matter what the grass will keep growing.
The dictionary will cough up its harmonies.
Love will pour out of phonemes and machines
and I will stand next to you, a glass of lemonade
beside a glass of lemonade, and I hope
by then you and I will finally be friends.

CONTRIBUTORS' NOTES

Andrew Foster Altschul is the author of the novels *Deus ex Machina* and *Lady Lazarus*. His work has appeared in *Esquire, Ploughshares, Mc-Sweeney's, One Story, Fence,* and anthologies, including *Best New American Voices* and *O. Henry Prize Stories*. He is the director of the Center for Literary Arts at San Jose State University.

Cole Becher was a sergeant in a Marine Corps Combat Engineer Battalion. He served in Habbaniyah, Iraq, in 2008, and has a BA and MA in English. He misses a world without cell phones and reality TV, and Kardashian-esque anything. He does not miss officers, drill, or dust storms.

Lucie Brock-Broido is the author of four collections of poetry, *A Hunger, The Master Letters, Trouble in Mind,* and, most recently, *Stay, Illusion,* which was a finalist for both the National Book Award and the National Book Critics Circle Award. She is director of poetry in the School of the Arts at Columbia University, and lives in New York City and in Cambridge, Massachusetts.

Jeffrey Cranor cowrites the podcast Welcome to Night Vale. He also creates theater and dance. He lives in New York.

Kyle G. Dargan is the author of *The Listening, Bouquet of Hungers, Logorrhea Dementia,* and the forthcoming *Honest Engine,* all published by the University of Georgia Press. He is originally from Newark, New Jersey, and currently lives in Washington, DC, where he teaches at American University and directs the creative writing program.

Kathryn Davis is the author of seven novels, most recently *Duplex*. She has been the recipient of the Kafka Prize, the Morton Dauwen Zabel Award from the American Academy of Arts and Letters, a Guggenheim Fellowship, and the 2006 Lannan Award for fiction. She lives in Vermont and teaches in the MFA program at Washington University in St. Louis, where she is Hurst Senior Writer-in-Residence.

Matthew Dickman is the author of *All-American Poem, 50 American Plays, Mayakovsky's Revolver, Wish You Were Here*, and *24 Hours*. He lives in Portland, Oregon, where he is the poetry editor for *Tin House*.

Yasmine El Rashidi is an Egyptian writer and critic. She is a frequent contributor to *The New York Review of Books* and an editor of the Middle East arts and culture quarterly *Bidoun*. She lives in Cairo.

Mona Eltahawy is an award-winning columnist and an international public speaker on Arab and Muslim issues. She is based in New York.

Joseph Fink is from California but doesn't live there anymore. He spends most of his time making a podcast, and also has a novel coming out pretty soon.

V. V. Ganeshananthan's debut novel, *Love Marriage*, deals with Sri Lanka and its diasporas. The book was long-listed for the Orange Prize and named one of the best books of 2008 by the *Washington Post*. Her work has appeared in the *New York Times, Granta, The Atlantic*, and the *Washington Post*, among other places. The recipient of fellowships from the Radcliffe Institute for Advanced Study, the National Endowment for the Arts, Yaddo, the MacDowell Colony, and Phillips Exeter, she previously taught at the University of Michigan. Next year she will join the MFA faculty at the University of Minnesota. "K Becomes K" is a part of her forthcoming second novel.

Janine di Giovanni is an author and essayist and human rights activist who has reported war for twenty-five years. She has won many awards, including two Amnesty International Prizes and a National Magazine Award. She is the author of five books, the most recent of which is *Ghosts by Daylight*. Di Giovanni is currently writing a book based on "Seven Days in Syria." In addition to Syria, she has worked in Bosnia, Kosovo, Afghanistan, Iraq, Libya, Somalia, Rwanda, Ivory Coast, Sierra Leone, Zimbabwe, East Timor, Chechnya, Egypt, Tunisia, and Turkey, among other places. She lives in Paris with her son.

A. T. Grant is the author of *Collected Alex* and *WAKE*. He lives in Virginia, where people call him Alex.

Gabriel Heller's essays and stories have appeared in *Agni Online, The Gettysburg Review*, and the *Stranger*, among other publications. He is the recipient of the 14th annual Inkwell Short Story Award as well as a notable story citation in *The Best American Mystery Stories 2013*. He lives in Brooklyn and teaches writing at NYU.

Adam Johnson is the author of *The Orphan Master's Son*, which won the 2013 Pulitzer Prize for fiction, as well as *Parasites Like Us*, a novel, and the story collection *Emporium*. His forthcoming story collection, *Interesting Facts*, will be published by Random House in 2015.

Rachel Kaadzi Ghansah is an essayist whose writing has appeared in *The Paris Review, Bookforum, Transition*, the *New York Observer*, and *Rolling Stone*. She has taught at Columbia University, Bard College, and Eugene Lang College. More of her work can be found at the-rachelkaadzighansah.tumblr.com.

Lally Katz is an American-born playwright living in Australia. After Shakespeare, she is currently the most produced playwright in Australia. She has written over forty full-length plays and won multiple awards.

Dan Keane served as the AP's last gringo correspondent in Bolivia, and received an MFA from the University of Michigan. His AP journalism has been published in the *New York Times*, the *Washington Post*, and dozens of other newspapers. His freelance work has appeared in the *Austin Chronicle*, *ArtForum*, and the *Village Voice*. He currently lives in Shanghai.

Ali Liebegott is the author of the following books: *The Beautifully Worthless*, *The IHOP Papers*, and *Cha-Ching!* The poem included in this collection was part of a project in which Liebegott wrote a poem every day for three months until she qualified for health insurance at her cashier job. The only rule was that each poem had to begin with the first thing that she rang up that day. She currently lives in Los Angeles and is a staff writer for the TV show *Transparent*.

Karen Maner is a graduate of the MFA program at Eastern Washington University and a winner of the 2013 AWP Intro Journals Project. After spending some time in Europe and Asia, she's back in her hometown, Dayton, Ohio, working on essays, paintings, and getting her mind out of the gutter.

Luke Mogelson lived in Afghanistan between June 2011 and December 2013, writing for the *New York Times Magazine*. He has also reported from the war in Syria for *The New Yorker*. He currently lives in Mexico, where he is working on a collection of short stories.

Maia Morgan's work has appeared in *Glamour*, *Creative Nonfiction*, and *The Chattahoochee Review* and is forthcoming in *Hayden's Ferry Review*. She just finished her first book, *The Saltwater Twin and Other Mythical Creatures*. Visit thesaltwatertwin.com for updates and posts on words, memory, road trips, yoga, and dogs. She teaches writing and theater in schools, health care facilities, and jails in Chicago.

Anders Nilsen is the award-winning artist and author of the books *Big Questions*, *Rage of Poseidon*, *Don't Go Where I Can't Follow*, and *The End*, among others. His work has been translated widely and shown internationally. He lives in Minneapolis.

Sylvan Oswald's plays have been produced around the United States and his web series is posted at outtakes.squarespace.com. He lives in Brooklyn and is a resident playwright at New Dramatists. Sylvan oswald.com.

Amos Oz was born in Jerusalem in 1939. He is the author of fourteen novels and collections of short fiction, and numerous works of nonfiction. His acclaimed memoir *A Tale of Love and Darkness* was an international bestseller and the recipient of the prestigious Goethe Prize, as well as the National Jewish Book Award. *Scenes from Village Life*, a *New York Times* Notable Book, was awarded the Prix Méditerranée Étranger in 2010. He lives in Tel Aviv.

Thomas Pierce was born and raised in South Carolina. His stories have appeared in *The New Yorker*, *Oxford American*, *Virginia Quarterly Review*, *Subtropics*, *The Coffin Factory*, and *The Atlantic*. His debut story collection, *Hall of Small Mammals*, will be published by Riverhead Books in January 2015. A graduate of the University of Virginia creative writing program, he lives in Charlottesville, Virginia, with his wife and daughter.

Nathaniel Rich is the author of two novels: *Odds Against Tomorrow* and *The Mayor's Tongue*. His essays and journalism appear regularly in *The New York Review of Books*, the *New York Times Magazine*, *Harper's Magazine*, and *Rolling Stone*. He lives in New Orleans.

Rebecca Rukeyser is a graduate of the Iowa Writers' Workshop and a native of Davis, California. She has worked in China, Turkey, Japan, and South Korea. She lives in Chicago.

Yumi Sakugawa is a comic book artist and the author of *I Think I Am in Friend-Love with You* and *Your Illustrated Guide to Becoming One with the Universe*. She is a regular comic contributor to the *Rumpus* and Wonderhowto.com, and her short comic stories "Mundane Fortunes for the Next Ten Billion Years" and "Seed Bomb" were selected as notable comics of 2012 and 2013, respectively, by *The Best American Comics*. A graduate of the fine arts program at UCLA, she lives in Southern California.

Matthew Schultz is a writer interested in both fiction and literary non-fiction. Originally from Massachusetts, he is currently living and writing in Tel Aviv.

Zadie Smith was born in northwest London in 1975 and divides her time between London and New York. Her first novel, *White Teeth*, was the winner of the Whitbread First Novel Award, the *Guardian* First Book Award, the James Tait Black Memorial Prize for Fiction, and the Commonwealth Writers' First Book Award. Her second novel, *The Autograph Man*, won the Jewish Quarterly Wingate Literary Prize. Her third novel, *On Beauty*, was shortlisted for the Man Booker Prize, won the Commonwealth Writers' Best Book Award (Eurasia Section), and the Orange Prize for fiction. Her most recent novel, *NW*, was published in 2012 and has been short listed for the Royal Society of Literature Ondaatje Prize and the Women's Prize for Fiction.

Nick Sturm is the author of *How We Light*, as well as several chapbooks, including the collaborative works *Labor Day*, with Carrie Lorig, and *I Was Not Even Born*, with Wendy Xu. He is from Ohio and lives in Florida.

Rachel Swirsky holds an MFA in fiction from the Iowa Writers' Workshop, where the California native took lessons in writing and being cold. Her work has been nominated for the Hugo and the World Fantasy Award, and she is a two-time recipient of the Nebula Award, including a 2014 win for the short story included in this anthology. Her second collection, *How the World Became Quiet*, came out in September 2013. If she were a dinosaur, she'd want to be a Caudipteryx, because they had feathers and looked ridiculous.

Reggie Watts is an American comedian and musician. He performs regularly on television and radio and in live theater. Watts currently appears on the IFC television series *Comedy Bang! Bang!*, which began airing in June 2012 and will enter its third season in 2014.

THE *BEST AMERICAN*
NONREQUIRED READING
COMMITTEE

The *Best American Nonrequired Reading* (*BANR*) committee is composed of a corps of high school students that meet at McSweeney's Publishing in San Francisco and a group of students that gather in Ann Arbor, Michigan, at 826 Michigan. Both groups meet weekly and spend the year reading (almost) everything that is published in the United States and, ultimately, selecting the work that ends up in this collection.

Nilo Batle, sixteen, is a junior at the Ruth Asawa School of the Arts in San Francisco. He is an avid rock climber and enjoys making short films in the media department at his school. He loves learning new skills: everything from building a wooden boat to editing a book.

Hanel Baveja is a freshman at Harvard University, where she hopes to become a better writer, thinker, and person. This was her fourth and final year on the *BANR* committee, and she feels very lucky to have been a part of the *BANR* team for all of high school. Her favorite authors include Junot Díaz, Jhumpa Lahiri, and Terrence Hayes. Aside from writing, she enjoys croissants and night driving.

Cassie Behler is a junior at Skyline High School in Ann Arbor, Michigan. This is her first year on the *BANR* committee. She's very interested in psychology and language, and she writes poetry almost daily. A huge coffee enthusiast, Cassie plans on staying caffeinated for the rest of her life, and attending many local punk shows in the process.

Lianna Bernstein is a graduate of Ann Arbor's Pioneer High School. She is spending the year on a kibbutz in northern Israel before heading off to college next year. She often discusses the transportation systems of various cities and sings Beyoncé way too loudly in public spaces. Her passions include lemonade with mint leaves, the rest stops along the Ohio Turnpike, and, of course, nonrequired reading.

Juan Chicas is currently a senior at June Jordan School for Equity in San Francisco. He is known by many as the Duke of the Excelsior, and he rules the neighborhood with a fist of steel. He also likes to play strategy games and destroy all the noobs. He will soon lead a revolution and it will be awesome. You have all been advised.

Claire Fishman is a senior at Community High School in Ann Arbor. This will be her fourth year on the *BANR* committee, and she couldn't be more excited for it. She continues to collect a motley assortment of items and has recently acquired Star Trek Band-Aids and a Martin Van Buren trading card. She also loves competing in Academic Games, something she urges you to look into.

Merlin Garcia is a sophomore at Pioneer High School. She loves chicken shawarma and Joe Biden. If she's not reading, she's probably watching *Scrubs*.

Sarah Gargaro is a freshman at Tufts University and a graduate of Greenhills School in Ann Arbor, Michigan. She is a firm believer in having a little dirt under your fingernails, and she has a highly freckled nose. Sarah thoroughly enjoyed her four- year tenure with *BANR*, stumbling upon some of her favorite pieces of writing in the Robot Shop's basement.

Neerja Garikipati is a sophomore at Huron High School in Ann Arbor. When she's not swimming, she can be found doodling on graph paper and playing flute. Most of the time she'd like to be listening to Imagine Dragons or eating sushi. If she had her druthers, she'd be living in Cambridge, England, or San Francisco. This was her first year on the *BANR* committee and it was excellent.

Sophie Halperin is a senior at Mission High School in San Francisco. She is a Jew. Her parents are still together. Her hobbies include television, baking, and working on her screenplay, *Santa-in-Law*.

Shalini Lakshmanan is a junior at Huron High School. Even though she is not British, she enjoys a good cuppa with a slice of lemon tea cake. Her heart is set on a quest to find the perfect book that can be read numerous times without boredom, and she wishes that more varieties of mangoes could be made available in the United States.

Rebecca Landau is a freshman at Columbia University. Her life goal is to read everything Ursula K. Le Guin ever wrote. She once entered fairyland with nothing but an iron skillet, but then she got scared and ran away.

Samantha Ng is currently a junior at June Jordan School for Equity. You're probably wondering how to pronounce her name because it has no vowels: It's like "ing" but without the "i." She loves YouTube and Hong Kong–style milk tea. This was her first year on the *BANR* committee and she loved it.

Annabel Ostrow is a freshman at Stanford University and a graduate of Lick-Wilmerding High School in San Francisco. *BANR* staff bios are written in May before the book is published, so Annabel is actually a senior at the moment and too busy studying for finals to write a witty bio. Please accept her profuse apologies.

Marco Ponce is currently a junior at George Washigton High School in San Francisco. He has been a *BANR* attendee for two years now. He picked up lacrosse this year and likes to write in his spare time.

Evelyn Pugh is currently a senior at Ruth Asawa School of the Arts in San Francisco. She's in the theater department at school and she spends her free time doing homework and thinking grand thoughts. She looks forward to applying to colleges in cities where people have to wear real winter coats.

Anna Sanford, eighteen, has been a part of the *BANR* program for two years. She is currently a freshman at Wesleyan University in central Connecticut. Anna desperately misses the smell of Mexican food on Valencia Street, the jumpy twine of the banjo at Amnesia, and those long discussions in the McSweeney's basement—all things that make her homesick for *BANR* and the Bay Area. In the future, she hopes to become fluent in French and write something that is worth reading.

Frances Saux graduated from the Ruth Asawa School of the Arts in San Francisco, where she studied creative writing. She is now a freshman at Kenyon College. Her favorite writers include Zadie Smith and David Foster Wallace.

Abigail Schott-Rosenfield graduated from the creative writing department of the Ruth Asawa School of the Arts in San Francisco. Now she attends Stanford University, where she plans to study . . . something involving words. She dreams of becoming a polyglot.

Hannah Shevrin is a freshman at Tufts University. She can safely say that, as a member of the *BANR* committee, she has learned more about Trader Joe's, octopods, and celebrity baby names than she would have anywhere else. She is a sucker for political TV shows. Her favorite is *The West Wing*, which might

be the reason she is such a speedy walker. You can probably find her reading feminist literature in a plush chair at a coffee shop.

Sarah Starman was a member of BANR for three years. She is currently a freshman at the University of Pennsylvania. She likes sports that don't require hand-eye coordination, like soccer, ice-skating, skiing, and running. Though she is enjoying Philadelphia, she misses many things about her life in Ann Arbor, especially the basement of the Robot Shop, where she and her amazing coeditors on the *BANR* committee would meet every Tuesday.

Tammy Tang, eighteen, graduated from Lowell High School in San Francisco and is now a freshman at UC Davis. When she isn't pondering the mysteries of life, she is busy mastering her piano skills, learning how to knit, and hanging out with friends and family. Her first and last year on the *BANR* committee was full of interesting conversations and previously unimaginable ideas.

Cynthia Van, sixteen, is a junior at George Washington High School. She enjoys rolling down grassy hills and writing poetry. Although she very much enjoys spicy food, she cannot handle it very well. This is one of the great struggles of her life. She aspires to skip through a sunflower field during a rainstorm. Is that too much to ask?

Grace VanRenterghem is a junior at Huron High School in Ann Arbor and this was her first year with *BANR*. She enjoys speaking in unison with her identical twin, like the twins in Harry Potter. She is also fond of drawing sloppy, crystal structures on her Spanish homework.

Hadley VanRenterghem is a junior at Ann Arbor Huron High School. This fall will be her second year with *BANR*. She moved to Ann Arbor this year from Grand Rapids and finds the weather much nicer here. She loves studying science, reading books, and watching sunsets on Lake Michigan.

Miranda Wiebe is a freshman at Carleton College. India.Arie is her role model, and nothing makes her happier than a good burger (with fries). She is incredibly grateful for the ways in which *BANR* has opened her mind over the past two years, and she hopes to continue to find ways to constantly redefine her perspective and opinions.

Very special thanks to Nicole Angeloro, Mark Robinson, Colin Corrigan, Matt Robinson, and Nora Byrnes. Massive thanks, also, to our intrepid intern, Charlotte Bhaskar, who provided essential help at every step of the way. And thanks to 826 National, 826 Valencia, 826 Michigan, Houghton Mifflin Harcourt, Laura Howard, Andi Winette, Jordan Bass, Jordan Karnes, Casey Jarman, Brian Christian, Clara Sankey, Ruby Perez, Ian Delaney, Dan McKinley, Sam Riley, Sunra Thompson, Mimi Lok, Cliff Mayotte, Claire Kiefer, Alyson Sinclair, Gerald Richards, Lauren Hall, Olivia White Lopez, Jorge Eduardo Garcia, María Inés Montes, Bita Nazarian, and Molly Parent.

NOTABLE
NONREQUIRED READING
OF 2013

SELENA ANDERSON
  Grief Bacon, *Agni*

LASHONDA KATRICE BARNETT
  Hen's Teeth, *New Orleans Review*

CHARLES BAXTER
  Charity, *McSweeney's Quarterly Concern*

Z. Z. BOONE
  The Buddy System, *The Adroit Journal*

PHIL BRONSTEIN
  The Shooter, *Esquire*

KATIE CORTESE
  Lexa Flying Solo, *Gulf Coast*

JOHN P. DAVIDSON
  You Rang?, *Harper's*

LYDIA DAVIS
  The Gold Digger of Goldfields, *Fence*

JOSHUA DAVIS
 Dangerous, *Wired*
MICHAEL DEAGLER
 Etymology, *Glimmer Train*
ALEXA DERMAN
 Variations on Ophelia, *Word Riot*
JAQUIRA DÍAZ
 Ghosts, *Kenyon Review*
TOM DRURY
 Multistrada, *A Public Space*

CHARLES EAST
 Virgo, *Sewanee Review*
BRIAN EVENSON
 The Dust, *McSweeney's Quarterly Concern*

JOSHUA FERRIS
 The Breeze, *The New Yorker*

AJA GABEL
 In the Time of Adonis, *Glimmer Train*
J. MALCOLM GARCIA
 Revolution Download, *Guernica*
BULL GARLINGTON
 Reliquary, *Slab*
ISABEL GREENBERG
 The Bible of Birdman, *The Encyclopedia of Early Earth*
SAM GRIEVE
 Curious Things That Happened to Her in Paris, *PANK*

JULIE HECHT
 May I Touch Your Hair, *Harper's*
CAROL K. HOWELL
 Bricks, *Alaska Quarterly Review*

ALAYA DAWN JOHNSON
 They Shall Salt the Earth with Seeds of Glass, *Asimov's*

ABOUT 826 NATIONAL

Proceeds from this book benefit youth literacy.

A PERCENTAGE OF the cover price of this book goes to 826 National, a network of eight youth-tutoring, writing, and publishing centers in eight cities around the country.

Since the birth of 826 National in 2002, our goal has been to assist students ages six to eighteen with their writing skills while helping teachers get their classes passionate about writing. We do this with a vast army of volunteers who donate their time so we can give as much one-on-one attention as possible to the students whose writing needs it. Our mission is based on the understanding that great leaps in learning can happen with one-on-one attention, and that strong writing skills are fundamental to future success.

Through volunteer support, each of the eight 826 chapters—in San Francisco, New York, Los Angeles, Ann Arbor, Chicago, Seattle, Boston, and Washington, DC—provides drop-in tutoring, class field trips, writing workshops, and in-schools programs, all free of charge, for students, classes, and schools. 826 centers are especially committed to supporting teachers, offering services and resources for English language learners, and publishing student work. Each of the 826 chapters works to produce professional-quality publications written entirely by young people, to forge relationships with teachers in order to create innovative workshops and lesson plans, to inspire students to write and appreciate the written word, and to rally thousands of enthusiastic volunteers to make it all happen. By offering all of our programming for free, we aim to serve families who cannot afford to pay for the level of personalized instruction their children receive through 826 chapters.

The demand for 826 National's services is tremendous. Last year we worked with more than 6,000 volunteers and over 29,000 students nationally, hosted 646 field trips, completed 220 major in-school projects, offered 387 evening and weekend workshops, welcomed over 200 students per day for after-school tutoring, and produced over 900 student publications. At many of our centers, our field trips are fully booked almost a year in advance, teacher requests for in-school tutor support continue to rise, and the majority of our evening and weekend workshops have waitlists.

826 National volunteers are local community residents, professional writers, teachers, artists, college students, parents, bankers, lawyers, and retirees from a wide range of professions. These passionate individuals can be found at all of our centers after school, sitting side by side with our students, providing one-on-one attention. They can be found running our field trips, or helping an entire classroom of local students learn how to write a story, or assisting student writers during one of our Young Authors' Book programs.

All day and in a variety of ways, our volunteers are actively connecting with youth from the communities we serve.

To learn more or get involved, please visit:

826 National: www.826national.org
826 San Francisco: www.826valencia.org
826 New York: www.826nyc.org
826 Los Angeles: www.826la.org
826 Chicago: www.826chi.org
826 Ann Arbor: www.826mi.org
826 Seattle: www.826seattle.org
826 Boston: www.826boston.org
826 Washington, DC: www.826dc.org

826 VALENCIA

Named for the street address of the building it occupies in the heart of San Francisco's Mission District, 826 Valencia opened on April 8, 2002, and consists of a writing lab, a street-front, student-friendly retail pirate store that partially funds its programs, and satellite classrooms in two local middle schools. 826 Valencia has developed programs that reach students at every possible opportunity—in school, after school, in the evenings, or on the weekends. Since its doors opened, over fifteen hundred volunteers—including published authors, magazine founders, SAT course instructors, documentary filmmakers, and other professionals—have donated their time to work with thousands of students. These volunteers allow the center to offer all of its services for free.

826NYC

826NYC's writing center opened its doors in September 2004. Since then its programs have offered over one thousand students opportunities to improve their writing and to work side by side with hundreds of community volunteers. 826NYC has also built a satellite tutoring center, created in partnership with the Brooklyn Public Library, which has introduced library programs to an entirely new community of students. The center publishes a handful of books of student writing each year.

826LA

826LA benefits greatly from the wealth of cultural and artistic resources in the Los Angeles area. The center regularly presents a free workshop at the Armand Hammer Museum, in which esteemed artists, writers, and performers teach their craft. 826LA has collaborated with the J. Paul Getty Museum to create Community Photoworks, a months-long program that taught seventh-graders the basics of photographic composition and analysis, sent them into Los Angeles with cameras, and then helped them polish artist statements. Since opening in March 2005, 826LA has provided thousands of hours of free one-on-one writing instruction, held summer camps for English language learners, given students sportswriting training in the Lakers' press room, and published love poems written from the perspectives of leopards.

826 CHICAGO

826 Chicago opened its writing lab and after-school tutoring center in the West Town community of Chicago, in the Wicker Park neighborhood. The setting is both culturally lively and teeming with schools: within one mile, there are fifteen public schools serving more than sixteen thousand students. The center opened in October 2005 and now has over five hundred volunteers. Its programs, like at all the 826 chapters, are designed to be both challenging and enjoyable. Ultimately, the goal is to strengthen each student's power to express ideas effectively, creatively, confidently, and in his or her individual voice.

826MICHIGAN

826Michigan opened its doors on June 1, 2005, on South State Street in Ann Arbor. In October 2007 the operation moved downtown, to a new and improved location on Liberty Street. This move enabled the opening of Liberty Street Robot Supply & Repair in May 2008. The shop carries everything the robot owner might need, from positronic brains to grasping appendages to solar cells. 826Michigan is the only 826 not named after a city because it serves students all over southeastern Michigan, hosting in-school residencies in Ypsilanti schools, and providing workshops for students in the Detroit, Lincoln, and Willow Run school districts. The center also has a packed workshop schedule on site every semester, with offerings on making pop-up books, writing sonnets, creating screenplays, producing infomercials, and more.

826 SEATTLE

826 Seattle began offering after-school tutoring in October 2005, followed shortly by evening and weekend writing workshops and, in December 2005, the first field trip to 826 Seattle by a public school class (Ms. Dunker's fifth graders from Greenwood Elementary). The center is in Greenwood, one of the most diverse neighborhoods in the city. And, thankfully, enough space travelers stop by the Greenwood Space Travel Supply Company at 826 Seattle on their way back from the Space Needle. Revenue from the store, like from all 826 storefronts, helps to support the writing programs, along with the generous outpouring from community members.

826 BOSTON

826 Boston kicked off its programming in the spring of 2007 by inviting authors Junot Díaz, Steve Almond, Holly Black, and Kelly Link to lead writing workshops at the English High School. The visiting writers challenged students to modernize fairy tales, invent their ideal school, and tell their own stories. Afterward, a handful of dedicated volunteers followed up with weekly visits to help students develop their writing craft. These days, the center has thrown open its doors in Roxbury's Egleston Square—a culturally diverse community south of downtown that stretches into Jamaica Plain, Roxbury, and Dorchester. 826 Boston neighbors more than twenty Boston schools, a dance studio, and the Boston Neighborhood Network (a public-access television station).

826DC

826 National's newest chapter, 826DC, opened its doors to the city's Columbia Heights neighborhood in September 2010. Like all the 826s, 826DC provides after-school tutoring, field trips, after-school workshops, in-school tutoring, help for English language learners, and assistance with the publication of student work. It also offers free admission to the Museum of Unnatural History, the center's unique storefront. 826DC volunteers recently helped publish a student-authored poetry book project called *Dear Brain*. 826DC's students have also already read poetry for the President and First Lady Obama, participating in the 2011 White House Poetry Student Workshop.

SCHOLARMATCH

ScholarMatch is a nonprofit organization that aims to make college possible by connecting under-resourced students with donors. Launched in 2010 as a project of 826 National, ScholarMatch uses crowd funding to help high-achieving, San Francisco Bay Area students who have significant financial need. But it takes more than money to ensure that students successfully complete college. That's why ScholarMatch also offers student support services and partners with college access organizations, nonprofits, and high schools to ensure that students have the network and resources they need to succeed.

More than 80 percent of ScholarMatch students are the first in their families to go to college, and over 50 percent of them have annual family incomes of less than $25,000. ScholarMatch students are resilient young people who have overcome harrowing challenges, and maintain their determination to seek a better future through college.

With commitments from donors, we ensure that young people in our community receive the education they need to succeed in a challenging economic landscape. To support our students' college journey or to learn more about our organization, visit scholarmatch.org.